WOLF'S PRINCESS

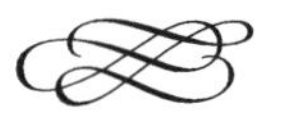

CASSIE ALEXANDER

KARA LOCKHARTE

Cover by the Bookbrander

ABOUT WOLF'S PRINCESS

Rough-and-tumble Austin knows better than to flirt with his best friend's younger sister—she's a princess, part-dragon, and 100% off-limits—he just can't stop himself.

Ryana Blackwood, Princess of the Realms, is coming out of the worst break-up of all time and looking for a rebound. Luckily, her werewolf friend Austin checks all her boxes: he's hot, easy, and nearby.

So when Ryana asks him to pretend to show her what a real relationship is like...how on earth is he supposed to resist? But what is he supposed to do when she realizes she's too good for him? And how can she convince him when it's not a game to her anymore?

Wolf's Princess is a sweet yet incredibly sexy paranormal romance between two complicated people who are fated mates—they just don't know it yet.

CHAPTER 1

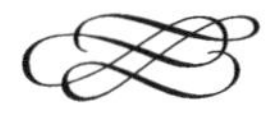

RYANA HEARD A KNOCK AT HER DOOR, AND SHE PRAYED IT WAS REAL even as she knew it wasn't.

If it *had* been real, she would've woken up inside her rooms at her brother Damian's castle. This late at night, it would've been him or one of his people asking her to come help them fight the monsters that made it through the rifts between the Realms.

But if it *wasn't* real, she would hear Baran's voice shortly. She would know she was caught in another dream.

A nightmare.

One in which she inhabited her body and got to watch herself make the worst mistake of her life again and again, completely unable to stop it.

"Princess?" asked a voice through her door, low and manly, and hungry with need.

And this dream version of her, the one she was trapped in, sat up quickly, snapping for her magical bird Lyka to turn on the lights.

She felt the thoughts her dream-version was having, almost like she was reading her own story on one of Earth's ubiquitous screens: if Baran was outside calling her, then it must be possible for them to be alone. He would know; he was the leader of her personal guards, the Kagaroth.

And back in reality, no matter how much she tried to pinch herself awake, or shout that she should stop, she was never able to change a thing.

The lights fluttered on in her dream, and a younger version of her —one she couldn't help but think of as hopelessly naïve—ran for the door in bare feet, her wings streaming out behind her with a smile on her face.

"Baran?" she whispered back through the door, just to hear his voice again.

On the door's far side, he chuckled. It elated the dream-her, knowing she'd made him happy, whereas the Ryana-of-the-now, trapped in this farce every night, wanted to shriek and cry. *Don't do it —don't open the door—don't go!* she screamed inside her own mind, but the dream-her never listened.

"Open the door, Ryana," he entreated, and dream-her, like the fool she had been, did it. Just a finger's width, to smile tantalizingly out at the man she loved.

Had loved.

Past tense.

A mistake she would never make again.

Baran smiled back at her, dark-eyed and handsome, with the sharp edge of a beard around his strong chin. "Come out and leave your Lyka behind." He didn't have his helmet on, so dream-her knew he must have something planned.

He does! Ryana pleaded with her former self. *Don't go!*

But dream-her never listened. She saw herself wave Lyka back, and then step into the hall with Baran, wearing nothing but a gossamer nightdress. She took his hand without thinking. "Where are we going?" she whispered.

His eyes had a devilish gleam to them as he leaned over to breathe, "Out," against her ear, and it made her shiver more than the night air outside her room.

She followed him, unable to believe him capable of any deception.

She assumed he'd take her to some quiet armory or treasure chamber that only he had the key to, where they would be away from all of the Palace's prying eyes as they pleased each other. Dream-her bit her lips in anticipation of being kissed—whereas somewhere on her bed-in-the-now, Ryana bit her lips to stop from screaming. She didn't want anyone else who lived inside Damian's castle to know a thing.

Baran led her through the palace, down narrow corridors and past guards he'd ordered to look the other way, until they reached the back of the building, with its vast gardens sprawling out behind them. The night air was heavy with the scent of watchberry blooms, and it seemed like she and Baran were the only people out beneath the moons. The whole thing felt terribly romantic, especially as he turned toward her, taking her free hand so that he now held both of them.

"Princess," he began, and dream-her smiled at him encouragingly, even as she writhed in her own bed, knowing what was coming. "Come with me."

His hands let go of hers and slipped around her wrists, getting tighter, with what she thought at the time was the possession of a lover. He tried to draw her further into the gardens.

She hesitated. It was night, yes, but if anyone saw her here with Baran—he'd be executed right away. Her personal guard weren't allowed to take their helmets off, much less touch her skin. "It's not safe," she told him.

"Let me be the judge of that," he said, pulling. Giving her one of the looks she'd become used to, the kind she craved when she closed her eyes at night.

"Baran," she whispered. "One of us has to be the sane one. You're already at enough risk."

"And yet I would risk more." He pulled her another step away from the safety of the palace. "Run away with me, Ryana."

This was always the dream's worst part. When she was trapped inside it Ryana was forced to relive exactly what his words meant to her, and how they made her feel.

That for once, someone wanted her, and not her power or her crown. That someone was going to listen to her and take her seriously, and not put her down as young or untested. And, more potent than anything else—that someone wanted to *be* with her.

Not just any someone, but the man that she knew she loved.

He wanted to be with her so badly that he would risk life and limb to do so.

At the time—in this hellish moment that she was forced to relive every night—it felt like a stunning blow. Like she'd summoned some magic she wasn't capable of controlling yet, and it had transfixed her, rippling through muscle, sinew, and bone. She knew she would be changed by it, forever.

She took several deep breaths, composing herself beneath the moonlight, before gently taking back her hands. "Baran. My mother would kill you. There would be no place we could hide. And the entire Realm would talk."

"What do we care for that?"

The dream-version of her gave him a smile so fragile it could've been made of glass. The thought that he was willing to risk himself, right down to his very life, for her—it was the most perfect thing that had ever happened to her…until it became perfectly awful. "I care that you live," she teased.

He took a step toward her, to stand taller than she was and look sternly down. "I love you, Ryana. And I would rather die in love with you than never be able to say it."

Her hands fluttered to her chest above her heart. "Baran," she whispered. "I love—" she began, and then Lyka was there, racing between them, a brilliant red streak, sizzling with magic as she changed from the size of a sparrow into a creature bigger than a human. Ryana stepped back instinctively and gasped, turning to follow Lyka's path with her eyes—and saw her magical guardian murder one of Baran's men, who'd been creeping up on them, one row of blooms over. Lyka dug her claws into his shoulder and shook him roughly, snapping his neck.

"Lyka!" Ryana shouted—and so did other men. She felt magical powers rise and burst, as Lyka whirled around her, protecting her from her own guards as they seemed to…attack?

Her?

She took a disbelieving step back inside her dream. "Baran—what is happening?"

He looked dismayed, but not surprised—and the dream version of herself realized just how far away from the castle she'd been lured. *Without Lyka!* No wonder he'd wanted her to leave Lyka behind.

Ryana drew her own powers to herself, readying to fight anyone who made it through Lyka's increasingly frantic barrier...including Baran.

"Ryana," Baran began, but she started shaking her head.

Her guards, the Kagaroth, wore terrifying-looking helmets, to indicate how vicious they were in battle. As they were never once allowed to take them off in front of her, so she didn't really know the men who were dying around her now.

Not like she knew Baran.

But if he'd managed to orchestrate this, after lying to her for years, then he didn't need his armor to be cruel to her.

"Kidnapping? Ransom?" she asked. "Worse?" Tears streaked down her face, as she attempted to strip her feelings away, like they were another entity entirely, like an outfit one might wear, instead of something innately possessed. Her mother was right. Feelings were an infection that caused weakness.

"It's not like that," Baran said, sounding stern. He didn't even have the decency to be shamed.

Ryana straightened her shoulders. "Then I don't want to know what it *is* like."

The on-going fight was making too much noise to not be noticed. There'd be no way to hide so many bodies, and here she was, in the palace gardens, barefoot, in a nightdress. The inevitability of what had happened, and what would follow, fell around her shoulders like a weight.

Every single person in the castle—if not the Realm itself—would soon know what a fool she'd been. That she'd been gullible enough to trust anyone. To love anyone. To have allowed herself such innocent hopes and unsuspicious dreams.

And even if she didn't die now, she might as well have, because she would be marked by this event for the rest of her life.

Ryana felt pulses of magic inside the castle start up behind her, and caught Baran's eyes looking nervously back. Lyka hovered nearby now; the rest of the traitorous guards were dead or gone, and Ryana knew, looking at Baran, that it was too late now for both of them.

There was only one way out of this.

Baran was going to die. Just like she had always feared—and they both knew it.

He sank to his knees in front of her and began unbuckling the armor that protected his throat. He was otherwise unarmed, and Ryana knew she was safe because Lyka was at her side.

"Do it," he commanded her, like he still had the right to. "Kill me and reclaim what little remains of your honor."

Ryana took deep gulping breaths in her dream, trying to keep down both her panic and her bile. Tears streaked down her face and her hands were weak.

"Do it!" he shouted at her, grabbing her hands, to put them at his throat. "If you ever had any true feelings for me—do it now!"

She could feel his pounding pulse beneath her fingers, and she knew why he begged: Death at her hands would be infinitely more merciful than anything her wicked mother could dream up.

"I truly did love you," he whispered, staring up, the light from the moons above reflecting in his eyes.

"Don't lie," she whispered back, openly sobbing as she started to squeeze.

CHAPTER 2

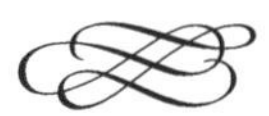

RYANA SAT UP WITH A START, FINALLY FREED FROM HER DREAMS. SHE panted, staring at her bedroom's far wall while Lyka hovered nearby. "Your nightmare, again?" Lyka asked.

Ryana settled her face into her hands. "Always." Her guardian bird was an improbably magical being, and not even Lyka could fix what was wrong with her.

She caught her breath, slowly, wondering what she always did: how long would her mind keep torturing her? And what could she do to make it stop?

"I'm sorry, princess," Lyka said.

Ryana swallowed, mouth dry. "Me too."

She slowly lay back down and turned towards the mess of books strewn on her bed's far side. What would she read now, until she could trust that her mind had given up, and she wouldn't have her dream again?

Lyka brightened the room, sensing her intent, as she stirred her hand through the books and let the thought of reading calm her. Some of them were Earth-books she was reading to try and understand her new home, others were her favorites from the past, which Lyka had recreated for her, and one of them was her new notebook.

She tugged it out. It was shamefully crisp; it would take years to acquire the comfortable worn look her old notebook had had—and maybe longer than that for her to recreate all the magical knowledge her prior notebook had held.

Ryana wiped her face and flipped through the pages to where she'd outlined the ingredients of her latest spell—the thing that she hoped might let her finally sleep. Only it wasn't a spell at all.

Just a name: *Austin.*

She sat with the thought for a moment, calming down. He was one of the werewolves in her brother's employ. He was strong, both physically and emotionally, doggedly loyal, and ruggedly attractive—but none of those qualities were better than the fact that he was utterly unconnected to anyone back home.

And what was better was that he seemed like he liked her. He *always* had.

She'd written his name down a week ago. Not to control him magically or any weird thing like that, but to firm her commitment to this course of action. To help make it real.

And, as if to push her into his arms, she'd had a horrible nightmare every night since.

Ryana flopped back flat and stared up at the ceiling. She was tired of feeling like a bad person for doing what she'd had to do, as awful as it was. She was tired, too, of feeling like a fool, beating herself up for being hopelessly naive.

And she was deeply tired of being tired.

She wanted someone else to be strong for her. Just for a moment. Even if it meant nothing, long term. Ever since she'd come to Earth, she'd kept mostly to herself, with only her own thoughts for company...but now that they seemingly hated her, she was painfully alone.

But there was an answer for that, one short flight of stairs and a walk down a hall away.

She got out of bed and pulled on a dress quickly, before she could lose her nerve.

Memories—and men—could be replaced.

All she needed to do was be brave enough to try.

CHAPTER 3

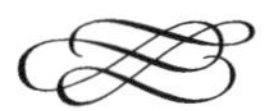

It was midnight the night after a full moon, and rather than being outside and feeling the moon's effects, Austin was killing his friends in a video game.

"What the fuck, Austin?" his brother Zach muttered on their earpiece after Austin shot him in the head.

"Lucky respawn!" Austin gloated from his higher position on a wall, before jumping back down and using an in-game tank for coverage. He'd already killed Max, which just left Jamison. The metal-armed bastard was around here somewhere, and if Austin took him out within the next five seconds, he'd win.

"Come on, come on," he muttered to himself, scanning the screen and the little radar window that gave each of them clues as to the other's locations. A red dot blipped—Jamison was nearby! Austin took his character into a crouch, raced around the back of the tank, and leapt onto his friend, cutting his neck with a knife and sending a gout of blood spattering just as time ran out. "Ha!" Austin shouted into all of their ears.

He heard his brother grumble. "Unfair."

"What, how good I am? Or that that's the tenth time tonight I've beaten you?"

"But not me," Jamison said with a laugh.

"Well, you're harder," Austin said.

"Because you cheat," Zach agreed.

"Please. If I were cheating, would I ever let you win?" Jamison said.

"That's exactly what someone who did cheat would say to play things off. You're too smart to win all the time," Max said.

"Oh come on, Max—you have magic eyes!" Jamison protested. Everyone knew the bear-shifter had to wear goggles all the time to hide them from people.

"Yes, but I still suck at this, so I'm non-threatening," Max said, laughing.

"Yeah, if Max won as often as you did, we wouldn't play him either," Zach added.

"Whatever," Jamison muttered. "I'm not sandbagging." They all knew he could plug his cyborg arm into the computer, though.

"He's not!" Mills, Jamison's girlfriend and their resident witch, piped up from somewhere behind the man, loud enough for them to hear via his microphone.

Austin snickered. He knew Mills was cursed not to lie. "In that case, good game, gentlemen."

"That makes it sound like you're out?" Jamison complained.

"Yeah. I should probably quit while I'm ahead," Austin said, sitting up straighter and arching his back.

He heard his brother laugh heartily. "When the fuck have you ever let being ahead stop you?"

Austin groaned. "I'm wounded."

"Not in the game you're not. Log back on," Zach demanded. It was much safer to do video game violence this near the full moon rather than train, when his and his brother's tempers were so easily riled.

But there was a knock at the door behind his back. Austin turned in his chair, wondering who'd be bothering him this late—especially as it was clear almost everyone else in the house was playing video games, or was game adjacent.

Damian?

"I'll be right back," he announced and set his mic down. He headed for the door, preparing to give Damian shit. The last time the dragon-shifter had visited this late, it'd been because he'd wanted to show Austin the ring he'd gotten for Andi, to make sure she'd like it, which'd made Austin laugh like hell. Yeah, they were cute as a couple, but since they were mates and all, Austin knew very well Damian could've given her a ring pop and she would've said yes.

Although how often did you get to see a nervous dragon?

Not very. He chuckled, remembering.

"Buyer's remorse?" Austin teased as he swung open the door, fully expecting to find his dragon-shifter friend outside...but instead he found Ryana, Damian's beautiful, curvaceous, sarcastic-as-hell-while-still-somehow-being-impossibly-naïve-about-earth-stuff sister. Who, because God was a prankster, had rooms just one floor away from him in Damian's expansive castle.

"Oh, hey, hi Ryana," Austin said, trying to play it cool. Hoping beyond hope that she didn't want to come into his room, which was a mancave at the best of times, but had recently verged into mancave-with-a-lot-of-visible clothing on the floor, because Damian's magical cat Grimalkin didn't always separate whites and colors if you asked for his help with the laundry when you were a werewolf. "It's late. Are you alright?" He stood just inside the door, trying to take up more space so she couldn't see around him.

She seemed to consider this. Her pine-needle green wings waved behind her as she thought, and today her magical guardian Lyka had taken the form of a tiny red hummingbird that was nestled just inside her collarbone, which he could clearly see because Ryana herself was wearing a low-cut scoop-necked dress, also green, a shade in between her dark-green wings and her light-green eyes. "I am," she said, like she'd come to a decision. "Can we talk inside?" she asked, gesturing to the room behind him.

Oh, fuck you Grimalkin for hating me so much. "Sure," he heard himself saying, taking a step back from the door, clearing a trail for her to take to the chair he'd just been sitting in. She stared at it for a second, and he realized it had a back, and why hadn't he gotten in some bar stools, something more gorgeous-woman-with-wings compatible, while he'd had the chance these past few months prior? She snapped her fingers, and her magical guardian Lyka made her the kind of chair she could use with her wings out, and he sat back down on his gaming chair nearby.

"So, to what do I owe the pleasure?" Austin asked, trying to fight the urge to cross his arms. He and Ryana coexisted, nothing more. Of course he flirted with her shamelessly, and he occasionally thought she tried to flirt back, but both of them knew the rules of reality as it currently stood: she was a princess from another world; her brother was a very temperamental dragon-shifter; and he, Austin, was a werewolf who liked to fight and who had a reputation for being a man-whore. There wasn't any way for their Venn diagrams to overlap, especially with the buffer of Damian's presence in the middle.

Ryana took a moment to rearrange her skirt so that it cascaded down her knees and covered up her ankles, only allowing a peek at her red painted toes, which matched her manicure, which matched her feathered guardian, perfectly. She appeared to come to a decision and nodded, either to herself or to him, he wasn't sure. "Hopefully the pleasure will be mine."

Austin took a moment to really look at her, while waiting for her to go on. He didn't get to see her sitting quietly very often—she spent most of her time in her rooms, which had been outfitted like the ones she'd left behind in the Realms, and studied magic and read books on her own. So usually he only saw her during battles, or eating dinner, if their schedules overlapped, or sometimes they passed each other in the training room. Behind him, he could hear Zach calling for him over the earpiece, and when she didn't say anything, he leaned back and grabbed the mic. "Hey, I'm out for the night!" he said and turned his entire gaming system off.

"Sorry about that," he apologized to her. "You were saying…?"

Her smile tightened, then relaxed. "Austin, you know I come from extraordinary circumstances, yes?"

RYANA SAT in front of him and braced herself.

This was it.

She would graciously offer to sleep with him, he would graciously accept, and then it would be the beginning of her making new memories here on *this* planet, slowly scrubbing away the old. Eventually, nothing else that came before would matter, and even if she ever did go back to the Realms, no one *there* would ever worry that she'd come *here,* tonight.

Because Austin was a nobody, in a good way. Born on earth, he had no subterfuge, no secret allies, and no one to tell about their escapade—lest her brother kill him—so overall?

He was perfect.

And there was no reason on this world or any other for him not to agree.

She watched his eyes trace over her wings and saw him frown lightly. There was a pockmark on one of them, from when she'd deflected a bullet meant for him. She'd saved his life, although it'd punched a hole into her wing that'd left a scar.

He owed her. *Yet another reason he'll say yes.*

"Yeah, wings, I'd noticed you're not from around these parts," Austin said with a soft sigh, relaxing in his chair.

Time to be brave!

You are part-dragon!

She pictured herself sleeping through a night. Not waking up with a knot in her throat, crying, feeling horrified or ashamed. Finding rest, true rest, in someone else's arms, no matter how briefly.

The thought of it gave her strength. "Yes, well…different places do things on different schedules. So it seems that on Earth, of course, I'm woefully behind in some components important to my future well-being." She crossed her legs and set her hands in her lap, doing her best to seem as regal as possible.

Austin's head tilted and he gave her a befuddled look. "I can give you more movies to watch, Ryana…maybe even watch them with you, if you wanted?"

"No. That's charming, though," she said with a nervous laugh. *He is going to say yes. Absolutely.* "No, Austin, the reason I'm here is because I'd like you to sleep with me."

And then she watched Austin—suntanned, rough-and-tumble, never met a fight he didn't like, Austin—slowly go as white as the t-shirts that were for some reason littering his floor right now. "Excuse me?" he said, and blinked.

Yes. Immediately to terms. This was exactly how she'd hoped. She sat straighter and smiled winningly at him. "This is an experience I desire to have. And so I am here, requesting your assistance."

"No way," Austin muttered to himself. "Did Zach put you up to this? Because if so, it's really not funny."

It was Ryana's turn to blink—and for the first time since she'd walked into his room, she had a feeling things might not go as planned.

Which was stupid, right?

Because her plan was flawless.

His name was in her notebook!

He was him, she was her, and they'd get together and get it over with. He would be the first in her no doubt many future conquests, which would erase Baran from her memories.

Wouldn't he?

"No, I haven't told anyone else. I've just told you. Just now." She crossed her arms—and he rolled his chair back against the carpeting to be further way from her, a disconcerting maneuver. "Although I have to say, this isn't how I imagined that it would go." Her lips fell to a pout.

One of Austin's eyebrows crawled up to meet his golden hair. "And just what did you imagine, wings?"

She took him in with all her senses—his heart was beating a little fast, but it often did around her—all the more reason she'd assumed this would work! "I thought—I thought there'd be a little more enthusiasm. On your part. Not mine. I'm plenty enthused. It is time for me to be done with this." *And back on the path to sleeping without dreams.*

"You're serious?" he asked her.

"As certain as when Eloph made the sun."

It was an expression from the Realms, and he squinted, getting her gist even if he didn't understand the reference. "When?" he asked her.

"Now? I guess?" She looked around his unkempt room. It wasn't exactly like she'd pictured things, but, well, none of her experience on Earth really was. She'd always imagined her older brother Damian had gone off to a magical place to rule in peace and prosperity. The truth about Earth so far was much more prosaic—and violent. "So," she said, standing. Austin's bed was underneath that pile of clothing over there, surely. *Somewhere*. "Let's set to—"

Austin shook his head, with his tongue dug in beneath his lower lip. "I haven't said yes yet."

Ryana turned to fully look at him. "But you're going to." She hoped he heard the threat implicit in her tone.

He crossed his arms. "Am I? Does having wings give you the ability to read minds?"

"Austin," she said flatly. "I'm not going to beg you." Her pride had limits. Ryana lifted her chin haughtily and arched her wings out, occupying more space. "Do you not want me? Because if that's so, I'm sure I can find someone else."

He swung up out of his chair then. "You think you can waltz into my room and ask me to perform on command?"

Ryana frowned, feeling herself lose power over the situation. "Yes!" she snapped. "Why isn't this easy?" In all the variations she'd run through in her mind, not a one of them had ever ended like this.

"*Because I'm not*," Austin growled. He didn't need wings to loom in front of her. He had a good half-a-foot on her, and his shoulders were quite broad. "Despite what you may have heard."

Ryana squinted up at him. Clearly she'd pressed some button she didn't even know he had. "Fine." She folded her arms in on themselves and her wings back. Surely sleeping with one creature from Earth would be like sleeping with the next. "I'll find someone else. Forget I asked. Forget I was even here."

Austin groaned and rocked back. "That's not what I'm saying, Ryana."

She hugged herself. "Then what are you saying, hmmm? I'm listening –"

"Ryana," he complained at being pressed.

She took a step toward him, glaring up. She knew she was very good at it; it was a family trait. "Perhaps I've surprised you. And perhaps you're not interested. Perhaps you can't even make up your own mind? You are half-hound, after all," she sniffed, then put her finger out to tap on his chest above his heart. "You have three weeks to figure yourself out, Austin. And after that? I will be taking my interest elsewhere."

Ryana waited for him to say something, hoping he would. When he didn't, she whirled and left the room.

CHAPTER 4

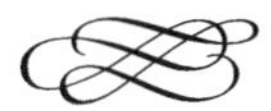

AUSTIN STOOD LOOKING OUT THE DOORWAY LONG AFTER RYANA HAD left. She hadn't closed his door behind her. Back in the Realms, she probably had servants to do that kind of thing.

He slowly sank back down into his gaming chair, so pleased he'd had the foresight to turn the entire thing off so Max and Zach and Jamison—and Mills!—hadn't had the chance to hear what had gone on.

Although if one of them had, it might've made it easier to believe that it had happened.

Had Ryana Blackwood, a princess from the goddamned Realms, just come to his bedroom in the dead of night and offered herself to him? If he couldn't still smell her in the room—her scent was so faint, but he was attuned to it from living with her. It was like soft moss, deep forest and spring water. Without that, he'd manage to convince himself it was all a hallucination. That he'd been drinking too hard —again.

But no, he thought, taking a deep inhale. She'd really been here.

And she'd really wanted him.Well…not precisely him, so much, as the idea of him.

He paced in a small circle, trying to figure out exactly what had happened and convince himself he hadn't fucked it up. *Goddamn his pride*. He should've just taken her at her word, picked her up, and thrown her on his bed.

Thinking about what he could be doing right now with her, if he had, was like a gut punch.

But—if all men were interchangeable to her—which made sense when someone was an *actual* princess—he didn't want that. Christ, he wasn't blind, or stupid—Ryana was a catch. No, she was more than that. She was the kind of woman that, once they came into your life, you grabbed onto with both hands.

She'd just made it very clear she didn't feel that way about him, though...which fucking sucked because, for maybe the first time in his life, Austin wanted to be more than the sum of his cock.

"I don't believe it," he murmured to himself.

"Believe what?" Zach said from the hall.

Austin jumped up and walked to his door. He and Zach had equal and opposite wings on this floor, and Zach was at the top of the stair. "How long have you been out there?"

"Not long—Jamison just kicked my ass another five times. It's totally no fair he sandbags with you and then slaughters me," Zach said, with a suspiciously fake yawn. "I was just going to go outside."

"And?" Austin asked.

"And none of your business," Zach said, flipping him off from the hall. Austin lunged out, grabbed him, and hauled him inside his bedroom, kicking the door closed behind him with his foot. "What? I'm not telling you," Zach protested, as Austin set him free.

"I don't care if you're going out to stalk Stella, Zach. I only care about what just happened here and now," Austin said, indicating the confines of his room. "What do you smell?"

"Laundry," Zach tsked, as Austin rolled his eyes. "And...Ryana." He gave his brother a pointed look.

"I know. Odd, right?"

"Did she come into your room while you weren't here?" Zach walked over and toed a tangled pile of jeans.

"No. She just left, in fact."

"Oh?" Zach asked, turning on him. "How did you manage to lure her in?"

"I didn't." Austin moved to sit down on his bed and indicated that Zach should sit down on his gaming chair and wheel closer, which he did. "She came of her own accord...with a business proposition."

Zach snorted. "Which movies did you tell her to watch this time? Or has she been watching Shark Tank?"

"No," Austin said with a frown and leaned in to whisper. "She wants me to take her virginity."

"What?" Zach's eyes went wide as his jaw dropped.

"Shhhhh!" Austin said, waving his hands.

"I can't believe you didn't swear me to secrecy first!"

"I can't believe you'd think I'd have to, when the alternatives are clearly death, death, and more death!" Austin hissed.

"Damian," Zach agreed, rocking back.

"Oh yeah, he'd kill me for sure. But she's not actually interested in me. She just wants it done—and she said if I didn't do it, she'd find someone else in three weeks."

Zach sucked air in through his teeth. "Really?"

"Yeah."

"Well then, easy. Just wait out twenty-one days, and you'll be in the clear."

Austin opened up his mouth but there were no words. His brother was being sensible, as always, whereas Austin...wasn't.

"Oh God," Zach went on. "You're actually thinking about doing it, aren't you?"

"Wouldn't you?" Austin said, then shook his head. "No, wait, don't tell me, I don't want to have to kill you—and everyone knows your heart's a block of ice."

Zach frowned. "I can't believe you're even considering it, Austin. Don't you get into enough trouble on your own? Can't you just go to another strip club and sweat this out?"

Austin searched inside himself. His life had a rhythm. Everyone who lived here trained hard, fought hard, and in the in-between times they had fun, hard. On full moon nights, he and his brother would go out into the forest and raise a little hell. And on moonless nights—he raised hell solo. Austin would go out to a few different bars he liked, or a strip club, and just be himself. He couldn't do the corporate song and dance the way Zach could; he was more interested in experiencing *life,* as defined by hitting on pretty women and going home with them...or fucking them in bathroom stalls. He wasn't hugely picky, and as long as he was getting off and they were getting off, who cared? Everything else was stressful enough. Even with all the training, he knew he might die at any time. So why not grab a little pleasure when he could?

Especially from someone like Ryana....

"Oh my God," Zach said, watching him. "I should kick your ass right now and save Damian the trouble."

Austin made a low growling noise. "I'd like to see you try." Zach answered him with a growl of his own, and Austin tensed at the same time as his brother did. While a fight the night after a full moon sounded like a really good time, them raising a ruckus was likely to attract attention, which was something that he did not want.

No, he needed time to think, in private. Ish.

He shook himself straight and stopped growling. "You can leave now," he told his brother.

Zach reached forward to grab his shoulders. "At least try to think this through, Austin. There's no possible way it can end well. You know that, right?" He shook Austin's shoulders for emphasis. "Let me hear you say the words."

"Fine," Austin said. "There's no way it can end well. Are you happy now?"

Zach released him and stood. "Not really," he said, giving Austin another glare on his way out the door. Austin watched him leave, sinking back onto his bed. His analytical—emphasis on the 'anal'—brother was right, as usual. But that didn't mean that he couldn't get some...right before he probably died.

He stared up at a ceiling that was depressingly not-spinning, odd considering how the rest of his world was—even odder when he thought of the fact that he hadn't had anything to drink yet today. Not unless he counted the beer he'd drunk three hours ago when they'd started their game, which he didn't really. It was just one beer.

For circumstances like those he'd just been exposed too, he needed at least seven more.

Maybe eight.

Austin stood and went over to his bar, which included a keg of Red Stripe, and pumped himself a pint. His room was sorted out rather like a college dorm, because he'd never seen the point in decorating. Everything he owed looked a little rough around the edges. Worn in. Kind-of like he felt most times.

He brought the cup to his lips, so deep in thought he hadn't tracked the acrid sent of it until he'd almost taken a sip—and then he cursed. "Grimalkin!" he shouted, knowing very well that Damian's cat was always listening, if not watching him—and that it had very deliberately turned his keg of beer into motoroil.

"Fucking cat," he muttered, setting his glass down on the bar. He grabbed his sheepskin-lined flannel coat and headed outside.

HE BOUNDED DOWN THE STAIRS—AND straight into Damian and Andi, who were thick as thieves, setting a tented note down on a table that hadn't been there prior, as they grinned together.

Andi saw him first. "Hey Austin!" she whispered with a smile, then put a finger across her lips to indicate he should be quiet. She was a beautiful girl—a bit delicate for Austin's tastes, especially in comparison to Damian's muscular bulk—and she loved Damian utterly. She had her own life and friends—and her own job still, even, which Austin found kind of bizarre in that Damian had an infinite amount of money—but most of her everything seemed to revolve around her mate, the dragon-shifter—and the same for him, for her. If you'd told Austin before this that a tiny girl was going to be able to wrap Damian *—and his dragon, no less!—*around her little finger, he would have found a bridge to sell you. But now, looking at the two of them, Austin knew it was too late.

Damian gave Austin a guilty look—which was probably the only reason the dragon-shifter wasn't reading the guilty look that Austin could feel plastered across his own face.

I'm thinking about touching your younger sister and not just with my hands—sorry!

"Austin," Damian said with a nod—and Austin finally realized that they had...luggage? And that there was a mirror behind them with a view of a hotel room, with windows that opened onto a balcony someplace where it was already daylight.

"Where are you going?" he asked, instantly concerned.

"Italy. At first," Damian said, reaching over for Andi's hand to give it a squeeze. "Things have been calm lately—"

"That's not a guarantee," Austin said. They needed Damian in fights more often than not.

"I know. But—nothing's guaranteed, really, is it?" he said, drawing Andi closer to him.

"We'll only be a phone call away, Austin. All of our hotels have full-length mirrors—and Italy's full of fountains," Andi told him.

Austin inhaled to protest—they still hadn't figured out when the Conjunction was going to happen, the astronomical event that would open up aligning rifts on all the Realms, with likely horrific monsters pouring through to Earth.

But—he swallowed his words before speaking.

Not because of Ryana—okay, maybe, some—but more because he finally heard what Damian had said. Damian's relationship with the dragon inside himself—who was a totally *other* creature, and not Damian at all—was a tenuous thing, caused by a curse. Damian was doomed to become his dragon eventually—everyone knew it.

Especially the two of them.

And while Mills had been working hard to figure out how to break the curse, she hadn't made any forward progress yet.

So throwing a fit and making them stay behind and miss out on an actual vacation together would just be a dick move on his part, even if letting them go abroad didn't feel one-hundred-percent safe.

Austin forced himself to drop his shoulders from his ears. "All right then, brother. Have fun."

Andi grinned. "We'll bring back souvenirs!"

"And I do mean it—if anything happens—just call," Damian said to him seriously, then looked back at her. Austin could practically watch a current pass between their eyes—if he kept watching this, he was definitely going to need more alcohol.

"Ugh," Austin said, waving his hands in their direction. "Go already. Your mirror's blocking my path to the door."

Damian laughed, picked all their bags up in one strong arm, wrapped his other around Andi, and then pulled them through. Austin could see them reappear on the far side of the mirror a few seconds later—and Andi leaned back to wave furiously, right before the mirror in front of him disappeared.

Austin pushed his way through the castle's main doors with a headshake.

CHAPTER 5

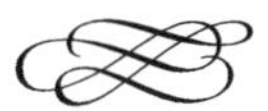

FIFTEEN MINUTES LATER HE WAS AT HIS SECOND FAVORITE BAR. IT WAS late, so the clientele was a little sketchy—himself included. He fit right in. He gave the bartender a nod, and a Red Stripe appeared in front of him, as if by magic and/or the fact that Austin always tipped well. He took a sip of the beer—it *was* actual beer this time—and then turned to look around and see who else was still up tonight that he could get into trouble with. He spotted a friend he hadn't seen in a long time—Dominic. The rhino-shifter gave him a companionable nod from across the room.

Not that kind of trouble. Even this close to the full moon, his wolf had some self-preservation skills, and knew that brawling with a rhino-shifter would only be fun for about thirty seconds prior to when he would begin praying for death. He knew Dominic from his old, pre-Damian-and-gainful employment days, after he'd left the Marines, when he'd spent most of his time beating other people up for money. Dominic never entered the ring, but Austin knew he'd won some sizable bets for the man before.

Before he could get detoured into reminiscing, though—*remember when I yanked that guy's jaw off? Good times!*—his preferred kind of trouble walked straight on up.

"Missy," he said as she stopped just in front of him.

"That's Melissa to you right now," she said, putting her hands on her hips. Missy had long dark hair and an angular face, with lips always on the verge of pouting, and she wore enough crystals to be a witch, even though she wasn't one. Her lavender aroma had always smelled good to him before, but right now…not so much. Must be the remnants of the motor oil Grim had tried to poison him with in his nostrils. "Where the hell have you been, Austin?"

"Around?" he guessed. Truth was, he always lay low the week before a full moon and, honestly, he shouldn't be out tonight so soon after one.

"That's not good enough," she said, taking the seat beside him. "Buy me a round and I might forgive you."

Austin snorted. "Of course," he said, giving the bartender a nod.

Missy caught him up on the local things he'd missed as he knocked back a few, trying to think beneath the thrum of her telling him stories. He managed to make the right sounds at the right places so that it seemed like he was paying attention—and usually he was. He knew his ability to listen got him laid just as often as his looks. But right now, his mind was whirling—trying to figure out what Ryana's angle had been, why, of all people, she'd chosen him, and if he was going to follow through. The bartender kept them coming, and any minute now he was going to forget everything that'd happened earlier in his room, because he'd either drink enough, or—

"In any case," Missy said, quite sloshed herself, as she put a meaningful hand on his knee. "You know I live nearby."

Austin did. He also knew her cat's names were Dawn and Dewdrops—he'd seen their names painted on their food bowls, even though the cats themselves had never made an appearance when he, a werewolf, had come over. And he knew that Missy's perpetually pouty lips looked good wrapped around his cock.

"Walking…distance?" she said, walking her own fingers higher up his leg, miming them going back to her place, as they so often had. It was a proposition which on literally any other night of his life he would've said yes to.

But not tonight. He had shit to figure out—or forget—but he knew hopping into bed with Missy wasn't going to help, plus she was nowhere near sober enough to be making up her mind.

"No," he said, gently, pushing her hand aside. "Thanks, but I'm good."

"I know you're good, that's why I'm trying to take you home with me," she said with a laugh.

"I mean it Missy. Sorry. Not tonight."

His words finally worked their way through her alcohol-sodden brain. "If not tonight, then...when?"

Austin looked down at her, unable to do that math for her, because his own brain was half-liquid at this point, too—and shit, figuring out things with Ryana was like calculus-level, and he'd only gotten through eighth grade before getting a GED. "I don't know." She pouted—for real this time—and then stomped off, looking for someone else to keep her bed warm.

Dominic walked over to where Missy had been, but didn't sit down—if he did, he'd break the barstool. "You gonna buy me a round?"

"Bounty hunting not covering the bills?" Austin taunted, as he gestured the bartender to Dominic's side. The rhino-shifter was built like a cross between the Michelin Man—the mascot of the tire company—and Butterbean, the almost-four-hundred-pound professional boxer. Pale-skinned and bald, other than a dark brown beard on the lower half of his face, Dominic was always sharply dressed, held himself well and, mystifyingly to Austin, had a posh English accent right out of Harry Potter. It was in high contrast to the size of the man, because Dominic didn't just take up space, he inhabited it, called it his bitch, and made multi-dimensional babies with it—he had to be that big to run bounties on other shifters.

"You know how it goes. Ups and downs. Not all of us can be cushy bodyguards to billionaires." No one else knew Austin helped Damian fight unearthly creatures from other Realms, so it was just as well to go along with Dominic's assumption, as the much-larger man clapped

Austin's back with enough force to make an echo. "I wouldn't think you'd be out this close to a full moon."

"I'm not immune to bad decisions," Austin said, looking at the bottom of his drinking glass, and wondering just how soon he could get back home to make one. *Or not. He could...just. Not.*

Somehow.

"Speaking of, then, mind if I go for your bird?"

Austin blinked and looked up. Missy was in someone else's lap, and she looked like she'd snuck in a few shots on her way there. And he knew her well enough to know that, if she saw Dominic chatting to him and then making a move for her, she'd jump on the other man to get back at Austin, her current level of inebriation be damned.

"Sorry man, but I do." He opened up his wallet and slid over two hundred-dollar bills to the bartender, pointing at the bottle of Red Breast Irish Whiskey behind him. "Give me that, close me out, and keep the change." The bartender handed the rest of the bottle over quickly, as Austin put his fingers to his lips and whistled loud. "Missy!" he shouted for her, like she was a bad dog. Her head snapped around, and she walked over with a sultry attitude, even though her eyes were glazed. "We're going home."

"About time," she said, tucking herself against him. Austin gave Dominic a curt nod, and then wheeled the both of them out of the bar, the bottle in one hand.

MISSY WAS on him like an octopus the second the doors closed behind him, trying to climb him like a tree, kissing his neck and clawing his flannel.

"Cut it out," he warned her, tempted to just put her under one arm and jog her home.

"What? Why?" she protested, walking faster to keep up with him. "Down to business?" she teased.

"Yeah," he grunted, swatting her ass, because he knew it'd make her go faster. She laughed, skipped, and almost fell. He caught her, and then gave up and scooped her into a cradle carry, marching her down the next block, her sucking on his neck and jaw, only letting her down to use her card to swipe them into her apartment complex, where he carried her up the stairs to her door.

She opened it, turned to look back invitingly at him—and he reached forward and closed it on himself, trapping her inside.

"Austin?" she asked. "Is this some kind of game?"

"Yep," he told her, sitting down on her doormat, holding the doorknob steady in his hand, despite her turning it. He tilted the bottle of Irish whiskey up—the bartender had left the shot-glass-pourer on, how kind—and started emptying it inside his mouth.

"Austin! Come inside! Right now!" she demanded. He felt her trying to twist the door handle, and when that didn't work, she started beating on the door.

"Cut it out, Missy," he said, slurring her name a little. "It's late. I'm just saving you from trouble."

Because that's what you did when you saw someone running out in front of a train. You stopped them.

But what if you were the train?

What was your responsibility then?

Didn't you owe something to all train-kind?

Shouldn't they have known better than to run out in front of you, anyways?

Austin listened for movement inside the apartment and didn't hear any. Missy had stopped trying to open the door, and they were three flights up, so he knew she wasn't going to go jumping out a window.

He took another swig of liquor, dialed up his car with one of Jamison's apps on his phone, and stumbled back down the stairs to meet it.

HE DIDN'T DRIVE himself home, the car did—God bless Jamison and all his toys—which allowed him to continue to drink freely, as the devil on his shoulder fought with an angel who was shouting in from somewhere in the trunk.

Ryana wanted him.

No, she wanted someone.

But maybe him.

Or...just someone!

But she'd come to him first, hadn't she?

Because she literally only knows a handful of people on Earth.

She was a woman, of course she had needs.

But why hasn't she done anything with those needs sooner?

Didn't she know that werewolves had needs, too? He sucked in air and fought not to touch the steering wheel out of habit. Right now —*Jesus*—could she have picked a worse time? Moonlight poured in through the car's windows, even through the heavy tint, and it was like it called to the wolf inside of him. He only had to change on full moon nights, but that didn't mean that the beastlier half of him wasn't always there and hungry. It wanted whatever he would give it and then some. Fighting, fucking; it did nothing half-way. He had no idea how his brother, who was practically a eunuch, coped.

And at the thought of being with Ryana, full speed ahead, damn the torpedoes and likely death at Damian's hand...it was enough to make him want to howl.

The car pulled itself into the roundabout with the fountain in front of Damian's castle. Austin got out, left the bottle behind, and went inside.

CHAPTER 6

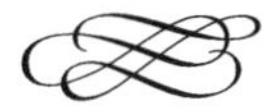

RYANA WENT BACK TO HER ROOMS, FEELING STRANGELY DISAPPOINTED. It was an unusual sensation, one that had few corollaries in her pre-Earth life, and she didn't like it at all.

Lyka had left the lights on, so she could easily see the sum total of all of her current possessions—an empty bed, a plain desk, and several overstuffed bookcases. Her few magical mirrors were safely fogged, and there was a door at the back of her suite that led to the laboratory where she performed her experiments.

This was it.

On Earth, this was all she was.

It didn't feel like much.

Ryana swallowed. She wanted to be mad at Austin for not saying yes—especially after he'd spent the last few months flirting with her so overtly—but maybe she wasn't as impressive as she had been, once upon a time. Back when she'd been a princess and had always had the trappings of power swirling around her.

She tugged at the neck of her dress, like she suddenly found it stranglesome, and Lyka took off from her shoulder, knowing what she needed—the safety of work.

Grimalkin, her brother's magical cat, had created her laboratory much like hers had been at home, where she could perform her magics and regain the knowledge that was lost with her old notebook. She'd had to leave it behind with all the rest of her possessions when her half-brother Damian had pulled her over from the Realms to Earth, saving her life during a battle. It was utterly unsafe for her to return, which meant that she was stuck.

Here.

Alone.

She bunned up her hair and pulled her wings in, disappearing them inside herself with magic, as Lyka hovered and found her dress's zipper with her beak. The bird tugged it down, so that Ryana could step out of the swishy fabric and pull on a shirt and jeans, and then her work clothes: gloves and a protective apron, which had panels of blastproof fabric sewn into it. Her helmet, which was lined with protective wards and had a panel of magically enhanced glass on the front was already waiting for her on her work bench inside her lab.

She'd started working with certain magicks on her own in the Realms prior to fleeing, trying to make the liquid-metal portals which, unbeknownst to her, had once been used to attack Damian. With the Conjunction coming up, she felt such a magical item would eventually be of use, and she trusted Damian's people to not betray him. So she'd restarted her work, even though it was hot and dangerous. Lyka could recreate certain ingredients from her, Damian had helped her to order other ones, and Mills had sourced a difficult few, but it was in combining them over certain temperatures with one another repeatedly, while exerting her will on them, that turned them into something *more*—if they didn't catch fire. Or explode. Which they had done, repeatedly—the whole process was just incredibly volatile.

Kind of like a certain werewolf.

Her gloved hand holding a glass beaker shook, and the contents erupted into flame.

Eloph-burn-it! she cursed in her native tongue.

Lyka sat safely up at the top of a bookcase ten feet ahead of her. "Are you sure performing magic right now is a good idea?" Her guardian was always concerned with her well-being and entirely unsure about her efforts, seeing as Ryana had gotten herself injured on more than one occasion.

Ryana set the flaming beaker down and put a lid on it to starve the fire of air. "Not in the least. But I need to do *something*." She couldn't go back to sleep just yet, not until she'd exhausted herself past the point of dreaming again.

And ever since she'd come to Earth she'd felt this hollow yearning. At first she'd assumed it was homesickness, but now that she was months out from her arrival, she was considerably less sure.

It was more like everyone else around her appeared to have a *purpose.* She trained like everyone else did, and she fought when they all went fighting, but it was not *enough.* And training and fighting didn't fill all of everyone's days—it was just that everyone else seemed to have someone else to spend their time with. Damian and Andi obviously belonged together, as did Mills and Jamison, and Zach and Austin got to leave the castle's compound frequently. Whereas all she had were books, and TV, and a world she didn't entirely understand just outside her door.

It just wasn't fulfilling—no matter how much fun it was watching the K-dramas Andi had turned her onto. And sometimes watching those even—*Goblin,* in particular, with its palace intrigue, fashion, and dramatic romances—made her feel even worse. Because then she got to see people living lives—albeit imaginary ones—that felt like they had more meaning than hers did.

She didn't know what else to do, so she did what it felt like she could: blowing herself up a little bit at a time—or managing to make another dram of the shiny metallic liquid.

Because other than that, her only choices felt like dreams that made her want to die, or aching while awake.

Ryana frowned and took her helmet off, her hair sticking to the nape of her neck in sweaty waves. "I'm heading to bed now," she announced.

"Would you like me to sing you a song?" Lyka offered.

"Please," Ryana said, and the bird followed her back into her bedroom, trilling.

. . .

RYANA DOZED in a short silky slip with only one sheet on, trying to cool off after her time so near the ovens in her lab.

Was she tired enough to be safe from dreams now, truly?

She'd never know until she closed her eyes.

She sighed, turned over, and risked it, willing herself to sleep deeply, without dreams. A moment later she heard her door crack open. The scent of wolf and alcohol washed in.

Ryana didn't sit upright—she'd had people watching her sleep her entire childhood; between her Kagaroth guards and Lyka, it wasn't threatening.

She was more curious why. She kept breathing in the same slow pattern, wondering just what Austin's game was.

Surely he'd just look in, find her asleep, and go back to his own rooms—but no. She could hear him coming closer—it was like he wasn't even trying to be quiet—and then she felt her bed shift as he climbed on top of it, knocking books out of the way.

And then he stopped. *What is he thinking?* She knew he was right behind her; she could feel the way the mattress pulled with his greater weight, so it was like gravity itself wanted her to turn to face him. She couldn't hear his breath, but she could feel it, fortified with enough alcohol to get *her* intoxicated. And even though her nose wasn't as sensitive as her brother's, or the wolves', she could still scent a feminine lavender radiating off of him.

Some other woman's perfume.

Austin aligned his body with hers, making contact slowly from her back down, his chest pressed first, strong and broad, followed by his hips and his—she bit back a yelp of surprise, at feeling his hard-on nestle between the cheeks of her ass.

"Wings, you up?" he hoarsely whispered in her ear.

"I am now," she whispered back. "Why are you here, Austin?" She fought the urge to turn around and slap him—she knew Lyka would kill him if she so much as snapped her fingers, so she felt completely safe.

He smoothed her hair back from her cheek and she felt the roughness of his hands against her neck, and while she knew she should be pissed, there was something about the contact that made her thrill—how long had it been since she'd let anyone touch her? He leaned against her with his entire body and her thin sheet and slip hid nothing from either of them. "I'm here to give you what you want." His voice was like liquid darkness in her ear, and it burned like the whiskey he'd surely been drinking, or the magical components which she'd earlier set aflame. "You want easy?" he asked, rocking against her again with promise. "I can give you easy."

Ryana blinked in the darkness. This...was what she'd wanted... right? It was certainly what she'd asked him for. After all, she'd proposed going to bed right then and there in his room.

They could do this now and Baran would be one step closer to being a distant memory, instead of the ghost that haunted her every night.

So why did she feel so sad now at the thought of it?

He rocked into her again—but now he was doing it to push off of her. "Jesus. My wolf—*fuck*—" he muttered to himself, backing away from her as she finally turned over to face him, despite the fact the room was black.

"You've been drinking, haven't you," she asked.

"I have."

"Have you considered that maybe you shouldn't?"

He chuckled low just next to her. He was still so close, just a hand's width away. "You don't get to tell me what to do, Ryana."

"I'd noticed." There was something about the rumble of his voice that confused her. It made her both want to listen to him, raptly, and also tell him everything. A long silence passed between them then. "I shouldn't be here," he said, finally breaking it.

"You're right, you shouldn't," she softly agreed.

"And," he said, while reaching out to find her wrist with his hand and somehow catching it at once, "you shouldn't want this from me." He brought her hand toward him, placing it on his erection. She could feel its firm outline, hidden only by his jeans. "I am not the man for you." He released her and she slowly pulled her hand back as he also pulled away.

"I'm not a fool, Austin. I know," she agreed, even softer. She knew she and the wolf didn't belong together. *That was the whole point of choosing him!* She reached out and put her hand on his chest. "But that doesn't mean that I want to be alone."

He paused, and she could almost feel him gathering his will to depart. "No. Not like this. And not tonight."

"Definitely not," she agreed. As ready as she was to be done with things, she still had *some* pride.

Another long moment passed between them, during which she could feel the slow and steady beating of his heart. Then she felt him move to sit up at her bedside. She snapped her fingers and magically illuminated the room, revealing a fully clothed Austin sitting right in front of a dangerously pissed-off bird. Lyka had shifted up into the size and shape of a phelleran, a mythical creature which their nannies used to threaten her and Damian with, when they were misbehaving children. Lyka's sharp beak was as long as Ryana's leg, all the better to snap bratty children in two. "Whoa," Austin said, sensing the danger he'd been in all along for the first time.

Ryana gave him a faint smile in this new light. "And maybe don't sneak in again. For your own safety."

WHAT THE HELLLLLLLLLLLLLLLLLLLLLLL.

Austin's conscience—mostly factory-sealed, mint-in-box—started yelling at him the second he stepped into the hall.

The girl just told you she was a virgin, you idiot. And you thought it was a good idea to haul your drunk ass up there and start to write checks with your dick?

What the fuck were you thinking?

He made it into his room, tossed even more clothes on his floor, and headed into his bathroom to take the world's longest, coldest, shower. He was already getting sober, his shifter-liver too strong for its own good, and the better it worked the more he realized how badly he'd fucked up.

Not only had he gone and ground up on her, but he'd somehow *agreed* to follow through on things? That couldn't be right, she must've just been saying things to get him to leave—but that moment when she'd put her hand on his chest—even in his currently freezing shower, he thought he could still feel its outline. That had felt *real.* And—her big-ass bird had been there the whole time. So as threatening as he'd felt he'd been…shit, in hindsight, was he really? It was one thing for Grimalkin to be an asshole who dyed his shirts pink, but he knew that if he ever really got on the truly bad side of Damian's cat, he'd be a goner for sure. Grimalkin would just open up a door to a closet that hadn't been there before, shut him inside of it, erase the door, and no one would ever hear from him again.

But just because he hadn't truly been dangerous didn't mean he was off the hook. He'd gone into her room with intent.

And his intent was…?

To either fuck her and ruin things preemptively—furtively, in the dark, with enough alcohol on board to kill a horse—or to scare her off of him.

Neither of which had actually happened.

Amazingly and completely no thanks to him and his self-destructive streak.

He dried himself off, remembering the way she smelled, like forest moss and light sweat, and how come was that? It wasn't like she'd ever had to work a day in her life. When he went back to his bedroom, he found his keg on his bed, leaking beer.

"Goddammit, Grim," he cursed, kicking enough of his clothes into a pile on the floor to use as a nest to sleep it off.

CHAPTER 7

KLAXONS WOKE HIM UP SOMETIME AFTER NOON THE NEXT DAY. HE blinked, coming too, feeling the familiar surge of adrenaline pumping him up before a fight—and then all his memories of the prior evening returned in full color, larger than life. He stood and realized his keg had returned to its prior location at least—maybe Grim was taking pity on him. He went to his closet where he kept the clothing he actually cared about—his black tactical gear—and hauled it on as quickly as he could, before running into the hallway and smack into Zach.

"Nice outfit," Zach teased, although he was wearing the exact same thing.

"Fuck you," Austin muttered, following his brother down the stairs. "What're we dealing with?"

"I don't know. Just heard the alarms, same as you."

And then, ahead of them, a scream of horror. The werewolves looked to one another and then practically flew down the final flight.

"He left me?" Ryana's voice rose an octave, as she held a folded piece of paper in a shaking hand. She was dressed all in black too, her wings magically tucked away, obviously assuming she was coming along—which, if Austin had had a say, *fuck no,* only he didn't—and her fingers were clamped around the note Damian had left like it was electrocuting her.

Austin slowed way, way down. *Shit.* "Yeah. I, uh, saw him and Andi leave last night. They wanted to go on vacation," he said, turning, announcing it to their growing crew, as Jamison, Mills, and Max arrived. The bear-shifter gently pried the letter away from Ryana and read it to everyone aloud—a note about how Damian and Andi needed a vacation, but everyone should feel free to call them at the drop of a hat.

Austin jumped in when Max was done. "Even though he said we could call if we needed him, I could tell he was hoping that we wouldn't."

Or was that just him, hoping it very fervently, now?

Mills blinked and took stock of things. "Really?"

"I think he didn't want to worry us. Or…." His words drifted as he glanced over at Ryana, who looked on the verge of throwing-up.

Max frowned. "Well. I suppose he is only a mirror's length away."

"And Italy is full of fountains," Austin quipped, just like Andi had. *If this works, Damian, your mate is a queen.*Mills seemed to consider this and nodded sagely. "True," she finally agreed, and Austin let himself relax. "What do you think," she said, turning to Jamison, whose eyes had glazed as he tracked whatever it was they were about to fight.

He returned his attention to their group with a grin. "I think we've got this. Let's let the lovebirds be."

Not long after that, everyone but Max was saddled up inside the 'tour bus,' their extraordinarily well-armed and armored SUV that Jamison had modded for them. But instead of what'd become their normal seating arrangement, with Austin right next to Ryana, just like he'd manipulated it every time he could since she'd arrived, she'd gone out of her way to sit on the other side of his brother. He couldn't say anything, but Zach noticed and gave him a pointed look.

"So, what are we up against?" he asked, leaning forward.

"A small rift the size of a dinner plate—should be a fast job," Jamison said from the front passenger seat as Mills drove.

"Why're we taking a full crew then?" Zach asked.

"We weren't going too, but...." Mills started.

"Because of Damian," Ryana said in an irritated tone. Austin couldn't tell if she was peeved at him or her newly absent brother, but he dearly wished the latter.

"Yeah," Mills agreed. "I think it's best if we travel in a pack while he's gone. I don't want to take any additional risks."

"Fair," Zach acknowledged. "Anything more?"

"Not really, no," Jamison said. "Just one of those weird ones, about an hour outside of town."

"Don't tell me—it's in a field of corn?" Austin guessed. They'd been to rifts in two of those crop-circle things before, and while most were borne of drunken college shenanigans, he was pretty sure the last one they'd closed had been a pit to hell.

"Farm yes, corn no. It's in a cow lot." Jamison angled the screen on his lap so everyone sitting in the back could see it.

"That's going to stink," Zach said, curling his lip.

"What do cows smell like?" Ryana asked, sitting forward. Lyka was draped around her neck, tail feathers on one shoulder, her neck on the other, her head resting on one of Ryana's breasts, giving Austin a baleful glare.

"Disgusting," Mills informed her.

"Ah. Just like booze?" Ryana asked.

Austin winced. Yeah, he was not in the clear yet. *Understandably.*

THEY COULD SCENT the cow lot before they saw it, and it didn't smell any prettier up close. Mills took the SUV onto the dirt road that led to the lot's back gate and popped it open with her magic as they went off road. The field ahead of them was immense, and the lot was bounded by distant warehouse-like buildings. It was dotted with cow patties, but there were no cows to be seen.

"I've got this whole area on blackout now," Jamison announced.

"And I called in a fire down the road just a bit ago—most of the farm hands went down there to help, and anyone who didn't Max can sweep up later."

Austin looked in the rear view and saw Max's truck pull onto the road behind them. The bear-shifter mostly travelled alone when he was carrying Forgetting Fire. It was safer. He took a strong left, towards the distant buildings.

"Where are the cows?" Ryana asked, looking eagerly outside—and Austin realized she'd probably never seen a cow in person before. Not an Earth-cow at least.

"More importantly, where's the rift?" Zach asked.

"Just ahead. Under that oak tree," Jamison said, pointing. It was past the hill they were on, so they could only see the top of it.

Mills aimed their SUV over the hill and once they crested it, she gasped.

There was indeed a rift there—a little diamond-shaped tear in the fabric of reality, hovering in mid-air with weird light pouring through. Jamison was right about its dinner-plate size, and there was a ring of dead cows in a circle around it, with what looked like stab wounds on each of their necks and with all of their bellies sliced open. He glanced over to see what, if any, effect that was having on Ryana, who'd put her hand to her mouth—and then she caught him looking. Her eyes narrowed.

Mills parked the SUV, and everyone got out, shouldering gear. Dead cows smelled even worse than live ones—but the part of Austin that was a wolf didn't mind. The sharp scent of so much carnage held a certain raw allure.

"I feel confident we can seal that rift...but what did this?" Mills asked, stepping forward. Her hands were out, as if she were pressing the air, and she was walking slowly up to the nearest cow.

"Hang on," Ryana told her, catching her shoulder. "I have a feeling." Austin watched her scan the cows' number—all of the cows had been beef cattle, so their hides were tawny red—until she found one that interested her. "Lyka, I need a stick."

Her guardian bird magically produced one, just as tall as Ryana was, and she advanced on a particular cow. Austin tensed—and then when she whapped the cow's side he almost laughed.

"It's dead, Ryana," he said, sure that it was—there was too much blood for it not to be—when something moved beneath the hide.

"Just as I thought," Ryana muttered to herself, squatting. She used the stick to prop open the wound on the cow's stomach. "I see you in there."

All of them heard a metallic shrieking, emanating from the dead cow's hide.

Ryana looked to Lyka, who squawked at her.

If Ryana's deadly-serious guardian bird wasn't concerned for her safety, did that mean it was safe? Or that he should take the fool bird's place? Austin came up to her side just in case. "What's going on?"

"Lyka, tell him he can come out now." Lyka perked up again, translating. The shrieking began anew, and then Lyka 'spoke' to Ryana again, and she laughed. "I don't care how warm and comfortable he is. He doesn't belong here, and he needs to go back. And tell him, if he doesn't hurry, he won't be able to."

Lyka did as she was told as the rest of them gathered around, and a creature rather like a clear gelatinous spider, but with far, far, too many legs emerged from the dead cow's side. It ignored all of them, with what Austin assumed was its...*face?*...which was dotted with milky white eyes.

"You've gotta be fucking kidding me," Jamison said.

"Ryana," Austin growled, ready to yank her back.

"It's okay," she said, waving everyone down. "He's full now, aren't you?" she asked and Lyka translated.

Being able to see the thing shrieking did not help—especially now that there weren't any cow organs muffling its tones. Ryana stood and dusted her hands on her thighs. "I saw the marks on the cow's necks. He bit all of them, drained half their blood, then started trying to figure out which one he wanted to nest in. We don't want that here, though."

"Does any place want that?" Zach said, keeping his gun out but safely pointed at the ground.

"Yes," Ryana said, putting herself between him and the creature. Austin moved around her to keep an eye on the creature. "They're quite rare in the wild. And they usually nest for years, quietly nurturing their young. They're distant relatives of our guardians, if you can believe it. That's why Lyka knows its language."

"How interesting!" Mills said, coming closer to her side.

"It looks like a space-spider," Jamison said, edging back.

"It kind-of does, doesn't it!" Ryana said with a laugh, and Austin belatedly remembered that he'd told Ryana to watch all the Alien movies. Now he wondered when she'd watched them whose side she'd been on.

Max strode up, with his lantern of Forgetting Fire swinging at the end of a pole, balanced on his shoulder. "None of the men remaining saw anything—or saw me," he said, reaching back with a hand to tap the lantern's side. Then he saw what Ryana was hiding. "A progenitor!" Austin heard surprise in the bear-shifter's voice, but not fear.

"I know," Ryana said, pleased. "Lyka, please—tell it to hurry. We need to close the rift so more creatures don't fall through and get lost."

The bird translated, and the tire-sized creature bobbed as it listened. Then it shrieked back to Lyka, who flew up in the air.

"What?" Ryana said, startling just like her bird. Lyka wheeled and grew in size, much as she had the prior night, as she cawed back to Ryana. Ryana gasped, dropped her stick, and reached for the gun strapped to her thigh. As everyone else cocked their weapons at the space-spider, she aimed for the rift. "It didn't fall through. It was shoved."

The rift ahead of them, that'd been so small and containable moments ago, started tearing wider—and men began pouring out of it.

Ryana's aim, which'd seemed so sure a second ago to Austin, faltered, as her gun shook in her hand—but the man who was stepping through the rift just like it was a fucking doorway had no such problem, and Austin watched him lift a weapon at her.

"Ryana!" he shouted, throwing himself at her and taking her down. He saw a flash of red wings as Lyka launched herself at the intruder, blocking any attacks. A firefight erupted above them, but all he could think of was Ryana, who was eerily still beneath his bulk. "Are you all right?" Why wasn't she yelling at him, pushing him back, doing any of the things that would be like her? "Ryana?" he asked her, holding himself up to see if she'd been injured. He didn't smell any blood, but shit, what did her blood even smell like?

She was below him, stricken, her eyes wide, as shots rang out both overhead and behind them. Austin grabbed her with one arm and hauled her over to where the nearest carcass could shield them both. "Are you hurt?" He watched her try to make a word, and when she couldn't, she just furiously shook her head—and he realized he didn't know if he could trust her. "Are you telling me the truth?"

She nodded, taking a shuddering inhale.

"All right. Stay here," he said, looking around. He still heard gunshots—he peeked over the cow's side and saw Jamison and Zach both at the rift's edge, firing into it, while Max guarded Mills as she performed her rift-closing magic. It seemed like they had it covered, so he stayed at Ryana's side.

"Done!" Mills shouted, and a second later the light-from-another-realm disappeared.

Austin looked down at Ryana again. "Can you stand?" he asked her, and she nodded again. He stood and offered her a hand.

"Are you all right, princess?" Max asked, striding over with a look of concern.

"No," Ryana answered him—and took his hand, not Austin's. *Goddammit.* Austin looked her over clinically, trying to find any wounds he might have missed, as she walked toward one of the corpses of the men that'd come through. They'd each been hit by multiple bullets, and one had massive gouges down his chest from Lyka's claws. Ryana stared down at the nearest body, then asked Max, "You see what I see, yes?"

Max nodded gravely. "Unfortunately."

Ryana shook her head and knelt down. The men on the ground all had similar armor on, black leather and metal breast plates, black meshed metal sleeves, and hideous faces carved on their helmets.

Ryana reached for one and seemed to have no problem undoing the many latches and buckles that kept it fastened to its armor, pulling off the snarling face of some unknown-to-Austin demon, and revealing a man underneath.

"I don't know him," Max said. "Do you?"

Ryana looked at the man again, and then at the mask, as though they were one and the same. "He's from the Lost Faction. They're Kagaroth. The royal guard. Or, they were," Ryana said, turning. She pointed to a spot on the man's chest where it looked like an emblem had been ripped off. "They're rogue."

"Rogue Kagaroth? That's impossible!" Max said, alarmed.

"It happened after you left, Maximillian, when things were beginning to unravel. Some of them behaved...distastefully." She licked her lips in thought. "Although honestly, now that everything's in chaos back home, who's to say they aren't all rogue, now?"

"What are they doing on this side of the rift?" Zach asked, as he reloaded his gun.

"I don't know." Ryana tossed the helmet on the ground.

Mills made a thoughtful sound. "Will the Forgetting Fire take care of them?"

Max groaned. "No."

"Go get the truck. We can toss them in the bed," Zach said. Max grunted assent and walked away.

"And then what?" Austin asked his brother.

"Figure out shit later, at home."

Ryana gasped again, looking around. "Did the progenitor go back? Did anyone see?"

"Fuck, I forgot about that thing," Jamison cursed, before full-body shuddering.

"Lyka?" Ryana asked. Her bird flew back down from where it'd been hovering, to land on her shoulder, and its beak pointed at another cow, which Ryana walked up to, picking up the edge of the wound on its belly fearlessly. "Can you come help us, ancient one?" The shrieking that made Austin want to cut off his ears began anew. "I know you're full. But can you do this favor for me? And then I promise you we will find you such a nice warm place to nest, until we can get you back home."

The space-spider reluctantly emerged from the cow's belly, red streaks on its clear carapace, and went over to the nearest Kagaroth. "Yes. Those are the ones. Please—and thank you," she told it, as it unhinged its mouth to wrap it around the Kagaroth's boots. Austin only looked for long enough to know what was happening, and then decided he was okay without imprinting the image in his memory, and turned.

"Oh, fuck no," Jamison said.

"You don't have to watch," Ryana told him. Some of her spirit was coming back to her, post-fight. Austin knew it must've been a tremendous surprise to see warriors from her home arrive, unexpectedly—but he'd feel a lot better if he could get another clear look at her green eyes, to try to read what she was thinking.

Max got out of his truck and saw what the progenitor was doing. "Well, that's certainly a solution," he said, then looked to her. "But it's still on the wrong side of the rift."

"It's all right," Ryana told him, before turning toward the others. "It can live inside a box; they fold up quite small. I'll just keep bringing it to fights until we have an opportunity to send it back. I'll handle it."

Jamison stormed over, angling himself so that he only saw Ryana and not what the space-spider was doing to yet another corpse. "Ryana, you're a fantastic addition to our crew, but there's no goddamned way I'm driving around with a monster in a box."

She finally spared Austin the glance he'd been longing for, and shrugged. "You drive around with him, don't you?"

CHAPTER 8

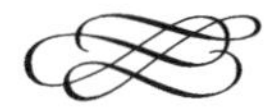

THEY DROVE HOME IN RELATIVE SILENCE, ALL OF THEM AWARE THAT there was a creature from another world 'nesting' in an empty munitions box beneath the back seat.

"Just how sure are you it's not going to come out in the middle of the night and eat our faces?" Jamison asked Ryana in the rear view.

"Very. It had a large meal. It needs time to digest. A few years." Ryana said, looking pensively out the window at the passing fields. "Probably."

"Probably?" Jamison said, his voice rising, as Mills set her hand on his arm.

"Shush," she said, before twisting back. "I think the next thing we need to decide is whether or not to tell Damian."

Everyone in the car looked to Ryana, Austin included, leaning forward to see her around his brother's wide shoulders.

Ryana returned her attention to her co-passengers. "The progenitor did say it was shoved...so that implies its appearance here was intentional. But I haven't known Kagaroth to be able to create rifts before. And even if they did create that rift, and weren't just acting opportunistically, having found one open—why would they shove a progenitor through?" She tapped a thoughtful finger against her lips, apparently unconcerned that it was streaked with blood. "I don't know, really," she admitted, then looked around their number, minus Austin, again. *He needed to apologize, and fast.* "But what I do know is that Damian's not going to know, either. He knows even less about the Realms, currently, than I do, seeing as he left the longest ago. So I don't think it's worth bothering him just yet. And besides—we don't want to give him reasons to turn dragon-y, if we can help it. It's not good for him."

Zach considered this and grunted. "We did seem to handle them just fine with the bullets you warded for us, Mills."

The witch nodded. "All right then, we're agreed," she said, then heaved a massive sigh.

"What's wrong, baby?" Jamison asked. "Other than the obvious, that I am transporting a spider against my will."

Mills chuckled and reached out to rest her hand behind his neck, familiarly. "People are going to think all those dead cows are from Satanists, and that's a shame. I know a few. They're nice people."

Usually Austin stuck around in the garage to help restock the tour bus, but this time he didn't—he followed Ryana straight inside the castle, and didn't care who saw.

"Wings," he said, trotting up the stairs after her. She had the box they'd put the creature in beneath one arm. "Wings—I need to apologize."

She stopped, halfway up the flight, and didn't look back at him. "Yes."

He walked up until he was in front of her, blocking her path—and able to see the closed door behind her, the one any one of the other numerous people who also lived in this house could just walk right through at any moment.

"I am sorry. I'd like to make excuses for myself, but I know there are none."

Ryana nodded, while looking at something about a foot to the right of his boots, which was apparently intensely interesting. "Go on?"

"And I meant what I said." Austin looked over her shoulder, at the still closed door. "I am not the right man for you," he whispered.

Her green eyes finally flashed up at him. "And I meant what I said —that you are good enough for now."

He sharply inhaled. That's all this was, of course. All that she wanted. One ride on him and she'd be finished. Pride and hope waged a battle inside him, and surprising even himself, pride won. He ran his hands through his hair. "Look—fine—let me take you out with me tonight. And I'll show you why even that's a bad idea, okay?"

She considered it for a moment, then agreed. "Time? And attire?"

Austin swallowed. "Midnight. And—anything. Just no feathers."

"I don't have feathers," she said with a pout.

"You know what I mean," he said. She sniffed as she sidestepped around him, and Austin paused to watch the hypnotic sway of her hips as she walked up to her floor.

If there's a god who watches over dragons—help save her from me, because I'm sure as hell not that strong.

RYANA RETURNED to her rooms in dismay.

Of course the wolf didn't want her.

He'd only come to her the prior night under the influence of alcohol, after his earlier refusal. Probably after taking another woman to bed, with the way he stank.

Did she somehow think she was more appealing now, covered in cow blood and scented with waste? There were sticks of straw in her hair, she knew; she could feel them jabbing her scalp the whole way home, but she hadn't wanted to pull them out.

Because part of her thought she deserved them.

She put the box with the progenitor in front of her oven's hearth, where it'd be comfortable, and sat atop it. She'd recognized each of the men who'd come through the rift by their helmets. The one she'd unmasked was Draegor—it was the first time she'd seen his face—and she'd once been so sure of his loyalty she'd had him pass notes from her to Baran. *Of all of their loyalty.*

They made sure her entire life that she'd had no reason to doubt it.

When she was a little girl playing hide and seek with Damian, there were Kagaroth at her side. When she was older, Kagaroth followed her in her garden, listening to her sing girlish songs to herself as she harvested watchberries—fruit with short-lived hallucinogenic properties that helped you pass the time—and they kept guard over her and her girlfriends once they'd taken the berries, their stern and upright presence in stark contrast to the passel of maniacally laughing girls writhing at their feet.

And when she was older yet, she'd given her heart to a Kagaroth, and he'd held it in his armored fist and crushed it.

Kagaroth weren't supposed to ever take their helmets off. They were barely supposed to talk. And so, when Baran did both in front of her years ago, she was taken aback. All of her mother's warnings about maintaining dignity and perpetually royal behavior fell by the wayside—after all, how could the same Kagaroth who'd watched her grow up, loyal to nothing but the throne her mother possessed, ever be interested in betraying her?

How little did she know.

In hindsight, she'd been an easy target. The Kagaroth came and went as they pleased and controlled their own schedules, and it was nothing for Baran to arrange to be alone in hallways with her, or the only one on guard inside her lab. She was certain now that all his squad was in on her attempted kidnapping, but afterwards she never knew precisely where Baran had stood. Had they drawn lots? Had he gotten shortest straw, so it was up to him to break her heart?

The worst of it was that, while it was happening, she didn't mind. All she knew at the beginning was that he showed a kindly interest. And at the level of her station, for all of the palace's attendants that surrounded her, very few had time or were brave enough to interact. She'd aged out of childish games and most childhood friends, and by the time the few suitors who her mother allowed arrived, it was already too late.

She thought she was Baran's.

The only person who claimed to want her for her. Who made her feel like she was worthy of love that didn't come attached to her station.

She'd made a devastating mistake, and now she was here on Earth, begging a wolf to be interested.

"Princess?" Lyka asked, spinning her head down on a long neck to peer up at her wet eyes. Her guardian ran her head alongside Ryana's cheek, brushing away the first tears that'd escaped. "Don't cry. I'm sure it was a coincidence. I do not think we'll see their like again."

Ryana savagely wiped her other cheek, where Lyka hadn't nuzzled her. "I hope you're right. But just in case you're not, Lyka—I will need a bigger lab."

RYANA SPENT the rest of the afternoon adjusting the size of her laboratory so it ate up most of her living space, communicating with Lyka and Grim in turn. If Kagaroth were truly coming to Earth on purpose, she was going to have to recreate some of her old magics from scratch, and they required more elaborate preparation and longer furnace time. She dearly wished she had her powerful old notebooks with the formulas she was trying to recreate, but she'd barely escaped the war happening back home with her life. She hadn't gotten to bring anything through with her but the Heart of the Dragon—the crystalline heart that represented her brother's curse—and Lyka.

Once her new laboratory was set up, she took a shower, finally pulling all the straw bits out of her hair. She wished Austin had given her more detailed instructions—in the Realms she'd never dream of asking anyone anywhere without letting them know what was expected of them, if it was not obvious by the time of the event, or the company they knew they'd be keeping.

But what did women on Earth wear to go out?

And where *were* they going?

She supposed she could just go up to his room and ask him, but he'd probably just try to dissuade her again, and she wasn't sure her pride could handle the blow. His body had wanted her last night, yes, but he hadn't been in his right mind then. It couldn't be trusted.

And honestly...neither could she.

She needed the worst mistake of her life to be firmly in her past. She couldn't ever let herself fall for someone ever again. If she was going to do this thing with Austin, in a desperate attempt to feel less alone, she had to do it analytically. She would get what she wanted out of it, no more and no less. Because from here on out, she would never listen to her heart again.

Hearts could lie. But princesses needed to deal in truth.

CHAPTER 9

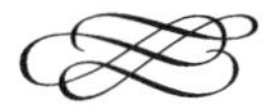

Austin knocked on her door at twelve-oh-one, and she went to answer it. She'd decided on a tight black sheath dress with a low top that hid nothing, accessorized with a wide red belt and high red heels. (The footwear on earth was so uncomfortable—but also so attractive!) Her hair was up in a twist, and Lyka had turned herself into a tiny red hummingbird that looked like a feathered hairpin to hold it up, and of course her own wings were magically hidden.

She opened up the door to Austin wearing a suit, which was as surprising to her as she apparently was to him. He took an appreciative step back and muttered, "Goddamn, wings."

Ryana tilted her head at what was obviously a compliment. "Thank you. I'm ready."

"I'll say," he said, backing up so she could come out. He offered her his arm on the stair like a gentleman, and she took it, slowly descending as he did.

Zach spotted them as they were coming down to the first floor, as he walked from one of the castle's grand parlors towards the kitchen. He then pinched the bridge of his nose, shaking his head as he walked away.

"What was that about?" Ryana asked, peering after him when they reached the foyer.

"He doesn't trust my intentions towards you," Austin said, walking forward.

"Which are?"

"Currently? Making you realize what a horrible decision you've made," he said, holding the front door wide. She bit back a sigh.

His particular car was waiting outside—she'd seen it in the garage before, something called a Jeep. "Betsy, Ryana, Ryana, Betsy," he said by way of introduction.

"Do you name all your vehicles?"

"Only the ones that matter to me," Austin said, giving her an easy smile. Then he looked between Betsy and her with a little bit of horror, as she noticed it was missing half its top. "Oh—hey, wait, wings. I'm not used to taking company. Let me go get her cover on."

Ryana took a step forward, gathering that he got to ride in this vehicle just as it was. "We can ride without the top?"

"Yeah, but it'll ruin your hair," Austin warned her.

She waved his concern away. "You underestimate Lyka," she said, turning her head to point to the bird in it. "And—I want to," she said. Her only trips to the outside world so far had been in the SUV, which had windows tinted so heavily they were almost impossible to see through.

"Well, all right then, sure," he said, opening up the Jeep's passenger door. "And tell Lyka not to come out, no matter what. We don't have any Forgetting Fire, and you're safe with me tonight."

"That's a matter of opinion, isn't it?" she said, getting inside the vehicle.

"Not really, no." He held the door open, looking down at her. "I'd die before I let anything happen to you."

Ryana felt a flush build that she didn't want to let him see. "Because Damian would kill you." It was the obvious response, and it was true.

"Sure, wings," he said softly, and closed the door on her.

. . .

Air, so much air, swooshing by—she put her hands up and felt it rush through her fingers—and she wished she could unfurl her wings to feel it. The air made it too loud for them to have conversation, but she didn't want that anyhow. This was her first time truly free of Damian's castle, she couldn't help but peer into the darkness outside, trying to see the other homes as they drove past them. She knew the place where they lived was at the apex of the Briars, an exclusive living zone, but she didn't know much else—and she was frustrated by how hard it was to see—only then they dropped through the final set of gates, and they were in the city.

Just like she'd seen it on TV. With crosswalks and people and other cars—everything! Brightly lit signs beckoned, and with the car missing the top she could smell so many smells—it didn't even matter if they were good or bad, they were *real,* and between that and the wind on her skin, and just seeing other people living life, she felt like she was out in the *world* again, a feeling she hadn't had for quite some time.

They didn't even have to go anywhere. Austin could keep driving them around just like this, and her evening would be perfect.

She looked over at him to tell him as much and caught him looking at her, before he quickly turned away. "We're almost there!" he shouted over, and she nodded, so he'd know she'd heard.

He pulled his Jeep in beneath a sign that said 'Platinum' on it, with a woman's silhouette giving a coquettish smile behind the word, and parked, coming around the Jeep to open her door up for her. Ryana realized the building had no windows—she'd seen these kinds of places in the Realms, but had never gotten to go in. "Is this a fighting establishment?" she asked eagerly.

"What? No. So much no," he said, once again offering her his arm.

She took it. There weren't stairs here, but there was a curb to step up to, and her heels were awfully high. She let him lead her to the door around the side, where a stern looking man was waiting—but his demeanor changed when he saw Austin.

"Yo! Austin, my man!" he said, standing. "Been awhile! The girls will be happy to see you!"

"I know," Austin said, letting go of her hand to reach into a pocket. He took out a wallet and pulled out money, handing what seemed like a lot of it over. "This is cover, for me and the lady—and I want you to tell everyone here to make sure we have an exceptionally good time."

The man gave Ryana an appraising look. "Usually we don't allow dames in here, but," he waved some of the money back in Austin's direction, "I think we can make an exception."

"Trust me, I'll make it worth your while."

"You always do," the man said with a chuckle, clapping Austin's back as he led them inside.

THE ENTRY HALL WAS DARK, and Ryana could smell many strange things. Alcohol, yes, sharp and pungent, sex, musky and dark, and... fruits of some sort. Andi had recently taken Ryana on a tour of Earthly food-things in their kitchen, with Grim's help, and some of those scents were definitely here.

"Cherries?" she guessed, as Austin directed them through a velvet curtain, into a dimly lit world with a thumping beat. Ryana read the room in an instant—there was a main stage with a woman dancing on it, and the stage was surrounded by seated men. Other women, scantily clad, moved among them, offering drinks, and some of them were in darkened corners, grinding.

She almost laughed. Did he really think this was going to scare her off? She'd been invited to orgies in the Realms. Just because she'd never gotten to go—she was smart enough to know that the invitations were delivered out of a polite sense of royal inclusiveness, rather than anyone actually wanting to have sex in front of her Kagaroth—nor would she want to have done so in front of Baran, once they were together—didn't mean she was unfamiliar with the situation.

He tugged her through other men and tables, until they were seated right beside the stage. The woman dancing was tall, lean, and muscular, although somehow she still had very nice breasts, which Ryana knew because the dancer wasn't wearing any clothing. She saw Austin and her face lit up. Austin wrapped his arm around Ryana's shoulder unexpectedly—she felt Lyka twitch a little in response against her scalp—and he waved something against her neck. The dancer grinned even wider at that, falling to her knees and crawling over.

"Hello!" she mouthed, because the music was too loud for real words.

"Hi!" Ryana mouthed back. The dancer's face was painted gloriously, with all sorts of glittery make-up and lips as red as Stella's, the female werewolf that used to go on missions with them.

"Don't mind me," the dancer told her, leaning forward like a cat, brushing her cheek against Ryana's as she pinched what Austin was waving—money—out of his hand with a delicate thumb and forefinger, before leaning back. Then she tossed it in the growing pile behind her, and went back to the pole to swing herself aloft.

"Oh my gosh!" Ryana said. "She's so strong!" She turned to Austin. "Magic?"

"Not hardly," he said. In the half-light emanating from beneath the stage, she could see the shadowed features of his face. His cheekbones were more sloped than his brother's, coupled with a wider jaw, and his lips had a devastating fullness to them, combined with the faintest hint of a scar at one corner that made some of his smiles look like a smirk. His eyebrows were strong and thick, and she could tell his nose, while well-healed, had been broken many times before. She knew if she ran her fingertip down it, she'd feel a little knot at where it bent.

Something was happening on the stage behind her, and she was sure it was impressive, as the other men in the room were hollering about it—but Austin's dark blue eyes were just for her. Suddenly her dress, which *was* tight, felt much *too* tight, and so she quickly turned. She just wanted to see what she'd missed. It had nothing to do with needing to look away.

The dancer who'd been so close earlier hoisted herself aloft again, spun, and then did what seemed like a death defying drop before catching herself right above the ground as her song ended and she spun safely down, dismounting onto heels even higher than the ones Lyka had made for her this evening.

Men cheered, some unseen man announced the dancer's name overhead, and Ryana clapped joyfully. It'd been so long since she'd seen a live performance of any nature. "I want to see more," she told Austin, without making eye-contact.

"Then you're in luck," he told her.

CHAPTER 10

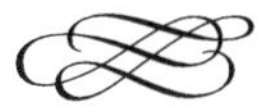

AUSTIN HAD ASSUMED TAKING RYANA TO A STRIP CLUB WOULD PUT A nail in her 'maybe I should sleep with a werewolf' coffin, but no. What he hadn't anticipated—and it was a shame he couldn't have asked Damian for advice, but he could literally never, if he wanted to stay breathing—was that as someone from the Realms, and as someone who had been a princess, she was entirely familiar with transactional economies and not scared in the least of sex work.

And when she found out she could have Lyka create more money for her to use to fund more dancing—well, that was game over. All the dancers wanted to perform for the delightful woman handing out wads of cash. Probably the only other club patron who didn't hate him right now was the man sitting directly across from them, and that only if he was an ass man. Ryana laughed as the women whispered encouragement to her, getting smears of glitter on her cheeks, and then she ooohed and ahhhed at their every move on the pole, telling Austin that, while she'd seen better acrobatics before, the fact that they were doing it without any magic made it, "so much more impressive!" One of the women asked for permission to touch Ryana's breasts, which she granted, and then the dancer held them up to bury her face in them, and Austin's dick just about figured out how to unzip his pants.

A stripper he knew—in more ways than one—came up to slouch across the back of their chairs between sets, popping her head between them. "Hey Sasha," he said, giving her a nod.

"Where did you get her from?" Sasha whispered in his ear with a laugh, and then squeezed both their shoulders. "Private room, private dance? You two interested?"

Austin blinked. In his prior life, getting ground up against would've sounded like all sorts of fun. And while there was usually no sex in the champagne room, he had personally experienced a few exceptions.

"No," he said.

Just at the same time, Ryana said, "Yes. Absolutely!"

Sasha rose up a little, looking perplexed. "Oh—well—which of us do you want? We'd assumed it was going to be a two-person job." Austin looked over his shoulder to find another 'friend' there, Tiffani. Ryana saw her, too.

"Both!" Ryana said, clapping decisively. "Let's go—where too?"

Austin definitely had outdated opinions about Ryana walking off with two strippers, but it was too late, she'd already bounced up to join them. He rose up without thinking, and Sasha gave him a sly look.

"And you're sure you're not coming?" she asked him.

He considered things quickly, and forcibly made himself downshift. "Yeah," he confirmed. What he wanted to do was drag Ryana back to his side and chain her to the chair—but that was not the point of this evening. He was supposed to be convincing her to run *away from him,* remember? And she looked so happy right now, besides. It was a rarity for her, especially when he was around. She was sparkling with second-hand glitter and had such a wide smile—somehow Austin found the strength to sit back down and waved the three of them off.

Tiffani blew him a kiss, and the girls started laughing, each of them helping the others to walk. They teetered away on high heels, and his baser instincts wanted to lunge after them, his dick planning some sort of Leverage-style escape from his suit slacks. He managed to stay seated though, and after his hard-on had subsided enough that he could safely stand, he made his way to the bar. The bartender greeted him with a smile and a strong drink. "Thanks," he said, after a sip.

"No, it's on the house," he said, waving away Austin's money. "I'm gonna get cashed out hard tonight, so thank you."

"You're welcome," Austin chuckled. He wasn't sure what to do with himself in Ryana's absence. He knew some—well, a lot—of the talent here, but he didn't want her to come back and find him gawking at another girl, or with someone on his lap, getting handsy.

Although—that was probably the surest way to end this. And this was the easiest place ever to orchestrate it, he thought as he turned around. He could spot three women milling amongst the men, who he knew would be up to job for free, even.

But...he found he didn't want to do that.

Not to her.

It was one thing to try and get her to ride someone else's cock—his own cock's thoughts on that be damned—and another to crush her spirit by kinda-sorta-cheating on her. She was having a good time, and so was he, watching her. She got so excited to see each new stripper's outfits and make-up, clapping along with the songs, all of which he knew she'd never heard before. And laughing, so much laughing. He'd never seen Ryana like this—in Damian's castle it was like she was a caged bird.

But out here?

She could fly, even if you couldn't see her wings.

"Thank god that stupid bitch is gone," muttered a man coming up beside him, waving the bartender down with a twenty.

Austin tensed. He was certain he knew who the 'stupid bitch' was, seeing as everyone else in here was a dancer. He clenched his drink tighter, all that was in him wanting to punch this asshat through a brick wall.

"You shouldn't say that," the bartender said, coming to Ryana's defense on Austin's behalf.

"She's been hogging all the girls," the man complained.

"Well maybe if you made it rain," the bartender suggested—because he was also on the house's side.

"It wouldn't matter," Austin said, sizing the man up, figuring out just how strong a punch he could throw without killing, two nights after a full moon. "You'd still be you. And she's a goddamned hurricane."

The man looked like he was going to try his luck against Austin for a brief second, and Austin wanted him to. If the man started shit, it was going down, but the other patron thought better of it and scurried off with his drink to make use of his Ryana-free time.

And thinking of that...just how long ago had Sasha and Tiffani absconded with her? Was she having a good time?

And just what the hell were they all doing, together?

RYANA LET the girls lead her into a small room outfitted with couches and a solitary pole. "What are we going to do here?" Ryana asked, looking around.

"Whatever you want, sweetheart," the darker skinned one said. She turned, sending her braids swinging, and rocked over, showing Ryana her entire ass.

"Really?" Ryana asked.

"Yes, really," the other one, Austin had called Sasha, said with a nod. "We can dance on you; we can dance together—pay us enough and Tiffani and I will even make out."

Tiffani rose up and gave her a look. "Enough-enough, and we'll even make out with you," she said, swaying.

"Okay, that's amazing," Ryana said, putting out her hands. "Both of you come here," she said, patting either side of herself on the couch. "And can you turn that music off?"

Someone somewhere above was listening in, and the music cut down substantially.

"It's harder to dance without music," Sasha said, giving her a worried look.

"I don't want to dance. I would like to talk." She waited half-a-beat and then remembered to add, "Please," like Damian had told her to, on many, many occasions since her arrival. "I will pay for the pleasure, as long as you're honest with me."

The dancers looked at each other, then sat down. The blonde asked, "Talk about what?"

"Austin," Ryana said, definitively. It was clear the women here knew him, and she had no problem with that—in fact it would make her life easier. "How do I make him want me?"

The women shared a look and then burst out laughing.

"What?" Ryana asked, feeling her soul fold in on itself, the butt of some joke that she didn't understand.

"He's been watching you all night, girl," Tiffani said, crossing her long brown legs.

Ryana frowned. If that was the case, she'd been having such a good time she hadn't noticed.

Sasha nodded in agreement. "Yeah. We know how he usually is in here. Whatever he is tonight, is the opposite of that."

He was probably just being polite for her sake. Or out of fear of Damian.... "That may be," Ryana said, "but—he keeps telling me we can't be together."

"That does sound like Austin. He likes to put out, but he's not one to stick around," Tiffani said with a sigh.

Ryana gleaned what 'put out' was from context. "But he hasn't even put a hand on me. Even though I want him to."

Sasha's brows perked. "Oh?"

"Are you pressing him for commitment first?" Tiffani asked.

"Hardly," Ryana scoffed. "I just want him for a night."

Sasha blinked. "Really? Because he's the kind of ride you want to ride twice, if you know what I mean."

Ryana felt herself lightly flush. "I don't need to ride him twice, as you say. Once will be enough."

Tiffani's head tilted, sending her braids rolling across her shoulders. "How do you know?"

"I just do." Austin was a werewolf, and she was a part-dragon princess. In no realm would they make sense, which was, again, specifically why she had chosen him. He knew where he stood, and she knew where she stood—slightly higher.

Little had she known he'd be so obstinate.

"Well, if he's not jumping at the chance to sleep with you, no strings attached, then there's got to be something else going on." Tiffani tapped at her teeth with outrageously long neon pink fingernails.

"He could be scared of my brother," Ryana sighed, sinking down.

"Or he could be scared of himself," Sasha suggested, coming near.

"Why?" Ryana asked. Austin was the opposite of scary. Another point in his favor. She could always see his face to read it—there was never a snarling helmet in the way.

"Because of you," Sasha said.

"But—why?" Ryana pressed.

"Because he doesn't want to hurt you," the dancer said gently.

Ryana's spine straightened as she rose up to her full height on the couch. "That's preposterous. He can't hurt me. No one can."

"Are you so sure about that?" Tiffani asked, squinting.

"Very." Ryana spared a glance down to make sure that her past wasn't written on her somewhere that other people could see. "But he did bring me here to scare me off. He told me as much himself."

Sasha laughed. "Is it working?"

"Not yet," Ryana told her.

"So he thinks we're going to do his dirty work for him, eh?" Tiffani said, giving Sasha a mischievous look. "Well, he's got another thing coming."

Tiffani laughed, catching on. "Can we give you a present? To take back to Austin?"

"Sure. What?" It wasn't like they had anywhere to hide anything beneath their skimpy clothes.

"Hickies. It'll drive him mad," Sasha told her.

Tiffani laughed. "Oh yeah—that is such a good idea."

Ryana wasn't entirely sure what a 'hickey' was, but she was part-dragon; there was no way mere humans could ever hurt her. So she shrugged and said "Sure," and then the two women descended on her, one to either side of her neck, like they were also relatives of the progenitor that had drained so many cows. She knew in an instant what they were doing, as she'd had to hide marks like the ones they were giving her from her mother before, and she laughed.

Who would've thought she'd get neck-kisses from two girls before she'd managed even one from Austin?

CHAPTER 11

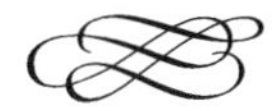

AUSTIN SAW THE WOMEN RETURNING JUST AS HE WAS ON THE VERGE OF going to look for them—Ryana had been gone for at least five songs-worth of time. Her hands were wrapped around the other dancers' hips, all of them helping one another balance, laughing—and as she neared, he spotted hickies on her neck, one to each side. The bruises themselves would've given it away, but they were both clearly outlined by lipstick marks. He gave both of the strippers a dry look, and then turned to Ryana.

"Ready to go?" he asked her, and she nodded, grinning. "And did you have fun?" He tried and failed not to sound arch.

It was all too easy to imagine Sasha and Tiffani descending on Ryana's neck like bikini-clad vampires, and he felt a surge of jealousy that he'd not only missed the moment, but that they'd kissed Ryana before he had.

Which, he reminded himself gravely, didn't matter, because he never would.

"I did," Ryana said, positively beaming, before turning back to the dancers. "Thank you, I had a wonderful time." She reached into her cleavage, which was where Lyka had been conjuring up her cash for her, and handed both of the women fistfuls.

"Those breasts are magic," Sasha told him with a leer.

"You have no idea," he said, taking hold of Ryana's hand to lead her away. Ryana leaned back and waved, and Tiffani blew her a kiss, and all Austin could do was shake his head.

He took her out into the much cooler night, gave the bouncer a nod, and then stopped himself from pulling Ryana tight against the cold. "Here," he said, taking off his suit jacket to hand to her. Their ride home in the Jeep was going to be freezing—he should've thought of that before he let her talk him into not putting on the top.

"Thanks," she said, pulling it on. She walked over to her side of his ride and looked up at him. "Did you really think that bringing me here was going to disconvince me?"

He thought for a moment. "I don't think that's a word."

She pouted. "Why not?" He knew she was using magic to translate herself until she actually learned English, just like Damian had years before. "It sounds right, doesn't it?"

"It does. And it makes sense. And yet, just because things make sense, that doesn't always make them right, Ryana," he told her, hoping she got his implication.

"Hey! You!" shouted someone from across the parking lot. The portly man from the bar stumbled over, slurring his words. "You fucking cunt. Your fat ass ruined my night."

Austin wanted to grab the words the man said out of the air and shove them back down his throat before Ryana heard any of them, but it was too late, so clocking the man into next week would have to suffice. The man's teeth clacked against each other like castanets, and then he pirouetted like the dancers they'd just left behind, to drop onto the concrete.

The bouncer rushed up right afterwards. "Oh shit, Austin, I'm so sorry—we'll handle this."

"You'd better," Austin said with a growl, as the bouncer dragged the drunken man away.

When he turned back to his car Ryana was looking at him strangely. "What did he mean by that?"

Austin swallowed and cursed internally. "Which part?"

"All of it."

Austin ground his jaw and he wished he'd punched the man inside, earlier when he'd had the chance. "Well…there were other men watching the dancers tonight, as you saw. We were spending a lot of money, so the girls all wanted to hang out with us, and some other men got jealous."

She was frowning. "But why did he use those particular words?"

"Because some men think that they can use rough words for women's genitalia as insults. They think it makes them strong, because they think women are weak."

"But they're wrong," she said.

"Oh, I know," Austin agreed. "I wouldn't want to be in a dark alley against you, Mills, or Stella. Maybe even Andi. I bet she's a biter," he teased, hoping he could steer this conversation away from a rocky shore.

Ryana snorted softly, amused. "So then, why did he say the rest?"

Oh, fuck that guy. Austin couldn't believe he was going to have to explain the worst of internalized misogyny to the heretofore innocent sister of his good friend. "You may have noticed the size differential between you and the dancers?"

She nodded, running her hands down the outline of her body in a way that made him wish they were his hands grabbing hold of her instead.

"Well, he was implying—because he was an asshole—that you are somehow lesser than they are."

"Even though technically, size-wise, I'm…more?" she asked, her head tilting, as her face scrunched up.

"Assholes don't always make sense, wings," he said, wishing he could apologize for, oh, the entire goddamned human race.

She took a moment to consider this, then looked pissed and stomped a heel. "I am as I am meant to be."

"Exactly. And that's what I told him. Only with my fist," he said, gesturing with it between them.

Ryana blinked and then laughed at that—and that's probably what broke him. Because she'd only narrowly avoided harm tonight, and the thought of anyone else ever hurting her, like whoever the fuck else she thought she was going to put on deck to sleep with her if it wasn't him—no.

There were not going to be any others.

Not if he had anything to say about it.

He moved fluidly forward, pressing her back against the window of his Jeep and lowered his mouth to hers. She smelled like the best things in the world to him, mossy forest and bright clean water, and the hint of stripper didn't hurt, and he felt his wolf inside him beating its tail low.

She melted against him for one-one-thousandth of a second, tilting her head up to match her lips to his, her mouth opening, and then…she froze.

RYANA WAS WELL accustomed to experimentation. She'd been taught by the finest minds the Realms had to offer, how to amplify her will and concentrate her magic, to imbue certain objects and liquids with her abilities. She knew how to consider her options and make snap decisions within milliseconds, channeling dangerous amounts of power down chosen pathways to ensure desired outcomes.

So when Austin's lips settled on hers, when one of his hands slid into her hair, upsetting Lyka, and the other slid around her waist to pull her near, as his tongue asked her lips for entrance, she knew she was at a turning point.

She could be the brash princess that she mostly was and say yes and give in and they would undoubtedly go home and do this thing and then never speak of it again….

Or she could allow herself to *be* herself when she was with him. A person who she hadn't been for years. The person who she wasn't even sure was still inside.

One path would be easy, though untrue. The other would be true, but very, very hard.

He read her body before she even thought she'd made up her

mind, pulling his mouth away from hers while staying near. "You okay, wings?"

Ryana shook her head and answered honestly. "No."

He nodded, his forehead close to hers. "Let's go home."

THEY DROVE BACK UP to the castle in blustery wind, as she held his coat tightly around her shoulders, staring out at the streets and the stars in turns. Her hand rose to her lips without thinking, pressing against them just like his lips had, and she wondered what he thought of her. Could she really go back to who she'd been before Baran? She longed to go back to that earlier her, when she never had to question whether or not she was right, because she always knew she was. But now that she knew she could be fooled so easily, hurt so easily, and she was on an entirely different fucking planet from her home, she didn't know. She didn't entirely like who she was now, but she also couldn't see a path to follow back behind her.

Austin parked his car outside the garage and there was finally silence as he turned to look at her. "I won't touch you again, Ryana. I'm sorry to have misread the situation."

She sat looking straight ahead but didn't take her seatbelt off or reach for the door. "You didn't." She could tell he was waiting for her to go on, so she tried to find the words to explain, embarrassed by how unsure they sounded aloud. "I thought I wanted one thing, but now I want another."

"You're allowed to change your mind."

She looked over at him then. There was more than enough moon out to see him. His seatbelt was off, and he was sitting loosely in the car, facing her, one hand on the steering wheel, one knee against some sort of mechanical knob between them. He'd undone his tie the second they'd gotten in the car, like the fabric had been strangling him, and had opened the top few buttons of his shirt, allowing a little of the strange art he had on the skin of his chest to show through.

"In any case," he went on, "I know you're just getting your feet under yourself here. I can still help you with that if you'd like, without touching you, I swear."

Ryana bit back a gasp. "You don't want to touch me?" Of course not. Why would anyone? What did she have to offer anyone on Earth, now that no one knew who she was and she had to hide her wings?

"I...didn't think you wanted that," Austin said slowly.

She frowned at him, and then reached over and put a finger on his knee, like she was pointing to the joint.

He looked between her and her finger. "Is this some Realms thing?"

"I'm proving a point," she said as she rolled her eyes. "Or trying too."

He seemed to consider things, then leaned over to touch her back, putting a fingertip on the point of her nose. "Boop."

She squinted, first at his finger, then at him. "It's awfully daring of you to put a finger so near my teeth, much less make an inane sound while doing so."

He grinned. "You didn't explain the rules of this game to me. I'm trying to learn as I go along."

"It's not a game," she said, and pouted.

"Then what is it?" he asked, suddenly serious.

She rose up, shaking her head, dislodging his finger. She should've just kissed him when she had the chance. Everything would've been easier then; they'd already be halfway up the stairs by now.

"Ryana," he said, his voice soft. "If I've done something wrong, I want to know. And if I've done something right...I want to know that, too." He inhaled deeply and seemed to take her in. "If I managed to disconvince you—your word, not mine—of us sleeping together tonight, then hallelujah. That's an Earth exclamation for a miracle having happened, if your magic doesn't translate it right." His head tilted, and he gave her a lopsided smile. "But I can't sit here and lie to you and tell you that I still want that, because I don't. That's why I kissed you, Ryana. Because I changed my mind. I don't want to disconvince you anymore."

Ryana felt a flush creep up, and wondered just how well he could see her in the moonlight. "You're sure?" she heard herself ask him in a smaller voice than she was used to.

"Completely. You?"

Her fingers bunched up the hem of her dress. "No."

She heard his intake of breath then, like he'd just gotten punched. "Okay," he said, and she saw him nod out of her corner of her eye. "That's fine. You just tell me what we are, if anything, and that's how I'll be." His even tone couldn't hide the disappointment in his voice.

She'd tried to shove Baran away once, near the end. When it was clear he meant too much to her, when her mother'd started to snoop, and one meaningful glance seen by the wrong person could've led to his death. He'd redoubled his efforts towards her, she'd capitulated, and not long after that he tried to steal her. At the time—and prior to the kidnapping—she'd thought him so brave, because he 'couldn't live without her.' But was it, truly? Being ridden by your passions like you were a horse?

Wasn't it braver to be the rider, always in charge, even if it meant having to steer yourself off your desired course?

Ryana finally met Austin's gaze, where he was still waiting for her answer. "If we do this thing now, wolf, it has to be slow. So forget anything I said or what I seemed like earlier. I countermand that."

He chuckled beside her. "Countermand, eh? Your magic gives you a big vocabulary sometimes, wings."

"That's what you're choosing to focus on?" She played with the hem of her dress anxiously.

"Yeah. Because if I focus on you, I get blinded," Austin said—and then they both heard the sound of the castle's front door opening up, and Zach was running out to the garage. He saw them and stopped.

"Do I want to know where you've been?" he asked, striding over—although it was clear from his prior path he'd been heading out to his own car.

"You can probably smell it," Austin said, taunting his brother as he got out. Ryana knew she had marks on her neck, and she'd seen the rings of lipstick on herself in the side-view mirror—not to mention her neck and breasts looked like they'd been dusted by a particularly large and glittery moth. "Do I want to know where you're going?" Austin asked.

"No," Zach said simply, giving him a look full of daggers.

Austin didn't care, though. He came around and opened her door for her, offering her his arm to get out of the car. She took it. In front of Zach. And Austin didn't shy away. She'd never once been able to touch Baran in public, so the novelty of this small gesture thrilled her.

"Have fun, wherever it is that you're going," she told Zach, giving him a wave indicating that he would be much happier over by his own vehicle, and Austin laughed.

The other werewolf grumbled something as Austin led her to the castle's door.

THEY STOPPED TOGETHER on the level of her own quarters, in front of her door. Austin released her arm and took a courtly step back. "All right, wings—I've come up with a plan."

"Between the car and here?" she asked, her brow rising.

"Yep," he said, taking her in. "I want to make sure that we're always on the same page."

"How so?" Ryana crossed her arms. "I do not consent to telepathy spells."

Austin's eyes widened and he laughed. "No. Sorry. This is way more old school—it's a game that kids here play. Red light, green light."

"Red like my belt, and green like my eyes?" She frowned at him lightly. "Did you just make that up?"

"It's based on streetlights. I'll point them out to you next time we're out. But in general on Earth, red means 'stop,' and green means 'go.' So if I ever check in with you, and you can't find the words, use the colors."

"So if I say, 'red'…." she asked, leading him on.

"Then I stop whatever I'm doing, the second it sounds like you're saying the word."

"And if I say, 'green'?"

"Then things are okay. Or if you don't say anything. Although I'll still probably check in a lot. I don't want to assume anything with you anymore." He ran a hand through his hair. "We're too different; it's not safe."

"Very true," she agreed, and licked her lips. "I think I can manage that. Two little Earth words."

He nodded, then backed off, to head down the stairs before pausing. "Hey, wings?"

"Yes?" she said, inside her open door.

"You think you can teach me your language?"

Ryana observed him through half-lidded eyes. "Depends on how good you are with your tongue," she said with intent, and closed the door. She heard him laugh to himself as he walked away, and she smiled in the darkness of her room.

GRIMALKIN HAD BEEN a dear and finished setting up everything she'd had Lyka ask him for, recreating her old laboratory almost perfectly while she'd been gone. "It's fantastic, Grimalkin, thank you," she said, assuming the cat would hear, and sat down atop a bench, wriggling her dress down enough to let her wings flare.

She wasn't going to perform any experiments tonight, it was too late, and her concentration was off after that business with Austin in the car.

But things were better, she thought, looking around. She knew where she stood with Austin, for now, and she had a practical goal again here.

If Kagaroth were going to come to this planet with intent—she would be ready for them. She pulled out her notebook to write down her thoughts.

CHAPTER 12

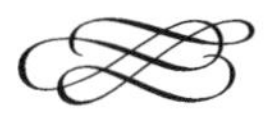

AUSTIN SPENT THAT NIGHT PLANNING OUT PLACES HE WOULD TAKE HER, things he wanted to do, and then the next morning, after getting up and putting the top back on Betsy and taking an invigorating and very cold shower he went to her door to knock.

It flashed red when he was two steps away.

He stepped back, and it went white again, matching the rest of the hallway's décor.

Forward—red.

"Fuck," he muttered. The temptation to knock and ask what he'd done wrong loomed large. But then he realized he probably...hadn't? At least he didn't think he had?

He walked by the door repeatedly throughout the day, and wondered if she knew how often he passed by. He didn't see her come out for food or drinks or training.

And it was the same thing the next day, too.

Here he'd been trying to prevent himself from making any untoward assumptions, when in reality he should've hopped back and not even assumed that Ryana wanted to be with him.

Except for the fact that she was 'playing' his game, which proved interest, of a sort. And he'd meant the rules as he'd laid them out for her. He wasn't going to broach a red. If she didn't feel like she could trust him, all was lost. So if she was in there hoping he was that kind of guy, well, she was out of luck.

Because, instead, he was him...the werewolf who made up reasons to walk past her door just-in-case, every two-to-three hours.

On the third day he detoured by in the afternoon out of habit, after hitting the training gym, and was surprised to see the door flash green. He stood in front of it, stunned and sweaty, and knocked.

"Come in," he heard her say inside.

He tried the handle and pushed the door open. Her rooms were quite different from what he'd remembered—it seemed like they were smaller than they'd been the other night even—and the scents inside were slightly unwholesome. Like burning plastic, or possibly worse.

She came into her main room through a door in the back, wearing an apron that made her look like she was about to get an X-ray, and she had a helmet in one hand. She crinkled her nose at him. "You're sweaty."

"And you're...at a dental office?" he guessed.

She reasoned her way through the words, although she still looked baffled. "No...I was working."

"On?" he asked.

"A project. It's in progress, so I don't want to say anything." She jerked her chin behind her.

So that's why the door was red.... "Have you been trapped in here for two straight days?"

"Yes," she said and nodded. "But now the potion is settling, and I've got some time. So I'm green, officially," she said, giving him a tight smile. "Are you?"

"Totally," he said. He watched her hoist the apron off of herself and hand it to Lyka, who somehow managed to hold the thing aloft in her claws while being the size of a common sparrow. Underneath, Ryana's clothing clung to her, damp with sweat, and tendrils of her hair were stuck to her neck in waves. "Should we clean up first?" he teased.

"I'd like too, yes," she said, giving him a slightly more genuine grin.

"Meet you downstairs in thirty minutes then?"

"Sounds good," she said, as he made to leave. "What kind of shoes should I wear?"

"Sneakers, if you have any."

"I have Lyka," she said with a derisive snort, and then shouted after him. "Wait—where are we going?"

He laughed and leaned in to close her door. "You'll see."

ONE MORE COLD SHOWER LATER, and Austin was downstairs with his hair still wet, trying not to pace. Ryana came down not long after, in a green halter top with a coat pulled over it and high-waisted jeans. Austin couldn't hide his surprise. "I've never seen you not in a dress before."

"I don't wear dresses when we fight, silly," she said with an eye-roll. "Or, when I work in my lab."

"Well—every other time than that."

"Stop questioning things," she advised, and followed him out to his car. "Oh, you put the top back on," she said, with clear disappointment.

"Because it looks like it's going to rain. I'm hoping we'll miss it, though." He held the door open for her, and closed it after she got in.

Austin took them out of the Briars and then north, and she was still plastered to the window. "See? Streetlights. Red, and green," he announced as they idled at one. "I didn't lie."

"Two of my favorite colors," she told him.

"So you like Christmas, then?"

She pondered this. "That's...that holiday, right?"

"Yeah, but ignore that—what kind of holidays do they have where you come from?" he asked, suddenly curious. Damian's patience for talking about the Realms usually only lasted for three questions, and then he'd start to growl.

"Oh, you know," she said, sitting back in her chair. "Mast Day, and Eloph's Day, and all the religious holidays, if you're into that sort of thing, plus all the ancestral days you're obligated to acknowledge, and birthdays, we still celebrate those until you reach like a hundred and then interest tapers off, so, the usual," she said, waving a casual hand.

"What do you do on Mast Day?" he asked.

"Carve masts for tiny boats and set them free in the harbor. Whichever one sinks last is lucky." She gave him a sly look from the sides of her eyes.

"Wow, that sounds awfully charming for the Realms."

She laughed hard. "You caught me. No—Mast Day is when we celebrate victory over the sun. It's an ancient ritual. The meaning's lost to time, but basically everyone gets drunk and parties and you're not allowed to kill anyone for one whole day. It only happens once every five years or so, years being your closest word, yet still imprecise."

"Sounds like my kind of holiday." Austin chuckled, looking over at her. Her auburn hair was in a ponytail, but there were still some free strands at her neck curling, above her halter, that his fingers ached to run through. The hickies the strippers had given her were long since healed away. "So, while I'm not gonna ask you what you were doing in your rooms there, I am going to ask why the hell you don't have Lyka or Grim install some air conditioning for you."

"It's hard to keep the ovens at the right temperatures as it is, and I don't want to introduce any other variables."

"You do realize that Mills has a really nice and modern lab set up in her wing?"

Ryana nodded. "Yes. She gave me a tour. But I'm trying to replicate things I've already made in the past—so I already know how to do it my way. I just didn't get to bring my notebooks over, so I'm having to recreate my process, is all. It should work soon, give or take a few more days of trying."

"Would Mills's way be safer?" Ryana's earlier outfit had looked like she was about to forge molten steel, which implied that whatever she was doing was dangerous. He still remembered the way she'd looked when Damian had brought her over from the Realms, how her body had been bruised, her wings torn, and her leg broken. It'd been bad enough caring for her then—caring for her now, if he hadn't done something within his power to shield her—the thought of it made his stomach churn.

She considered his suggestion. "Possibly? But—I have to get the formula down first. I can try to optimize things afterwards." She flashed her green eyes at him. "Do I get to know where we're going yet?"

"Soon," he promised, taking the next exit.

THE FOREST where Austin and Zach roamed on full moon nights was pretty far outside of town. He was intimately familiar with it as a wolf, but it'd been a long time since he'd come here as a man. He parked his Jeep in the gravel lot and walked over to get her door, then reached behind her seat to grab their water bottles as she got out.

"I thought we could take a hike," he told her, but it was clear she hadn't heard him. She was too busy looking at the trees.

"We're going in there?" she asked, eyes wide.

His head tilted. "Yes, if you're okay with that."

"Green," she announced emphatically, and started striding for the trail. Austin laughed, locked up his car, and jogged after her.

After her first fifty questions, Austin realized he should have gotten them a ranger for a tour-guide—only a ranger would've realized that Ryana 'wasn't from around these parts' by question twenty. She touched everything, fearlessly: the loam at their feet, rocks, ferns, leaves, the rough bark of each of the trees they passed by. Luckily, he managed to catch her before she lunged for poison ivy. She stood and watched, rapt, as a spider built a web, and compared it to some other creature called a *lachrony* back at home, which wasn't the progenitor, but sounded much, much worse. She grinned at the squirrels racing overhead and the chipmunks running around below, and squealed at seeing a lizard basking on a rock.

"A tiny dragon!" she whispered, pointing it out to Austin.

"Not hardly, wings," he laughed.

"Really?" she asked, disappointed.

"It's a lizard. More like a snake with legs."

She sighed heavily. "I know what snakes are."

Austin knew that her mother—Damian's stepmother—was called The Snake in the realms. A very dangerous magical...woman? Creature? Austin had never asked Damian to specify. "Do you miss home?" he asked her. They'd been following the trail for the past hour. Austin knew it went deep into the forest and then circled back again.

Ryana's face scrunched up, and he saw Lyka peeking out of one of her coat pockets, likely because he'd upset her. "Parts of it. In many ways, it was easier there for me."

"What with all the servants and the guards?"

She nodded, then looked to the ground near her feet and not their surroundings. "Something like that."

"The...Kagaroth?" he went on, using the same strange word she and Max had for them.

"Yes. I used to have a fleet of them. There was always at least one of them assigned to me, and they followed me like shadows, watching over my every move. When I was tutored. When I worked in my lab. They tasted everything I ate before I did." She blew air through pursed lips. "Sometimes they even watched me sleep."

"That sounds...awful?" he guessed.

"I knew no better at the time. But I was younger then."

He could tell from her bearing—and by the fact that they'd stopped walking—that her memories upset her. "Hey, wings. Do you need to say red?"

She blinked, looking up, her full lips pinched flat together before relaxing. "No. But, thanks."

"Any time," he said, taking a step forward, so she'd follow.

THEY REACHED the half-way point where the trail began circling back, or you could detour for the lake. He would've taken her to its rocky beach, except rain threatened: the skies turned dark and he could smell it in the air. Ryana paused and looked up at the clouds, too, in a clearing.

"I take it the Realms has rain?" Austin asked.

"We have weather," she said, cocking one hip and rolling her eyes. "It's just been a long time since I was out in any."

"I like it when it rains when Zach and I are out here as wolves."

"Why?"

He inhaled, and tried to think of the best way to explain. It wasn't something he ever thought on. As a wolf, it was just a truth he knew. "When you run, your paws catch the ground differently. And it washes all the other scents away, which is fine, because it replaces them with...something cleaner. Something new."

"Cleaner than this?" she asked, sniffing lightly.

"Yeah. It's like God's taken out an eraser, and he's wiped everything away, and he's about to turn a page—and if you don't run fast enough, you won't make it to the next one. It just feels extra...alive, I think." He shivered at the memory. "I've never asked Zach though, so it's possible he has an entirely different opinion."

She smiled softly at him. "Well, I was smart enough to bring a coat...so what're you going to do?"

"Get caught in the rain," he said, grinning back.

"Won't you be cold?"

"Not really, no."

One of her eyebrows rose. "So I'm going to have to sit with a wet dog in an enclosed space all the way home?"

"You have dogs in the Realms?"

"We use them to hunt down smaller *lachrony*, in fact." His eyes widened, and she quickly added, "Don't worry. We give them armor."

Austin laughed. "Well, I'll be a wet wolf. It's totally different."

Ryana snorted, shucking her coat off to hand to him. "Here, you fool." Lyka squawked and tumbled out of her pocket, fast, to fly overhead.

"It's cute you think that this will fit me," he said, holding it between them.

"It's cute you think I didn't bring my own umbrella," she said, and shrugged her shoulders. Two perfect leather wings unfurled, and she made them meet above her head. There was no way she'd get wet now.

Austin was in awe for a moment, then returned to his senses. "It's not safe, Ryana. What if someone sees?"

"I've got Lyka for a look-out," she said, pointing up. "I'll be fine." She gestured that he should hold her coat over his head, as the first drops spattered.

THE RAIN STARTED SLOWLY in a fine mist, then matured into a sprinkle, finally becoming the kind of downpour where the raindrops hit like pennies, and he wasn't entirely dismayed to be shielding himself with her coat, especially because it smelled like her.

The rain still had the same effect on him, though. It was like he could feel it washing away everything unwanted—all the fights, all the danger, all the women, all the booze—finally leaving him whole and clean. The second the storm's ferocity lessened, he moved her coat down and just stood for a moment, face up, letting himself feel it.

"Everything's better out here, isn't it," she whispered from beside him. He looked over at her, whipping his wet hair from his face, as if resurfacing.

"It is," he said, at seeing her. She was in the alcove of her wings, the raindrops that landed on them beading down their dark green leather. She was partially hidden, but he could still see her much lighter green eyes, and it was like she was a literal force of nature, like everything that grew and was good was captured in them.

"What're you thinking?" she asked him, staring back.

"You probably don't want to know."

She pouted, only barely shadowed by her wings. "Green," she demanded.

"So it's like that, is it?" he asked with a head shake. He wanted to be honest, but he also didn't want to scare her off. "Fine. I'm thinking I'd like to kiss you, wings. But I don't have to. I'm entirely okay just standing over here." He held her coat and his water bottle in one hand, and made a gesture towards the ground with the other.

When she didn't respond, he was still for a long moment, wondering if he should try to take the words back.

"Do you think that all the time?" she asked him, right before he wanted to die.

If the rain hadn't washed him clean, he might have attempted lying, but he found he didn't want to dirty his soul back up. "More often than not," he admitted. She swung her wings back behind herself and stepped closer to him, finally looking up at the sky. The rain hit her face for the first time, and she closed her eyes, which made him feel free to gawk.

Her face was a perfect oval, and it was like her features were carved out of his dreams. Her cheekbones were high, her nose was pert and button-like, and her lips were full, although her mouth was narrow, which made him feel like she was always holding words away from him, inside. Raindrops met and traced down her skin and were trapped in her long, light brown eyelashes, the same color as her hair.

She was so beautiful it hurt.

And he was him.

A dented werewolf, who knew so much better, even as he couldn't stop himself from taking this one chance. "May I kiss you, Ryana?"

Her eyes flashed open, and he watched her lips intently then, to see if they'd say *red* or *green*—but instead they just came closer as she rose up on her toes, and brushed his.

Her lips were just as soft as he remembered from the night outside the strip club, and he had to fight not to devour her. They were in the woods that he roamed as a wolf; he was used to being hungry here, and wild. Fierce instinct and long habit wanted to grab her and press in, to make her mouth open for his, to claim her with his tongue. But somehow he managed not to, and just trailed his closed lips across hers, then ran his oft broken nose down her straight one, before pressing his lips to hers again. If hers had opened, even for a moment, his will would have snapped and he might have tried for more, but they didn't, and she rocked back.

She put one hand to her own lips and her other to his, and while he wanted to catch her wrist and keep it there, he forced himself to stay absolutely still.

See, wings?

I don't bite.

I may think all the fucking time about biting...but I can control myself.

You can trust me.

Then she swallowed and pulled her wings in at the same time as she pulled her hand away. "It's stopped raining."

It had. He had the stupid thought that their kiss had made the sun come out again, but managed to keep it to himself.

By the time they were back to Betsy, it was as if nothing had happened, Ryana was back to her old self, and he didn't know what to think about that. And then on their way home they visited a gas station and its candy aisle, so the rest of their trip was spent debating the relative merits of all the different kinds of candy that he'd bought her.

They were parked in the garage and heading in, when Austin realized he had another question. "If the Kagaroth were worried about your food being poisoned...did they kiss lips before you kissed them, too? Just to see?" He meant it as a tease, but as he watched her mood fall and her lips frown, he knew he'd said the wrong thing.

"No, they did not," she told him. "But they should have." She turned on her heel and started walking to the house.

CHAPTER 13

THE FIRST THING RYANA DID WHEN SHE GOT BACK WAS CAST THE 'RED' spell on her door and check on her experiments—but all the alembics she'd left running were fine. She sat on the progenitor's box in front of her oven with the remnants of her candy, let her wings emerge, pulled her notebook out, and tried to think.

Baran had never been so…gentle?

Then again, when Baran had approached her as one of the Kagaroth, he'd known that if she refused his advances he might die. And what point was there in being gentle besides, when death was a Kagaroth's constant companion?

But it wasn't that Austin didn't have roughness in him—she'd seen him in enough fights, and she could read it on his face. She'd felt it when his nose had brushed hers, and she'd covered the faint scar at the corner of his mouth with her fingers. And there was a heat inside of him—she'd felt it against her hand. He'd wanted more. He'd as much as confessed it to her…and she wondered what other things she could've gotten him to confess, if she'd only had the patience.

So—yes. He continued to be perfect for the purposes of her experiment. He—and all the others after him, surely—would help to keep her dreams away. She'd only had the nightmare once, since she'd started painting her door red. She traced something called a 'twiz-il-er' over the path his lips had taken across hers, and then bit it savagely. Austin desired her company, while she desired company in general, but yes, he would do. He was no Baran, but that was a good thing.

She flipped to the next empty page of her notebook to capture her thoughts, feeling herself gaining power. The more she understood him, the more she would understand all of her future men, of which there were certain to be many. She opened the lid to the progenitor's box, tossed the rest of her candy in for the beast to snack on, and then sat back down to start writing.

THREE SWEATY DAYS passed before she got to leave her experiments unattended and could change her door to green—and then three hours passed without anything from Austin.

She didn't expect him to be hanging around outside her door just waiting on her...but at the same time, she only had so long a window before her experiments would require her attention. So she showered quickly and made her way through the rest of the house.

When she knocked on his bedroom door there was no answer—and his precious Betsy was still in the garage—so she realized he must be fighting. In hindsight, she probably should've looked there first. She ran back to her rooms and pulled on her own clothes for training. Maybe they could work through one of Grim's simulations together, and wouldn't that be fun? Excited by the thought of company—any company, not just his company, she tried to tell herself—she jogged lightly down the hall.

Sure enough, she'd caught him inside the gym. She opened the door just wide enough for herself to pass, went in with a smile, and then gasped.

Austin was wearing the gear that he always did, all black, with his favorite gun in his hand, hiding behind a magical boulder—and he was fighting warriors in black armor with helmets that had faces that looked like they were screaming. More bodies in armor littered the floor.

"Stop the simulation!" she shouted, and Grimalkin, paying attention from somewhere, did so. Austin turned to look at her, surprised, as she stormed up. "What are you doing?" she accosted him.

He gave her a mystified look and took off his shirt to blot his face with it, revealing all of the intricate artwork he'd had placed on his body. "What's it look like I'm doing, wings? Training."

"But—why against Kagaroth?" Of course Grim had been able to make them look completely accurate. She looked around at where the bodies had been, but they'd disappeared when the simulation ended.

"I just thought if they were going to come through again, I should be prepared." He'd almost caught his breath.

"Prepared?" she scoffed. "No. You beat them last time because they weren't expecting you. If we see them again, we need to call Damian. It doesn't matter where in the world he is."

His brow furrowed as he frowned. "Did I ever make you watch Predator?" he asked her. She shook her head. "Well allow me to quote good ol' Arnold to you—if it bleeds, we can kill it." He squinted at her. "Look, I know seeing them again had some sort of effect on you –"

"You don't know anything!"

He stood up straighter, as if preparing to accept a blow. "So why don't you tell me?"

"Red," she snapped, and he took a deep inhale, biting back whatever he'd been about to say.

His body was so different from Baran's—Baran's pale torso and arms had been covered in wiry dark hair, with odd raw patches where his armor had worn the hair down. Whereas Austin was tan with a light mat of golden hair across his chest like an emblem, then it was absent over his shoulders and upper arms only to thicken on his forearms like light-colored fur. And so many drawings on him, too, just like his brother Zach, whose purpose she didn't understand.

"All right then, wings," he said, jerking his chin toward the door. "If you don't want to talk, let me finish my training."

"Are you going to fight them again?" She couldn't keep the worry out of her voice, and she knew it didn't make sense, these were just Grim's toys, but—

"They're just simulations."

"Red," she implored him.

"Is it that important to you?" His eyebrows rose and met on his forehead, and then his eyes widened. "Why are you scared of them, wings?"

She wasn't, of course. She was a princess of the Realms, and she wasn't scared of anything, nor could she ever be. But for some reason when she opened up her mouth all her bravado evaporated instantly. "Red," she whispered.

He wanted to do—*something*—she could see his muscles tense in synchrony with the urge to take action, for or against her she couldn't say. Then he controlled himself and calmed. "Okay, wings," he said softly, and gave her a lopsided smile. "I'll have Grim turn them into unicorns or something. Unless you have strong feelings about them, too."

"No." She crossed her arms. "Unicorns are fine. I'm sure they're assholes."

"I have a feeling the Kagaroth are as well, but you won't tell me," he said, while scratching at his stubble. "So are you green now, or did you just decide to hunt me down to yell at me?"

"I am." She gestured to her outfit, clearly meant to join him. "I thought it might be fun to fight together."

"Yeah?" he said, perking up.

"Yeah," she said. "Only we just did." She shrugged, and turned on her heel back to the door. She knew his eyes were on her as she left and started walking down the hall.

"Hey! Wings!" he called after her a moment later. She stopped but didn't turn. "I just want you to know that I'm not chasing after you because I'm trying to respect your boundaries. But if that's what you want—you let me know—and I'll fucking run you down."

His words echoed in the hallway, chasing her even if he wasn't, and she closed her eyes for a second, just listening to them. Then she started walking without looking back.

. . .

HALFWAY BACK TO HER ROOMS, she realized there was a chance that she'd been unfair.

He was prying in her business, yes, but ever since they'd seen the Kagaroth it'd become team business, hadn't it? Wasn't it natural to want to protect the people you cared about, the ones you counted as your family? Even more so, now that Damian was gone?

The closer to her rooms she got, the...well, bad wasn't the word for it, because in general princesses of the Realms did not feel bad. There was no reason to second-guess yourself when you were always right.

Unless you had had intense personal experience that suggested otherwise.

Like when, at the end, she'd had her hand on Baran's windpipe, watching the light drain from his eyes.

"I don't want to have to kill him," she muttered to herself.

"Kill...who?" a woman's voice asked behind her.

Ryana whirled to find Mills not far behind her on the stair, giving her a kindly smile. "If there's someone that needs killing, and you're not in the mood, there's two or three men in this house that could handle it for you."

Ryana forced a laugh. "Yes, I'm well aware."

"Austin in particular. I think he'd be mad if you picked someone else, honestly."

She chuckled in earnest, this time. "What if he's the one that needs to die, though?"

Mills leaned against the railing beside her. "Then we might need to have a team meeting first. Why would you be killing him?"

She inhaled, ready to list all his flaws, and found there weren't many, past that first night. "For doing exactly as I ask."

"You're a princess. I thought you were used to being obeyed?"

"It's different." When she'd propositioned him, it'd been as transactional as the dancers they'd gone to see. Or like any number of her experiments—or her entire prior life. You perform A, you get B in return. B just didn't arrive out of nowhere and act all B-like and not expect anything from A.

Did B?

Mills walked up and rested a hand on her shoulder. "I'm well aware of how powerful you are, Ryana, even without your guardian. Please don't kill him. I'm very fond of him."

"Fine," she muttered, instead of saying what she was thinking very loudly: *Increasingly, me, as well.*

SHE WENT BACK to her chambers, pulled in her wings, and changed into a tight purple sweater and a skirt that matched it and nipped in at the waist. Afterwards she headed up to Damian's empty quarters. There were TV rooms in the house, but she wanted privacy, even as she wasn't sure she wanted Austin in her bedroom. She then requested Grim's help in performing a small magic on Austin's room, to which he readily agreed.

She had Lyka rearrange all the furniture in her brother's room to accommodate her desires, and by the time she was done there was a wide screen TV on the wall in front of a large green couch, with a green path from Austin's door leading all the way up to it.

Austin opened the door not long after, cleaned up in dark jeans that clung to his body and a tight dark gray t-shirt, which showed more of the art on both his muscular biceps and forearms. "Here?" he asked, looking around.

"You should be happy I forgave you, rather than questioning things," she said, sitting down on the couch.

"Well, I do have to take into consideration that, now that you hate me, you're setting me up for Damian to murder, since we're in front of half his mirrors."

Ryana squinted at him. "Did you talk to Mills?"

His eyebrows rose. "No...should I?"

She quickly rolled her eyes. "No. How were the unicorns?"

"Not as strategically proficient as I had hoped." He'd reached the couch by then and was looking down at it, dusting his hands on his thighs. "Is the entire couch green, or just one section of it?" he asked her, clearly teasing.

"You may sit here," she said, putting a hand beside herself. "But that's all."

"Got it," he said, sitting down. "So what's on our agenda, wings?"

"I had Grim find your movie for you. The Predator one," she said, gesturing to the TV which turned on.

"All right." He leaned out. "Think you can make a coffee table about this high? And ask Grim to get me my favorite drink? He knows what it is." She did as he requested, and then watched him fold his long body out, putting his feet on the table, rocking back against the couch beside her with a beer in his hand. "Let's see some old school Arnold."

They watched the movie—which was ridiculous, but no more so than other movies she'd watched at his request—and it was entertaining to see the monsters on the screen. His shoulder was next to hers, and it brushed her as he leaned in. "That kinda looks like your buddy in the box," he said, after the monster in the movie unhinged its face.

She resisted the urge to sidle up against him, but only barely. "It does," she agreed. "I'll have to tell him when he wakes up next."

"Which...won't be for years, right?" He sounded concerned.

"I'm not entirely sure. I think being on earth may be affecting him. He's brooding over eggs."

"He's...brooding? Not a lady space-spider-friend?"

She looked up at him. "Of course. If you want your inheritable traits passed on, then you should be the one in charge of making sure that happens."

"I am learning more and more about the Realms by the moment." Austin made a thoughtful sound and nodded sagely. "Do me a favor and don't tell Jamison that, though."

"I won't," she promised. "Also—he likes chocolate. I gave the rest of that bag of Whoppers to him."

Austin blew air through pursed lips. "In that case, we'll have to buy him more."

They watched the movie in contented silence for a little while—and she'd had Lyka make her another package of Twizzlers—then he asked her, "Hey, wings?"

"Yeah?"

"How do you do this, where you're from?"

She looked over at him, sure she wouldn't miss some crucial piece of action on the screen. She knew what he was asking. "Depends on who you are and your station. I'm sure common people do whatever they like…but in general…you have your servants talk to their servants, to arrange a meeting. Some people send letters of intent."

"Letters of intent, you say?" Austin asked, laughing lightly.

She grinned at him. "It's no different from using the internet now, I think. I mean, I guess it depends on what your aims are." She tucked her feet up on the couch with her. "Damian had it a lot easier, when he was back home. Not as many guards followed him, and the women he was with were all aware on some level that they were being used, much in the same way they themselves hoped to use him. To gain power, or status, or accrue future favors."

Austin looked momentarily confused. "So nobody in the Realms gets together just for fun?"

Ryana thought and shrugged. "Common people? Maybe. Not when you're a prince." He looked at her meaningfully. "Or a princess," she added.

"So I'm common, eh?" he teased her and smiled.

"You did say you were easy. Your words, not mine." She found herself smiling back without meaning to. She tilted her head at him. "So—on Earth, what would be next?"

Austin's lips pulled to the side. "You have no idea how badly I'm tempted to lie to you."

"I would know." Would she though? Her stomach roiled as she frowned.

"I'm kidding," he said, and she felt immense relief. "What happens next, most times, is that I wrap my arm around you. And maybe you lean in. Right here," he said, holding his arm up and indicating that she could duck beneath it.

"And that's…it?" she asked.

"Yeah. Then we watch the rest of the movie. And there's like three after this one, although we'll skip the really shitty Alien crossover one, if you don't mind."

Ryana looked up at him. His face was open to her—well, not as open as the monster's on the screen—but she felt sure she could read his intent. He wanted her to trust him.

Wasn't that what everyone who wanted something from you wanted?

But…she'd picked him for a reason. Because he was disposable. He was common—and he knew it! He didn't have any delusions of grandeur. (Not like Andi, whom she'd somewhat disliked, until she found out that Damian had *given* her princess as a nickname, and not, as Ryana had assumed, that she'd taken it.)

"Or not," Austin said, and gave her a bemused look. "Which is fine. We're still not watching the one with the space pyramids though. It's too embarrassing for everyone involved." He moved to put his arm down and she caught it, scooting closer, pulling it over her head, to rest between her neck and the back of the couch. She arranged herself against him, rather like a cat, nestling her face against his clavicle.

From here she could smell him. He smelled like being outdoors, with a faint hint of something darker, something wild, like a musk. She leaned even closer to him and inhaled, and both heard and felt him laughing.

"You smell like an animal."

"Strange," he told her. "I guess I am one." He didn't take his eyes off the screen, but she could see the corner of his lips curl up, and he stroked a short line down her shoulder with his thumb. Beneath the safety of her long-sleeved sweater her skin broke out in gooseflesh.

CHAPTER 14

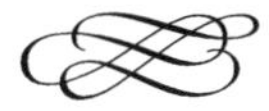

THE MOVIE BECAME MUCH MORE TOLERABLE WHEN SHE WAS LYING against Austin's side. She could feel the soft rise and fall of his chest as he breathed, and imagined that she could hear the beating of his heart. She knew if she closed her eyes and tried hard enough to summon that side of her which was dragon, she might actually be able to.

But for him...what was he getting out of it? He continued to brush her shoulder with his thumb. Was that one point of contact all he craved?

"I like this," he said, as if answering her thoughts. "How are you? Still green?"

She frowned a little, then remembered that he'd warned her he'd check in. She nodded against him and heard him rumble, pleased.

This entire moment, here, with him...was nice.

Which felt untrustworthy.

She looked up at him. "Why aren't you angry with me?"

"For what?" he asked, tilting his head.

"For this," she said. She moved sideways, dislodging his hand. "For everything."

He gave her one of the looks he so often did, like she was a surprisingly locked door. "We made a decision to try this, Ryana. So I'm doing as you've asked me to, to the best of my ability."

"But...why?" she pressed.

"Why...aren't I busy trying to put moves on you or tear your clothes off?" His eyebrows arched up as he chuckled deeply.

"No. Why are you being kind to me?" she demanded before she could stop herself. Better to hear his lies and free herself now, than any of the alternatives.

She watched him inhale, slowly, and his blue eyes became more intense. "Because you deserve someone who can be," he explained slowly. "I've played games before, Ryana. I know how to rile a woman up, and how to stop one cold. But I don't want to do any of that with you. If I'm going to be your first time and all, I want to –"

It took a moment for her to fully register the words, but the second she did she pushed off of him with both hands and stared at him openly as her stomach fell.

He read her expression quickly and inhaled. "Oh, no. I thought –"

"*You thought*," she snarled, yanking her hands away from him like he was on fire. Suddenly everything fell into place. Why he'd been fighting her so hard—and why he'd wound up giving in. Their past few interactions had all been based on lies.

She'd been played for a fool.

Again.

"What?" she challenged him, her voice rising. "That no one else would want me?"

"Ryana," he said, his voice low. "That is unfair."

She started shaking her head in disagreement. "No—what's *unfair* is you trying to be nice to me, thinking you're gaining access to some *priceless treasure*. I've seen enough of your media here on Earth. I know how much emphasis people here put on their virginity. And you think that you're going to be *the one?*" she mocked, before rearing back to the other side of the couch. "That's all you want from me?"

He paused on his side of the couch, breathing hard and looking wounded, and then surged over after her, surprising her utterly. She squeaked and rolled back as he held himself above her, straddling her thighs.

"Technically this whole couch is green, wings," he warned her.

"What, so now that you know that you're not my first, you think I'll be your whore?" she hissed.

"Ryana!" he snapped, close enough she could feel his breath on her cheek. "If anyone here on this couch is a whore, it's me, all right? And I actually have some friends who are whores. You shouldn't talk bad about them. Life is hard and money's nice." She squirmed for the couch's edge and he blocked her in with his elbow. "Listen, and I'll let you go."

She fought against him, and while he wasn't much stronger than she was, he was much, much faster. "I should have Lyka kill you."

"If you were going to, I'd already be dead," he growled.

It was true. She could've snapped her fingers at any time, it was all the bird was waiting for. "Fine. Talk," she demanded, then looked away.

One of his hands sank behind her head to take a fistful of her hair and make her look up at him as he spoke. "I don't care who or what you've slept with in the past or how many times," he said, and she snorted. "All I care about is now." He let go of her and used the cushion by her head to press up. "I'm trying to do right by you. I don't know why you can't see that. Jesus." He stared down at her and swallowed. He was hard, she knew, because she could very well see it through his jeans—and then he dismounted the couch and her in one smooth athletic motion to stand. "When, and if, you make up your mind—you know where to find me," he said, and walked out.

AUSTIN STALKED down the hall to his own quarters, the green path Ryana had created for him evaporating as he did so.

He should've known better than to even try. He'd been in enough hopeless situations before—he knew exactly what it felt like when there was no way to win. He'd been too busy listening to his dick to hear his gut when it chimed in, but it was there now, loud and clear, saying he *shouldn't have bothered* and *he knew it would end like this, all along.*

After his and Zach's pack was murdered when they were kids, and their mother went on her vengeance kick, their lives were fucking hard. But he'd been smart, and even then, he'd paid attention.

Because he'd wanted to be normal. So he'd spent so much of his childhood watching, figuring out exactly what that was like—only to realize somewhere in middle school that he'd never have it. He could pretend, sure, even now he could put on a suit and play along—not as well as Zach could, but he knew that was *why* Zach was good at it, because they'd been in the same boat—but unlike Zach, he knew he'd never win.

Not in the places where other people thought it mattered. Sure, he could beat the hell out of people, and sure, he could save lives—at the time, he'd thought Damian was an idiot for forcing him to go through paramedic school, although he didn't complain about going to school on the dragon's dime—but of course Ryana could see through all that, to the real him. The part that really was just an animal, only after one thing.

Perhaps, because, up until her, he had been.

But had he really been, all his life? Or had his existence just been one big self-fulfilling prophecy, where people had assumed the worst about him, and so he'd given it to them? Because he was always that kid on the outside, moving from place to place, school to school, the one everyone knew didn't fit in, that everyone thought it'd be a fucking great idea to beat up, until he proved them wrong?

He shook himself like he was shaking away a fly and slammed the door to his room behind him. "Don't fuck with me tonight, Grim, I am in no mood," he announced, and pulled on clothes that wouldn't smell like Ryana to go out in.

AUSTIN WOUND up at his second-favorite bar again, because it was closest—and once again Dominic was there. The rhino-shifter had procured himself a booth seat along one wall, and Missy was talking animatedly to him, sitting on his lap, her arms slung about his thick neck. On spotting Austin, Dominic waved him over—as did Missy.

He could hardly ignore the both of them, although he dearly wished he'd already had a buzz on to deal with this nonsense. He sat across from Dominic, as the other shifter pushed Missy off.

"Go, dear. Men are talking."

Missy blinked at this, and looked to Austin to take some sort of affront on her behalf. Finding none forthcoming, she sat up and bolted as Dominic waved a waitress over.

"Are there not any English-style pubs open this late?" Austin asked, slightly more relaxed now that he knew he wouldn't have to have a fight.

"Not with werewolves I want to talk to in them," Dominic said, placing an order for the both of them.

"Make that a double," Austin said, before the waitress could get away, as Dominic shot him a look. "Tonight I am going to drink a lot," he explained. "But you're welcome to join me. Especially if you keep women away."

"Bird trouble?" Dominic asked with a laugh.

"No." Because Ryana was, and would never be, his girl. "I just don't want to deal with any bullshit right now is all."

"Which is why you don't give anyone your phone number, eh?"

Austin frowned as the drinks arrived. Dominic really had been looking for him. "I'm more of a word-of-mouth operation," Austin said.

"So I hear," Dominic said with a snort. "But now that you're here—I have a business proposition. It's a money-is-no-object kind of thing."

Austin knocked the first glass of whiskey back, and then laughed. "Which usually means that whoever hires you doesn't care if you live or die."

"It's this kind of perspicaciousness that I've missed in conversation lately, Austin," Dominic said, and grinned.

"Too bad for you, I'm still generally interested in life, and I get paid just fine, Dom, as you know."

"I do. Which is why I'm not just cutting you in on cash—I'm cutting you in on a challenge."

Austin swirled the whiskey in the second glass, his gut telling him he could *use a distraction* and that *listening wouldn't hurt.* "Go on?"

"Some men from the Realms are looking for something of value on our earth, and they need local help."

Austin steeled himself to look vaguely disinterested the second Dominic said the word 'Realms.' "Yeah. I don't need the money, again —and anything involving other Realms is trouble."

Dominic sighed dramatically, like an actor might, with a wrist up to his forehead. "And to think, all this time Melissa's been telling me that you were 'fun.'"

"Did they say what it was?" Austin asked, pretending to be nonchalant. The Heart of the Dragon, the physical object that embodied Damian's curse, was somewhere in their castle, where Mills was performed experiments on it periodically, trying to break Damian free. If people were after it, Damian would want to know.

"What, I should tell you what it is, and then you go and snake it out from under me?""You greatly overestimate my free time," Austin told him, setting into his second drink.

Dominic grinned, showing a line of straight white teeth. "Honestly, the people who've hired me, they're quite coy. They haven't told me what it is yet—could be a person, for all I know—or how to find it. But it sounds interesting. Maybe even fun. Which is why you should give me your phone number—in case watching an old man sleep gets boring and you change your mind."

"Fine," Austin snorted, pulling out his phone. He was texting his number to the other shifter when it both alarmed and buzzed, and he saw a text from Mills come in. A rift had opened, and it was all hands on deck immediately. Austin looked up and saw Dominic considering him. "The old man woke up, gotta go," Austin said with a shrug, standing and finishing his text. Dominic's phone buzzed with Austin's number, and Austin told him: "If you give that out to a girl, I'll kill you."

"I'd like to see you try," Dominic said with a rich chuckle as Austin ducked out the door.

He jogged down the block and saw the cherry of a lit cigarette near Betsy—no, from inside. As he neared, he could scent lavender twining with cigarette smoke, and found Missy sitting in Betsy's driver's seat. She'd climbed in because the top was off.

"Missy, get out," Austin growled, opening up the door. He didn't have time to play games; he was going to have to meet the others as it was. "Now."

She clung to the steering wheel defiantly. "No! You owe me for ditching me!"

"I did not ditch you—I stopped you from making a bad decision." Austin's phone buzzed again. "But I really need to fucking go, so get out of my car."

"Make me," she said.

Austin lunged in and grabbed her, picking her up and putting her down outside his vehicle, as she tried to punch him with her free hand and kicked at him ineffectually. "Go back to Dominic. His lap is empty," he said, releasing her.

"I don't want him. I want you," she said, throwing her cigarette down and stomping it out.

"There's not an *us* Melissa. I'm not *with* anyone—and I never will be." He got into his car and yanked the door shut behind him. He'd meant to sound dramatic, but as soon as the words left his mouth, they felt depressingly true.

He turned Betsy's engine over—and because the top was off, he could easily hear Missy shout, "Because you're an asshole!" after him as he drove off.

AUSTIN DIDN'T RECOGNIZE the address Jamison had sent him. It was just outside the city. He stepped on the gas, and he texted Zach to say he'd meet them there. Zach was too busy to text back, so he didn't know what he was heading into—he just hoped they'd had the wisdom to call Damian if the dragon-shifter was needed.

He pulled over where his map told him to, into the serpentine parking lot of an outlet mall, wrapping around assorted buildings. He had no idea which one the rest of his friends were inside, but he knew he was in the right place because he could see the tour bus and Max's truck. He cut his headlights and cruised down the first empty block of shops, to do two sharp lefts and turn into a U-shaped cul-de-sac, where everyone, Max, Ryana, Jamison, and Zach were standing guard in the middle of the asphalt while Mills repaired a rift and—he saw movement on his right. Something dark was darting between shops and making its way towards his friends. He saw Zach and Ryana turn and knew they'd be the first in danger—he whipped his brights on to blind the intruders, changed gears, and hit the gas.

Betsy launched over the curb, aimed straight for the two stark outlines of armored warriors now casting massive shadows on the wall of the store behind them. One of the warriors jumped in time, but the other didn't. Austin bailed out of the Jeep right before impact, and even with the crunch of the metal, he could hear the sickening sound of flesh tearing wetly. Austin landed ungracefully, rolled, and then came up to race after the warrior he hadn't hit, but Zach was already pumping rounds into the man.

"Stop! Stop!" Ryana shouted at both of them.

"Why?" Zach growled, saving Austin the trouble of questioning her, as both werewolves stalked to the downed fighter's side. It was another one of the Kagaroth—Austin figured as much with his headlights, but this time he wanted to see the body for himself.

"Because I need to ask him questions!" she said, coming up beside them, kneeling down. "One encounter might have been an accident, but two times shows intent!" She was working on the buckles to the man's armor. "How are they causing rifts? And why?" she asked, yanking the helmet off the man on the ground, but it was clear he was already dead, Zach had shot him too many times.

Lyka took off from her station around Ryana's neck to fly toward Betsy, and Austin watched Ryana rise from her knees to run for his car.

"Princess!" Max shouted after her, chasing her quickly, and Austin followed.

BETSY HAD TRAPPED the Kagaroth against the wall but hadn't killed him, although, from the scent of blood hanging in the air, Austin suspected the man was bleeding out. Ryana held up her hand and her magic illuminated the area around them, letting Austin see just what he'd done to his poor car—and the much, much worse-off man pressed just above the level of his hips to the brick wall in front of it. Ryana went for the injured warrior without hesitation.

"It's not safe!" Max shouted, pulling her back.

She shrugged him away. "You know how they are—I have to talk to him fast!" She grabbed the man's free arm, pinning it against the brick wall behind him, and blocked their view of him as she pried this one's helmet off, too.

Austin came up to her side without thinking—he didn't care if she was still pissed at him, or how helpless the warrior currently seemed—and so he was able to see the man's reaction as Ryana levered his helmet off, dropping it to the ground.

The dying fighter definitely recognized Ryana. And then he said rough things, shouting at her, with flecks of blood in his spittle, getting it on her face.

Austin had no idea what the Kagaroth was saying, but he could see the effect it was having on Ryana. Even as she fought back, repeatedly asking questions, he could tell by her inflection.

The fighter continued to...what...curse at her? Austin gave Max a glance, knowing that the bear-shifter also spoke the tongue—and found him much paler than normal, which was saying something because Max's skin was so light already it was almost see-thru.

Ryana said something back—pleading, almost?—which the fighter ignored, to spew more invective.

"That's enough of that," Austin said, stepping forward, grabbing hold of the Kagaroth's throat, ready to tear it out. "May I?" he asked Ryana.

"It doesn't matter now," she said, as Austin felt the Kagaroth sag forward into his hand. She peeled back a portion of the man's armor to reveal what looked like a needle. "He'd already done it himself by the time I got here."

"He could've used that needle on you, Ryana," Max said, his voice grave.

She inhaled to fight him on this point and then laughed ruefully. "I was going to say 'he would never'...but, my old Weaponsmaster, yes. You are right."

CHAPTER 15

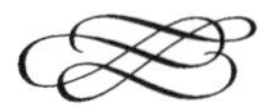

THEIR GROUP RECONVENED UNDERNEATH A STREETLIGHT TO DISCUSS what to do.

"First off, we need to call Damian," Mills said. She was leaning on Jamison. Closing rifts always tired her.

"No," Ryana said.

"You said it yourself, Ryana—one attack might be an accident, but two's an incursion," Zach said.

"We can't. We don't need him," she said, and Austin watched her shake her head and not stop as she went on. "This is just a small rogue group. A handful. We've probably already killed half of them," she said, looking to Max for back-up.

The bear-shifter's color had not gotten better in the meantime, but he considered Ryana and then sighed. "I agree with Ryana. So far, we're fine."

"So far, they're opening up rifts to play peek-a-boo. What happens when they send more men or monsters?" Zach pressed.

"We'll deal with it then," Ryana said, definitively. "Not now. My brother deserves a vacation."

This version of Ryana was a lot different from the one who'd been pleading with him to not even fight imaginary Kagaroth earlier in the day. "What'd they tell you?" Austin asked.

"Nothing useful. Just a lot of curses and nonsense." He watched the muscles of her jaw tighten, and she wouldn't look his direction.

"Well, whatever we decide to do—we don't need to do it here," Jamison said, returning his attention to them. "I've wiped all the security cameras, and put in a stolen vehicle report with the police on Betsy three hours ago, which'll explain why she's here. Someone was out joyriding into the wall."

Austin grunted. "And what about the bodies?"

"Into the truck with them this time, for sure," Max said.

"In that case," Austin said, looking around the group, "you all go ahead—Max and I will catch up."

AUSTIN AND MAX shouldered the Jeep off the wall to retrieve the Kagaroth's body. The leather—he guessed, although because it was from the Realms he knew he could be wrong—armor it was wrapped in was hard and unforgiving. He scanned around with the flashlight from his phone afterwards—most of the blood he'd scented seemed to have disappeared, which was good from a forensic standpoint, but fucking odd.

"Where'd it go?" he asked Max.

"Don't ask questions you don't want the answers to," Max said, picking up the Kagaroth's legs so that he and Austin could sling it into the waiting truck's bed.

"Why do I get the feeling you're talking about more than a few blood stains?"

"Because you volunteered to stay behind for clean up."

"I do clean up duty all the time Max. That's unfair." Austin said, dusting his hands on his legs. The surrounding area was back to normal now—no rift with strange light pouring through, and no more armored bodies. He ran back to the Jeep, gave it a final affectionate pat. "Sorry Betsy—but thanks." Then he returned to Max's truck to pull himself into the cab. "So about whatever that thing said to Ryana," he began, buckling his seatbelt.

"I knew it," Max muttered. "It's not my story to tell, Austin."

Austin considered this. "That may be true. But surely you can tell me more about the Kagaroth—now that we've seen them twice, it seems important."

Max tilted his head at Austin, and Austin knew, were it not for the bear shifter's omnipresent goggles, Max would be giving him side-eye. "They're rabid warriors. Supposed to be loyal only to the throne…."

"But?" Austin prompted.

"This group isn't. Ryana said they're rogue, she knows them better than I do." The bear-shifter's lips narrowed.

"Come on, Max," Austin said.

Maximillian shook his head. "Sorry, Austin. I only have the princess's best interests at heart."

"What I say next is going to surprise the hell out of both of us but, hey, Max?" Austin said, waving a hand in front of Max's goggles, forcing the other man to look over. "Me too."

Max returned his gaze to the road to consider this while wringing the steering wheel. "If you hurt her, Austin, I will take the Forgetting Fire and erase your entire life's memories from you, right down to the day you were born."

"I promise, I won't."

The second the words left his mouth he knew they were true. Ryana could hurt him, for sure—she could scrape his heart out of his chest with a bottle cap—and he'd fucking let her before he hurt her in return.

Max pulled his truck onto the highway. "It was clear she and this group of Kagaroth have some sort of history."

"Well, yeah, if they were royal guards—she already told me about that. Sounds like the things stalked her, growing up."

"No, I mean history of a personal nature. Which, by the rules of the palace, is strictly forbidden. The Kagaroth are neither supposed to take off their helmets nor talk while on palace grounds, unless it's an absolute emergency. Which would make having a relationship with one rather difficult…." Max's voice drifted, as Austin's stomach clenched.

"And yet?" Austin asked him.

"That guard knew of Ryana. They were…quite insulting to her personal honor, let's say, without going into particulars."

Austin twisted so he could see into the rear of the truck's cab, where Max's travelling brazier of Forgetting Fire was kept, along with the two Kagaroth's bodies, and he wished he knew some resurrection spell so he could kill the men a second time.

THE ONLY THING Ryana could think on the way home, staring out the SUV's window, was, *May Eloph's bright light shine down on Max for playing along.*

Because Mills was right, they absolutely should call Damian—which would not only ruin his much-deserved vacation, but also, most likely, his entire impression of her.

Welcome back older brother! You may be wondering why we asked you home so quickly? Well, it's because my old honor guard has decided to reappear, and all their members know that I was an easily played lovesick fool and an embarrassment to the throne. And guess what, on top of that? They bet amongst themselves on how long it'd take me to fall for Baran—and because I fell in love so quickly, this elite group's decided that I'm an idiotic whore.

Their words, not mine!

So, how was Italy? What'd you bring me?

She could taste the acid at the back of her throat and swallowed it down, and when the SUV parked, she was the first out of it and first back inside the castle. She'd let the others call Damian once her experiments were finished in two or three days. She just needed *one* thing to prove her worth to them. She was getting close to replicating her old formula, she knew it—if only the Kagaroth would give her a little bit more time....

How dare they infect not only her dreams, but her current reality?

She was half dressed in her work clothes, with only her helmet left to pull on, when there was a rap on her door, and a muffled voice saying, "Yo, wings," from the other side.

Austin. Her shoulders sank, and not just from the weight of the blast apron she'd just slung over her shoulders. "The door is red!" she shouted, loud enough for him to hear.

"Fuck what color the door is," she heard him mutter, as she came near. "I'm checking up on you as a friend, we don't need to play games," he said, much louder. "Open up, wings. I'm not going away until you do."

Ryana sighed, and pulled the door open without saying anything. Austin stood straighter in her presence, looking down, and it felt like he could see all her flaws and imperfections. The outside of her was beautiful, she knew, but the inside? Not so much. "I'm only going to ask this once," he told her, "but I need you to be honest with me. Is there someone out there I need to kill?"

Ryana swallowed and looked away. This whole thing would be a lot more impressive if he didn't smell like some other woman. But he had told her that he 'was a whore' himself mere hours ago, so maybe they had that in common, if you asked the Kagaroth. "Perhaps I should be asking you the same thing. I don't think Betsy favored lavender perfume before her untimely demise."

She watched his eyes roll back and heard him groan. "You know I went out earlier."

"In search of more compliant women?" she snarked.

He laughed—for real, without a drop of irony—and she was taken aback for a second before regaining her composure. "Just because I am easy doesn't mean I'm only interested in easy," he told her.

"Yes, well, as you can see, I'm just fine." Ryana gestured at herself with one hand, and went to close the door.

He blocked her from doing so with his boot. "I don't believe you."

She fought the impulse to just have Lyka bite his foot off. "Why not?"

"Because. It's like there's two of you, Ryana. There's the one that you project into the world—and then the one underneath, that I can barely see. This one," he said, making the same gesture at her as she just had, "says she's all right, sure. But I don't trust her for shit. So let me talk to the other one, the one she's hiding. I know that she'll be honest with me." He tilted his head, looking down at her. "Take off the armor and tell me you're actually okay. And my offer to go and kill whoever hurt you still stands. I'll even let you watch if you want."

She looked down at the blast shield that was covering her up. "I need this armor for my experiments."

"We both know that's not what I meant."

She would've crossed her arms only, with her heavy gear on, she couldn't. "It's charming that you think that I haven't killed them already, myself." She shrugged again and looked away. "I achieved revenge, and it didn't change anything, because it came too late. And the person that you're looking for inside me? She's not there. I lost her."

He reached out and lifted her chin up, making her look up at him. "I refuse to believe that."

"I don't care what you believe. You don't actually know me, Austin." She stuttered out a harsh laugh and took a step nearer him. "How can you trust me, when I can't trust myself?"

"I don't know, wings, I just do." His dark blue eyes, the color of the sky just before dawn, stared down at her.

The look he gave her then made her stomach feel like that one time that Damian had taken her flying. Like she wasn't sure if she should shriek in delight or throw up. Her hands clenched into fists. *Enough with these games.* "Stop being so nice to me! I hate it!"

"Fine," he said. "How do you want me to be instead, Ryana?" His voice was preternaturally calm as he stepped up to her now, staring her down, boxing her in against the door behind her. She moved to shove him back and found his chest was like a warm wall of steel. He looked down at this point of contact between them. "I may smell like an animal—and I may turn into an animal—but I am not an animal," he growled, taking a step back, leaving her hands empty—like the rest of her—and suddenly the thought of being alone became slightly worse than dealing with his presence.

"Kiss me or else," she demanded.

His eyes narrowed, but the corners of his lips quirked up. "Or else what?"

"If you don't, I will hate you even more."

"Well we can't have that, can we," he said, coming back into shoving range. He bent his head to meet hers and she rose slightly up. Their lips pressed together and his opened, his tongue asking hers for entrance, sweeping across the line of her lips, and she let him in.

The chorus of cells that made up any smart part of her sang that it was such a bad idea, if they let him near, they would get hurt, that there was no good way for this to end, but his body covered hers against the door behind her like a blanket, momentarily quenching the fire of her fears. He held her face in his hands, and he was tasting her, slowly, deliberately. Each time he pushed his tongue in, it made her shiver, and each time he pulled it out she followed with her own, tasting him back, and that was all he did; his hands didn't roam. It felt like he was learning her, and by the time he broke their kiss and pulled up she was sure he could've drawn a map of her mouth with his tongue.

"Green?" he asked her.

She knocked the door behind her with an open palm and changed its color to match her eyes. She felt his laugh more than heard it, he was so close. "How do I know if you're for real?" she whispered.

He bent down and ran his nose along hers. "Because I'm going to somehow go back to my room without you right now."

"You could just be luring me into a false of security." She didn't finish the rest of the sentence the way she wanted to—*so we should just sleep together, now.*

"I could," he admitted, still so near. She was glad for the blast apron's protection, so he wouldn't see her flush or her nipples tighten. "So don't be with me till you're sure," he said, finally standing up. "Let me know when you're green next, wings. Don't make me haunt your door."

She nodded as he took a step back out into the hall. "I'm sorry about Betsy, by the way," she called after him.

"Me too," he admitted, "but keeping you safe was worth it."

CHAPTER 16

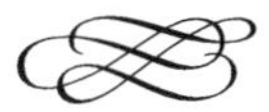

More than ever, Ryana wanted her experiments to *work*. She tried to tell herself it was because she wanted protection against the Kagaroth's plans, but a deep-down part of her knew it was because she wanted to see Austin again—even as everything sensible inside of her counseled against it.

But on the second day of her experiments he put a letter underneath her door—she found it when she woke up, just wearing the slip that she slept in.

The envelope said 'Letter' in strong handwriting on the front—and inside was a folded-up piece of paper that said, 'Of Intent—Austin.' It was so ridiculous she had to laugh. She folded it up and put it inside of her notebook.

"What do you think about him, Lyka?" she asked on the third day, setting the potion she prayed-to-Eloph was in its final stages in a device that would keep it gently spinning 'round, so its contents wouldn't solidify. She'd already finished changing into normal clothes after her shower—a somewhat slinky burgundy dress, ruched on one side, with low-heeled sandals—and was about to go find Austin. In her heart of hearts, she knew it was probably too late for a check in.

Her guardian changed into a sizable red parrot and took its place on her shoulder. "My only desire is to see you safe and happy," the bird told her, which she knew was Lyka's way of withholding judgement on the man.

"I know," Ryana told her. Lyka nuzzled her little feathered head against her temple as Ryana opened the door.

IT DIDN'T TAKE her long to find Austin after that—he was in the castle's grand foyer, looking at his phone, wearing jeans, his boots, and some kind of plaid flannel, and he had a worn brown satchel strung over one shoulder. He looked up on hearing her, and his face lit up with an open smile as he stood.

It was so much better seeing men who didn't wear helmets.

"Green," she announced, smiling back at him.

"You have impeccable timing, wings. I was just about to catch a ride out, looking for Betsy's replacement. Want to come with me?"

Out in public with Austin in the daytime? "Sure."

He offered her his hand instead of his arm, and she took it.

They walked together outside the castle's last set of gates. "And you're sure they're not going to mind Lyka?"

"Nah. As long as she behaves," he said, giving the bird a mock glare. Lyka rustled her feathers in response and squawked, and Austin chuckled. Their ride arrived, and Austin led with enough cash to keep the driver calm, while holding the back door open for Ryana. "Lyka's much nicer than Grim."

"You just haven't pissed her off yet," Ryana said, getting in.

THEIR DRIVER, a girl not much younger than Ryana, wanted to know all about her bird, and also where Ryana had gotten her dress, and it was nice being the one asked questions for once—especially because Austin had retaken hold of her hand. His fingers laced with hers, and he'd brought both their hands to the outside of his thigh, and his thumb stroked hers up and down. Just that small amount of friction sent little thrills up and down her spine. It felt right. Just like being with him did. She watched him laugh quietly the next time she had to lie to their driver, and she caught him giving her a secret smile—the kind of smile she felt the need to draw, so it would be hers forever.

And then he told the driver to change their destination to someplace called a car dealership, named after someone named Bentley. The people there also had questions about Lyka—asked much more rudely, though—and seemed to not want to talk to them until Austin had produced some sort of black card from his wallet, after which everyone was obsequiously polite.

"So, as I was saying," the man explaining the vehicle went on, cornering Austin, who shook his head.

"Talk to the girl. It's going to be hers."

"What?" Ryana said, looking up from the car she was peering into. "I thought we were replacing Betsy!"

"So did I, but this seemed much more fun," Austin said, grinning at her.

"I still don't know how to drive, Austin," she reminded him. Ryana watched the man who worked for Mr. Bentley blink and swallow.

"You're going to teach her how to drive on a Bentley?" he said in a small, high voice, possibly meant only for himself.

Austin gave the man a wolfish smile. "Yeah. Make it an automatic. We'll start there."

HALF AN HOUR LATER, they were out on the road in a candy-red convertible with the top down. She'd wound her hair up into a bun and Lyka was acting as a hairpin again, and Austin was driving them outside of town.

"Are we going to the forest?" she shouted over the wind, feeling exuberant. She'd have Lyka make her different shoes, if so.

"No, now we're killing time," Austin shouted back.

"Why?" she asked, although she was sure he wouldn't answer.

"You'll see."

She squirmed impatiently. "I'm not sure I like that phrase."

"It's good for surprises."

"I know." Back in the Realms, if someone had told her 'you'll see' she would've assumed she was about to be assassinated. No one liked surprises there, least of all royalty. Maybe that was another point in Earth's favor.

Austin slowed the car down and took a side road. "This seems like another forest," she told him. "I'm not complaining though. I like forests."

"Stop guessing, you'll take all the fun out of it," he laughed, and then the road they were on dead-ended into a magnificent view of the city below. He stopped the car, got out and came around for her door, and then they both walked up to the edge where someone had left a large woven basket. She leaned over the metal railing to see better, and felt his hand catch at the back of her dress, just in case.

"I have wings," she reminded him as he gently pulled her back.

"Damian said you couldn't fly?"

"I could glide a little bit. Plus, Lyka."

"True," Austin said, letting go to kneel down and open up the basket at his feet, placing his satchel beside it. Inside the basket was a large checkered blanket, which he brought out and snapped open on the ground right in front of the car, before pulling other things out of the basket: cold water, fruits, and cheese.

"How did you do that?" she asked him, moving to sit by his side.

"I may not have magic—but I do have Instacart," he said, smiling.

Ryana smiled back. "Is this place another wolf-thing?"

"You could say that." He bit into an apple and leaned back against the vehicle. "My brother and I used to live right over there." He jerked his chin behind them.

There wasn't much there—just a field of waist-high grass, laced with wildflowers, and a small grove of trees.

"All the way up here?" she asked. It was beautiful but desolate. "Alone?"

"With my mother. When we were kids. In a barn not too far from here."

Ryana looked around at the waving grass and the butterflies

dancing between flowers. "No wonder you two are close, then. My mother just tried to make Damian and me fight."

"Did it work?"

"We both survived childhood, so, no," Ryana said with a chuckle. "There were times when it was touch and go, though." She popped another grape into her mouth and opened a water bottle. "My mother almost beat him to death once because of me." She watched Austin's eyes widen in horror. "Want to hear the story?"

"Of course."

Ryana kicked off her shoes so she could more comfortably sit with her legs tucked beside her. "So...it took a while for Damian to find his dragon inside of him, but after he did, when we were kids, he used to change into it all the time." She closed her eyes for a moment, remembering her own jealousy. It'd seemed so unfair that Damian was able to change into an entire dragon, when all she'd gotten from their shared father were her wings—but that was before either of them had understood that his dragon was a curse.

"I can imagine," Austin prompted her, and she opened her eyes to catch him grinning. "He's impulsive enough now—teenaged Damian must have been a real jerk."

"Precisely," Ryana agreed. "But actually—he wasn't a jerk that particular day, though there were plenty of others. I think we were fighting, although I can't remember what about, and then I wanted to see if I could fly." She shrugged her shoulders, where her wings would be, if she let them out. "It seemed like a good idea at the time. And none of the Kagaroth stopped us, so we figured we were safe."

She and her brother had gone up to the tallest portion of the palace together, Damian changed, and then as a dragon, he'd swooped her up. "He flew me up, up, up, and then when I told him I was ready he let me go."

Ryana went still at the memory of trying to make her wings hold her—how the wind had caught against them, and how she'd flapped, but the most she could do was a semi-coordinated drift.

"And he caught you, right?" Austin asked, sounding concerned, even though she was sharing distant history.

"Of course," she said, smiling. "And then we did it again, and again, just to be sure—and basically, all I can do is glide."

One of Austin's eyebrows quirked up. "Where'd the beatings come in?"

Ryana winced. "Eventually one of the guards must have gotten worried and told my mother. When we saw her on the roof, we knew we were both in trouble."

"And?" he prompted.

"And Damian brought me back to the roof, changed back to human, and my mother just launched herself at him." Ryana remembered the moment vividly. She'd been so certain her mother was going to murder Damian. "The only reason my mother didn't kill him was because our father intervened—as a dragon. I'm not sure the human version of him could've pulled her off."

Austin's expression clouded at that, trying to understand. "Well... she was scared for you, right?"

"Only kind of." Ryana reached down to pluck at the checkered blanket beneath them, remembering. "At the time, yes, I'm certain. But after that—and when I was older—I realized we'd been experimenting out in the open, where everyone could see."

"Couldn't you magic-up the ability to fly?" he asked, waving his hand in mid-air.

"No. I mean, I could, but it would take so much energy it wouldn't be worthwhile. But the part my mom was pissed about was that I'd basically announced to the entire countryside that I didn't have a dragon inside of me, like Damian does." Ryana frowned lightly. "My mother thought it made me seem weak, and maybe she was right."

"Weak is not ever a word I would use to describe you, Ryana," Austin said.

Ryana searched his eyes for a moment, with words on her tongue-tip that she would never speak. *That's odd, because sometimes? I feel weak around you.*

Austin was oblivious of this as he polished off the rest of his apple. "Want to hear about the time my mom got the most mad at me?"

"Sure," Ryana said, wondering how on earth Austin's mother would begin to compare.

He nodded and tossed the core of the apple over the edge of the railing. "It was right before we moved here, in fact. We were living in a little apartment in town, and it had a phone that we were supposed to use only for emergencies, and we were never, ever, supposed to pick it up." She watched him stare off into the distance. "Well, I'd decided to play hooky one day and stay home—Zach didn't, because Zach's a good kid, unlike yours truly—and while I was trying to make the most of it, eating all the cereal and watching TV, the phone started ringing." A quietness descended on Austin then, a strange seriousness that was very unlike him. "It wouldn't stop. I mean—it would—but then it'd start up again. And this was an old school phone; you probably haven't seen one before, but trust me, they're loud. There was no way I could do anything else I wanted to with it ringing in the background. So after listening to it for two or three hours, blasting the volume on our little TV to try to hear my cartoons over it, I gave up and answered the call."

Ryana had twisted toward him without thinking, sensing something ominous in the air. "What then?"

Austin was still staring out at the view ahead of them. "I heard the sound of a man breathing. Then he said, 'You're alone, aren't you,' to me, and hung up."

"Oh, no," Ryana breathed.

He nodded subtly. "Yeah. I went and got every knife we had and barricaded myself in my closet. Then, just as I finished, my mother came home, calling for me—the school had finally called her, Zach had ratted me out—and I told her what happened. We packed up and left, picked up Zach, and we never went back. We lived in our car for two weeks, then we moved up here, and didn't finish the end of that school year."

Ryana was genuinely unsure what to say. "Austin, that sounds horrible."

She watched him take a deep inhalation, leaving his memories behind and returning to her side. "In hindsight, it was, although it didn't feel like it at the time. We'd lost a lot of members of our pack to an enemy pack—Stella's, which is why I give her shit—and our mom spent a lot of time out…doing things. Killing people, honestly, although she did her best to hide it from us." He snorted. "It took us awhile as adults, after she died, to piece everything together, because you know, as kids, you never get the whole story, right? Or you only get one side."

Ryana nodded, and looked past him at the field that the butterflies were playing in. "I can't believe we're sharing such dark stories under such bright sunlight."

His gaze caught hers. "Sometimes dark stories are all you have, until you make new ones." His hand came up for her chin, and she moved closer without thinking, knowing what he wanted and wanting it as well. Their lips met and opened, and he tasted lightly of the apple he'd been eating, and without the blast apron on she was free to run her hands into his hair. His hands gently, hesitantly, found her hips, and as he pulled his head back she already knew what he'd be asking.

"Green," she whispered, smiling at him, his presence eclipsing everything around her—except for the sound of two things, the buzzing of his phone, and a sound she hadn't heard in quite some time:

A sharp intake of breath behind a helmet.

CHAPTER 17

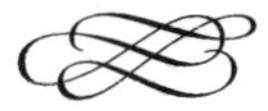

Ryana snapped her wings out without thinking, tearing her dress, and shielding Austin's back just in time as she felt a magical bolt hit her wing's leather.

"Ryana?" Austin asked sharply as she hissed.

"Lyka—up!" she commanded. Her hair fell down around her shoulders as her guardian flew free, spotting the Kagaroth shooting at her, squawking their location down.

By then, Austin had his hands in the satchel he'd brought, pulled out a gun, and was grabbing her to haul her to the car's far side. "How many?" he asked her.

"Lyka says four." Her wing ached; the reverberation of the magic blast was intense.

"Are you okay?" he demanded, looking up at her.

"I'll be fine." She didn't dare peek over the car, as the Kagaroth kept shooting more bolts. "Why are they here?"

"For you, obviously," Austin grunted. "Do they have to reload those things? Whatever it is they're shooting us with?"

Ryana thought fast. "They have to recharge them with magic. It's almost the same thing. It takes about thirty seconds."

"Will Lyka know when that is? And can she tell me?" Ryana nodded. "Okay then. You stay here. She and I will handle this."

He crouched beside her, making ready to run on Lyka's count, and she grabbed his arm. "I need one of them alive, Austin."

"What? Why?"

"For my experiments. Only if you can—but if you can—please."

He grunted again. Lyka squawked and he lunged up, leaping over the hood of the car, racing over to where Lyka darted, as she herself sized up into a much, much larger bird.

AUSTIN WAS glad to have the red blur of Lyka flying into the grove of trees beside him. He was angry, but Lyka sounded pissed, and he heard her make contact with the first of the intruders, landing against one's chest and then sizing up to take him down, pecking at the underside of the man's helmet with a sharp beak the size of a fist. Austin listened to the man's bones snap as he sank into the wolf inside himself, breathing, being—he knew this place well, even after so many years.

What else was out here that didn't belong?

The wind brought him a scent he didn't recognize. He triangulated where it'd come from and shot three rounds in that direction, instinctively, then heard a man groan and fall. He sidled over to the sounds of harsh breathing, using trees for cover, until he found the man, face down. He kicked him over, and fuck, their helmets made it hard to tell if they were still alive. But judging from where the bullets landed, he was going to guess he was successful.

He heard Lyka take off again and wheel behind him, then crow with triumph. He was guessing she was on round two—which left him with Kagaroth number four, the one that Ryana needed alive.

He paused, crouched, and felt magic blast his shoulder—his whole arm instantly went numb, and he dropped his gun. He dove to hide behind the nearest tree, then peered out, spotting the oncoming Kagaroth easily. The man looked like a living shadow, which was strange beneath the sunlight. Austin watched the warrior walk up to his gun, surely wondering what'd happened to him, and ran to slide out in front of it on leaf litter, to snatch with his left hand at the man's knee. He couldn't get the kneecap, what with the armor, but the warrior stumbled forward as Austin bounced up, shoving him down by his back, stepping on his hand and kicking his magical weapon away, trying to keep him alive for Ryana's sake, even as the numbness in his arm kept creeping higher.

Then Lyka was there, the size of a St. Bernard, clinging onto the back of the Kagaroth with both claws and beak, as Ryana raced up.

"You're brilliant!" she shouted, and even though Austin wasn't sure which one of them she meant, he was going to assume it was him. "Can you flip him over, without letting him touch himself?"

"That sounds naughty," Austin muttered.

"They come equipped with poison," she reminded him, then watched him try to help Lyka with concern. "Are you hurt?"

"I got shot." He tried to shrug his arm and couldn't.

Ryana looked between him and the Kagaroth like she couldn't make up her mind, and then decided. "It's going to get worse before it gets better, but you *will* be all right." Then she knelt down and started taking pieces of the Kagaroth's armor off, while Lyka held three of the man's four limbs still with two clawed feet and her beak.

And that was when the pain set in. "Oh, *fuck*," Austin hissed. It felt like his entire arm was coming back to life after having been asleep for centuries.

"I know," Ryana said, not looking up from her task. "Incapacitators."

"How'd you know they weren't using live rounds?"

"First off, because they wanted something, clearly. Secondly—because I still have a wing." He remembered the moment when she'd flared them out to protect him—he hadn't realized she'd taken a hit as well.

"So you feel like this too?" he asked her, holding his arm, which was so numb it felt like it belonged to someone else, in between streaks of excruciating agony.

"On and off, yes. I'm concentrating, Austin, please." He realized she hadn't taken this Kagaroth's helmet off yet, although it was shouting invectives at her—and then she held a piece of armor up and laughed in triumph. "There," she said, separating a glass vial and some delivery device from the leather. "Now he can't kill himself," she said, and Austin realized he hadn't asked her a vital question.

"What do you want him alive for?"

She moved to standing and snapped to Lyka, who started to lift the Kagaroth into the air with strong sweeps of her wings. "I'll explain later. Promise. But I've got to take him home now." She looked around, spotted the car, and nodded. "That's reflective enough. Lyka—take him there."

"Ryana," he warned, as Lyka flew the thrashing man over to the Bentley's hood, and then dove into it, using its reflection to travel just as Damian might through a mirror or still water.

"Don't worry, Austin. Lyka's with me, and I've prepared for this—I'll be fine. See you later." She stepped onto the Bentley's bumper, and before he could stop her with his good arm, she jumped into the reflection to disappear as well.

Austin ran up to peer through, but it was too late: the car hood only showed him his own image, as he realized he was alone with three dead bodies and an arm that felt like it was in a fire. "Fuck," he growled, then started picking up the cast-off armor.

HE WAS glad Ryana's new car was an automatic, because he couldn't have shifted with his right arm if he'd wanted to. He'd put the convertible's top up to hide the one body in the backseat that wouldn't fit into the trunk, and drove five miles under the speed limit, following all of the traffic laws precisely.

Halfway to home he realized they hadn't done a good job of checking for local rifts—but also that his phone hadn't buzzed again, like it would've if Mills had needed him. He pulled his phone out at a red light and swiped it on before he needed to use his good hand again, calling the witch quickly.

Mills answered the very first ring. "Austin?"

"Hey," he said. "Ryana and I were just attacked. We're fine—but—there aren't any rifts open right now, are there?"

He heard her conferring with Jamison before answering. "No."

All right then. That meant that those Kagaroth had come over via an earlier rift, and had then been lying in wait for an opportunity. "Runner up question—have you seen Ryana? She took a prisoner home via magic. Can you check on her?"

"Of course," Mills said.

"Thanks. Call me back if I need to drive faster, eh?" he said and hung up as the light went green. Before he turned his phone back off though, he saw a text from Dominic, the one that'd come in right when everything started.

Have a lead. Could still use your help.

Yeah, Austin thought. *Maybe I'll text you back when I can use my fucking arm.*

He parked the Bentley inside the garage at Damian's castle, in Betsy's old spot, and found his brother leaning against his own vehicle, waiting and clearly angry. "First off," Zach began, the second he got out of the car, "who the hell authorized you to buy a Bentley?"

Austin gave his brother an I-don't-want-to-hear-about-it sigh. "Ryana needed a new car."

"She doesn't know how to drive, Austin."

"I'll teach her," he said, walking around to open the door so his brother could see the body in the back, before he also popped the trunk.

"Oh, *fuck,*" Zach said.

"Yeah. And I'm going to need some help getting them out of there. It was hard enough getting them in with one arm." His right arm felt only slightly less excruciating than it had—the tingles had shifted into a million bees stinging-him-all-at-once feeling.

"Are you okay?" his brother asked, suddenly brother-like again.

Austin knew Zach always had his back, no matter how much they bickered.

"Just got shot with magic is all. Ryana said it'd get better, so I'm sure it will. I called Mills to check on her—Mills didn't call back, so I guess she's all right." He hovered, torn between helping Zach and checking on her. "I'm going to…." he began.

"Go," Zach said, understanding and nodding quickly. "I've got this."

AUSTIN JOGGED for the castle's doors, across the cobblestone and past the dragon-headed fountain, ignoring how each jolt brought fresh pain to his arm. Once inside, he ran up the stairs to Ryana's room, where the door was closed and most definitively red.

"Wings!" he shouted, pounding on the door with his good hand. "You all right?" He pressed his ear against the door, listening. "Ryana!" he shouted, pounding again.

"I'm okay!" she announced as she opened the door up. She was wearing her strange protective gear again. "I've got him locked up, and Lyka's watching him."

"Are you sure?" Austin said, looming, trying to look over her shoulder.

"Yeah. I've been preparing for this for a while now."

"Why didn't you say anything?" he asked her.

"You'll see?" She gave him a tight smile.

He groaned. "You should only use that phrase for good surprises."

"This might be, if everything works out. But I've got to get back to it, Austin." She looked over her shoulder like she'd left the oven on, and Austin started shaking his head.

"I don't like it. You, in there, alone with that thing. Let me come help you," he said, putting his hand on the door and preparing to shove.

She placed her gloved hands on his chest. "No," she told him. "Nothing personal, but I find you quite distracting. And this is high intensity magic I'm doing, wolf. I can't think the wrong thought or look away."

He made a growling sound then without meaning to, the wolf in him acknowledging how little it liked this situation. She gave him a sympathetic smile. "I'll be all right, I promise. How's your arm?"

"Hurts like a motherfucker," he admitted.

She tilted her head adorably. "Someday you're going to have to explain earth curse words to me fully. But today is not that day," she said, gently shoving him back.

"If you need anything—" he began.

"I know where to find you," she finished for him, and closed the door.

Austin spent some time in the hall pacing after that, not sure what he should do. "Grim?" he asked aloud, and shortly after that Damian's Siamese cat came drifting down the hall like it had better places to be. Austin knelt to get on its level. "Look, I don't like you, and you don't like me, and I'm okay with that."

Grim sat on his haunches and rolled his crossed blue eyes: *What else is new?*

"Lyka's in there and I'm sure she's got that shit on lock, but—can you keep an eye on things too? I know Ryana's tough—but I can't let anything happen to her." Austin looked at the red door beside him, then refocused on the cat. "*Anything,*" he reemphasized.

The cat got up and seemed to shrug—but afterwards it walked through the door like it didn't exist, and Austin assumed it was keeping an eye on Ryana on the other side.

CHAPTER 18

"SO LET ME GET THIS STRAIGHT—YOU WERE OUT ON A JOYRIDE, AFTER dropping a quarter of a million unauthorized dollars on a new car, and Kagaroth attacked you?" Zach asked him, although honestly it was way more of a statement.

"Pretty much," Austin agreed.

Everyone else in the house, minus Ryana, Lyka, and Grim, was in the conference room a few hours later. The assorted weapons that Zach had liberated from the Kagaroth, with Max's help, were in the center of the large table, along with a large metallic net, and Austin could actually use his arm now, though it still hurt occasionally.

"But no rifts," Mills said, tapping a finger against her lips.

"I'm assuming they came over with the others, earlier. It's the only thing that makes sense," Austin told her.

"Most likely. But that still leaves the question why."

"Because they want to get to Ryana, obviously." The only reason he wasn't inside her room right now and shadowing her every move was because he knew their house was rift-proof. Her not wanting him there ran a very distant runner-up.

"Why though?" Mills wondered aloud.

"She's in line for the throne," Austin said.

"Then why aren't they attacking Damian?" Max asked. "Technically he's first in line."

Austin rocked back. "They seem to have it out for her, for some reason." It was close as he would get to disclosing what Max had told him in confidence, in the truck.

"Whatever it is, they want her alive," Jamison added, glancing meaningfully at the pile. "Otherwise, you'd be dead, and..." he let his voice drift, reaching out to finger the strange netting Zach had taken from one of the Kagaroth. It'd unfolded to cover up half the table, and even Austin, with his mostly non-magical life beyond his innate wolfness, could tell that it radiated power.

"Can we assume that that's the last of them, until there's another rift?" Austin asked his friends.

"As much as I hate assuming anything...that would make sense," Max said. "If they had a chance at capturing her, wouldn't they go all in?"

"So if she stays indoors until all this is sorted...she's safe?" Zach prompted.

"Except for the fact that we may not be able to sort it until we know more," Jamison said with a frown.

"Well, she's got a prisoner in there. She's doing something," Austin muttered.

"I checked in with her on that. She seems to have it handled, and she'll let us know if she learns anything valuable," Mills said.

"Damian always says confessions under torture are suspect." Austin frowned.

"I don't believe she's torturing him," Mills said, like that was somehow better. "Not yet, at least." The witch looked around the table. "So are we all right, for now?"

At least no one else looked particularly pleased with the situation —and Austin remembered Dominic's text on his phone. "There's one more thing," he said. "A friend of mine from back in the day wants to cut me in on a deal involving the Realms. Says he's getting paid to search for something magical. I don't know if it's for the Heart or what."

Mills made a thoughtful noise. "I don't like it."

"Me either," Max agreed.

"I've been avoiding him but, given our current circumstances, maybe I should learn what I can, and just not get involved," Austin said.

"Avoiding trouble's not your strong suit, brother," Zach said.

Austin shrugged. "It's Dominic. We go way back."

Zach grunted. "Well, he's better than most."

"All right. I'll check it out and let you all know." He made to stand, but then gestured to Mills. "Can I ask you something? Alone?"

"Sure," she said, giving him a generous smile.

AUSTIN WAITED until everyone else was gone and the doors were closed, before turning to the witch.

"She knows what she's doing Austin," Mills told him. Her magical, floor-length hair was wound up in a casual bun, and she was wearing a black t-shirt that said "Necrophobic" on it in a death-metal font.

"This isn't about that...well...not precisely." He slouched on the table in front of where she stood, so they were eye-level with one another. "I want you to cast that language spell on me. The reverse of the one that Damian and Ryana use. I want to understand speech from the Realms."

Mills blinked. "Why?"

"So I can understand what those fuckers are saying. If they talk to each other in the field, I need to know."

Mills's lips pursed. "Really?"

"Mostly," Austin said. "Come on, Mills. I just want to make sure she's safe."

The witch put her hands on her hips. "I will only do this if you swear to me that you will tell her that I did it, right away."

"I will. Swear." Austin patted his chest twice, right over his heart. "So—zap me?"

Mills snorted and rolled her eyes, and then reached out to put her fingertips on Austin's temple. "I hope you're not planning on going anywhere else this evening."

"Why?"

"Because in about thirty seconds you're going to have the world's worst headache," she said. Then she whispered something in a language Austin couldn't understand and—

"Oh God," he whispered. It felt like someone had shoved an ice pick in through one ear and out the other side.

"I warned you," Mills said, taking her hands back.

"You did," he gritted out, holding onto the table for dear life.

"I'm sorry today has been so rough for you," Mills told him, gently patting his shoulder—which was still stinging, intermittently, although the time between stabbing bursts of pain was getting longer and longer.

Austin's head hurt so bad he almost couldn't see straight. But... between fighting Kagaroth and disposing of bodies one handedly while his arm felt like it was in a volcano, and the chainsawing sensation he had inside his brain right now, courtesy of Mills...he remembered the way Ryana had looked at him, sitting on the picnic blanket, right before he kissed her. That one memory blotted out all the pain. "Actually?" he told the witch, squinting against the conference room's suddenly too-bright light. "It hasn't been that bad."

THERE WAS no way he could go out with Dominic tonight, so he didn't bother texting the rhino-shifter back. He took the stairs up to his room, and walked by Ryana's out of...longing? Hope? Habit? But the door flashed red.

He didn't want to interrupt her—God forbid she ever needed to use any of that gear she wore—but he did lean against the door, trying to hear inside. If anything bad happened to her, surely Lyka or Grim would come get him.

But his rooms were an entire floor away.

What if she needed him more quickly?

He took a step away from the door—and then a step back toward it, and slowly lowered himself down to the ground. His head was going to hurt no matter where he slept tonight. So he might as well sleep here, nearby, just in case.

He pulled off his jacket, turned it into a pillow, lay down, and closed his eyes.

THE NEXT DAY he woke up stiff, but his head had stopped hurting and his arm didn't hate him anymore. He rolled up to standing and shook himself loose before leaning down to pick up his coat. Ryana's door was still red, of course, but at least it was daytime.

Although that didn't really change anything....

Austin went up to his room to take a shower, and then down to the kitchen to grab food, and then he returned to his station outside Ryana's door—this time with a few pillows, a blanket, and a book.

"Are you camping?" Zach asked him, coming by a few hours later.

Austin answered without looking up. "Let the record show that I am a hundred percent up for s'mores, but that Mills says I can't light things on fire inside."

"This is insane, brother, even for you."

"Look, I didn't judge you for sleeping with a Starry Sky pack member—at least not for very long. How is Stella these days, anyways?" One of Zach's eyebrows rose precipitously as Austin continued. "All I'm saying is, stay out of my shit, and I'll stay out of yours."

"Damian won't be on vacation forever."

Austin shrugged. "I'll deal with that when the time comes. Now can you move?" he asked, pointing at the book in his lap. "You're blocking my light."

Zach snorted, but walked up to their shared floor.

Not long after that, Austin stretched out to take a nap. The lights dimmed considerately, which he thought might've been a trick of his imagination—but then he woke up to a small plate of Grimalkin's favorite food: cheese.

He had no illusions about Grimalkin changing his mind to like him, but they did have one thing in common—they both liked Ryana.

"Thanks, Grim," he said aloud, in case the magical cat could hear, and tucked in.

CHAPTER 19

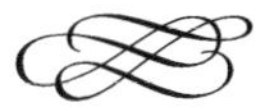

THE SOUND OF THE RED DOOR BEHIND HIM OPENING WOKE HIM UP FROM a semi-legitimate slumber late that night, and he found Ryana peering down. She was dressed in just a short silky pink slip that did nothing to hide her curves, and from his location on the ground he could see up it just enough to note that her panties matched. "What're you doing?" she asked him, stepping back with surprise.

"Being worried about you," he told her, sitting up quickly and pushing the hair out of his eyes.

Grim came to sit by her feet and meowed something. "I'm sorry for not believing you," she told the cat.

"Were you coming to make the door green?" Austin asked in hope.

"No. I only have a few hours off. I was just going to get some sleep. But then Grim told Lyka, who told me that you were stationed out here." She gave him a lopsided smile. "Go back to your own room and be comfortable, silly."

"I'm totally fine right here." He made a show of fluffing his pillow. "Sleeping on hard surfaces is great for my back."

"Uh huh," Ryana said, crossing her arms. "Are you that convinced that I'll screw up?"

"This has nothing to do with you, and everything to do with me," he said, moving to sit across from her, putting his back against the hallway wall.

"Is that right?" she asked, looking him up and down. "You're just fine hanging out out here? For as long as it takes?" He nodded. "Three or four weeks?" she asked.

He winced. "I might need to bring a gym up here if it's going to take that long. And also I'll need a time-out in a week and a half, for the full moon. But other than that, yeah, I'll be fine." He jerked his chin at the room beyond her open door. "You go do your thing, wings. Don't worry about me."

She stepped back into her dimly lit room with a headshake, hesitated, and then laughed softly. "If you swear to not ever come into my laboratory, no matter anything you hear...I suppose I can let you come inside."

Austin stood, sweeping up the things he'd brought with him in an instant. "It's a deal."

RYANA MADE room for him to pass, and then she knelt down to Grim's level, making her slip ride up. If Austin hadn't already been holding a blanket in front of his lap, he would've needed to quickly readjust. "Grim, you know Lyka's busy. Can you please make my errant werewolf friend here an actually comfortable bed for him to sleep in?"

Grim closed his eyes, and created a narrow twin bed for Austin—likely so he wouldn't get ideas—against Ryana's room's wall nearest the door, then disappeared. Austin put his things down beside the bed and sat down on it. "This is nice," he said, surprised, as the bed gave under his weight.

"Why wouldn't it be?" Ryana wondered.

"No reason." If the cheese Grim'd set out for him this afternoon hadn't poisoned him, he wasn't going to question the cat's sudden turn toward generosity. He kicked off his boots and swung himself into the bed.

"Is that what you wear to sleep?" Ryana asked him, heading over to her own bed, and looking back.

"No," he told her.

"Lyka could—" she began to offer, sinking into her own bed and pulling up her sheets.

"Usually I don't wear anything." He heard her make a little 'oh' of surprise. "Good night, Ryana," he finished.

"Good night, wolf."

AUSTIN LAY in his newly made bed, listening to the steady sound of Ryana's breathing. Everything in her rooms smelled like her, which he liked. And while normally being this close to a beautiful woman —*much less Ryana*—would've tormented him, he found he wanted her safe more than he needed any satisfaction. Physical things would come in time; he knew they would, he could be patient for that—but right now it was more important that she sleep restfully.

He only wished that somehow, instead of her all the way across her room, she could be sleeping at his side. He imagined his arms around her, the way she'd felt leaning against him on the couch, one of his hands wound with hers like they'd been in the backseat of that car.

Was it normal to want to protect someone this badly? Because it wasn't just keeping her safe from the Kagaroth she had somewhere behind her laboratory's door—it was more than that.

It'd started to feel like a calling.

And whenever he was near her, he wanted to stand at her side and somehow take all her pain away—all the hurt that he could see reflected, sometimes, just inside her light green eyes—and make sure that no one ever injured her again.

"Austin?" she whispered. "Are you still awake?"

He thought about lying for her sake, but found he couldn't. "Yeah, wings, I am," he whispered back, turning toward her bed in the dark.

"I'm having a hard time sleeping."

"Why?" he asked.

He heard her inhale, and knew that she was thinking. "I'm nervous that my experiment won't work. And then I'm nervous that it will."

"Want to talk about it?"

She seemed to consider this for a bit, then said, "No." He nodded, even though she couldn't see it. "But can we talk about other things, if you'd like."

And even though he wanted to be strong, he was not a martyr. "Yeah, wings," he answered. "Of course. Anything."

He heard her bed shift as she did. "Is it hard to learn how to drive a car?"

He chuckled. "Not for you, it won't be. I'll teach you."

"I'd like that," she said, and then a pregnant pause. "But then I'd owe you."

"Is that so bad?" he asked, before realizing in the Realms, yeah, probably it was. "You can always teach me words, like you promised, wings." He hadn't gone through all that headache for nothing—and he remembered his promise to Mills to tell Ryana about the spell, quickly. Nothing wrong with teasing her some though, first.

"What do you want to learn?" she asked him in the mostly dark, her voice light.

"Anything you'll teach me."

Ryana groaned, but she was exaggerating, he could tell. "Be more specific," she complained.

"Okay, how about, hello and goodbye."

She laughed melodiously and then said the words in her Realm's language. He heard her say them, even as his mind translated them—and then he tried to say them back, his tongue tripping over the syllables. The magic didn't fix that part, it seemed. "Try again," she prompted, and he did. "Better. What else do you want to learn to say?"

"That you're very beautiful." She snickered at that, and said something quickly to herself. *Such a silly wolf,* he translated quickly, before she said the words she meant for him. "You're very beautiful," he repeated, to her, in her own language.

"Why, thank you," she said. "What else?"

And even though he knew he shouldn't, and that he should let her rest—"I want to ask if I can kiss you again." She threw a pillow across the room at him. He caught it. "This is how you ask? Strange. I've never seen Damian throw things...well...actually, I have...."

Ryana broke into peals of laughter at that. "Okay, fine," she said, then told him how to say it in her tongue. He repeated the phrase back to her, and then the room was quiet, like they were each holding their breath.

"Can I?" he whispered to her, after far too long had passed.

"Green," she whispered back.

Austin got off of his bed softly and walked to stand at the bottom of hers. There was just enough light in the room for him to make out the outline of her curves on the bed beneath the sheets. He brushed a lock of hair out of his eyes, waiting. "I didn't say where I wanted to kiss you."

"Ask," she told him, and he heard, but could not see, her smile.

He knelt down and untucked the bottom of her sheets, pushing them up to reveal the top of one foot. "Here," he said, drawing a circle on it with his finger.

Foot, she told him, and *foot,* he repeated back to her, before leaning down to kiss the spot he'd just touched. He heard her gasp.

"What about here?" he asked, stroking a finger atop her opposite knee, feeling her shiver.

Knee, she told him, and *knee,* he repeated back, bowing himself between her legs to lick the hollow behind her knee.

He looked up at her, and pulled the sheets aside, so there was nothing hiding her from him but her soft pink slip and the underwear she had on that matched it, as he drew a finger up the inside of her thigh. "And here?" he asked, pulling his finger down the fabric that hid her pussy from him.

"Don't make me say the word," she whispered.

"Then say red or green, wings," he whispered back.

He heard her lick her lips in the dark, and breathe "Green." He ran his hands up the outside of her thighs and underneath her slip to help her take her panties off. She squirmed and helped kick out of them, and then she waited, watching him, he knew, as he pulled himself forward on his elbows, using his hands to push her legs open and her hips down. He went for her with his mouth, dragging his tongue up her slit until it opened for him, and he heard her moan.

She wasn't trimmed or waxed like most girls, and he liked that; it was like he could bury himself in her essence, as he pulled his tongue up her again, from the cusp of her crack all the way to the soft nub of her clit, and then he started to go at her, gently at first, warming her up to the idea, nuzzling and licking and kissing, until she started to rock against him, clearly wanting more, so he reached in with his thumbs to spread her wide and pushed his tongue in.

At that, she gasped, and he listened for anything that might mean that he should stop, but all he heard were moans. So he did it again and again, fucking her with his tongue, feeling her open up, tasting all her pussy had to offer. She made soft noises over him, one of her hands wringing her slip up, the other grasping for his neck and in his hair, and she started speaking in her own language again.

Don't hurt me, don't hurt me, don't hurt me, he could translate, and he pulled up. "Ryana?" he asked her, feeling her writhe. She lifted her head and swallowed, looking down at him as she panted. "Are you good?" he asked.

"Green—please—so green," she said and used his hair to pull his head back down so his mouth would meet her—and he realized that it wasn't that she was worried about him physically hurting her, which he knew he wasn't, he could see it and taste it and smell it, everything about her was turned on. No—she was whispering it like a kind of prayer, hoping to find a man she could believe in. "Green?" she told him, her voice rising up, because he'd stopped while he'd been thinking and oh, if she even for a second took that personally—he growled low, like an animal, and feasted on her.

Her hips started to shake beneath him, and he moved his mouth to follow. He knew she was winding up, and he wanted to be *right there* and feel her come all over him, every shudder and quake, every juicy drop—he dropped his jaw wide, pinned her thighs down with his arms, and rode her with his tongue as she cried out with words that were in all languages and no language at once, moving with her as she rocked beneath him, until she was nothing but soft breaths and sighs and had fallen limp against her bed.

He pulled up, licked his lips, and wiped his mouth against the inside of her thigh. "What's the word for that, wings?" he asked her quietly.

She stroked a hand through his hair, and told him a word she didn't translate, *Everything.*

CHAPTER 20

Ryana knew she could've banished him back to his own bed, or even the hallway, but she didn't want to anymore. She reached down, grabbed his shoulder, and pulled him up to lie beside her, still in all his clothes, facing her.

She touched his lips where they were still a little wet. "No one's ever done that with me."

"That's a shame," he said earnestly. She felt him smile against her fingertips, and heard it in his voice. "I'm sorry then—you're just going to have to trust me that I'm good at it."

"I believe you," she told him.

He caught her wrist in his hand and kissed her fingertips. "I love the way you smell and taste. I could lick all of you for days." She laughed. "What?" he went on, pretending to be offended. "It's the wolf in me."

"Hmm," she said, wiping a tired hand across her face. She'd been exhausted before, and him kissing her *there* hadn't helped, because now she was an awkward mix of sleepy and turned on. "And you're not just saying that because of the hard-on I'm betting you have right now?"

"No," he told her, using her arm against her to push her flat down. She expected him to mount her then—sex with Baran had always been short and fierce, on borrowed time. It'd seemed exhilarating in the moment, always hiding, but now....

Austin brought himself up beside her and she let him move her like the sleepily-pliable woman that she was, until she was on her side and he was lined up again against her back, like that first night weeks ago. "Ignore that please," he said, wrapping himself around her, and she could definitely feel the outline of his erection beneath his clothes. "I'm a big boy. I can handle myself later."

Ryana blinked in the dark, wondering what his goal was, then decided to give up on guessing. "What is happening?"

"You said you needed to sleep, and I want you to be safe," he said, his voice low in her ear. He was lying right behind her; he'd joined her on her pillow.

"So...we're not having sex?"

"Yep," he said, nuzzling his face into her hair. He bent his knees behind hers, and ran a hand around her waist, catching her hand in his and twining fingers.

"And...you're staying?"

She felt him chuckle. "Shh, go to sleep."

She tensed, with rising panic. Yes, she wanted this...but what if she had a nightmare here, tonight, in front of him?

Then again...what if him being here meant the nightmares went away?

"Wings?" he asked her, and she heard the concern in his voice.

"I've...never done this before, either," she confessed, because it was true, even if it was less true than other things she could say.

"Well, I'd call you a virgin, but I know how you feel about that already," he murmured. Ryana snorted, and rocked her hips against his to punish him—and in an instant his hand released hers, his arm trapped her against him, as his teeth pressed against her neck. She froze and he released her, some. "Don't do that," he warned, and his voice had gone from teasing to rough.

"Why?" she whispered back.

"Because I ask it of you."

She found his hand with hers again and felt him relax as their fingers laced. "All right."

He nodded his head, she felt it, and then he softly kissed the spot where his teeth had just been, where her neck met her shoulder.

She closed her eyes and fell asleep a lot more quickly than she'd expected.

RYANA WOKE in Austin's arms a few hours later, feeling Lyka nudge against her hand for her alarm. She thumbed across Lyka's feathered cheek to let the bird know that she was up.

She hadn't had a single dream. Austin's arm was still wrapped around her, and one of his legs was over hers, and she could feel the rise and fall of his chest against her back. He seemed so…restful. So trusting. It felt a shame to wake him, so she looked for a way to escape quietly, but found none.

"Austin." She said his name softly, rocking her back into him, and felt him stir. "I need to get up," she said, turning in his arms, lifting them to free herself. He growled a complaint in his sleep, and she tittered quietly until his eyes opened—and it didn't seem like they saw her. No—it didn't seem like they were his. "Austin?" she whispered, her voice rising. And then he blinked and pushed back.

"Ryana?" he asked softly, as if seeing her for the first time.

"I'm here," she told him, gently stroking his hair off of his face. "I've got to get up, it's time," she said, extricating herself from him.

"Yeah, it is—I mean, that's a good idea," he said, moving away from her and wiping his face with a hand.

"You're welcome to stay here," she told him, moving to stand beside the bed. "I'll be in the other room. It's relatively soundproof."

"In the other room with a Kagaroth," he complained.

"And Lyka and Grim," she reminded him.

"Still doesn't feel safe."

"Too bad," she said lightly. "Go back to your own room and sleep for the both of us."

He made a disgruntled sound and then sat up. "Maybe."

"Or shower. Or eat," she also offered.

"What I want to eat for breakfast isn't in the kitchen," he told her in the kind of tone that made her shiver. She felt herself flush and was very glad the lights were dim. Her slip wasn't very long, and her underwear were still lost somewhere beneath her sheets.

"Red. Go," she told him, gesturing him away. "I'll talk to you again tonight. I promise."

"Good," he said. "I'll be nearby."

She went to the door of her bathroom, then paused to look back at him, still waking up at the side of her bed. She smelled like him, after he'd been pressed so close to her the whole night, and if she closed her eyes she thought she could still feel the weight of his arm, wrapped around her waist. "Wolf?" she asked him, and saw his head snap up. "Thank you."

"Any time, wings," he said, moving to stand as she closed the bathroom door.

By the time she was out of her shower and awake enough to control her magic properly, he was gone. She found herself wistfully thinking of him, and then shook her head—she needed to forget everything that'd happened and concentrate on what came next—in a few short hours, if nothing exploded, she'd be able to use her truth serum on the Kagaroth they'd captured and finally find out what he wanted.

She went into her laboratory and pulled on all her gear.

Austin was so lost in his own thoughts he stumbled down the hall like a drunken man, though he hadn't had a drink in days.

This morning…and then the night before…. He put a hand to his stomach, feeling a gnawing in its pit that grew every step he took away from her.

He went through a mental list of everything it could be—he was hungry, thirsty, he'd slept too much, he hadn't slept enough—until he reached the safety of his bedroom and sank into his bed—trying to...*disconvince himself*...that anything had happened.

That something inside of him hadn't changed.

He rested the heels of his hands in his eyes, watching blurry lights flash, but it didn't stop him from revisiting the prior night. The way her flesh had felt beneath his fingers: soft and yielding, with just the right amount of firm. The way she'd tasted: salt and sweet, tart and perfect. The way her scent had risen up around him and was still covering him now.

And the way he'd had to make her stop wriggling before his wolf came out to claim her.

Oh.

Fuck.

No.

He sat up immediately and almost ran for his door.

AUSTIN DIDN'T STOP until he was outside, with dawn rising in the east and a light breeze playing against his hair. He reached the edge of the dragon-headed fountain in front of the castle, leaning in to splash himself violently with its cold water, trying to shock himself into common sense.

What the fuck had he been thinking?

He kept splashing himself—he needed to get her scent off of him, to drink Listerine and then beer, to run a rag through his brain like the ice-pick of Mills's magic and somehow wipe *her* from his mind.

He'd been so intent on being the perfect man, to somehow show Ryana everything she needed and deserved and then pull one of those 'if you love someone'—where the person you loved was royal, and you sure as fuck were not, and part-dragon, *same-fucking-same*—'let them go' type things.

He'd only wanted to teach her enough to want better when she inevitably moved on.

But...now?

He stopped splashing himself and stared down at the rippled water, seeing his face blurred in its reflection, and knew the truth.

He wanted more.

There couldn't be more.

This wasn't supposed to happen.

Inside himself, his wolf howled its discontent, struggling to get free. They were already outdoors; it wouldn't take much to *shift* and run away from all his anger.

But would his wolf really run from her?

After last night, he didn't think that he could trust it.

"Fuck!" He punched the water of the fountain like he couldn't punch himself, then clutched the fountain's stone side, panting with his thoughts.

He was fucked. Royally—literally.

Ryana was a *goddamned princess.*

And he was just some werewolf who wanted to have a good time, most of the time, and who could fight like hell when the times were bad.

That wasn't enough to offer someone like her.

He shook his head like a dog, sending droplets of water spattering around him.

He never should've gone down this path. He knew better, he fucking did. And as the waters of the fountain in front of him stilled, he wondered if there was a way he could use it to call Damian to come home and put him out of his misery.

Austin tried to sleep more, didn't, and wound up texting Dominic, because he was supposed to, as per their last group meeting, and because he needed to get the fuck out of the house. Ryana was right, Lyka and Grim were all the protection anyone could ask for, surely. But Dominic didn't text him back, and training endlessly did nothing to distract him from the fact that she was just a few flights of stairs away. He showered late that night, saving Damian so much money on heating bills, what with all his showers being cold while he tried not to think of *her*, and walked back into his bedroom—only to find Lyka perched on his bed, with a green feather in her beak.

"You left her alone?" Austin asked, rushing the bird, who squawked and let the feather drop, wheeling up to the ceiling. "Get back there right now!" he commanded it, and the bird disappeared.

He dressed himself quickly, hardly bothering to dry off, and ran upstairs, his wolf ready to claw out of him if anything had happened to her.

He burst in through her now green door and found her standing behind a small table covered in food he didn't recognize. She was wearing a jeans and a dark blue shirt with a deep V, front and back, that had room for her wings to be exposed, and she was smiling winningly at him.

Being in her presence hit him like a brick wall—like if he'd stayed in Betsy a few nights ago, and had been going at a hundred. No seat-belts, no airbags, just getting slammed against his steering column at speed, knocking the wind out of him and stopping his heart.

"I have slightly longer tonight," she said, then picked up on his mood. "Did you already eat?"

"No—I," he began, running his hand through his wet hair. "When I saw Lyka, I assumed the worst."

Ryana blinked her confusion. "I told her to show you a green feather."

"She did—but Ryana, you shouldn't let her leave your side."

"Grim was with me," she told him, sitting down. "And my prisoner is quite incapacitated."

Austin frowned, at her or at himself, he wasn't sure. "Due to something you did?" The sooner the man was dead, the better, in his book.

"Yes. I gave him a potion. It didn't really have the right effect, though." She looked meaningfully between him and the seat in front of him. "Did you want to...stay?"

If he hadn't been worried for her, if he'd managed to lose that feather in his own bedroom, there was a—fuck no, *who the hell was he kidding*? He pulled the chair across from her out and sat down. "Yeah."

There was still tension in his shoulders and chest as she tried to explain food from the Realms to him—it was all a good deal more rubbery than Earth food, a fact which he found disconcerting—but he managed, he hoped, to keep his stress out of his face, because she didn't deserve that. His feelings were his problem, not hers.

She sensed it nonetheless, however. "Are you all right?" she asked him.

"Yeah, why wouldn't I be?"

"You're not eating." She looked between him and his plate.

"It's all…a little chewy," he said, pushing himself back. "I'm sorry, Ryana," he started saying, and he watched her wings lower in disappointment as she ducked her head down.

Because she liked him, too.

This realization hit him stronger than a brick wall—it was more like an orbital re-entry landing without a parachute. He realized pulling the brakes—somehow, Christ—wasn't just going to hurt him, it would also hurt her.

She didn't even know she was too good for him.

Fuck.

"I'm just thinking about a thing I've got to do tonight," he lied. "I left my phone back in my room—it's making me anxious."

"All you had to do was say something, silly," she said, relaxing in an instant. She snapped her fingers, and Lyka appeared, with it in her beak. He took it, wiped a sleeve across it to get off any bird spit, and then swiped it open. Nothing from Dominic to help save him from himself. "Did you need to go?" she asked, politely.

He inhaled to lie, again, then looked up at her eyes. By the light of her room, they were the color of green sea-glass, and her small full lips were a light ruby. She was the most beautiful woman he'd ever seen, and he knew she was smart, and she was magical—so why the fuck did she trust him?

Only because he'd never given her a reason not to.

"Austin?" she asked, sounding concerned.

"I don't need to go yet," he admitted.

She smiled wickedly at him, even as her cheeks turned an innocent pink. "Good. Because I have an idea for dessert," she said, and he knew he was in trouble.

CHAPTER 21

It was all Ryana could do not to clap her hands in glee.

After her abject failure to get the Kagaroth in her possession to tell the truth this afternoon—the man had told her Baran was alive, which she knew was a lie, because she *herself* had killed him—figuring out what she was going to do with Austin while she let her next truth-telling potion simmer had brought her hours of delight.

And honestly? She'd been so distracted that she was lucky she hadn't burned the whole castle down.

Although, if she thought about it harder, there'd been something grounding in knowing she was going to see Austin tonight. It was like knowing he was in her life had stopped a part of her mind from spinning quite so hard. And there was power in that freedom—it was like the wobbly table from which she created magic inside herself had gained a stabilizing leg. It was...nice. And she was fairly sure it was because of him—she hadn't added any other variables to her life. She'd been very careful to keep track of everything in her notebook.

She smiled at him across the table full of food he hadn't eaten, wondering if that was because he was as nervous as she was.

"I don't know that I'm a dessert person, wings," he told her, and she shook her head dismissively.

"I can almost guarantee that you will like this one," she said, standing up.

His eyes followed her readily. "Yeah?" he asked.

She nodded quickly and came to his side of the table. "Push your chair away more."

He did as he was told, but then started trying to talk again. "Ryana," he began, and she put a finger atop his lips.

"Green or red?" she asked him, batting her wings slowly behind herself.

His blue-eyes clouded and then cleared. "Green," he softly said, licking his lips the second her finger pulled back.

She slowly knelt between his legs, and took one hand to each knee, pushing them wider so she could come close, and then started unbuttoning the rough shirt he wore, from the top on down. "Wings," he hissed when she was three buttons in, right before she sent her hands searching up against his chest, feeling his dense muscles tense at her touch beneath the softer fluff of his chest hair.

"Hmm?" she asked, as he rocked his head back.

"Never mind. Keep going."

She chuckled richly and did as she was told, finally opening up his whole shirt, running her fingers over his chest again. Someday she was going to get to trace all the drawings he had on him, and he would tell her what they meant, but not today. She wound her finger tips down the muscles on his stomach one by one, until both her hands rested on the waistband of his jeans.

"You don't have to do this, wings," he told her, looking down, as she unlatched his belt. "Last night was just a gift. I didn't expect anything in return."

"I know," she told him. "And I appreciated that. As a princess, I like presents very much." She undid the belt's leather tongue and started in on the buttons behind it. "At the same time though, I'm on Earth now, and I don't have to be a princess anymore. Which means I can do whatever I like to whomever I like for however long I want."

"It's funny, wings," he said, his voice low. "I would've thought being a princess got you all that, too."

"You would, wouldn't you?" she pondered, peeling back the denim that covered him. "But not really." Stretchy dark blue fabric continued to hide him from her beneath it, though she could see his erection straining up. She traced its outline with a fingertip and heard him take a sharp intake of breath. She looked up at him and saw him staring so intently down at her that she almost wanted to lift her wings to hide herself from him. Then she watched and heard him swallow as he briefly rose up to push all the fabric down for her, setting himself free.

She stroked down his shaft with her fingertips, feeling his cock bob beneath her attention, like it was a separate living thing. It was hard and warm and dark red, and she let the pads of her fingers trace each ridge and vein, taking her time and learning him like he was a spell in an ancient book.

"You don't have to do anything else, baby," he murmured overhead, as she finally encircled him with her hand.

Baby was new. And good…right? "But I can…if I want to?" she asked, looking up. His eyes were on her and his face was somehow torn between hopelessness and desire—his expression told her yes, while his eyes warned her no. "Red or green?" She needed to hear an answer before she went on.

"Green," he whispered, and the second he began the word she stroked. He moaned and shuddered, and she stroked again, keeping the contact of her skin on his so light. "Just like that," he murmured, and she nodded, watching her hand, watching him. A clear bead of fluid gathered on his tip, elicited from her stroking, and she leaned in to kiss it off of him, taking the tip of his cock into her mouth and wiping it away with her tongue.

"God," he whispered, as she kissed the head of his cock like it was his lips and tongue, pulling and sucking, running the tip of her tongue across his sensitive opening. "Baby," he panted, as she took more of him in, and she pulled off of him slowly.

"What do you mean when you say that?" she asked him.

He curled his body towards her then, running a hand up into her hair, making her look up at him.

Everything, he told her—using her word from the prior night. Even though he didn't know what it meant, he'd remembered, and his pronunciation was decent too. Like he'd practiced in the meantime. She grinned, and returned her attentions to him, licking up the bottom of his shaft before placing him in her mouth again, sucking him back in. His hand in her hair tightened, guiding her, and she moved her whole body closer to let him. He groaned as the head of his cock hit the back of her throat and she went up on her knees slightly, rocking her jaw open to take more of him in.

"God, Ryana—this—I don't—" he kept saying words, but not red, and not making sentences, and she could very well tell from how hard and hot he was inside her mouth that he was happy, plus the sounds he started making, guttural and low. Then he put both hands in her hair and started making her move with him, and she groaned along with him, a deep purr in her throat, knowing what was next.

His hips rocked up as she went down. Almost all of him was inside her and what wasn't she had circled with her fingers and thumb and he growled. "I'm gonna make a mess, baby, I'm warning you," he said and let go of her hair so that she could escape but she didn't, she just sucked harder, wrapping her tongue around the bottom of his shaft and pulling him with her throat. Then she heard him growl again as his hips beat up beneath her, and she felt his cock pumping as hot liquid surged, him coating her mouth in his thick, sticky salt. She took her time then, catching her breath through her nose as she sucked off of him, swallowing every drop, as he fell back into his chair.

"Wings," he whispered. "What am I going to do with you?"

She sat back, kneeling in front of him, wiping her lips daintily with the back of one hand. "Only good things, I hope." She arched her wings wide. "Did you like that?" she asked, even though she knew he had; she just wanted to preen.

"Yeah." He reached down and set himself back inside his jeans, lifting his hips just enough to drag them back up. He licked his lips, staring down at her quietly, and she started to feel confused.

"I keep seeing words in your eyes, wolf. Why won't you say them?"

"Because I don't want to hurt you, Ryana."

She swallowed and pulled back, suddenly feeling very exposed in this strange position in front of him, kneeling on the floor like some kind of servant. She gracefully stood and tucked her wings down. "I wouldn't worry about it, if I were you. I'm part-dragon. Hurting me's impossible."

"We both know that's not true," he said, shaking his head and leaning forward. "Ryana—you know this is never going to work, right?"

Only years of royal training saved her. She'd been trained not only for battle but for verbal blows—her rhetoric instructors had ensured it. So she fell quiet with practice now, her eyes half-lidded, her upper lip lifted in just the right amount of disgust. She could lace her words with poison, even if she couldn't taint her kisses.

"Yes," she scoffed. She'd just abased herself for him—*no matter how much she'd liked it at the time*—and for what? His...rejection? "It is why I picked you, after all." She let her eyes unfocus as she looked at him, as though he were not even there. "Another experiment, of a sort." When she deigned to give him her attention next, she found him frowning, and decided to try and hurt him more. "In fact, I can't wait to write this down."

"In a...book?" he guessed.

"Precisely," she said, sounding clinical and cold. "I lost all my notes when I came here, Austin—I don't want to lose anything ever again." *Not my heart, and not my pride.*

"But...this?" He sounded even more confused. "Why?"

"Because. I'm still learning." *To trust myself—and I shouldn't have. I've gone and made the exact same mistake now, twice.*

"Practicing," he said quietly, with a nod, before standing. "Well—that was good. You're good. You're a fast learner."

"I didn't say I hadn't done that before." She didn't look him in the eyes. "I think you should go now."

She heard him cross the room, then stop outside her door. "Stay safe, Ryana. Please."

She didn't respond.

How dare he ask her to stay safe when he was the only thing that could hurt her?

AUSTIN WENT BACK to his own room, feeling like a heel. *Yeah, it's always great to semi-break-up with someone after they give you the most spectacular blowjob of your life.*

But had it really been a break-up? Had they ever been a thing? Except for in his fevered imagination?

He knew he'd hurt her at the end, but she'd seemed to recover quickly, and there were a million and one guys out there who'd want to be with her. Now that he wasn't trying to help her safely lose her virginity, any other guy could do exactly what he'd done.

Even if the thought of anyone else touching her made his wolf want to leap out and kill them.

It didn't matter.

She was still a goddamned princess.

His phone buzzed, and he looked down, fully expecting there to be some note from her, telling him to never talk to her again, or Damian, saying something like 'meet you outside at dawn'—but instead it was Dominic.

TOOK you long enough to come around, wolf.

I'll arrange a meeting with the others tomorrow night.

AUSTIN HID in his rooms the next day, not wanting to risk the temptation of walking by Ryana's surely-red door, waiting impatiently for Dominic's texts, when one finally landed, with an address, at 8 pm.

He got dressed and went down the hall to knock on Zach's door.

"Come in," his brother said, and Austin saw him sitting on a couch with a laptop on his lap. He closed the lid as Austin walked in.

"Don't worry, I'm not here for hot stock tips. Dominic texted me. I'm heading out."

"You need back-up?" Zach asked.

"No, I think that'd seem strange." And, if anything happened to Ryana in his absence and there weren't other people in the castle who could save her, he'd never forgive himself. "It's only a meeting, sounds purely informational. I just figured I should tell someone, just in case."

"Look at you being all responsible, brother," Zach said with a snort before eyeing him. "How's camping life?"

Austin inhaled deeply. "I broke it off. Yesterday."

Zach groaned as if he'd taken a blow on his brother's behalf. He stood up to cross the room to Austin. "You know you did the right thing, right?"

"Yeah. Doesn't mean it doesn't hurt, though. And if Grim or Lyka so much as peep while I'm gone—"

Zach set a hand on his shoulder. "I'll keep an ear out. Promise."

"'K. See you in a couple of hours—I'll text on my way back."

"Sounds good. Be safe—and if things go south, let us know."

"Will do," Austin said, shaking his brother's hand off before leaving.

He hadn't replaced Betsy yet, and he was not driving a Bentley to a mysterious rendezvous, so he grabbed the keys to the least conspicuous of Damian's cars—Jamison's very old little Prius. It was green, which made him think of Ryana, and in hindsight playing the color game with her had been a hugely bad idea, considering just how many freaking things in the world were green—he should've made their game be 'neon-orange and magenta' and he'd have been safe outside of carnivals.

The address Dominic had sent was over in a rundown area of town, not far from where they'd first met Stella, and it occurred to him that he'd had his head up his ass about Ryana for so long, he really needed to bug Zach for a check-in. As far as he knew, his brother hadn't seen the Starry Sky werewolf ever since she'd ditched them at the arena after their last big group fight, but Zach had been acting a little off occasionally since then.

Austin got to the right address—a series of empty lots with

nothing but weeds sticking up, usually used for a flea market on the weekends. The lots were blocked off by rusty chains locked to metal pylons, and he parked outside, stepping out of his car to sniff the air.

"Dom?" he asked, scenting the rhino-shifter easily—the man couldn't help it; he always smelled a little bit like zoo, although under no circumstances would Austin tell him that.

"Austin," Dominic boomed, coming up out of a shadow. "Glad to see you—can't wait to have you aboard."

Austin leaned against the side of his car. "Tell me what's up."

"What's up is you and me splitting about four million dollars," Dominic said, low. "So just roll with this, all right?"

Austin tensed as four other men came out of a nearby van. They were dressed like he was, in comfortable, casual stuff, but the way they held themselves was military—especially the way that they sized him up, and Austin would've bet his left nut that they were Kagaroth.

"Austin, my friend, meet these nice gentlemen from the Realms, who are here after an object of power."

"Yeah, you told me that already," Austin said, pushing away from his car.

"Between my strength, your nose, and their magic, I know we'll figure out its location in no time, but, alas, before they include you in our circle, they want to try you out." Dominic spread out thick hands. "I tried to avoid this—I told them you were the toughest motherfucker I knew, myself excluded, but they wouldn't believe me without a personal demonstration." Dominic placed a palm on his chest and turned toward the strangers. "You don't want to know the fights this man got into and survived."

"Or how much money Dominic made, betting on them," Austin said, like he was playing their game, and then he lunged in and cold-cocked the closest one, hitting him right at the point where his jaw met his neck, knocking him out and sending him to the ground. "Sorry, gentlemen," Austin said. "But three against one seems like much better odds."

The nearest man said, *You bastard!* in Ryana's native tongue, leapt at him, and the fight was on.

It was hard because he didn't want to kill them—if he did, either all bets would be off, or they wouldn't share what they knew—but they didn't offer him the same compunction. After he'd so easily downed their comrade, they needed to fight him for their pride.

And Ryana—and Max!—hadn't been lying earlier. They were fucking good. He could tell because they were hitting him, and when they did—they didn't have were-strength, but they were stronger than normal men, and they were precise, and they knew exactly where to hurt him. His kidneys were bruised, and his stomach ached, and he could feel at least three broken ribs grating. One of them had busted his knuckles across the top of Austin's face in a brain-rattling lucky shot that'd opened up the skin over one eyebrow and sent a slick river of red pouring down. Austin shook his head like a dog and sent blood spattering to the ground.

"Are we done yet?" he growled. He'd downed one more of them, temporarily, but the other two were still circling—and while he hadn't been paying attention a fifth man with dark hair had joined their group and stood by Dominic, watching the proceedings with a cold disdain. He was the one in charge, Austin knew, because the remaining fighters looked to him.

Finish it, this man told them, and the nearest fighter leapt at Austin, who side-stepped him, only to leave himself open for the briefest second, and have the second man take advantage, hitting him where Austin already had broken ribs, the man knew. Austin bellowed, whirled, punched, and then felt himself get hit as he was harried from behind—the first man he'd knocked out had rejoined their small arena, only this time with a metal pole, and had just used it with enough force on Austin to break a normal man's femur in two.

His wolf was just under the surface now as they pummeled him. It was all he could do to protect his heart and head and keep standing straight, because if he fell to the ground then the kicks would begin. The animal inside of him begged for release, and he heard himself snarl in warning. His hand lashed out and grabbed a man's windpipe without thinking and Austin only barely stopped himself from crushing it. The metal pole came down on his arm, Austin could feel the reverberations from it hitting him, running up and down his body, but he didn't let go—if he was going to go down, really go down, then it was no holds barred and every single one of these bastards would pay—

Hold! their leader commanded, coming up. All the fighters but the one whose throat he held stepped back.

"You show remarkable restraint," the man complimented him.

"It's not what I enjoy," Austin stated. The man whose throat he held was turning blue.

"Can you release him?" the man asked.

"Depends. Are we finished?"

"For now, yes," he said, and Austin let the fighter go. The man sagged to the ground, gasping for air.

"We good?" Dominic asked, coming over to survey things. "I think we're good. Austin—meet Baran. Baran, meet Austin."

CHAPTER 22

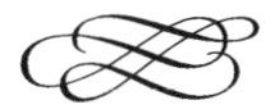

"I don't understand why you keep lying to me," Ryana told her semi-conscious prisoner.

She was in his cage now, and she'd blown enough sleeping powder at him to make a *jorgian* pass out—it was the only way to get in with him safely, take off his helmet, and get the newest version of her truth serum into him. She poured a precious spoonful of the potion into his mouth, then held his mouth closed until he swallowed it.

The Kagaroth didn't think he'd eaten or drunk anything since he'd been captured, but Ryana knew that was untrue—she'd made him drink water and broth, while half-drugged, because she needed him alive. And he'd had three separate variations of her truth-telling potion now…none of which had worked.

Because each time he woke and saw her, he recognized her—he knew who she was, of course, although she didn't recognize him—and started telling her all the horrible things about her that he believed were accurate.

But any time she pressed him for facts—why he was here, what they were planning—all he would say was that he didn't know—but Baran did.

Which was entirely impossible!

She'd strangled Baran personally and had watched him die—not only in real life, but in a million subsequent nightmares. As it'd been the most horrible moment of her life, she was sure she remembered it correctly.

She frowned at the man, finishing buckling his helmet to the rest of his armor, then stepped outside the cage and locked the door. "Call me when he gets up," she told Lyka, and then went to work on round four.

HOURS LATER, she was almost finished. She was getting faster now at creating the base potion, but she still didn't feel herself making any mistakes. It made it hard to know what to fix, and that made her feel suspect about all of her magic, and wasn't that just what she needed? Broken magic and a semi-broken heart.

She sighed, made an annotation of what she'd changed this time in her notebook, and then rose up to take a shower and go to bed. She'd try the newest version of the potion out on the Kagaroth tomorrow—it wouldn't do to give him too much, too often, otherwise her experiments might cross contaminate.

Then Grim appeared, yowling something at her. She walked back in, to where Lyka was guarding her prisoner. "Well?" she asked the bird, after Grim repeated himself.

"Grimalkin says that the wolf is injured."

Ryana felt something settle inside her soul. "Well, the wolf knows where my door is, doesn't he?"

But her door *was* red; she'd tinted it that way ever since he'd left the other night, so she wouldn't know even if he had tried to come by.

"Is it bad?" she asked Grimalkin.

Grimalkin meowed.

"He's a wolf, wolves are stupid, who can say?" Lyka translated, quite directly, Ryana knew.

"Yes. Wolves *are* stupid," Ryana agreed, reaching down to knuckle Grim's head. "Which is why I probably should check in on him," she sighed. She couldn't just let Austin *die* while Damian was gone. She might actually feel bad.

She pulled on a thick white robe to hide her sleeping slip and walked down a flight of stairs and over to his door.

"Hello?" she asked quietly, knocking. No one answered, which was a worrisome sign. The door was unlocked, though. His room looked much the same as when she'd first been in, weeks ago, except with less clothing on the floor. "Austin?" She tried his name and, after no response, stepped in.

He wasn't on his bed, nor at his desk—she should've asked Grim to be more specific—but through a doorway to her right she could hear a sound she recognized.

The clinking of ice.

She followed it into Austin's bathroom, and found him naked in a tub, half-covered in ice. One of his eyes was swollen shut, there was blood on his face, and his chest was bruised beneath all of his skin-drawings. "Austin?" she asked, kneeling down—she reached into the cold, cold water to pull out his hand and feel his pulse. Slow, so slow, but steady. "Austin—Austin, wake up," she told him, reaching in to shake him, but she wasn't sure where she could safely touch. "What happened to you?" She leaned over and brushed his hair off of his face. "Are you going to be all right?" she asked him, well aware that he wasn't going to answer.

"Grim!" she called aloud. "I need your help!"

Damian's guardian reappeared instantly. "Help me get him to his bed?" she begged, and the cat closed its crossed blue eyes, levitating Austin out of the ice and through the door, placing him down on his own bed in the next room. "Thank you," she told Grim. "Please go help Lyka," she said, and the cat disappeared.

Ryana walked over to where Austin lay on his bed, and the view wasn't any prettier. *Who did this to him?* she thought, and, *How could she make them pay?* It didn't help that his skin was so pale from how chilled he was, showing the mottled outline of his bruises—she went into his closet and found sheets and blankets and piled them on top of him, trying to warm him up.

"Stop being cold," she said, like he could hear, and sat down beside him on the bed.

She couldn't just leave him here, could she?

Oh, she totally could. In fact, she probably ought to. Whatever reason he'd had to go out and get beat up tonight most assuredly had nothing to do with her.

But…when she watched his chest rise, she knew she had to wait for it to fall again, and then watch the reverse, because if something *happened* to him it was going to crush her. No matter that he'd basically blown her off, that was him and he was fucking stupid. (Grim was right about that.) But she still wanted to do the right thing—no, right *by him*—and if something bad happened to him after she left tonight….

She lay down in the bed beside him, on top of all the sheets. Her face was near his shoulder, and she could feel it sucking heat from her it was so cold.

What he needed was a fire. Or that thing Andi had shown her in the kitchen—the microwave.

But she didn't have any of those right here, she just had herself.

I still hate you, she told him in her own language, and then untied her robe, flung it on top to act as yet another layer of fabric, and got beneath the covers with him.

She wasn't sure where she could put herself and not hurt him, but since he didn't move no matter what she did, she gave up and aligned herself alongside his body, putting her cheek to his shoulder and her thigh across his hips. She turned into him enough so that she could unfold a wing around him to wrap him up, trapping both their body heat inside.

It was like being in bed with an icicle, but somehow, despite everything, she managed to sleep.

CHAPTER 23

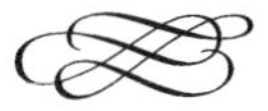

"Baby, what are you doing here?" Austin woke her by talking. His voice was thick with sleep and confusion.

"You were hurt." She had no idea what time it was. The room itself was dark, but daylight was seeping around the edges of a curtained window. She blinked awake, resisting the urge to nuzzle him, and wiped her face with a hand.

"I just needed time to heal was all," he said.

"You worried Grim," she said. "And me."

"I'm sorry," he told her, twisting his head to kiss her brow. She pulled her head back afterward, to take him in, cupping a hand to his cheek and running her thumb over his swollen eye. His lips lifted into a crooked smile, the tiny scar she knew he had lost in all the rest of his recent damage. "I probably look like you did, when you came through Damian's mirror."

From this close, and with him still healing, it was hard to remember why she'd been so mad at him. "Was I this busted up?" she asked.

"Your leg was broken, and your wings were torn." He shook his head lightly and winced. "I was so scared."

"Why?"

"Because I knew if I let anything happen to you –"

"Damian would kill you, I know, I know," Ryana said, blowing him off and pulling back.

"No," he said firmly as he pulled her close again. "I just knew that if I let anything happen to you—I would hate myself."

She went stock still beside him. "How come?" she asked, suddenly very intent on his answer.

He rubbed his thumb against her hip. She could feel it sliding over the satin of the slip she wore. "I don't know, I just did. I saw you, and I thought, shit, if I let anything bad ever happen to that girl…." he said, and let his voice drift.

Ryana looked down at him in confusion, trying to understand. "Is that…why you left me? You thought you were bad?"

Austin closed his good eye and let his head sink back on his pillow. "You're a princess. I'm a person who comes home looking like this every few months." He relinquished his hold on her waist so she was free. "I can be what you want, Ryana, but I can't be what you need."

She stared at him angrily, all of her rhetoric lessons cast aside. "*How dare you,*" she hissed at him, and watched him swallow as she spun more toward him, putting herself on her stomach and elbows beside him, rising up, sending the blankets over them cascading down her back. "Even now, do you think I'm some sort of spoiled child?"

He pulled away from her and put a hand behind his head to prop it up, grunting in pain. "No, wings, I don't—and never have. But I'm just me, Ryana. Don't make me spell out all the ways that I'm not good enough for you."

And what if I say that you are? The words came out of her mouth in her own language when she least expected and she saw his eyes widen, in confusion no doubt. But after she'd said them, she knew that they were true. "So let me get this straight, Austin. Either I'm a child who doesn't know what she wants, who you have to protect, or I'm a woman who is telling you she wants you. Which would you rather me be?"

His good eye searched her face before he answered. "Mine," he said, with a deep intake of breath, his voice almost a growl.

She closed her eyes at him, as slow as Damian's cat. "Well," she told him. "We'll see."

She rose up higher on her arms and snapped her wing back in as she brought her mouth up to his. He opened for her instantly and his strong hands rose to cup the back of her head, holding her there to kiss, taking her deeply with his tongue. Then his hands slid to explore other places on her body he hadn't touched yet. She felt them atop her slip, stroking down her back, then forward, lifting the weight of each breast, his thumbs brushing each nipple through the fabric in turn, and then down and over the curves of her hips and the roll of her stomach, to find the hem of the thing and lift it. "Can I see all of you?" he pulled his head back to ask, when he'd already worked it halfway up.

"It'd only be fair," she whispered, glancing down at how naked he still was, post-ice. His color was better now—and she could trace any of the drawings on his chest if she'd wanted to—but she reached for the edges of her slip and pulled it off of herself, listening to his breath catch as she did so.

"You have no idea how badly I wish I could see you with both eyes," he said with a laugh, raising a hand to brush her cheek.

"I'll still be around when you're whole," she said, twisting her head to kiss his palm.

"You'd better be." He considered her for a long moment, and then lifted himself towards her, curling his stomach, before hissing in agony. "Fuck," he said, falling back at the same moment as she pushed him down for his own good.

"How hurt are you?" she asked him, resting a hand on each of his shoulders to pin him down.

"I've got like eight ribs broken," he groaned. "Conservatively."

"What the fuck happened, Austin?"

"I'll tell you later. Just—for now—don't stop." He slid a hand up her thigh to grab her waist and pull her toward his side. His grip was strong and his want was as clear as the hard-on curving up his stomach.

"You know, ever since I got to Earth, I've been told to say *please*, to make sure I get what I want," she informed him, even as his hand grabbed her hips again, as if to prove that she was real.

"Baby, saddle up, or I'm gonna die," he said, grinning wickedly, then added, "Please."

She wasn't entirely sure what 'saddle up' meant, but she did have some ideas. She licked a line across her upper lip and then finished shoving the covers back and off of them both, running a delicate hand lightly down his stomach, careful not to hurt him, following the thin trail of fur down to the thick head of his cock.

"Ooooh, straddlc is very like saddle, isn't it?" she asked, wriggling free of her underwear, before moving up to swing a leg over him, hovering above his hips.

"It is," he told her, glancing down at the space between them. "Ryana –"

"No," she said, gently lowering herself against him for his sake. "No more warnings. No more changing your mind." Her heat found his shaft and she drew herself along him, feeling her seam open to reveal the slick stickiness inside. "I want this, Austin," she said, putting her hands very carefully on his shoulders, where she was almost sure she wouldn't hurt him.

His hands found her hips as his jaw dropped. "I do too."

She waited then, slowly rubbing herself up and down him, feeling his fingers grab her with restrained intent. Then she moved up slowly and tilted her hips just right as he did, angling his cock to press against her. He bent his legs behind her and pushed up as she rocked back, and then he was sliding inside her, making his way in. She felt herself part for him, opening up, as he hissed, "Wings." She closed her eyes. It'd been so long, and the last time had been with the wrong person. "Baby, look at me," he said.

"Your good eye or your bad?" she asked, because even though she'd wanted this, body and soul, she knew it was so much safer to tease him than be serious.

"Shush." His hands urged her hips on, not forcing her, just showing her what to do, and she went with them, sitting back as he lowered his and she was straddled over him, feeling every inch of him deep inside of her.

I'm scared, she whispered, pinned above him. It was safe to use her own language, she could tell him whatever she wanted that way, and he would never understand. *I want to be with you.* She rocked against him and felt his hips thrust in turn beneath hers, the head of his cock deep inside her where it felt so good. *But I don't know how. I've never done any of this before. I've never been with someone who really wanted me. This doesn't feel real half the time, and then when it is real, it's frightening. It's like carrying around a lachrony and waiting to be bitten.*

Below him on the bed, his clear blue eye searched hers. "Come here, baby," he said, opening his arms up, and she fell into them as carefully as she could. He played his hands up and down her back, his lips kissing her face and hair. "Hold on," he whispered, and turned them over roughly with a groan, so that now he was on top.

"Austin!" she said sharply. "You're going to hurt yourself."

He looked down at her then, and kissed her as he thrust again. "No —I'm not."

After that there were no more words, only movement—he held himself above her with one arm and used the other to hold her breasts for him to kiss, then his lips were at her jaw and throat, and the entire time he kept thrusting, slow, deliberate, strokes that used the length and width of his cock to its full advantage, making her feel him moving inside, and the sensations made her moan. None of it was like anything she'd ever done with Baran at all. For all that Baran was human and Austin was part-animal, it was like their personalities were reversed—and she felt more human below this werewolf than she ever had with Baran.

"May I talk?" he asked her.

She blinked beneath him, her mind switching from sounds back to words. "Now?"

"Yeah."

"Why?"

"Because," he told her, his voice half-a-growl. He left himself pinned inside her as he kept himself high on his arms. "You remember that night outside the strip club?" She nodded, wondering where on earth this might be going. "That guy tried to make you feel bad for having a cunt. You know I never would—but I have to tell you, baby, from here on out—*your* cunt is mine." He gave a sharp thrust that made her gasp, and Ryana was sure it hurt him, what with his broken ribs, but he didn't let on. "I'm not giving this up," he said, filling her again. "Not now—not ever." He stared down at her. "Do you hear what I'm saying?"

She nodded helplessly, reaching her hands up between them to bring his face to hers for kissing. "Say it again," she whispered.

"This cunt—the one that I'm fucking," he said, punctuating each phrase with a thrust, "the one I'm gonna make come—it belongs to me."

"More," she whispered.

"It's not just your cunt, baby," he growled low in her ear. "It's your breasts, your waist, your hips, and your ass," he said, tracing a hand over her to grab each part in turn. "All of you is mine now. Every single piece of you. Mine." He set his forehead to hers as she felt things that she hadn't even known were fragile breaking inside her heart.

"Even my wings?" she asked him genuinely, and he laughed, his breath was warm all over her face.

"Especially your wings, wings," he teased. "The next time we fuck, I promise I'll let you finish your ride so that you can have them open on top of me. I can't wait to watch them shudder when you come." He brought his thumb to his mouth and licked it then sent it in between her legs. "God you're so wet, baby. I feel so fucking good inside you."

Her breath caught in her throat. "I like you inside me too."

"Say it again," he told her.

"I like you—inside my cunt," she said. He grunted as he thrust up to take her and she moaned. "Your cunt," she amended.

"That's right. Mine. Like all of you. Don't worry though, I'll give you back at the end of the night. We'll work out some kind of lease-to-own." His body got heavier over hers then, and his strokes became more intent and the spot that he rubbed with his thumb started to feel like it was on glorious fire.

"Wolf," she warned him, throwing her arms around his neck where she knew she wouldn't hurt him. "Wolf—you're going to make me—" she tried to tell him, but it was too late, she was already coming, her body curling up beneath him as she shouted out his name. He rode her through it, never stopping his thrusts or his hand until her final shudder, and then he reached out and took one of her legs and put it over his shoulder, pinning her down.

"Ryana," he hissed, and she knew he was emptying himself inside her, as he beat her with his hips. "You—*fuck*—goddamn," he cursed, thrusting himself into her again and again, and he was right, she thought dreamily, her cunt was his. It was only right that he should fill it up.

CHAPTER 24

I don't think I've ever come that hard, Austin thought above her. *I feel like I poured my soul into that woman.*

He had one sharp moment of clarity and then—it was too late.

"Oh, fuck, fuck, fuck," he said, rocking into her again, releasing her leg carefully. She blinked her sex-glazed eyes and looked up at him.

"What's happening?"

"It's…I…," he started, but he really had no idea how to explain. "Don't get scared. And—don't move. If you move I think it makes it worse."

"Makes what worse?" she asked him, and then moved exactly like he'd asked her not to, and gasped. "What is that?" she wondered.

"It's a thing that happens sometimes." Austin had slept around indiscriminately with hundreds of women—and never once so much as felt a twitch from his mating knot, the thing that would've outed him to any normal human. But after he'd finished fucking Ryana, it'd flared, and now his cock was trapped inside of her, too swollen to pull out.

Just like he'd been afraid of—and now it was too late.

"Is this some Earth thing?" she asked, wriggling a little.

He grabbed her hips tighter to stop her. "No. It's a wolf thing," he growled. He couldn't tell her what it really meant though. How on earth could he?

Hey, Ryana, yeah, it's just me, Austin, your werewolf neighbor from down the hall—no pressure or anything, but I want to mate you.

In fact...I already have....

She tried to read his face. "Does it hurt?"

He shook his head and looked away. "No. It feels good." *Better than he could ever afford to tell her.* "Which is why I need you to stop moving, because otherwise I don't think it'll ever subside."

"Hmm, in that case, why would I want it to?" He could hear the wickedness in her voice.

Now would be a great time to explain all this. Right now. Any minute. Just be honest.

Or...wait until she at least wasn't locked to him, bodily....

She rocked her hips again, and he glanced up, catching her giving him an evil grin. "You're not...horrified?" he asked her.

She blinked, forgetting to be a temptress for a moment. "Why would I be horrified about anything from you?" she asked earnestly.

Shows what you know, wings. He grunted and let himself fall over to his least injured side, making sure to pull her hips over with his hands, so they were both lying down, side by side, her upper leg over his. "Ryana, first off, I appreciate you being understanding about this," he started.

Her eyebrows rose. "Are other people not?"

Austin closed his eyes. "It's literally never happened before," he said, more to himself than to her.

He heard her laughing. "Austin, are you telling me that in this very moment, you're a virgin?"

He groaned. "If my dick weren't trapped inside you, I'd be tempted to use it to stop you from talking." She laughed again, against him, and the sensations were delicious, inside and out. "Fuck, Ryana, don't move. I mean it."

One of her fingers traced his lips. "Why?" He was going to tell her, he was, *he was,* ***he was***—but then she rocked against him again. "It's strange...but good," she said, her voice rough.

He finally opened up his eyes to look at her again. If this was the last time he got to be inside her, because surely the second he confessed, she would have to run away.... He thrust his hips up and heard her gasp. One last time, one last kiss, one last fuck, because there was no possible way Ryana Blackwood, princess of the Realms, could ever be mated to him.

No matter how badly every single piece of him wanted her to be.

He kissed her, and pushed her back down, ignoring the shooting pain from his ribs along his side—broken bones were nothing compared to the thought that this would be their final time. "I want you again," he warned her, bowing his head down to run his teeth up her neck.

"Then have me," she whispered to him.

There wasn't much room between them then for movement, locked like they were, but he made the most of it, pushing into her with sharp quick thrusts, only pulling out until he felt a slight resistance, but it was enough, because every nerve he had—and not just on his cock (but mainly? *on his cock)*—was paying attention. He was sheathed so fucking deep and hard inside her, right where he belonged, and how hadn't he known it sooner? Zach was right; he *was* a fool.

She made perfect noises beneath him each time he landed, and he'd have sworn his swollen cock inside her could feel her own puffy g-spot as he took her good—so good—God, he wanted to change into a wolf and howl. "Oh Austin," she moaned, as he raised himself above her, holding onto her plush hips and driving deep, watching her full breasts jiggle with every stroke. He licked a thumb and forefinger quickly and pinched both her nipples hard enough to listen to her hiss, as her heels kicked by his side. Her cheeks were red, and her hair was getting tangled as she tossed her head back and forth, like she couldn't believe what she was feeling. *No one's ever made me feel like this,* she confessed in a whine, not opening up her eyes while speaking her own tongue. *Oh wolf, don't stop, never stop, please!*

Austin growled a low carnal sound that he hoped didn't need

translation. His balls, which'd felt so empty earlier, had somehow found another load, and all he wanted in life was to give it to her.

Yes, yes, yes, yes! She cried out beneath him, and he felt her clench him tight as her hands wrung the sheets beside her head, only opening her eyes up at the last moment to see him panting over her.

"Ryana, baby," he warned her, and then thrust in to seal them as her pussy milked him, feeling his own cum jet inside her as he groaned. Even small movements were impossible now, but it didn't matter because all of him knew he was exactly where he was meant to be.

Inside of her.

His mate.

He only barely held himself above her, catching his breath, and felt his knot subside with a deep sense of sorrow. She was free now, and there was no way she would ever come back to him. He steeled himself and shifted, sliding out, and heard her make a satisfied sigh.

"Oh, Austin," she purred, as he fell down beside her. "I liked that."

"Yeah, wings?" He forced himself to sound light, pushing a sweaty lock of hair off her shoulder. "You gonna write about it in your notebook?"

She nodded, staring at the ceiling with a satisfied smile. "For science," she said.

"Of course," he agreed, and swallowed.

In the drifting silence that followed, he tried to gather up his courage. He would've rather fought a hundred Kagaroth than try to explain one moment of what had just happened to her.

"So...in the Realms...what would come next?" he asked, on the off chance that it was anything good.

She looked at him out of the corner of her eye without moving her head. "You would gift me three fine horses and a deed to arable land."

For a second he thought she was serious, but then he saw the corners of her lips lift, and he laughed. "I'm fresh out of horses, wings."

"It's just as well. Wolves make horses nervous," she said, grinning, then she suddenly turned her head toward him. "What happens next on Earth?"

"Well," he said, and took a deep inhale, turning toward her. "We should probably talk about that," he began—as he heard the door to his bedroom open up behind him.

"Austin—Jesus. Why do you always smell like sex? And here I was, worried about you, since you didn't answer my texts," Zach said, barging in. From the doorway, Zach had an excellent view of Austin's naked back and not much else. "What the fuck happened to you?"

"Yes, Austin," Ryana teased. "What did happen to you?"

Austin shot his brother a death glare over his shoulder, and Zach's eyes went wide, realizing that Ryana was there, too, hidden by Austin. She pulled sheets up to her neck and laughed at both of their discomfort. "Good morning, Zach—or is it afternoon now?"

"I, uh," Zach began, back-peddling, so that Austin wouldn't have to climb out of bed and murder him.

"No, no, Austin was just about to tell me who broke eight of his ribs last night." She pouted and put her hand up to Austin's face. "And also who did this to his eye."

Austin blinked his whole eye shut, bracing for impact. "Kagaroth," he said.

"What?" Ryana sat up, scooping most of the blankets from the bed with her. "How—wait—why didn't you say anything?"

"I'm sorry. I was recuperating and then I was a little distracted," he gave her a meaningful look, but she gave him no quarter.

"Or, you neglected to mention them because you knew if you did I'd go back to my lab and finish what I was doing. Which is probably where I should be right now, anyhow," she said, pushing to stand, taking all of the sheets with her. He reached out and grabbed the end of them.

"Don't go, Ryana—we still need to talk."

She frowned between the men—but mostly at him. "We can talk later. When you're ready to explain yourself, and after I check on Lyka," she said, and strode out the door with all his bedding.

Zach moved aside to let her go, and then retook his spot, closing the door behind her and locking it, like Ryana had apparently not done hours ago. "What, and I mean this with all sincerity, Austin, *the fuck?*" his brother hissed.

"I didn't ask for it," Austin said. "She gave it to me."

"Oh, no, you just camped outside her door for days. She didn't have to ask for shit, you were already leaving your heart on her doorstep." Zach growled.

"Since when is what I do any of your business?" Austin asked, sitting up, and reaching for some clothing on the ground, hopping into jeans with a pained grunt.

"It's my business when you come home looking like that!" Zach pointed at him. "What if a rift opened right now? How the fuck would you be able to fight?"

"I'd make do," Austin told him, buttoning his jeans closed. He needed to shower. He knew he smelled—fantastic, actually, if you were into sweat and sex—but before that he needed to hunt Ryana down and talk to her.

Zach sat down in Austin's gaming chair and blocked his path. "Tell me exactly what happened with Dominic?"

Austin hesitated, heading around him for the door. "More of the same—that they're looking for something magical and to stay ready for his call. This," he said, gesturing at his naked chest, the art of his tattoos now hidden by his bruises, "was to earn the Kagaroth's trust."

"Well I'm glad it wasn't just for fun," Zach said, frowning. "Now onto problem number two—what the hell business do you have sleeping with Ryana? She's—"

"Perfect," Austin cut him off. "She's fucking perfect and I won't hear you say otherwise."

Zach's ice blue eyes narrowed at him.

"What?" Austin growled.

"You've never fallen for a girl like this before."

"Well, I've never met a princess of the Realms before now, have I?" Austin made to leave, then decided to stand in front of his brother instead. What he was going to tell Zach now—it might be the only time he got to tell anyone. And as pissed as Zach would surely be... there was a chance his brother might actually understand.

It was Zach's turn to growl, "What?"

"I mated her, Zach."

His brother's already pale skin became more so, and his eyes closed as he took a deep inhale so as not to yell.

Austin continued. "We were fucking—it was the first time—and it happened. One minute I was coming inside her, the next we were locked, and I've never felt more right." He swallowed roughly and drew a hand through his shaggy hair. "It felt like I was home."

Zach nodded slowly, like the hinge of his neck had a thick coating of rust. "What did she think of that?" he asked, in a very flat tone.

Austin walked to sink back against his bed. "I panicked. I told her it was a wolf thing—and I was just about to explain everything, when you came in, so thanks for making this even harder than it was already going to be."

"Oh, Austin," Zach said, with the exact same pained intonation as he'd used when he'd told him their mother'd died, and suddenly it felt like they were kids again, just the two of them, back-to-back, against the entire world. "What are you going to do when she refuses you?"

Austin stared blankly at his carpeting, and answered with the truth: "Want to die and get fucked up." Zach stood up and crossed the room to him, setting his hands on Austin's shoulders.

"I know. You told me, and I know," Austin said. His brother stood there with him, just breathing in their shared moment, supporting him as best he could. "I didn't have a choice, Zach," Austin explained. "You saw her come through Damian's mirror, same as I did. The second she needed me then, I needed her back." He'd taken care of Ryana for days before she'd come to, thinking of nothing but her the entire damn time, sleeping in the same room with her in case she stirred. "And remember that night we were all in the library when she was comatose, giving Damian shit for being mated to Andi?"

"Yes—and you were the worst about it," Zach said, with a rueful snort.

"I know." Austin thought back to the moment, remembering. His voice went quiet. "I think I was scared."

"And all your talk of pussy?"

Austin groaned and ran his hands through his hair. "I straight up took her to a strip club, Zach, trying to convince her not to be with me. It didn't work."

"Clearly," Zach said, his tone dry.

Austin looked up at him. His brother was neither angry, nor accusatory—just disappointed, which was vastly worse. "She's the one who got into bed today with me. I woke up to her practically naked beside me, what the hell else was going to happen? I'm not a fucking saint."

Zach slowly let Austin's shoulders go. "I would've bought you ten Bentleys if it would've kept your dick in your pants."

"Well, the cat's out of the bag now." Austin pushed himself up to standing. "And I've got to go tell her. I can't put it off."

Zach considered him then, with a concerned look and pursed lips. "Good luck, brother. However it goes. And if you need someone to drink with later—pick me."

CHAPTER 25

IN ROUGHLY EVERY SINGLE VIDEOGAME AUSTIN HAD EVER PLAYED, there'd been a part where the protagonist had do a timed run down a hall and somehow miss getting sliced by spinning knives.

All of those halls and this hall now felt exactly the same.

He realized halfway down the stairs that he hadn't even bothered to put on a shirt, and it didn't matter.

There was no magical way to make what he was about to tell her more palatable. There was no point in bringing her flowers or taking her out to dinner, trying to pussyfoot or pretend.

It just was what it was what it was.

He wanted her, not just for a night, but for forever, even if sometimes he didn't fully understand her and she couldn't stand him.

The second he walked near her door it flashed the same color as the blood he'd spilled the night before. He knocked on it regardless. "Wings, let me in." When he couldn't hear anything on the other side, he tried again. "Ryana. We need to talk."

No response. He gritted his teeth and remembered the old saying, a gentleman is simply a patient wolf—well, his wolf had run out of patience.

"Goddamnit, Ryana," he shouted, hitting the door with a hand, making it rattle in its hinges—and then after that, he tried the handle.

Apparently princesses of the Realms did not believe in locks.

Or, more likely, she trusted him.

He put his head against the door and breathed bodily, trying to talk himself into waiting for her, again, even if this was exactly the part where he'd misstep and die in a videogame. It felt like he could almost hear the knives coming for him.

What was worse, barging in now, trampling over the rules he'd given her to gain her trust—a thing he genuinely wanted to keep—or waiting for a week while she stewed without him, and then try to explain what his knot had meant?

He was nowhere near figuring shit out when he heard a shout from inside. "Ryana?" he asked sharply, setting his ear against the door's wood.

Another shout—and it wouldn't have mattered if the door had been locked, covered in rubies, and made of cement—he would've punched his way through.

As it was, he slammed the door open and ran to the back of her room for her laboratory. He pulled up short at the open door, and he could hear the shouting far more clearly, as Ryana stood in the back of the cage where her prisoner was chained.

What have you done to me now, bitch? the prisoner demanded.

Austin stood, stunned. The word the Kagaroth used for Ryana wasn't exactly bitch—he could feel Mills's magic scraping his mind to come up with an equivalent in English and finding none, because what the Kagaroth had called her was much, much worse.

I've given you another dose of my potion. It compels you to speak—and now it is time to tell me the truth, Ryana said calmly.

Fuck you and fuck your magic and fuck your potions! her prisoner shouted at her.

Why are you here?

Because Baran ordered us, the Kagaroth snarled.

Austin heard Ryana make a sound of frustration. *What color is the ground?*

Brown.

And my eyes?

Green.

Lie to me! she demanded.

I...cannot. Austin was sure he heard the other man spitting, though.

You are! You must be! Baran is dead!

If I cannot tell a lie, princess, should I tell you what the Kagaroth think of you? Of your poor broken heart and the gaping hole between your legs? How we laugh at how we tricked you?

Austin wasn't consciously aware of moving—just one second he was outside Ryana's laboratory door and the next he was in the middle of her lab, inside the cage with the Kagaroth chained at the back of it, one hand wrapped around the other man's throat, and one hand holding a table leg that he'd snapped off on his way in. *Disparage her again and I will take this stick and wrap your body around it from the feet up.*

The Kagaroth's eyes were bugging out of his head. *Who the fuck are you?* he hissed. *And how do you understand me?*

"Austin." Ryana said his name from somewhere behind him. "Unhand my prisoner." He slowly let the man down, and took two steps back. The chains holding the man seemed solid. He turned, and saw Ryana dressed in a simple green dress and standing stiffly, with Lyka the size of an eagle sitting on her shoulder. There was a wet mark on her breast, and if she'd been close enough to get spit on, she'd been close enough to be in danger; he didn't care how fast her guardian was.

Her eyes narrowed on him beneath her arched auburn brows. "So," she began, every bit as stern with him as she had been with her prisoner. "When did you learn my native tongue?"

His stomach folded in on itself and sank. He was tempted to crack that he'd learned it while licking her, but realized making a joke now would just set things between them on fire. He also realized if he lied and she found out, there'd be no coming back from it. "The night we captured him." He jerked his chin at the prisoner behind him.

Her eyes widened and her nostrils flared. "How?"

"Mills. I asked her."

"Because you knew you were going to fight Kagaroth last night? And didn't tell me?"

"Wings," he began, trying to sound reasonable, "we had already fought them, when we caught this one. It seemed wise for me to be able to understand them."

"And that's all, right?" she asked, half of her lips lifting into a cruel smile. "It had nothing to do with you wanting to spy on me?"

"I should've told you that same night." He held his hands up between them. "Your door was red and—"

Is this a lover's spat? the prisoner asked, lunging to the end of his chains to leer at Ryana. *Oh you idiot-girl-child—you went from Baran to this beast-creature here? We all knew you had poor taste but at least—*

Austin casually swung the table leg out and backhanded the Kagaroth in the stomach, making him gasp for air. Ryana appeared not to notice.

"Answer the question, wolf." She held her chin up to look down her nose at him, and he saw the selfsame ice in her that he'd so often seen in Damian before a fight. "Or were you just going to spy on me like everyone else?"

"I came to tell you now," he said. Because he was going to tell her everything now, and why the hell-fuck-goddamned not.

She snorted softly, to let him know what she thought the chances of that were. And he could see her then, her eyes flickering over him, calculating every moment that they'd spent together, when she'd been honest and open, and he'd been...not.

It was only fair to tell her how badly he needed her, to share all of himself with her, to even their playing field again if nothing else. He glanced over at the prisoner. "If you're done with him, Ryana—I need to talk to you."

"I'm *not* done, and I may never *be* done, because he insists on lying. I might be in here for several more weeks, during which you are free to sleep in the hall."

Austin blinked back to the conversation he'd overheard them having when he came in. "And just what is he lying about?"

"It's no concern of yours," she told him, striding out of the cage. He moved to follow, and Lyka kept her gaze on him.

"I met a Kagaroth named Baran last night, Ryana. He's not lying about that."

At him mentioning that name, Austin watched the color drain from her face, and she whispered, "No."

"I shook his hand."

"You," she sputtered, before looking at his hand like it'd betrayed her. "You what?"

"He was the leader of the men who jumped me. Dominic—the friend who set me up—he said they needed to see if I was serious." Austin moved closer to her, and Lyka fluttered her feathers in warning. "Who was he? Is he the man I need to kill?"

"I already did," she breathed to herself. She was staring at the ground, lost in thought, and Austin wanted to grab her shoulders, but knew if he did Lyka would attack. "He's—I killed him," Ryana said to herself. "He's dead. He has to be."

There was a sound behind them like sifting sand, and then the prisoner bolted past Austin's shoulder, out the open cage door, dragging his chains behind him like the Ghost of Christmas Past. Austin protected Ryana instinctively, grabbing her wrist and pulling her behind him, as Lyka flew up, intent on the prisoner. He threw the heavy table leg at the man with his free hand, and it caught the prisoner square in the back, flinging him forward to the ground, but before Lyka could get to him, the munitions box on Ryana's hearth opened up and the progenitor leapt out, jumping onto the man's face.

Ryana shook herself free of Austin's grip and ran for the prisoner. "No!" Austin could see the Kagaroth's face, very blurrily, through the progenitor's clear carapace and internal organs.

It chittered something back to her in metallic tones, which Lyka translated.

"How can you still be hungry? You drained ten cows!" Ryana shouted.

Austin heard the creature's bitter complaint, and saw Ryana...give up. He could tell from the way her shoulders had slumped and her head bowed and *who was this* and *what had they done to his Ryana?*

"Fine," she agreed. "Carry on."

"Ryana?" he asked her, trying to figure out just what had transpired.

"He's already injected poisons." She frowned and kept frowning.

"Disgusting—but that's not what I meant." He moved to stand in front of her again. "What happened, wings?"

"You mean how did he get out?" She hugged herself. "They're not without magic." She glanced back inside the prisoner's cage, and Austin saw where a portion of each chain had been melted through. "That's why whatever it was you did last night, fighting them, was foolish."

"I didn't know who they were for certain, when they started. They were out of their armor –"

"You could've died," she cut him off. "And Baran would not have cared."

Austin brought the image of the man to the forefront of his mind. "Who is he to you, Ryana?"

Her eyebrows rose and she laughed sharply. "You don't get to ask that."

Austin raked his hand through his hair, trying to ignore the repetitive slurping coming from the progenitor's direction. "We need to talk. I need to be honest with you."

"Yes?" she asked, her voice going high. "You think? You think it's okay to lie to me for over a week, and now that I'm the one withholding, it'd be a good time for honesty?" She rolled her eyes like someone well-practiced with the expression. "Please. Get out Austin."

"No. Ryana, I mean it—I really need to talk to you." The slurping increased in speed and volume. "Can we get somewhere the hell away from that," he said, waving his hand behind him, "and just sit down and have a conversation?"

She shook her head. "I have nothing to say to you. And you've already apologized—oh wait, you haven't, actually, and you're probably not going to, because why should you?"

"Ryana, I am so sorry, you have no idea—"

"I don't," she cut in. "And what's more? I don't care, Austin." The way she said it was like a knife through his heart, and he could feel his soul bleeding out as she went on. "I trusted you. Do you have any idea how hard that is for me? Maybe you might! Seeing as you've been able to hear me *this whole time!"* She flung her arms out at him—the space between her hands was occupied by a green flickering light. "And now —I can't trust Mills, because she gave that power to you and didn't see fit to tell me—"

"That's on me, I swore to her I would—"

"What is for me in this place, Austin? With my brother gone, why am I even here?" Her pain was legible on her face, same as if she'd written it down.

Because I need you, is what he wanted to say, but before he could manage a word, she told him, "Red."

"Wings, don't," he told her, his chest heaving, each breath making all of his ribs ache.

"Red," she said again, simply, lowering her hands, the light between them quenching.

"Please," he begged.

"Red," she said quietly.

He knew what she was asking for. Either his promise to her meant something...or it'd meant nothing all along, just been some kind of ploy. This was the last chance he'd have to prove that he respected her —enough to leave her when she asked.

Announcing how he felt to her right now would be the opposite of that.

So even though it killed him, he said, "Okay." He took a step back. "Whenever you're green, next, wings—please come and find me. Immediately." He turned on his heel.

"*If* I am ever green again," she called her correction after him. He paused, fought the urge to turn around, and then walked out her door.

Somehow he made it back to his own room. Zach wasn't there anymore, which was good; he didn't need anyone else to be disappointed in him tonight. He stripped off his jeans and hesitated before getting into the shower.

If he showered, he wouldn't smell like her anymore.

If he didn't...her scent would torture him.

Which was worse?

He got into the shower and let the cold water slap him.

CHAPTER 26

"Is Baran truly alive?" Lyka asked her, echoing her own disbelief. Ryana reached her hand up to idly rub her guardian's feathered cheek while in heavy thought.

"It seems so. I don't know how, though." Ryana would have vividly remembered killing him, even without her nightmares—the weight of his neck had seemed to occupy her hands for months after she'd done the deed. And at the time, she'd listened against his chest and hadn't heard his heart so much as flutter—which was when she'd had Lyka take him outside and thrown into the moat for the *sluciers* there to eat.

By then the entire palace was up in arms about the coup. She'd had to tell her mother, and listen to her mother shame her. They discovered that an entire squad of the Kagaroth had run away, clearly complicit in Baran's sins. And then all of the rest of them were imprisoned, until Ryana was able to complete her first course of potions—the truthtelling serum that made releasing some Kagaroth possible. They'd tested it under extreme torture conditions, and it'd seemed accurate. By using it, they were able to clear most of the remaining Kagaroth's names.

The deed was already done, however. That a coup had even had a chance—it was a massive dent in the palace's metaphorical armor and, correspondingly, in her mother's reputation.

Not to mention her own....

They'd done their best to keep what'd happened under wraps, but without the rest of the Kagaroth there to cut out talking tongues... tongues talked. About her. Mocking her for falling in love, especially with a simple servant who had nothing to offer. How simple-minded she had been.

But now, if Baran was alive, and on Earth.... Ryana frowned, unable to make heads nor tails of it all. She knew she needed to tell the others what the Kagaroth had told her the night before, though, back when she'd assumed that he was lying, when he actually couldn't.

She changed into a clean dress and went to go find Mills.

RYANA KNOCKED on the witch's door not long after. "Mills?" she asked. Mills's door was painted a cheerful yellow, which Ryana felt sure did not fluctuate with the witch's mood.

"Is it important?" came a muffled shout from inside.

"Yes!" Ryana shouted back. *Unfortunately.*

After being forced to wait far too long in the hall, wondering whether or not she should send Lyka in after the woman, Mills emerged, hopping out and setting her back to the door behind her quickly. "Ryana! How can I help you?"

She was wearing a robe and appeared disheveled. *How nice it must be to be in a relationship without lies.* Then she remembered that Mills had been the one to spell Austin into understanding her language and frowned. "The prisoner is dead," Ryana informed her.

"Should I say I'm sorry?" Mills asked.

Ryana made a face. "No. I'm not. But—before he died, he told me things you need to know. They're opening rifts to create instability between Realms, hoping to cause a Conjunction. Can I come in?"

"Oh—oh my God." Mills put her hand to her mouth, opened the door enough to shout, "Jay, put some clothes on. You need to hear this!" and then dragged Ryana inside.

"Tell me everything," Mills said, as she indicated Ryana should sit down on her couch, and Ryana felt a sudden urge to confess.

Not about the Kagaroth, or any danger from the Realms, but about Austin, and what he'd meant to her, and how badly she'd just been hurt.

"You okay, Ryana?" Jamison asked kindly, joining them, looking just as rumpled as the witch did as he hauled up a chair to sit across from her and Mills took a place by her side.

"I'm fine," Ryana said, definitively. She took a brief look around their shared rooms. One half was all technological gear from Earth that she didn't yet understand, the other was pleasant wood, warm colored stone, and hanging herbs drying from the ceiling. Somehow their space managed to be the combination of the two of them, disparate as they were. Ryana knew she was in a home, she could feel it, and it made everything slightly worse for her.

Not because she missed the Palace—she didn't.

It was just that, for all of the gilded throne rooms and treasure chambers and libraries that seemed endless in her past, she'd never had something as simple and good as what they had, here.

"Ryana?" Mills asked, touching her knee gently. "Did you need some tea?"

Ryana blinked back to attention. "No. I just need to tell you what I learned."

"Would you rather tell everyone in the conference room?" Jamison asked. "We can round everybody up, no problem."

"No," Ryana said, shaking her head. She had no interest in seeing Austin again right now. It would only make everything cut deeper. "I'll just tell you, and you can tell them."

RYANA WENT through everything her imprisoned Kagaroth had told her, before he died. Which he wouldn't have done, if Austin hadn't distracted both her and Lyka long enough for him to melt his chains.

Then again, without Austin's interruption, she'd never have

known that Baran was alive somehow. While Austin might *be* a liar, there was no particular reason *for* him to lie about that.

As she explained that Baran and his men were interested in creating rifts to trigger a Conjunction, Mills and Jamison looked increasingly horrified.

"But...why?" Mills asked, when she was through.

Ryana shrugged. "The same reason they went rogue back home, I guess. Regime change, and the opportunity to grab power."

"And your prisoner never once mentioned they were after you?" Mills pressed.

"Not directly, no." Although she'd never asked it, but why would they care? Both of the Kagaroth she'd managed to speak to before they died seemed to hold her in little regard. They'd been opening rifts, they'd been found near rifts, there was nothing personal about it—other than Baran's unending ambition, haunting her. She'd elided her horrible betrayal and its cause, as it didn't seem currently relevant. "I guess things are just particularly chaotic there, and they're trying to make the most of it."

"We've concentrated on closing rifts for so long, I've never given opening them any thought," Jamison murmured as he rubbed his chin with his metallic hand. "How is that even possible?

"The magic energies required alone boggle me," Mills said, sinking deeper into the couch at Ryana's side, before looking at her. "Had you ever heard of such a thing in the Realms? As some sort of attack, perhaps?"

"Never," Ryana said, because she hadn't. "But if we capture another prisoner, I can ask?" she offered. Mills nodded.

"And just how did this one die?" Jamison asked her.

Ryana sighed. "An unfortunate accident." There was no need to recount a blow-by-blow about why Austin was in her lab with her. "He freed himself, ran, and the progenitor got hungry."

His eyes widened precipitously. "What? *No*." He did a full body shiver, turning to Mills. "I *told* you that thing was dangerous."

"Well, it would never eat me," Ryana said, coming to the progenitor's defense.

Jamison stared at her, his eyebrows furrowing so hard they almost met. "That's not as comforting as you think it is."

Mills laughed. "Jay," she said, reaching out to take his metal hand in her own to comfort him, and Ryana watched him let himself be calmed. He gave Mills a tender smile, and Ryana felt like there was a snake twisting inside her gut.

"In any case, there you have it," she said, standing suddenly, needing to get away.

"Ryana," Mills called after her, before she could escape. "Shouldn't we tell Damian?"

Ryana paused and looked at the ground. Technically...yes. Her brother was far more suited to dealing with incursions from other Realms than the rest of them.

But he was also out there, somewhere, on vacation, with Andi looking at him just like Mills had Jamison. And even as much as she didn't want to be around it, especially when no one else would ever feel like that about her, truly—she couldn't bring herself to take that chance away from him.

"To do what?" she snapped, and then shook her head quickly in apology. "You can talk to your other wardens in his absence, can you not? And start to ready supplies?" She tried to make herself sound reasonable, as Mills hesitantly nodded. Jamison inhaled, to disagree she felt, so she went on quickly. "Does he actually need to be here, or would we just find his presence comforting? Let my brother have another day and night of freedom—it's likely the last he'll ever get."

"Fine," Jamison agreed. "But tomorrow—"

"Is tomorrow," Ryana finished for him, squashing all dissent. She looked between the two of them, politely flicked the line of her dress's skirt, and said, "Good night."

SOMEWHERE ON THE way back to her own room, she decided to detour and go outside. It didn't matter how massive and impressive Damian's castle was, it wasn't big enough for her to be in right now.

Where would she go?

What would she do?

Why should she stay here?

She hesitated on the stairs once the front doors were closed behind her. Almost every time she'd left the castle, she'd left with Austin, which meant that everything outside reminded her of him. But staying indoors was even worse—how had he managed to make it so that there was no place she could go without him in her thoughts?

It wasn't fair.

"Princess?" Lyka asked her, running her small feathered head softly beneath Ryana's chin.

"Can you get me my car keys, Lyka?" Ryana asked her. The bird disappeared in an instant, and then returned, keys in hand. "Thanks."

RYANA HAD SEEN cars in use on TV and in movies, and she'd watched Austin drive. It didn't look that hard, and Earth was large. Surely there was some space out there that didn't feel like Austin—she only needed to go find it.

She opened the door, got in, played with the pedals, and figured out how to turn it on—and how to take the top back down, which felt important. She experienced a brief thrill of success when she managed it, and then more so as she edged out of the garage, feeling the night air wrap around her.

Her hands wrung the steering wheel, and she realized that never in her entire life had she ever driven her own contraption. Even back home in the realms, the magic that made the carriages run hadn't been her own.

This was happening. She was going to go drive off into the night and just be *away*. If she couldn't get free from her nightmares, she needed to at least be free from her formerly hopeful dreams.

"Ryana—wait!"

She heard her name called over the sound of the engine and ignored it, pulling the car further out, heading for the compound's gate.

"Ryana!" someone shouted after her.

If it was Austin, she didn't want to see him, and if it was anyone else, she didn't care.

But a black blur raced in front of her vehicle and she slammed on the brakes to stop from hitting it, making the entire car lurch forward. She turned on her headlights slowly—after making the screen-wipers work first—and illuminated Zach, wearing the black suit she'd seen him in in Austin's room, earlier. He now had his hands on her car's hood to protect himself.

"I know how to drive," she preemptively told him, afraid he'd try to stop her.

"I'm not debating that," he said, standing to straighten his sleeves before he looked at her. "Although you need to put on your seatbelt."

Ryana frowned. "You can't make me be safe."

Zach groaned and put his hands up to his face so their heels were in his eye sockets. "Maybe you two are perfect for each other," he muttered, before lowering his hands and shaking his head once. "Can we talk?"

"No. I'm going. Get out of the way." She made the engine rev threateningly.

He gave her a look. "I don't think you're willing to run me over, Ryana."

"No—but I'm not above having Lyka forcibly remove you."

She raised her hands to snap her fingers, to do just that, but he spoke low and commandingly as he leaned forward on her car: "Which one of us do you think is older, Ryana? Austin, or me?"

Ryana's hand paused at his unexpected tack. "Why could it possibly matter?"

"Indulge me," he said, pushing on her car and shaking it. "Please."

She sighed and stared off into space. "You, probably." Zach had suits on all the time, and he was responsible for bearing the burden of being the face of her brother's large company, wearing the magic that made him look like her and Damian's aged father as a disguise. Zach clearly took his life and his position more seriously than Austin ever had. She didn't think she'd have believed them brothers, if she hadn't seen their matching tattoos.

Zach nodded, finally taking his hands off the car's hood. "You would think that, wouldn't you? But no—Austin is three years older."

"So?"

"So—the only reason I can do this," Zach said, while gesturing at himself, "by which I mean stand up in board meetings and pretend to be another man, pretend to give a shit about other wealthy people's vacations on islands I've never been too, and feign interest while they tell me about which boarding school they've picked out for their mistress's child, is because Austin protected me." Zach stared at her through her windshield, as if willing her to understand something via telepathy, which she'd been trained to be immune to. She frowned deeply at him as he went on. "Our childhood was...well, to say it was bad is an understatement. I was a smaller child; we were always moving, always different, always poor. Our mother was more interested in vengeance than in raising us—when our pack was slaughtered, she was too blinded by her grief to act like a mother." His gaze dipped down to the car's red hood, which looked like old blood beneath the moonlight. "I think perhaps mothering was hard, whereas murder came easy."

Ryana tilted her head, unable to begin to imagine what emotion Zach was trying to evoke from her. "When I was five, I watched my mother pull an enemy's arms off like the wings of a fly." She remembered the hot horrific spray of blood across her skin. She'd screamed in terror—and then her mother had screamed at her for screaming. "So just what are you trying to say, Zach?"

She watched the werewolf's jaw tighten. Telling her this story was clearly costing him. "I just...I just want you to know that our entire childhood, Austin protected me. Made sure I was fed. Didn't let anyone make fun of me. Woke me up from nightmares. He told me I was smart and made sure I took my books home. And if I didn't do my homework? He would beat me up."

Ryana wanted to be pissed at Zach—and via him, Austin in absentia, she knew—but the thought of two little were-boys fighting over homework made her bite back a smile. When Zach finally raised his gaze to catch hers, his blue eyes shone, as if their usual ice-blue was slightly melted. "Ryana, no one ever did that for him."

Her lips parted, finally understanding Zach's point. That there'd been no one watching out for Austin. No one who'd ever protected him. Made him do homework.

All of Austin's nightmares, he'd had to go through alone.

And no matter how pissed she was at him currently, the thought of him hurting as a child made her soul ache, and she longed to somehow move back through time, to be that person for him.

Zach took an emotional inhale before continuing. "Ryana…while I know he may not be the mate that you've dreamed of—he is still a good man. So perhaps you can find room in your heart for him."

Ryana double-blinked, her empathy for Austin blindsided by Zach's phrasing. She swallowed and sat still, her blood rushing in her ears, looking around at her car's well-lit dashboard and all of its fiddly little controls, wishing one of them could make the world stop.

"Oh, no," Zach whispered, breaking the silence between them first.

She looked up at him, stricken. "Did my magic translate you right?" She knew it had. She was just basically daring him—begging him?—to lie.

"He told me he was going to go tell you," Zach said, and nervously swallowed, an action she knew she had never seen him take before.

"Did you," she began slowly, keeping her voice even, although it was hard, "just claim…that Austin…thinks he's my mate?"

Zach closed his eyes, trapped. "He doesn't just think it. He knows it."

A panoply of emotions raced through Ryana, one after the other so quickly she couldn't begin to pull them apart. Elation, terror, disgust, yearning—it explained why Austin had rushed into her room, and then why he'd been so reluctant to go. Not out of fear for her, or to confess that he could understand her, but because he'd wanted to tell her…that.

She hoped.

But if he had…what would she have told him in return? She held onto the steering wheel like it was a life preserver because it felt like she was drowning.

"Ryana," Zach began, and she shook her head at him to cut him off. "Where is he now?"

He walked to her side of the car and put his hand out for the keys. "Let me drive—"

"No!" she said sharply. "I can do it! Just tell me where to go."

"He's likely at the Whistle Stop, 99 Bottles, or The Aqua."

Ryana nodded, and snapped her fingers. "Lyka, go get my phone."

Her bird disappeared to bring back her phone with the precious mapping program that she'd figured out how to use, while Zach looked on with increasing dismay.

"May I ask what you are going to tell him?"

She gave him a half-lidded glare. "I'm far more interested in seeing what he'll tell me."

CHAPTER 27

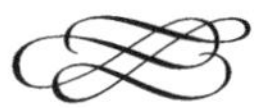

THIS TIME, AUSTIN TOOK THE PRIUS OUT TO WHAT HAD ONCE BEEN HIS first favorite bar but had since been downgraded. The Aqua—formerly Rebar—was in the process of attempting to go upscale, which meant that the owners had closed it for three months and remodeled everything in chrome and black and given it a new name. The wall of liquor behind the bar was lit with gleaming white lights from below, and the ice cubes in drinks had grown to the size of baseballs, an affectation which Austin found annoying.

But even though he now felt out of place there, in his jeans and his flannel jacket, he'd come, nonetheless.

He didn't have anywhere else to go. Austin got himself a shot of Red Breast at the bar and then found himself a booth, settling in to do a thorough soul searching with a dash of self-loathing. People he recognized gave him companionable nods, which he didn't return, and waitresses must've kept swinging by because the glasses on his table multiplied like see-through rabbits.

When would Ryana allow him to talk to her next? By then, would her anger have solidified her heart into impenetrable stone? Would she ever forgive him? And if she did...how the hell was he going to bring up being mates?

Hey wings, yeah, so—what's the etiquette in the Realms for when someone has accidentally given you their heart, not to mention other organs, and they don't really want them back?

What then?

What business did he have wanting to be mated to her, anyways? Why hadn't his wolf given him a choice?

He was staring at the table with one hand curled into his hair when someone sat across from him.

"Found you," said a familiar voice, at the same time as he scented lavender.

He slowly looked up. Missy had taken the seat across from him, and if he didn't concentrate, there were five of her.

"Not now, Missy," he told her, swiping a finger across his phone. He'd been here about two hours, and at this rate he'd burn through all their whiskey by midnight.

"Yes, now," Missy told him, giving him a pout. "I'm sorry for smoking near Betsy."

Austin looked her straight in the eyes, until there was only one of her. "I have a girlfriend."

Both her eyebrows rose. She guffawed, then made a show of looking over both his shoulders. "Is she imaginary, or did you leave her at home?" Then she took his bruised face in. "And what kind of woman would let you out of her sight, looking like this? Unless she did it to you, maybe?" She snaked a hand over the table and caught his. "Blink once if you need me to save you from her, Austin."

"Missy, don't," he told her, but he didn't pull his hand back fast enough because the table was littered with empties and—

"Austin?" said another familiar voice.

One that he would recognize forever. He turned, slowly, as his liver kicked into high gear. "Ryana?" he asked, just to make sure she was real, and not some apparition conjured by too much whiskey, and yanked his hand away from Missy's to fully face her.

"Is this her?" Missy said in her most challenging tone.

Ryana's gaze flickered over the other woman coldly. "Am I who?"

"His girlfriend."

Austin held up his hand before she could answer. "No," he said aloud, and he could've sworn he saw Ryana's expression clouding for a moment, before it returned to its regal bearing. "But I want her to be."

She stared at him—and then she stared at Missy. And without saying a word, she turned on her heel, revealing Lyka tucked against her hair like a hairpin as she walked quickly to the back of the bar. He started up and trailed after her, until they were both outside in the ill-lit parking lot, and the second the door was closed behind them, he yanked off its door handle so that no one could follow them out. The street in front of the bar had loud road noise from cars driving by, and he knew Ryana's would be among their number soon if he didn't manage to say the exact right thing.

"Ryana, wait, please," he told her, as she strode over to the Bentley. She turned and leaned against it, crossing both her arms to take him in.

"You have my attention for a brief moment, wolf. Speak." He needed to tell her to run back home. If she and Baran had history—he needed her safe more than he needed to spew his feelings. "Nevermind, wings—you need to go home. Right away. It's not safe out here for you."

"No?" she said. "Where is safe for me then?" Her wings weren't currently out, but it wasn't hard for him to imagine them above her, arching. "Tell me what you were going to say, wolf. Before you decided to try to boss me, again."

He inhaled to yell at her to leave—then realized he didn't know when he'd be able to talk to her again after tonight.

Maybe never.

"Ryana," he began slowly, "I don't want to just be what we are." He paused and prayed for clarity. The night had been overcast so far, but he knew the waxing moon was up there somewhere behind the clouds and he willed it to give him strength. "I'm sorry to change the rules on you—on us. When I started off, my intentions were good. But then every time I was with you...." Why hadn't he spent the last few hours practicing this conversation instead of drinking? He swallowed dry.

"At first, I just wanted to protect you. To show you Earth, and teach you. But who am I kidding? You don't need either of those things—you're plenty strong and you already figured out how to drive." She frowned at him and he felt like he was dying, but he kept going because he didn't know how to pull up. "Then I figured out what I really wanted, Ryana. Just to be by your side. To help you if you need helping—and to watch you in awe when you don't. To always be in your corner, and always have your back."

"I already have wings on my back," she told him, her frown growing deeper.

"It's a metaphor." His stomach soured, and not because of all the whiskey he'd ingested.

"What else?" she demanded.

He shook his head lightly. "I don't have other things to offer you, Ryana. I know I don't deserve you. I don't think anyone truly could. But looking at you makes me feel like I'm running beneath the full moon on a clear night." He dared to take a step toward her. "And like any good werewolf, I would follow my moon anywhere."

He watched her waver, and he was sure it was real, not just a trick of the light, but then her eyes narrowed. "Which is why you're here and smell like lavender, no doubt."

Her words slapped him, and he knew he deserved it. "No—I'm here failing to drink myself unconscious. Missy being here is just a coincidence."

"I don't know that I believe you, Austin, seeing as I've scented her on you three times." She began shaking her head. "There was a time when I might have believed you, yes. Are you full of good intentions, and do I like your words? Possibly. But?" she said, and gave him a look of infinite pity, and the moon chose that moment to break through the clouds so that he could see her absolutely clearly by its light. "When I look into my future, I don't see you in it."

Austin inhaled, to say something—anything—to ask for more time, or another chance—but he was interrupted by Missy. She'd found someone strong enough to shoulder bump the door open for her, and she and another man tumbled out of the bar and onto the asphalt, laughing hysterically.

Ryana looked down her nose at the pair of them. "Stay with her, Austin. She suits you," she said, and got into her car.

"Oh my God, is that a Bentley? Here?" Missy said, coming to enough to register Ryana's vehicle as she put it in reverse. "No wonder you wanted to date her, Austin."

"Never talk to me again," he growled at her, letting some of his wolf through, and the alcohol allowed the primal part of her to register that. Missy and the strange man both scooted back, realizing they were in danger, even if they couldn't have pinpointed why. "I mean it," he warned her, and then got into the Prius.

CHAPTER 28

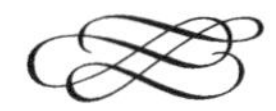

AUSTIN DIDN'T KNOW WHERE HE WAS DRIVING TOO. HE WAS dangerously sober and entirely aware of what had just transpired. He'd told Ryana everything and gotten nothing in return.

Worse than nothing.

He'd been dismissed.

Which is what he'd been afraid of this whole time. Somehow, he'd managed to convince himself he had a chance, when in reality—no. She really was like the moon. Cold and indifferent. Just enough light to make you think you could find your way, but in reality all she was doing was casting deeper shadows.

He couldn't go home; she would be there, and everything would smell like her—but he couldn't go out to another bar and risk running into Missy again, or any of the other numerous women like her.

So when he found himself on the interstate driving to nowhere and his phone buzzed, he checked it, of course. It was a text, from Dom.

Can you go out? Or are you too broken?

He took his eyes off the road long enough to type back one word: *Where.*

. . .

TWENTY MINUTES LATER, Austin was parked two spots down from Dominic's ridiculous Humvee at a rest stop.

"I know you need serious shocks, man, but really?" he asked, slamming the door of the Prius shut behind him and walking over—just as an unexpected passenger emerged from Dom's ride.

Baran.

He got into the back of the vehicle without saying anything.

All of Austin's muscles flexed in sinuous synchrony, as visions of killing Baran and taking his head home to Ryana on a platter as a peace offering danced in his mind.

"You look a damn sight better than I thought you would," Dom said through the door the Kagaroth had left open. Austin knew if he killed Baran now, he'd cost Dominic four million dollars—and he had no question that the rhino-shifter would, in turn, kill him. "Come on," Dom prompted, patting the seat. "Load up—the bird is on the move."

"The bird?" Austin asked, grabbing hold of the door to pull himself inside the cab. Dominic's Humvee smelled like him, posh cologne with an undercurrent of zoo and gun oil. His Humvee looked much the same as Damian's 'tour bus', and Austin had no doubt there were weapons under every seat. The only thing that spoke kindly of its owner was a brave hula girl wobbling on his dash with an arm out, like she was waving at men gone off to war.

"Yeah, they finally told me what they're after," Dominic said, giving him a grin and clapping his shoulder with a meaty hand. The sensation of it rippled painfully through all of Austin's bruises and his still healing ribs. "I made him let you ride shotgun." Dominic laughed and pulled his absurd vehicle back on the road.

DRIVING for the first time was hard enough. Driving while crying was harder.

Tears made everything blurry, and Ryana was tempted to disobey speed limits so that the wind whipping by would dry them. *If she drove fast enough, maybe she wouldn't be crying at all.*

She felt Lyka rearranging her position in her hair to bring her beak to her ear. "Princess? Are you well?"

"No, Lyka. I am not."

Because everything that Austin had said had burned her like she'd opened the furnace door in her laboratory without her blast shield on. It'd been so bright and white and felt so unreal that she'd been relieved when the stupid human girl had reappeared to eclipse him and all his horrific generosity of spirit. His intolerable kindness. Naming her his *moon*—tantamount to admitting he was in love. Worse than mates even; at least with mates there was magic and fate involved.

But love? Love you talked yourself into, *all on your own.*

Who ever said such things to anyone else, without looking to gain?

Even Baran had not lied so fluidly as that!

But Austin wasn't lying. That was how he actually felt, she knew. She could feel the honesty radiating from him like some sort of bumpkin peasant in a comedic play. Because who else got to admit their feelings without armor?

People who had nothing to lose!

Pathetic people. People who were weak. People who could let other people hurt them.

And she was none of those.

Not anymore. Not ever again.

And that's why she was crying, she told herself. She wasn't hurt by Austin, by his earnest attempts to make her let him in. No—she was crying because once upon a time she'd been the girl those words could have worked on.

But now that girl was dead, and all there was for it was to mourn her.

"I wish to be dressed in black, Lyka," she told her guardian—and then looked down, and it was so.

"So about this 'bird,'" Austin asked, knowing full well that Dominic called all women *birds*, because American women found his English accent charming and didn't realize it meant he'd forgotten their names.

Dominic jerked his chin at the rear view. "I'll let the boss explain," he said. Austin glanced up and saw Baran's dark eyes narrowed, and peering back.

"We can trace her magical energy, when it's present—but it hasn't been present for quite some time." Austin fought not to tense. *Because the vast majority of the time, Ryana was safe inside Damian's castle....* The Kagaroth leaned forward. "So we need to make the most of it."

"Where are we going?" Austin asked.

Baran flashed a glowing blue object at him. "Don't know yet. She's on the move. We're following her. Head northeast, Dom."

"Sure thing." Dominic took a sudden turn at speed, which made his hula girl shimmy.

Austin pulled out his phone. Dominic, missing nothing, glanced over. "Sorry—the old man buzzed," he explained.

"Look at you, all leashed," Dominic teased.

"Pays the bills," Austin muttered, swiping his screen on, quickly texting Jamison.

I'm in a car with Dominic and the leader of the Kagaroth. They're tracking Ryana—take control of her car and drive it home immediately.

The three dots of Jamison's imminent response spun up: *Bentley's not wired up for remote driving yet—no can do,* followed by, *Need a team?*

Yes. Trace her phone. Bring everyone. He ground his teeth together. What did it matter now? *Even Damian.*

On it, Jamison texted back.

"So domestic," Dominic said with an eyeroll as Austin put away his phone.

"I'd tell you I like the health insurance, but we both know I don't give a shit," Austin growled. He turned in the seat to allow himself to take Baran in like he hadn't been able to after the fight. He was shorter than Austin, but not by much, though his chest and shoulders were just as wide. What history did he have with Ryana, and just how fast could he wring it out of him?

"I'm surprised you made it out tonight," Baran said.

"You mean you're surprised your men didn't kill me," Austin corrected him. The thought of surging into the backseat and pummeling the other man until he confessed to whatever had hurt Ryana loomed large—but Dominic's presence stopped him, again. "How many of them are there, and where are they, anyhow?"

"My men will meet us there," Baran said, without admitting to their number. "We were out canvassing when we got the signal, and we're closest, but no one's going after her alone. She's much too dangerous for that."

Austin grunted. As much as he hated the other man, he was right.

AUSTIN WAS surprised when they took the off-ramp for the forest. "Out here?" Why on earth would Ryana come here without him?

"Birds like nature, perhaps?" Dominic shrugged, pulling onto the final dirt road that led in. There was no light except for the same half-full moon up above that'd watched him get turned down in a parking lot. Austin got out of the Humvee and spotted Ryana's empty Bentley with the top down, parked by the trail head.

Before he could process that, two vans drove in. Their doors slid open and armored Kagaroth poured out with boxes of supplies on their shoulders, and Baran began ordering them in his own tongue.

Each team gets a net. No one goes out alone. You spot her, you signal the rest of us, then you take her down. She's dangerous—she'll kill you without a second thought. But we need her alive, so if you kill her—I'll kill you.

Baran went from group to group, double-checking the signals on the blue-glowing objects they each had, then returned to Austin and Dominic. "These are for the two of you," he said, handing over what Austin realized now was some kind of magical compass. "They'll help you find her." Austin swung the device around, but its blue glowing arrow was pointed straight into the woods.

At Ryana.

Austin looked between the compass and the moon. He knew the trails here like the back of his hand, or paw, depending on the night, and Ryana's safety depended on him being the first to find her. He wouldn't be able to do that though, as a human—but he wouldn't be able to hold the compass, as a wolf. He stared into the darkness of the woods and felt something stirring inside of him, not his wolf's familiar anticipation of *running!* and *hunt!* but the knowledge that his mate was out there, and she needed his protection.

And maybe because the moon was half out, and he was chasing *his* moon, he felt her presence. No matter what she'd told him in the parking lot, they were still connected by a solitary silver thread that would, if it were real, glint beneath the moonlight.

She'd never be able to hide from him again.

"Thanks," he said, putting the compass into his pocket—and then started to take off his shirt. "If I see her—I'll howl."

He undressed quickly, kicking his things to the side, and then felt the moonlight hitting his skin. Dominic knew what he was doing immediately.

"This is why I wanted him along, see?" Austin heard the rhino-shifter tell Baran as his wolf sprung out of him.

Yeah it hurt, and yeah, it tore, but like so many things in life—tattoos, childbirth (he'd been told), and love (he didn't know if this was true yet, but he did fucking hope)—the pain was worth it, once he was on the other side. He and his wolf didn't have any hang-ups like Damian and his dragon—for him, being his wolf was always thrilling. It washed away all of his problems with humanity. His wolf never had to pay bills, or figure out what was for lunch, or wonder if anyone else liked him.

All he had to do was be himself and live in the *now-now-now.*

He made a show of sniffing the air, like he couldn't already scent her, then raced into the underbrush where he knew they couldn't follow.

. . .

OTHER CREATURES of the night startled from his path. He wasn't worried about scaring them; finding *her* was paramount. He lowered his head and bowled through brush, feeling shrubbery scrape against his sides and face and leaf litter slide beneath his claws. He took a path on purpose that he knew the others wouldn't be able to follow—he had to get to *her* first.

His mate.

The urges and sensations he'd felt as a man were now so much more—because his wolf didn't question itself, and it didn't live in denial.

She was meant for him. Of course she was his. Just as he was hers.

And he wanted *her.*

His wolf cared nothing for his human reality, his lies of omission, or the way she'd just pushed him away. It had no doubts. It only knew *want* and *desire* and *protect* and *live* for *her.*

Her light, mossy scent was even easier to follow now as a wolf, and he could hear her running from him up ahead. She'd probably heard him coming for the last quarter mile and he couldn't help it, all he wanted to do was to see her again and be known and—he raced alongside her, up the side of a hill and past her until he could leap down in front of her in a clearing.

She stopped, with one hand to her chest, and the other with Lyka the size of a vulture on her wrist as she held the red bird out like a weapon. She was dressed in all black, but the moon's light still hit her face and—she was breathtaking. He sat on his haunches to take her in, his jaw at the level of her chest. He licked his chops and whined before panting again, tongue out, muzzle open, in the way that made it easier for him to breathe all of her in, her light sweat and panic and oncoming anger.

"Austin?" she asked quietly. He watched her eyes go wide by moonlight, frightened before recognizing him. "Austin!" she hissed. "Why are you here? You scared me!"

He went still and listened. He'd raced ahead of the others, but he knew with their compasses he wouldn't beat them for long. He rose up and took a step nearer her—and she took a step back.

Even though she knew it was him.

Possibly *because* she knew it was him.

But his wolf wasn't worried even by that—he just went to his belly and crawled up to her, as though he were digging his way underneath the walls she'd erected around herself, until his head was at her feet, looking up.

"What are you doing?" she asked him.

She wasn't running anymore, but he couldn't read her in the moonlight. He rose up slowly, running his head beneath her free hand.

"No, I will not pet you," she said, making to cross her arms again—when he nipped her wrist. Biting it, without breaking the skin. "Austin!" she said, turning his name into a curse.

He growled in warning, hoping she would keep her voice down, as he tugged her forward. She'd already been going the right direction on accident, they just needed to keep taking this trail on purpose, but they had to hurry—

"This isn't funny," she said. Lyka had hopped onto the top of his head, her claws digging into his scalp as she clamped her beak on his ear in retaliation when they all heard the sound of a distant twig breaking. Followed by a second one, and a man shouting a direction. Ryana gasped quietly, then put her hand over her mouth. "Is that why you're here?" she mouthed to Austin, rather than breathe it.

He let go of her wrist and urged her on, running the side of his body against her thigh in the direction she should go.

"Lyka, to me," she whispered, and followed him.

He jogged as fast as it was safe for her to travel down the trail—they had to get to their destination before any of the men—but it was dark, and for all her draconic traits, Ryana was not meant for moonlight. He had to bite back a whine of worry any time she stumbled, but using magic to light their path would as good as announce them. She started to put her hand on his back to guide her, and it was all he could do to not lean into it, wishing she would stroke it down the length of him—and then she lost her footing again and used it to hold on.

He wound himself around her in an instant, so that she fell against him and not the ground, as she caught her breath, both arms braced against his side. He lay down again in front of her, nuzzling her thigh with his muzzle, hoping that she would understand.

She did. "Won't I hurt you?"

He thumped his head against her leg and stared at her.

"No. I guess not," she whispered to herself—and then grabbed hold of the fur over each of his shoulders, and straddled him.

There was no dignified way to do it; a wolf was not a horse no matter how large, and she had no saddle besides—so Ryana was just lying across his broad back with her arms wrapped around his throat, clinging with her thighs and knees. Her heels dug along his sides, but he could travel faster and safer this way, and all he had to do was clear another half mile.

He could've been worried about the oncoming threat, or how he would manage to get back out again alone, but while his wolf was cunning it was also exuberant. Feeling his mate pressed against him, trusting in him as he kept her safe—was there anything else in the world more pure?

The trail he was running on ended, opening out to a rocky beach about a hundred feet from the edge of the lake he hadn't shown her in the rain.

"Oh no," he heard her whisper, as he pulled up short, not bounding out into the open flatness between them and the water's edge. He could see faint dots of glowing blue to their right—a group of Kagaroth he hadn't accounted for had come in at the park's far entrance, much closer to this side.

We're near! shouted one of them, urging on the others.

"Why did you bring us here? To be trapped?" she asked him, sliding off of his back to land quietly on her feet, one hand still wrapped in his fur.

He looked out at the water and whined. He knew that Damian could use water like mirrors for transport, and tonight was a still night. The moon's reflection on the lake's surface was perfect—until one of the oncoming Kagaroth picked up a rock and threw it in with a plunk.

Austin nudged her sideways, into the trees beside the trail, before shaking himself free of her and sliding out into the darkness. He'd fought four of them as a human and survived, perhaps because they hadn't been allowed to kill him.

Now it was time for him to take on four of them, as a wolf.

The fur of his belly dragged along the rocky shore, its mottled browns and blacks serving him in good stead—he probably looked like an aggregation of larger stones that wind and time hadn't chipped down. He slunk in parallel to them as they headed for Ryana, excitedly following their compass, until he'd circled around behind them and he could see their backs.

They were covered in that stupid armor, but he would have the element of surprise, and as a wolf he was double any of their individual weights.... He rose up and raced at them, and they heard him, but by the time they turned around he'd already leapt on the closest one's back, knocking him to the ground and grinding him sideways so that the eyeholes of his helmet filled up with gritty rocks.

He sprang off of that one's back, rammed his full weight into another's side, and heard a knee pop and break—then whipped his muzzle around to snarl at the remaining two, before jumping forward and taking the next nearest man down, twisting his head to grab the man's helmet inside his jaw, crushing it with an impossibly strong bite as the man inside screamed and blood poured out. By then the last one was running and shouting in panic—straight for the trail where he'd hidden Ryana.

Austin raced after him, and it was clear he was going to catch up—when Lyka flew out, heading straight for the man's chest, looking like a blood-colored comet, changing up to the size of bird that'd threatened Austin that first ill-fated night in Ryana's bed. Her talons pierced the man's chest easily, before lifting him up in the air with two strong wingbeats and shaking him as he screamed until he was dead.

Austin scanned their surroundings and made out more flickering blue lights heading for their location. He ran for Ryana's side—he had to get her to the water *now*.

Then he heard a familiar howl, travelling across the park.

Zach!

He howled back, urging his brother to hurry, as he reached Ryana. Lyka had hopped away from the man she'd killed, to finish off the others he'd downed. Austin grabbed Ryana's wrist and tugged, and she ran alongside him toward the water, the rocks of the beach sifting loudly beneath her feet.

I've got her!

I see her!

Kagaroth started reporting in as Lyka flew back to protect Ryana, downsizing to circle warily overhead.

They reached the water's edge and he willed her to understand, as Kagaroth began pouring out of the woods and running for them, the moonlight glinting off of the weapons and nets they held evilly. Lyka sized up again as the first one tossed its net at them, diving aside to caw her defiance as the others approached.

And then one of the Kagaroth shouted, "Ryana!"

Austin heard her catch her breath, as Lyka wove and dove as she was able, dodging their attacks, stopping their thrown weapons, trying to protect her mistress at all costs.

Ryana, come here! Baran called for her, as Lyka killed another Kagaroth, and Austin felt the water at his feet. If he backed up much more he'd make too many ripples—he knew the water needed to be flat and smooth for magic work.

You're still mine, Ryana! Baran shouted. *And we both know it!*

Austin fought down his anger at the other man, his wolf's urges to *kill* and *tear,* and he whined instead, running his muzzle up the outside of Ryana's thigh, begging her to release whatever hold Baran had on her and realize that escape was close.

And then there were too many of them, too many nets, too much magic, and Lyka shrieked a warning, before looking back—not at Ryana, but at him, and he knew in the manner of beasts what it was she wanted done. He watched Lyka splinter herself into a hundred smaller birds, a whole flock of them swirling and attacking, providing perfect cover, as he rounded in front of Ryana and shoulder bumped her into the lake.

She screamed in surprise and frustration as she fell into the water and—thanks to Lyka—disappeared without a splash. He caught a glimpse of her room in the water, and then the lake was just a lake again, reflecting only the moon.

By the time Austin's attention returned to Lyka—she was bound up in netting and the Kagaroth were congratulating one another.

On…what?

Then Dominic was there and—Austin realized that he'd assumed wrong.

They really had been after the bird, the *actual* bird, all this time.

One of the Kagaroth put his hand on the netting that held Lyka and pulled a line down through the night, like he was undoing a zipper—and eerie rift-light poured through. He took the ball of netting containing Lyka and stepped into the light, then zipped it up behind him.

Austin sat back on his haunches, stunned. He knew Ryana was safe, but Lyka had just been kidnapped.

CHAPTER 29

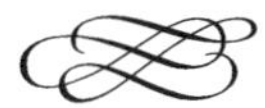

RYANA WAS UNCEREMONIOUSLY DUMPED ONTO HER BEDROOM FLOOR, still dressed in black, and now freezing. She whirled to look at the mirror behind her and saw nothing but the surface of the lake and the moon—and as she ran bodily back toward it, it went black and she only barely stopped herself before crashing into its glass.

"Lyka?" she looked around the room, and felt the looseness of her hair. "Lyka!"

Lyka was back there—with Austin. Surely he would look out for her, and she for him.

She knelt in front of the mirror and waved her hands at it with magical power, wanting to see them. But the forest she'd just left was dark and there'd been nothing reflective in it but the water, which of course she wouldn't be able to see them in—but surely everything was fine.

It had to be.

But the longer she waited to hear news of them, the worse things felt—not having Lyka near her for the first time in almost her entire life—it felt like she'd lost part of herself. Her guardian's steady companionship had gotten her through so much that she couldn't imagine living without her.

"Lyka?" Ryana whispered to the mirror, and cast her powers out again, but there was no response. "Grim?" she asked, and her brother's cat appeared. He took one look at her and bounded into her lap.

SHE WAS STILL CASTING out with her magic an hour later, with Grim nearby, when she heard her name bellowed from the lower level of the house. "RYANA!" She ran out of her bedroom and flew down the stairs, Grim racing by her side. Damian stood in the house's foyer and she flung herself at him. He caught her and held her tight, smoothing back her hair. "Are you all right?"

Ryana looked up at him—and then at everyone else who came in the door, one by one, each of them somber—Jamison, Mills, Max, Zach, and Andi. Grim inspected each of them in turn. "Where's Lyka?"

Damian glowered down at her—angry not at her, she knew, but the situation. "Is she not with you?"

"No."

He made a low rumbling sound in his chest—one which Grim picked up and made as well, a much larger sound than should've been possible from a cat his current size. "Where is she then?"

"She sent me home through the lake." Ryana pointed up the stairs to her bedroom and the mirror, but her hand trembled. Was this place really home? Could any place be, without her guardian? "She and Austin were fighting the Kagaroth, and there were so many of them—did you see them?"

Damian's frown only grew. "No," he said and looked to Zach. "Austin's second howl sent us away."

"He said you were safe, and that we needed to leave," Zach said. "I'm sure of it."

"Then…where is he? And where is Lyka?" she asked.

Grim yowled concern at Damian as Zach started pacing.

"Surely they're with each other," the other werewolf said.

Everyone else started talking amongst themselves, but Ryana could only hear the sound of her own blood rushing in her ears, like she was submerged beneath a waterfall. How could she survive without Lyka at her side? Who would watch out for her? Who could she trust?

And then the front door opened one more time, revealing Austin. She disengaged from Damian's arms to run for him, but she knew just by looking at his face that he hadn't brought Lyka back. "Where is she?" She still had to ask, because she needed to hear him say the words.

"Ryana," he began, holding up his empty hands, as Grim shifted himself to be hip-height beside her, staring the werewolf down, a Siamese cat the size of a tiger.

But before Grimalkin could attack, she threw herself at Austin, pummeling his chest with her fists and not caring that his ribs were barely healed. "Where is she? What did you let happen to her? How could you?"

He stood there, implacable, as she took all of her frustrations out at him, until she was sobbing in her grief and hitting him just because she didn't know what else to do or how to act.

"Ryana," he tried again, setting his hands on her shoulders, but she shook him off and stepped back.

"What happened?" Damian demanded from behind her, as she sagged into Grimalkin's furry side.

"The Kagaroth weren't here for you, Ryana." Austin answered her, and not her brother. "They were here for Lyka, all along. They wound her up in some sort of magical netting, and then took her away, through a rift."

"Where?" she demanded.

"I didn't get to see through it, to the other side." He looked to Jamison for confirmation.

"We did register a small rift, but then it healed itself—and it didn't trigger a Conjunction…."

"A Conjunction?" Austin asked.

Ryana blew past his concern. "She's…gone?" The words were like rocks in her throat. Lyka's absence explained why she felt so hollow, why her heart ached, why her eyes burned. Austin reached for her. Grimalkin growled, but she stepped back. "Don't you *dare* touch me."

"Wings," he said, in an apologetic tone—and then Damian stepped in.

"And whose amazing idea was it to not inform me that there were Kagaroth on earth?" he asked, twisting to include their full assembly.

Ryana closed her eyes. Once again everything was her fault, and she had no one else to blame, and this time instead of costing her her pride, it'd cost her her only friend.

"Mine," Austin said.

Ryana felt Damian's hand on her shoulder, gently moving her aside.

"And why the fuck would you do that?" he asked the werewolf.

Austin met his gaze with equal steel. "You know why."

Damian's jaw ground as his nostrils flared. "Get out of my house."

"Damian," Andi said, running up to put a hand on his arm.

"He endangered my sister, Andi—and all of the rest of you," Damian said, looking at everyone else, daring them to question him. One by one their gazes flickered to her, to see what she would say, if she was going to tell her brother the truth or just let Austin hang there —and what she wanted more than anything else in the world, apart from Lyka's safe return, was for that to be true. It could be, *should be,* Austin's fault, because the thought that it was hers alone was just too much to bear.

"I'm not letting you kick him out, Damian," Andi said, in a tone that was clearly used to being listened too.

"No, I need to go. It's better this way," Austin said, shrugging off Andi's concern. He gave Ryana one last look that said everything—how sorry he was he'd hurt her, and how sorry he was she'd hurt him —and then he was out the door, with Zach running after.

Damian stared after him for a time, fuming, with Grimalkin at his side in complete agreement—and Ryana knew if Damian so much as moved, Grimalkin would bound out and bring the werewolf down.

But while angry…her brother was not cruel. Which was good. It meant he wouldn't hate her later, when he found losing Lyka was her own fool fault.

Andi looked back at her. "Are you going to be all right, Ryana?"

She stood there, feeling empty, inside and out. She didn't belong in the Realms, she didn't belong here, and there was no one she belonged by. "I don't think so."

Andi let go of Damian to wrap an arm around her shoulders and pull her away. "Come on, Ryana. Let's go sit down."

ANDI PULLED her through the castle until they wound up in one of its libraries, which somehow, even paneled in dark wood, managed to be warm and inviting. There were leather couches and chairs with just the right amount of wear to be comfortable, the red rug on the floor was a little scuffed, and perhaps most importantly, it had a small sink and hot tap in the corner, to facilitate making tea.

Andi put Ryana in a chair and then went to make her some. Soon the scent of brewing Earl Grey filled the room, and the human returned with Ryana's favorite.

Ryana realized with a little shame she couldn't even return the favor if she wanted to—she had no idea which kind of tea the dark-haired girl liked.

"Don't think I don't know what you're doing," Ryana told her, as Andi offered her the mug.

"What's that?" Andi asked, sitting nearby.

Ryana frowned down at her reflection in the tea. "Being nice to me on purpose. I know that it's your job." When she next looked up, she caught Andi giving her a lopsided grin.

"That's what you think my job is?" Andi inquired, clearly trying not to laugh.

"Yes," Ryana said, frowning harder. "You go to work and are nice to people. By keeping them alive."

"Ahh. Well, I'm not *always* nice," Andi confessed. "Sometimes, I get to pull off band-aids really fast."

Ryana knew Andi was teasing, she could see it glittering in her eyes, but she wasn't in on the joke. *Again.* "I don't think I know what a band-aid is."

Andi gently took the mug from Ryana's hands and put it on the floor beside their feet. "Ryana, can I tell you something that I tell my patients' visitors a lot, in a professional capacity?"

Ryana sighed. "I suppose—as long as you charge my brother for the pleasure."

"Oh he'll pay, no doubt," Andi said, before continuing. "But really, Ryana, it's this—it is not your fault."

Ryana took a deep inhale. *The presumption of this human!* The only thing standing between Andi right now and certain death was the fact that she was mated to her brother and that Lyka. Was. Gone.

Otherwise, if someone else had treated her like that, back in the palace, she'd have had her bird go and snap their neck.

Of course it wasn't her fault, everything that'd happened to her—except for all the times it incontrovertibly *was.*

Because if she'd never fallen for Baran, Lyka would still be here! And maybe she and Lyka would be back in their palace still, where they belonged, and people would be forced to be nice to her, and she would feel safe knowing that they were nice to her because they had to be, not for all the reasons Austin played along.

"That's it? All you have to tell me?" Ryana felt her eyebrows crawl up her forehead. She gestured behind herself blindly. "They're all out there planning retribution, while I've been relegated to take advice from a mere human, and that's all you've got? 'It's not my fault?'" she said, making fun of Andi's tone.

"Yep," Andi said, with a soft nod. "I know how you and your brother were raised, Ryana. He's told me enough stories. All of that shit? Was *not your fault.* And anything happening now because of that shit? Same-fucking-same."

"I have agency, human," she snarled.

"I know it. I've seen it. But I've also seen this before, so many times," she said, before biting her lips and looking at Ryana. "If you can't stop whipping yourself over whatever it is that you think you've done—you're not going to heal. And neither are the people that you care about. You're not God, Ryana, you can't predict everything, and you made the best decisions you could in the past. I know you're a good person, and I know you'd never do anything cruelly wrong.

Mostly. For the Realms versions of that, at least." Andi reached over and caught her hands. Ryana frowned at the familiarity of the gesture, but didn't pull away. "It's just that sometimes bad things happen anyhow, despite all our best efforts. And then you have to choose, whether or not to live in the past or to work toward the future."

"And what if you don't have a future anymore?" she asked. It would explain why living in her past was so much more comfortable....

"Then you make one. And you let us help you." Ryana looked down at the ground as Andi squeezed her hands tight. She could finally understand why this was the other woman's profession—and why there was nothing like it, in the Realms. "You're not alone, Ryana, okay? I know it may feel like that, especially now, but you're really not."

Grimalkin bounded in and jumped up on her lap as if to agree with Andi, and Damian came in shortly after. Ryana shook herself free of Andi's grip and composed herself as a princess should.

"Mills told me the truth Ry," Damian said, dragging another chair over. "Don't be mad, she couldn't help herself." He took a long moment, studying her. "Did they hunt Lyka in the Realms, as well?"

She closed her eyes tightly. Even more humiliating than the thought of her being kidnapped for ransom was the thought that Baran had only gotten close to her because of her guardian. "Yes," she admitted. "Not that long ago. When things began to splinter. At the time...I thought they were after me. Now, though, I realize they were always after her."

Her brother suddenly seemed three sizes larger as he loomed with concern. "Did they hurt you?"

"Nothing but my pride." She'd heard Baran's voice in the woods tonight, she was sure of it—she hadn't even managed to kill him right!

And if she had, Lyka might still be here.

"And are you going to apologize to Austin?" Andi asked him. Damian made a grumbling sound—echoed quickly by Grimalkin in Ryana's lap. "Cut that out you two," she tsked.

Ryana had no idea how her brother had found someone who was both willing to put up with him and who was strong enough to do so

—and Damian looked to her for a response. "I would appreciate the space, if it's all right."

He nodded. "I warned Austin once that I would always take your side—I meant it."

"Thank you." She inhaled deeply and then let the breath go. "What's next?"

"I'm not sure. Obviously we don't want the Kagaroth causing a Conjunction—but if we don't know where they are, or what they're doing with Lyka, I'm not sure that we can stop them. We'll warn the other Wardens accordingly, but Austin was wrong to howl us away tonight." Damian's mood darkened like their father's used to, taking space up in the room around them, just like an oncoming storm. "I should've changed and flown in."

Andi tilted her head and gave him a pointed look. "Austin wouldn't have wanted you to change unless you absolutely had to."

His eyes narrowed. "But if I had changed, we might know where Lyka is."

Ryana scooted Grimalkin down and stood. "Don't worry, Andi; beating ourselves up is a familial trait."

"I'd noticed," Andi said, also standing, giving her a soft smile before taking Damian's arm. "Come on, dragon. I'm jet-lagged, and we didn't even use a jet." And despite knowing that the world might explode in terrors at any moment, Damian smiled at Andi as though she were the sun and the moon and all the stars in the sky. Watching them together set something that was not pretty seething inside Ryana's stomach. She didn't want to destroy what they had—truly, for her brother, she only wanted good things—but she also didn't want to have to see how much she was missing.

Especially knowing that she was going to be going up to her bedroom alone for the first time, ever since she was a small child.

"Good night, Ryana," Andi called back when they were halfway across the room. "We'll see you tomorrow."

Ryana looked down at Grim winding around her ankles in concern. "I suppose that just leaves us, then," she told him, and much to her relief, he followed her.

CHAPTER 30

ZACH HAD FLUNG A KEYCARD TO BLACKWOOD INDUSTRY'S PENTHOUSE suite into his car before he'd been able to get away, so Austin knew he had a place to stay—he just didn't want to go there.

He drove down from the Briars at speed, putting the Prius through its paces, and then zoomed off into the night, using all of his shifter senses to keep him safe while he barely paid attention to any traffic rules.

After he'd feathered the Prius's breaks to briefly acknowledge a third red light, he heard the sound of sirens coming up behind him.

Fuck.

Given the choice between spending the night in jail for going 105 in a 25 zone, versus Damian's penthouse suite, he definitely would've chosen the latter.

The red and blue lights approached in his rear view, and he pulled over, knowing that he'd been caught—*how much worse could tonight actually get?* Then the cop, on a motorcycle, blazed past him, lights still flashing, racing after someone else.

He pulled back onto the road and kept driving, this time at a more reasonable speed. The relief he felt at not getting a ticket was just a drop in an ocean of pain—it changed nothing, really.

Nothing could.

Three blocks later, he found what the cop had been flying toward —there was a car in the middle of an intersection. It'd been hit and had flipped over. Whatever had hit it was gone, but there were other cars stopped nearby with horrified drivers milling about, unsure of what to do.

Austin parked his car and strode up, his boots crunching on glass, and the cop that'd just passed him looked back at him. "Stay back," the cop warned.

Austin held both hands up. "I used to be a paramedic," he explained. "Anything I can do?"

The cop's eyes were shadowed by his motorcycle helmet. "Not unless you've got a jaws of life on you," the cop said.

"No," Austin said, but walked up to the wreck nonetheless. He crouched down and looked in, where an elderly woman was trapped, moaning, half dangling from the ceiling. There was no way to get her out—the ceiling of the car was half-collapsed on her.

"The guy who did it just drove off!" one of the onlookers was telling the cop, who was busy tapping the radio on his shoulder and calling something in. Austin gave a quick look around, noticed no one was watching him, and went for the door. Metal whined as it slid over metal, forced open by his shifter-strength—enough for him to get inside and hit the seatbelt button, catching the woman as she fell to pull her out.

"How did you do that?" the policeman asked him, disbelievingly.

"The door hinge must've broken in the crash," he said, carefully laying the woman straight. He didn't smell any gasoline, and he heard the sounds of distant sirens—real paramedics would be here shortly.

In the chaos that followed as a firetruck pulled in, he went back to his car, wheeled it around, and drove away, thinking the whole time as he headed for Blackwood Industry's skyscraper.

He'd probably just helped saved someone's grandma.

And that should actually make him feel good.

Only it didn't.

Because what good was saving other people if he couldn't save his relationship with his mate?

RYANA TOSSED and turned that first night, and the next, and while Grim tried to be helpful, she couldn't always understand what he wanted and she knew he was just a stand-in, anyhow. There were no more rifts, according to Mills and Jamison, and she knew there was always the chance Baran had just taken Lyka back home, never to be seen again.

She contemplated going back to the Realms herself, through a mirror, but if Lyka couldn't come to her, her chances of being able to find the bird and free her there were small—and she couldn't ask Damian for help, if Baran was on the cusp of causing a Conjunction. Their conference room had become a war room, and Damian had had Grim line it with mirrors so all the wardens could coordinate. Zach was embroiled in gathering funding and shipping supplies, Max was creating contingency plans, Jamison was monitoring the entire planet it seemed, Mills was warding munitions and teaching other wardens rift-closing spells. Even Andi was helping by keeping Damian sane as he paced and prepared, his dragon just beneath the surface—because it'd been all hands on deck ever since their first night back from their vacation…for everyone else.

Just not her.

Andi did check in on her, and she ignored the rules of the door color, knocking once or twice a day even if Ryana's door was red, as she'd kept it ever since Austin had gone. But she was easy enough to put off, even if Ryana did appreciate the offers of company and food.

It was despicably kind of her to keep trying, and Ryana wondered when exactly she'd give up—and it occurred to her that maybe she should be rooting for the Conjunction to actually happen, just as something, anything, to put her out of her misery, when she went into her laboratory again.

Out of habit, really, nothing else. She'd let one furnace quench and only left the other on enough to heat the progenitor. She rapped on its box and heard the creature inside tap in the same rhythm back, then sat down atop it like she used to and picked up her notebook from where she'd last set it down.

She'd lied to Austin—she'd never written her final entry on him, about their last time in his bed. She held the notebook in her hands, knowing everything that'd happened to her since her time on Earth began was inside of it—including everything with him. Every touch, every feeling, every hope. And she knew at the time she'd been using it to hide her feelings, even from herself—they were safer from a distance, colder on a page. So she didn't dare open it; it would only make her ache.

But as she shifted the notebook in her hands, the corner of a piece of paper poked out. She tugged it free and realized what it was—an envelope from Austin, his Letter of Intent.

Her first instinct was to protect herself, crumple it up, and throw it into the low furnace behind her, to slowly burn to ash.

But at seeing his handwriting on the outside, announcing that it was a *'letter'*—and then opening the silly thing to find the slip of paper stating: *of intent—Austin*, inside....

Was he still intent on her now, she wondered? Probably.

What a horrible fate it would be to be mated to someone who didn't want you back.

And what a worse fate still to be mated to someone who maybe did—but couldn't show it.

She spread the notebook flat upon her lap and started reading, from the very first page.

By his third day in hiding, Austin had demolished the Blackwood Industry penthouse's extensive bar, but all the alcohol in the world couldn't make him forget he'd been rebuffed by Ryana.

Repeatedly.

It was ironic that he could heal up from almost everything, barring actual decapitation, and yet there was nothing he could do about the wound she'd created when she'd pulled herself out of his life.

The penthouse's alcohol actually didn't cut it. It just applied a thin layer of numbness over the pain, like the skin on a cold gravy, irreparably damaged by thinking too hard—so he did his best not to. He read every book in the penthouse, even though they'd all clearly been supplied in bulk by CEOs-R-Us when the place had been outfitted, and there wasn't a single crack in any of their spines. He was a slow reader, and they weren't that entertaining, but they were words, a trickle of life left by somebody else, like a trail of breadcrumbs to another world where it was still worth breathing.

While he read, he had the TV turned on, so the rooms didn't feel so empty. It'd been a long time since he'd been this alone—even though he was on the top floor of a busy skyscraper, he had no connection to any of the people working below, despite the fact that they all knew Damian by name.

A maid or a secretary—he wasn't sure which—delivered food outside his door three times a day, and he did his best not to ever run into them.

And at night he looked at the moon.

It was hard to avoid—his wolf felt its time coming nearer, he could sense when the moon rose and when it set—and the penthouse had floor-to-ceiling windows all around. There were ways to smoke the glass in the bedroom by twisting dials, but he never wanted to—if he could, he would sleep beneath the moon all night.

And one night he went out and up to the roof, where the helicopter pad was, just to feel it beaming down.

He walked to the edge and looked at the distant ground below. The wind whipping through the cables for the assorted antenna and windsocks sounded like a siren's song, summoning him to jump, and it would've been lying to say he didn't want to.

Then he had the wisdom to look up. It was three nights out from the full moon, and so she was grand above him, and all his thoughts of falling were forgotten—replaced by the urge to fly.

Too bad he'd lost his wings.

But he lay down on the cold cement and watched the moon glitter down and felt its light start to heal him, and when he used Zach's gold card to let himself back into the building an hour later, he felt slightly more whole. He walked down the stairs, down the now-familiar carpeting—and through an unexpected scent. Like clean water, green leaves, and the soft moss of the forest floor.

Half of him rose up to attention, springing up in hope, while the other, wiser, half of him reeled back. He didn't want Ryana to hurt him more—and he didn't want her to lie to him, either—because every single fucking thing she'd said had been true. He'd known they didn't belong together ever since he'd first seen her.

It just hadn't stopped him from trying.

He looked to the end of the hallway, at the elevator's polished, mirror-like doors, and wondered if she was watching him through them. He went into the penthouse, to the office suite where all the books were, grabbed a black marker, and took it back outside to write 'RED' in big thick letters on the door.

He opened the door for his dinner the next day, and beneath the hearty smell of the roasted vegetables and filet mignon the secretary left out for him, he scented someone far, far more delectable.

"Wings," he muttered to himself, glancing up at the penthouse door. Sometime that afternoon an intrepid cleaner had attempted to wipe his 'RED' away and had instead made it ominous and blurry, like half of 'murder' spelled backwards in a horror movie. He sighed, picked his tray up, and wondered just how long she'd keep trying—and what her trying even meant. She had his phone number, like everyone else in the castle—Mills and Andi texted him every day and Zach visited occasionally, just to make sure he was still alive—so she had to know he was doing all right, if she could be bothered to ask anyone.

The next day he woke up late, worked out, took a shower, and walked with a towel wrapped around his waist to pick up his lunch in the hall—and on his way there he found the corner of a green notebook, tucked under his door. He pulled it free—he didn't recognize it, or the handwriting inside, but he knew it had to be Ryana's. It was written in the Realm's language, and he could feel Mills's magic working in his mind to translate it as he began to read her flourished handwriting on the very first page.

Ryana Blackwood's Notebook
Woe be to unauthorized eyes.
Return at all costs or utterly destroy on event of her death.

AND HERE HE'D been thinking she'd been keeping a diary...hopefully his eyes were 'authorized.' He flipped the page—and found a surprising gorgeous, fist-sized, anatomically correct drawing of a heart.

Austin set the notebook down and got dressed quickly. Zach's abominable suits were the only clothing stored here, so he was forced to wear slacks and a dress shirt he didn't bother to button as he returned to the couch. His food outside forgotten, he flipped through pages of her delicate handwriting as he slowly read. They swung from personal memoirs to academic thoughts: one page she was missing her home, the next was full of her feelings about whether or not Andi was good enough for Damian, and the one after that was an overview of the three different ways Mills might be using magic to move her hair, each one with their own separate...prescriptions, almost. Like a kind of algebra, a separate language all its own—annotations that even his magically amplified mind couldn't understand. The entire notebook was like that—she dissected her feelings with the same precision that she considered her magic—and then used her drawings to illustrate them both. The pages spent in supposition on Mills's hair were edged with curly-ques of it that looked lifelike enough to writhe off the page. There were illustrations for the furnaces she ran, or the glasswork she'd had Lyka create for her, so crisp they looked real life

—and two whole pages showed one of Lyka's wings, apparently drawn without any cause, because they were unlabeled. The detail was so incredible it made him gasp.

This was why she was so interested in the tattoos he had, clearly—he'd caught her looking at them more than once. He'd assumed she wasn't used to the idea of tattoos, but now he realized she'd just wanted to see the art more clearly.

All this time, all of this was in her, and he had never known. He was more convinced than ever that she was right, he needed to stay away—it didn't matter how much he wanted her, when he knew there was nothing as deep to him as this, that his whole life could fit on a single page.

Then he got to the part where she started thinking about him.

Not him, really, not at first—he was right—it could've easily been someone like him, interchangeably.

I LAY AWAKE AGAIN last night. There's no use closing my eyes when I'm not interested in sleep.

I don't know what I want instead though.

I just feel...hollow.

Is that a real feeling? Or is that just how I am?

I don't think I know.

But I don't like it.

NOT LONG AFTER that there was a page on which it was clear she was about to make a decision—she'd created four columns, two for her, two for him, and they each had their own 'yesses' and 'nos'. Under his 'yes' was a running list of things she apparently found pleasant about him: *strong, loyal, kind* and underneath his 'no' was the word *wolf* strongly underlined three times. He laughed.

Whereas for her—the reasons he'd say yes to her, when she proposed what she proposed—*beautiful, curious, smart*—and beneath her 'no', only *Baran.*

Austin's hand tightened on the page. He should've killed the Kagaroth when he'd had the chance, his own safety be damned—it didn't matter if he wasn't going to be with Ryana anymore; she just deserved to live freely—and the rest of her notebook only reinforced his beliefs, as she slowly opened up.

On a page with a close-up of an eye, gleaming with glitter and magic, heavily lined, just like the women from the strip club:

Every time I catch him looking at me, he looks a moment too long.
Why does he do that? What does it mean?
What does he gain by staring?

Above a careful drawing of a poison ivy leaf, that she'd also labeled 'Do Not Touch':

We both got rained on today. It was lovely.
The candy on earth is very good.
I wish to be caught in the rain again.

On a page that had a comparison of a Kagaroth's helmet to a Predator's face:

He thinks I am a virgin.
Considering what happened with Baran—I wish I was.
Is it possible to erase your past?
Perhaps that will be my next potion.

The next page he turned he saw himself. She'd drawn him well enough that it could've been a reference for a tattoo—not that anybody had any business getting his face on them, but it had that charisma that good artwork had to it—like she'd somehow managed to capture a little piece of his soul. *There was no rain this time and it was still good,* was the caption beneath it, and he ran his finger over her words.

After that came pages and pages of magical annotations—and then a drawing of her new car. She'd taken her time in shading it, till it looked like it gleamed, and titled it with just one word: *Freedom.*

And then more of her science and experiments—but up in the corner of a page she'd sketched one of his boots. Much like him, it didn't belong there, but it was on her mind, nonetheless. Then the words on the next page faded away halfway down, becoming waves; no, rumpled sheets, like on her bed that night, when she'd first let him in—and several pages after that, two hands entwined. One was clearly his and one was clearly hers, like when he'd held her hand in his above her belly, and he had to flip the page quickly because it was breaking his heart.

There wasn't much after that—just more magical science, and then empty pages, so much of her life without him yet to come.

He heard a soft knock at his door. "Austin?"

He looked up. The day had faded around him. It was evening now, and he was stiff from sitting still so long—and clearly hearing things because—he set the notebook aside and took a deep breath.

Another gentle tap. "Austin? I didn't mean it."

He stood without thinking, like he was compelled, and walked for the door, opening it without undoing the metal security latch.

Ryana was outside, dressed simply for her, in a high-necked red top and a loose knee-length navy skirt. He wondered what she did for clothing now that Lyka was gone, and frowned.

At seeing him frown she licked her lips and looked down. "Were you not hungry?" she asked, trying to tease, as she looked down at the lunch and dinner trays near her feet.

He ignored this tack. "Ryana—why are you here?"

"I thought you'd be happier to see me," she said, daring to look up.

Part of him was. The part of him that she was everything to, the part he'd spent the past five days trying to drink into oblivion and block off with other people's words revivified, attempting to claw out of his chest like a zombie.

But the rest of him was glad they'd left the door latch shut. If just seeing three and a half inches of her did this to him, he knew he wouldn't be able to control himself if they were in the same room.

"I didn't mean it, Austin," she said again.

"Which part?"

"The part where I was mean to you. You didn't deserve that. Assuming there's not some lavender-scented brunette in there right now with you, that is."

"There's three of them. So you should go," he said, summoning all of his fortitude to close the door.

She put her hand out, stopping him. "We both know that's not true." And then she let go.

It would be up to him.

He pushed the door shut and leaned against it on his side with his eyes closed. He couldn't live with himself if he opened it up—but he also couldn't live with himself if he pushed her away. He opened his eyes, and the rising moon loomed large in the penthouse's windows, as if taunting him.

He swung the latch over and pulled the door open. "Come in."

CHAPTER 31

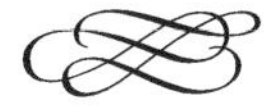

RYANA STEPPED OVER THE TRAYS OF NEGLECTED FOOD IN THE HALLWAY and walked inside, following him toward a couch that faced out over all of downtown, with a fantastic view of the moon. She perched on a cushion, ankles crossed, as he went behind a bar and returned with two full glasses.

"Sorry, it's water. After a few days, Zach cut me off." He gave one to her and then walked to the window and leaned against it, so that it looked like the moon was rising by his side.

"I don't mind," she said, taking a polite sip, leaving a wisp of her lipstick behind. Her notebook was just two cushions away on the couch, and of course he'd read it, he'd had to. "I didn't mean to intrude. Although, officially, you should know that someone painted over the 'red' on your door this morning, and so technically that meant you could be green...." she said, her voice drifting as she shrugged carefully and gave him the world's most fragile smile.

It bounced off of him completely. "Ryana, you know you're not wrong—right?"

She tensed. "About what?"

"How you don't see me in your future. It's because I'm not there."

He considered her from a safe distance, and it was hard to read his face.

"You said I was your moon," she said quietly, more to herself than to him.

"I did—and you are. But I had a chance to reflect on things here alone, Ryana," he said, sweeping his tongue across his teeth. "And I still think you were right."

"I see." She set her drink down on the table beside the couch and folded her hands into her lap.

"I read your notebook, wings. I know you care. Even if you don't know how to let anyone else know that you do. And I think...that that's what I'm meant to be for you. That you were right, maybe I am the man you practice on, so that next time you do this, you're not scared."

Every one of Ryana's instincts kicked in. A lifetime's worth of disappointments and experiences burbled up, remembering everyone who'd betrayed and left her, her so-called friends who'd only tolerated her to be near the throne, Damian's abandonment—even though he'd had to, it still hurt—and culminating in Baran, a man she couldn't even be trusted to kill properly—

And yet somehow this was worse.

Each of his words hit her like a piece of the glass she wanted to pick up and throw across the room at him. She wanted to whip her wings out to shield herself from him, and let them take his blows instead, even if it meant leaving here in tatters—because it would be easier to heal their leather than her soul.

"I understand what that's like, Ryana," he went on. "I'm scared, too."

"Of what?" she asked him venomously, only wanting to strike back.

He stared her down as if he was soaking her in. "Of the moment that you realize you're too good for me."

I already do—the words leapt to mind in both languages, so ready to bounce right off her tongue. If Lyka wasn't around to protect her, then it was up to her to protect herself.

But then she looked at him and her anger wavered. Everyone else in her life may have deserved it...but he didn't...not yet. She roughly exhaled.

"What if...I promise that that won't be tonight?" she asked him.

She watched him hold his breath—and then hold out his hand.

SHE STOOD, crossing the room to him, her spiky heels sinking into the plush carpeting beneath her feet. She put her hand in his first and let him pull her close to stand against him as he wrapped his other arm around her, feeling the heat of his body against hers, and the chill of his glass brushing against her upper arm. His shirt was open, and she liked that, liked feeling the give of his chest hair against her cheek, like it was trying to stop her from coming too close and then relenting, giving up, because close was where she belonged, and he was *stupid* for thinking that he should push her away.

But how could she convince him that he was good enough? That he was wrong? His head bowed over hers, and she knew he was smelling her hair—and all there was for it was to show him.

She ran her hands up his chest at the same time as she looked up into his eyes, and she didn't see any questions, no greens or reds, just shining need. She rocked further up onto her toes, so her lips met his in a silent kiss, and she was afraid for a moment that he might not answer—then he tossed his glass aside, she heard the thump of it landing as his hands came for her hair, to press her mouth to his. She tilted to meet him, to make herself more his, and opened willingly for his tongue, eager for him to taste her and remember everything that he'd forgotten in his silly time alone.

Because she was here, wasn't she? She knew how alchemy worked, how metals could be heated and cooled to transmute into other metals when magic was carefully applied—so couldn't she make him understand that he was good enough for her, by virtue of her wanting him? Using the magic of her presence, the crucible of her body, and the heat that they would surely go on to create?

"Ryana," he said, lifting his mouth from hers to breathe her name like a prayer, and she felt his chest rise and fall beneath her hands.

"Yes?" she asked him, rubbing up against him. The skin of his chest wasn't enough, she wanted to touch much more of him, and wanted more of him against her. As if hearing her unspoken plea, his hands started to roam, but then they paused as he tried to speak.

"The moon—" he began, then shook his head.

"What about it?"

"Nevermind," he whispered.

She cupped his face in her hands. "I'm your moon tonight," she told him. He growled, and his hand rose up her skirt to grab her ass.

After that they were in a tangle—she pushed his shirt back to kiss his shoulders, as his hands tugged her shirt up, while they were both somehow sinking slowly to the ground because the couch was too far away when the floor was already *right there* below them. He undid her bra as she got to feel the strong muscles of his arms again, pulling his shirt down, until he let go of her for long enough to toss it off, kissing her lips before diving his hot mouth against her breasts as she held him to her, gasping as he took her nipples in one by one, sucking them until they pebbled for him, the sensation of each lick travelling through her body to her hips like shooting fire.

"Wolf," she murmured for him and he growled again for her, licking up, pressing her to lie down as his fingers sank to the edges of her skirt. One of his hands dove beneath it as he lay beside her, his one hand protectively beneath her head as he kissed her neck and shoulder, while the hand she couldn't see rose up from below, rough against the inside of her smooth thigh, to cup it at its widest point, and stroke her center with his thumb, up and down, up and down, just like he had her shoulder that one night on the couch, only this time she was aching—and maybe she'd been aching that night, too, she just hadn't known it yet. "Please?" she whispered, running her hand down his wide back as he kept kissing a slow line across her neck, rocking her hips with intent. He bit her breast lightly in response, which she thought might be a 'no'—and then he nodded.

"Yeah. C'mere," he murmured against her, laying back, roughly pulling her on top of him.

At last she could finally see the artwork of all his tattoos clearly—it wasn't a stolen glance, nor was he covered in bruises—and even though his hard-on was firm between her thighs, she couldn't resist asking, "What do they all mean?" as she traced her fingertips against them.

His hand caught hers as if her touch burned and he stared up at her. "It's like your notebook. Only I carry it on my skin."

She let out a soft gasp in wonder. "Why?"

"So that I can never leave it behind. And no one can ever take it away from me."

Ryana blinked, knowing how much of her notebook was dedicated to him currently, and wondered if there were some analog for that, of her, now, on his skin—or maybe all his former girlfriends, if she could only read it properly—but even if that *were* true, he still had some blank skin, left. She carefully leaned forward and kissed the first of the mysterious symbols, tracing it with her tongue, and he moaned.

When he didn't fight her—when she felt him rumble—she moved on and did the next, like she could learn his language this way, using some magical osmosis with her tongue-tip. Her hair spilled out across her shoulders, trailing as she moved her lips, as her breasts rubbed and pulled against him.

"Fuck, Ryana, the moon—" he growled.

"What about it?" she asked innocently, finding a very moon-like symbol above his heart to kiss.

He made a strangled sound and then his hands were on her again, lifting her up easily, spreading her legs higher up his waist as he arched his hips below her to reach around her thighs. She heard the clank of his belt opening, and then the zip of his fly, as she nuzzled her face against his, purring. She licked a line from his neck to his cheek and felt him shudder.

"Please," she whispered into his ear, and Damian was right, it was such a useful word, because a moment later, Austin's hands were under her skirt and tearing her underwear out of his way. She laughed at that, wriggling intentionally against him before lifting herself above him like a cat, holding her heat spread above him, wide.

"God, Ryana," he growled, reaching beneath her skirt to rub

himself against her, and suddenly reading his language was forgotten —she wanted him to write inside of her.

She clawed her fingertips against him as she rocked back, taking just the head of his cock inside. "Wings," he said, moving his hands to grab her waist. "Baby," he hissed, as she slid down.

She threw her head back and ground her hips against him, feeling his hard cock stir inside. Being with him felt right and good—and she realized that she'd taken off her shirt. There was no one else here but the two of them. She rose up so that only the tip of his cock was in her, then dropped down, and heard him grunt in satisfaction as she snapped out her wings.

His hands tensed at her waist. "Jesus, Ryana" he whispered in awe. "Just when I thought I couldn't get harder."

She smiled impishly down, running her hands through his chest hair and back like a kneading cat. "Is that a good thing?"

"Fucking someone who looks like they just stepped out of a Frazetta painting? Yeah, wings. Real good."

She laughed. "You know there used to be portraits of me all over the palace."

His hands stroked up and down her thighs. "I bet. Did you draw any of them?"

"No." She shook her head quickly. "That's just a thing I do, for me."

"You're good at it."

"Thank you. I know."

"You know what else you're good at, Ryana?"

She gazed down at him warily with half-lidded eyes. "I suspect you're about to tell me."

"Making me change," he told her.

She felt herself grow warm, an unexpected sensation deep inside her chest, rocking herself back against him. "Isn't that what your moon is for?"

He nodded below her on the ground, pushing his hips up. "Yeah it is, wings. Precisely."

They started moving against each other then, like the warm-up before a concert, not always perfectly, but soon they shifted to be in tune, each of them playing off the other's movements, her knowing when he pushed up to roll down, and vice versa, until her hips and his thrusts rolled in an undulating wave. She'd never known this kind of friction before, where she wasn't sure where she ended and where he began, more so when she lowered herself on top of him and gave into everything, as he wrapped his arms beneath her wings and around her body, one arm around her waist, the other pressing against her thigh, holding her hips in the perfect place for him to fuck. He kissed her soulfully, his tongue hot and deep, capturing her moans with his mouth and echoing them back to her, and she realized that this, right here, was the closest she'd ever been with any other being, skin to skin, mouth to mouth, heart to heart—heat flooded her body and she twisted her mouth away so she wouldn't bite his tongue. "Austin," she warned him.

He hissed, "Yes," in her ear, and it was too late, she was coming. She screamed into his chest, shuddering against him with each wave, like her hips had a life of their own, as pulses of pleasure ripped through her body, each one stronger than the next, until she was breathless and hoarse. He held her tightly to him, his hips pressed up so she could finish on his cock, until she started to unfurl, slowly relaxing, from her hands on in, gasping for air.

CHAPTER 32

"AUSTIN." RYANA SAID HIS NAME AGAIN AND LIKED IT. MAYBE HIS NAME was the only name she'd ever need to say when she felt like this. For now…for tomorrow…for forever.

He grabbed her ass and pulled her off of him and it took her a moment to process what was happening. "Wait—" she protested. He was still hard, and his wet heat wasn't leaking between her thighs. She rose up above him. "Why?" She'd never come so hard before in her life. For the first time ever she'd held nothing back and—

He shook his head below her. "Because, wings. You only think you want me."

Her hands curled into fists against his stomach as her wings arched. "How *dare* you, Austin."

"Wings," he began, trying to…apologize?

No. That wasn't good enough.

Not when she'd been so close to falling for him.

"So you don't want my *pity?*" she asked, her voice rising, although it hadn't been that at all, and how couldn't he know? She'd done everything tonight but write it for him on a page! "If that's not good enough for you—then you can have my wrath!" She pounded her fists down on him—he caught her wrists before they landed.

"Ryana," he began, in soothing tones, like there was any way he could make it up to her as she tried to wrestle them away from him to hit him, because the only thing she could think to do was to try to hurt him the same way that he'd just hurt her. *How could she have ever done this to herself a second time?* She tried to get herself free and dug her high heels into his thighs until he yelped in surprise and let her go, and then she almost landed a punch on him, but he dodged, yanking himself sideways and sending her tumbling to the ground. She screamed in frustration and kept trying to hurt him—he was stronger than she was, and faster too, but she wasn't interested in her own safety and definitely not fucking his. "Ryana!" he shouted at her, as she spit at his face. "What the fuck?"

"You!" she shouted at him. "I can't believe—I –" she sputtered, unable to finish the sentence, shoving him back with both hands with all her strength. He went with the motion, letting her rock him back bodily, then she turned to crawl away on hands and knees—how could she have been this *fucking stupid twice*—all she had to do was get to her clothing and a mirror—but one of his hands wrapped around her ankle, catching her to drag her on her stomach to his side.

He threw himself on top of her, knocking the wind out of her to pin her down, her wings helplessly splayed out. She gasped for air below him, feeling his greater weight on top of her, trying to get purchase on the ground to shove him off.

"Wings!" he shouted, right in her ear. "What is happening?"

"What is happening is you!" She hit a fist against the ground. "Why?" She twisted her face away from him so he couldn't see her tears. "If I tell you I won't go, why won't you believe me?"

"Because! Ryana—you've walked away from me more times than I can count!"

"But I always came back!" she whispered. She wiped her wet cheeks roughly on the carpet. "Haven't I?" She felt him sag above her, bowing his head to hers. "Haven't I?" she repeated, hoping that he'd realize she was right.

"Ryana," he began slowly, and she braced herself, because even though she was already on the ground, this was going to be it, the second death of all her dreams. "Wings," he said, as she felt him above her, his weight so heavy over her that she had to breathe opposite to him to even get a breath in. She had no idea what he was thinking or doing, or if they were going to spend the rest of the night just like this, and she hated all of that. She wanted answers or, at the least, for him to never know he'd made her cry.

He lifted himself up a little, but she made no moves beneath him—then he traced a tentative hand up her flank and down her wing. It made her shiver, and she pressed her forehead into the carpeting. If he was going to humiliate her, it was no fair for her body to betray her.

"I can't do this, wings." He rose up off of her, and she slowly pushed herself up from the carpeting, not turning around to face him. "I want to make you happy, Ryana. But I also can't let you break me."

She looked over her shoulder and a wing at him, swallowing down a rising sense of betrayal. "Break *you?* How?" When it felt like she'd done all the breaking?

His eyes traveled up and down her, as if he were worried he might never see her again. "By being with you halfway. I can't do that to myself again." His chest heaved and she looked down at the ground, because it was safer. *Oh God, killing Baran was somehow easier than this.* At least his betrayal was a known thing, and she hadn't had to hear him reason through it. "I need something more, Ryana."

She tucked her heels under her skirt and covered herself with her wings, trying to feel both protected and demure.

"Something real," he went on. "Something forever. I can't fuck you like this, this close to the full moon, feeling the way I do, and make it not count." She heard him swallow and take a measured breath. "I can't knot you again, Ryana, and then just walk away. I'm not that strong."

Ryana looked at her empty hands and longed for the simplicity of her lab, where magical chemistry was so much easier than trying to understand an entire other person. "I don't want you to walk away," she whispered. "And I don't want to walk away, either. I don't know if you'd noticed, but it's very hard to walk in these shoes," she said, with a soft snort.

There was another long pause, and then he came near and took her shoulders to gently twist her towards him, ducking as she raised her wing out of his way. "I'd prefer you to stay eagerly, rather than because of a poor choice in footwear," he said.

"This is eager for me, Austin." She moved into a slightly more comfortable position, kicking her legs to be beside her. "I'm sorry if it's not what you're used to. But I'd hazard that I'm not what you're used to either, so—"

"I know," he said, tapping his lap with one hand, and giving her foot a meaningful glance. *Foot,* he told her in her own language, just like that one night.

She delicately kicked it out at him, making sure not to accidentally kick him anywhere important, and he undid all of its fussy buckles, leveraging it off of her foot and throwing it behind his shoulder to wherever his cocktail glass had gone earlier in the evening and she bit back a smile.

Next, he demanded, and she took her foot back, replacing it with the other. It was hard to ignore his thick cock at half-mast as she watched him undo all of the shoe's tiny buckles, before pulling it off and tossing it, too.

There. Now you're free, he told her.

Through the panoramic windows behind him the moon was at his back, higher now, beginning to rise out of view. She stared at it for a long time, wishing it would grant her the strength that it gave him. If only she could just go get her notebook from the couch and draw how she felt for him, because words could be used against you, but art was safe.

Which was why she'd drawn so much of it. Of him. Why she'd willingly gone out with him repeatedly, why she'd invited him into her bed, and why the fear of losing him had truly hurt, once she'd given it the space to.

What if I don't want to be? she asked him, hoping he could hear it in her words.

"Then stay and mean it, Ryana," he said, his voice a low growl—not angry at her, but full of promise. "And don't walk away from me again.

Or run—or crawl. Toward me, maybe," he teased, giving her an easy grin as she finally dared to look down at him. "But never away."

The tension that'd lined his body all night relaxed, shifting into something else, far more legible than his tattoos.

Need.

Desire.

Lust.

She'd mistaken his honesty for simplicity, when the truth was, he'd merely known all along what he wanted: her.

All she'd ever had to do was slow down for long enough to let him catch up.

She flashed him an equally teasing look back, and then intentionally preened, doing her best to sound princess-like without laughing. "In general, I do not crawl." She dusted off the rug burn on her knees dramatically.

"And I would never ask you to, wings," he told her, as his full lips curved into something far more wicked looking than a grin. "That said though—you've ridden me twice now. Fair's fair." One of his hands sank to stroke up his shaft and watching him do that was so raw it made her ache.

She restrained herself, barely, tilting her head, feeling her hair trace over the base of one wing, and pretended to contemplate things. "Fairness is a concept that really only applies on Earth. If you asked people to be fair in the Realms, they would laugh at you."

Then are you saying I should just take what I want? he asked her, momentarily frowning.

Oh no, she promised him. *I'm saying there is no need for you to ask, when what you want is freely given,* getting on her knees to turn around.

AUSTIN WATCHED her turning in front of him, the moonlight glowing off her skin, her wings like angular pieces of night sky in the penthouse's dim light, her scent heavy in the air—he rose up, crossing the short space to be behind her, his cock ready in an instant. He reached down to drag it up between her thighs, anointing its head with her juices, before shoving it into her roughly.

"Ryana," he tried to apologize as she cried out, but he couldn't finish the words, not when he'd needed her this badly. How the *fuck* had he survived this long tonight? His hands grabbed her hips and held her steady for him, taking her in fast deep strokes, making her feel all of him.

She braced herself against his onslaught, her hands planted against the carpet, her back arched, making low moans each time he bottomed out inside her, her wings swaying with the force of his thrusts. He'd spent so long dallying with humans, he'd forgotten what it was like to be with someone who could handle him—and then he realized if he had his way, he was going to get to fuck Ryana madly for the rest of his life.

"Wolf," she groaned, as he sank himself inside of her.

"Wolf," he agreed with a growl—and leaned down to pick her up, turning them both toward the tall windows before setting her back down. "I want to fuck you where she can see." He grabbed her hair into one hand and pulled her head back, making her look out the windows with him. "Under the moonlight, Ryana, so the moon knows you belong to me." He licked a line up her wing and felt her shudder, and then came to some vague form of his senses. Just because she was sticking around didn't mean he shouldn't check in. "Please fucking God be green."

Ryana laughed beneath him, and he loved it. She collapsed onto her forearms while leaving her hips high, and looked back at him through the veil of her hair, smiling openly. "Very green," she promised.

He stroked his hands over her hips, up her back, and down again, while leaving himself hard inside of her, as if trying to convince himself she was really there. "I don't know what I did to deserve you, Ryana."

"I don't think you had to do anything. I think I just needed to believe you." She reached back and found his hand with her own, briefly twining their fingers, like she'd drawn them inside her notebook, and that soft touch meant more to him than anywhere else they met.

She was really here, with him, and she wanted to be.

And even if it was complicated sometimes, or hard, they would both manage to work it out.

He made a joyful noise and leaned down to grab her waist, hauling her back up to all fours, before flipping the hem of her skirt up so that he could see where they joined.

"Don't tear it!" she laughed. "I can't go home naked!"

"Don't tempt me," he mock-growled, leaning over her to lick up the shell of her ear. She gasped at that, and everything inside him took a hairpin turn—common sense had had its moment, but it was through.

He started thrusting again, reaching his arms beneath the curves of her wings to grab at her breasts and hold her to him. Her nipples were hard against his palms and she kept breathing in small sharp bursts with every stroke.

"You feel so good," she confessed, twisting her head to the side like it was something to be ashamed of. "You make *me* feel so good."

He held her pressed onto him then, and found her ear with his lips. "I'm your mate. It's my job." She made a small helpless sound and shuddered against him, not because she was coming, but like she was letting something go. "I can't get enough of you, baby, and I never will," he said, breathing her scent, rubbing his face against the nape of her neck, wishing he could smell like her, always—and then he realized the wolf in him wanted one thing more.

He pulled out of her with a growl.

"What?" she gasped, falling forward as he released. "Austin –" she complained.

But he moved himself to lie down quickly behind her, and then wrapped his arms around her thighs, using them to aim as he kicked forward, his head between her legs, grabbing her ass to pull her pussy down onto his mouth.

In Eloph's name, Austin, she whispered, and he still didn't know precisely what Eloph was, except that it was a deity, and he guessed that was a good thing, as she started to moan. She lifted the hem of her skirt to look at him working her, and he could tell by her expression of shock and awe and maybe a little horror, that this was perhaps the dirtiest thing she'd ever done, no matter that he'd already done it once before.

He grabbed her hips and briefly lifted them up so he could speak. *Any man who didn't want to taste you was a fool,* he said before bringing her back down.

Oh wolf, she whispered as his mouth took up kissing her again. *You may taste me every night.*

He growled up against her, licking her delicious juices, basking in her scent, his hand stroking his cock and keeping it rock hard. She spread her legs wider for him and flung a hand out against the window glass to steady herself, as he took her ass in both hands and made her give him her clit, sucking on it, and then put two, then three, then four fingers inside her, readying her for his knot.

"Austin," she said his name again, breathless and high, ready to cry out.

He snarled and took one last long lick of her, and then pushed himself away and up and back to his knees so he could sheath himself inside of her again. He slid back into her deeply, easily, because this was where he belonged, inside her, the woman he smelled like, the taste of her on his tongue, his name on her lips.

His mate.

He fucked her fiercely as her voice rose, then he curved over once more, settling a hand between her legs to rub her clit as he bit her wing, and then he felt her start to come, hips pulsing as she cried out. He rode her through it for as long as he could stand, feeling her pussy grab him until it was his turn and he plunged himself deep. But even though he knew she knew what she was in for, he still felt compelled to warn her: "Ryana –"

She placed both her hands against the window glass and pushed back, giving all of herself over. "Fill me like only you can, wolf," she gasped.

And then he was cumming into her as pleasures wracked through his body in violent waves, and he thudded into her again and again until his knot flared and that didn't matter; he still wanted to keep fucking her, here, beneath the moonlight, for as long as she would let him, until all of him was empty as he howled.

"Oh, Austin," she sighed when he was finished, breathless and drowsy.

He sagged above her, holding her up by her waist as she removed her hands from the glass one at a time. He kissed a line down her spine. "Can you fold your wings inside?"

She didn't answer, but she did it anyways, and he pulled them both to the ground, catching her with his arm so she could use it for a pillow. The moon was gone now, risen too high to be seen through the windows anymore, but that didn't matter.

He had his moon in his arms, right here.

CHAPTER 33

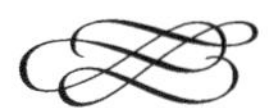

"I've never done anything like that before," she murmured minutes later, after she'd caught her breath. Austin had one leg over her, his hips were twisted against hers, he had an arm around her side, and they were both still on the carpet in front of the panoramic windows. He should've fucked her on the couch, it would've been more comfortable, post-coital.

"Which part?" he asked her.

"All of it."

"Me either," he said and chuckled. He nuzzled his face into her hair. "But I want to do it again. So—be patient with me."

"What do you mean?" she asked, trying to twist to see him.

He closed his eyes and wondered what the hell he'd been thinking, bringing this up now of all moments, but it was definitely too late. "Sometimes…you just seem to assume the worst, is all. But—you don't have to do that with me. I'm never going to hurt you on purpose, Ryana. I may do something stupid, yes, but I can already tell you now, whatever it is, I didn't mean it."

He felt her tense and he tensed too—and then she laughed. "You can't apologize before you've done a thing!"

"Can too," he grumbled, kissing her neck.

"No. That's...it's cheating, is what it is."

Her laughing made him laugh. "Fine. Can't blame a wolf for trying though."

She lifted a hand to run through his hair, scratching her nails against his scalp, and he shivered. "I understand what you're trying to say. I think. And I appreciate it."

"Thank you."

He felt her take a long inhale and then give an even longer sigh. "Do you want to know why I'm like this?"

He smoothed her hair back. "Yeah, wings. I want to know everything about you." He swallowed after he said it. Even though he knew she was his mate, it was still sometimes frightening to be so honest.

"I've only had one other relationship in my life. If it can be called that, really." She squirmed in his arms and he held onto her more tightly, trying to help her settle. "The Kagaroth you met. Baran."

"I figured." After tonight, Austin only knew two things to be true—Ryana was his mate, and the next time he saw Baran he was going to kill him.

She inhaled deeply, as though pained. "He was one of my guards. He took his time. And he made me love him."

Hearing her sum up a relationship that'd clearly caused her so much pain so simply made him ache on her behalf. He started running a protective hand up and down her side.

"It would've been one thing, Austin," she went on, staring out at the clear black night, "if he had been dark and cruel. And then there would've been an excuse. Heavy magic, curses, that sort of thing." He watched her lick her lips and drift with memories.

"But he didn't need to use any of those on me. I went with him willingly. No matter how many warnings my mother gave me, or how often Lyka told me—in her ever-so-polite terms—that it was a bad idea...." Her voice dropped low, and he knew she was feeling the loss of her guardian again. Austin knew he was a poor substitute, but he'd spend the rest of his life protecting her, nonetheless. "Everything was *so* elicit, and I thought we were *so* clever. When he took—no—when I gave him my virginity—we were in my father's throne room. At the time I thought myself quite the rebel, when in fact it was probably just a taste of things to come."

It was easy to imagine headstrong Ryana doing whatever she pleased—just as it was easy to imagine someone else taking advantage of her less jaded, younger self. Austin wished they had a blanket he could wrap her in—lacking that, though, he wrapped her tighter against himself. Ryana nestled back into him, accepting his kindness for what it was and finally letting him give it to her.

That one simple motion was almost as important to him as the sex they'd just had.

"It was years, Austin," she went on quietly. "Years of him making me trust him, and years of him whispering his love. Sometimes he'd take me into the Kagaroth guard room and let me play the gambling games that they all liked, calling me his good luck charm. I turned down the suitors my mother brought on his say so, and then as things fell apart it didn't matter, strangers didn't want me anymore. But that was okay. Because I still had him, I thought." She twined her fingers safe with his. "And then one day he told me to send Lyka away, so it would just be us, and of course I did—I would've done anything to make him happy. I think...maybe you know how that is, yes?"

He nodded his chin against her shoulder. "Yes," he agreed. "Completely."

"Then he pulled me out into the castle garden, and I was so in love I thought we were playing a game. I had no idea I was under real threat—until Lyka flew out and started killing men I didn't even know were there." She paused, and a chill ran down Austin's spine. "And then we both knew we were through."

She freed her hands from his, and he didn't like that, but she needed to look at them for some reason. "He...let me kill him. At the time I thought him offering himself for me, for death, was still some kind of kindness...." She stared at her hands in front of her in disbelief. "And I had to do it." She clenched her hands into fists and looked back up at him. "You have to understand that. In the Realms, there, there is no leniency, no forgiveness. If you show weakness, you are as good as dead. And I had done nothing but been exposed as weak by him, for years." She sank back into the carpeting, as if she'd given up. "I know it must all seem foolishly bloodthirsty to you, but that's how it is."

Austin grunted. "Remind me to explain pack politics to you someday."

"I will," she said with a sigh, gathering her thoughts. "And the worst part of it, Austin, was that even as I was strangling him…I was still in love with him. Even though he'd betrayed me, utterly, and ruined me in every way—"

He growled and held her down. "You're not ruined, Ryana."

"Maybe not on earth, wolf. But after that, I could never rule. No one in the Realms would take me seriously. I'd be mocked—worse than Damian's human mother, even," she said, and Austin felt her give a full-body shudder. "I don't know how Baran survived," she whispered. "And then I come to find that not only was the entirety of our relationship a lie, but he wasn't even doing it for me—he was actually after Lyka?" Her voice went high as she shook her head in dismay, rocking it against Austin's arm.

He had replayed that night in the forest a million times in his mind these past few days, searching for a way it could've ended differently. All he could do now was settle his head against hers and tell her the truth. "I am sorry that she's gone, wings. But I know she would've wanted you to stay safe."

"I know that too. It doesn't make it any better, though." He felt her sigh. "I just wish I hadn't been such a fool. If I had been stronger, or more brave—or even slightly more thorough!—then I could be home right now, ruling it as I was meant to, with Lyka at my side." He felt her shrinking in on herself. "Instead I had to go be simple and weak and fall in love."

He pushed himself up on his arm to look down at her. "Is that what you think I am?"

She pouted. "No. But you have to admit, falling in love means that other people can hurt you."

Which was why she'd gone on to arrange her entire life in an effort to not let it happen again, until she'd gotten lonely, and he'd made her let him in.

"Wings, I'm only going to say this once: fuck that 'weak' shit. Falling in love is the bravest thing you can ever do. It doesn't make you weak—it makes you stronger. Strong enough to do whatever is right for the other person, no matter how it breaks your heart."

"Oh?" she challenged him. "And just how many times have you been in love? How many women are littered behind you, in your illustrious past?"

"I haven't. Been. Before," he admitted reluctantly, and then realized two things—one, being mated definitely meant he was in love with her, so fuck it, why not let her know, and two, she was probably tied to him for another two to three minutes, so he might as well go for broke. "I've been with hundreds of women, wings. But...not in love. Until now."

She gave a sharp intake of breath and he knew she was trying to quench a rising sense of panic for his sake. "Well, scientifically speaking, a sample size of one is a poorly constructed experiment."

He laughed. He couldn't help it. "I never claimed to be a scientist, baby," he told her, and then she was laughing too, and he knew everything was going to be all right.

"How did you even find me that night in the forest?" she asked.

"I knew where to look for you," he told her.

"No, really, Austin," she said, swatting at his leg.

"Baran and his men had some sort of compasses that pointed at Lyka. Inside the castle, she was shielded by the magical dampening field Mills has erected to protect against attacks. Outside of it...not so much."

He could almost feel her thinking. "What'd the compasses look like?"

"Black metal rings with rotating blue lights. He gave me one—I can show it to you later, when we're not tied."

"And you...carried it in your mouth to find me?" she asked him, her voice rising with her disbelief.

"No. I meant what I said earlier." He drove his face against her hair to hide. Somehow this confession felt even more intense than love, because it verged on stalking. "I hope it doesn't weird you out...but I honestly think I could find you anywhere now, even across an ocean."

"Oh," she said, with a soft gasp.

"Yeah."

After that they both quietly watched the city lights and the crossing of a distant plane. "So many surprises for one night," she whispered, leaning back into his chest. Her fingers entwined with his, and he knew their hands were just how he had seen them in her notebook.

"What are you going to draw for tonight, wings? I noticed you're a few entries behind."

"Hmm." She nestled into him in thought, and he decided that was his new favorite thing. "I haven't decided yet. Usually I wait to see how I feel in front of an empty page."

"Can I see it, once you do?"

She smiled. He could see the corner of it, as he kissed her temple, looking down. "I think so." She turned a little to look up at him. "Sometimes it's scary to have empty pages...but right now I can't wait to fill them."

He let go of her hand to bring a finger to trace her lips and then he was kissing her again, he couldn't help himself. She moved against him, so soft and subtle, but he knew she wanted him—and he knew she was his world. Now, and forever, and always. He sank a hand between her legs to touch her gently while he rocked her, and her hand followed, using his fingers to rub herself, making soft exhales of delight. He kissed her jaw and ear and shoulder, reveling in the way her body responded to him, the slightly rough sound of her breathing, the way her lips curved when she moaned. Ryana was right, the sample size of women that he loved was indeed small, but that wasn't going to stop him from learning everything he could that turned her on. And whatever she needed to feel loved and cherished, somehow he would find a way to show her, until she felt safe enough to reflect it back.

She started whimpering against him—and then he scented tears—"Whoa, whoa, whoa."

"Don't stop," she told him, capturing his hand.

He shook his head against hers. "I'm not going to ignore you crying, Ryana."

She pouted and twisted away from him. "It's just," she said, sniffling. "This is hard for me."

"That's okay." He kissed her shoulder as his knot subsided and he slipped out. He made to kneel, and picked her up as he stood up, holding her to his naked chest, carrying her into the bedroom, carefully putting her on the bed where she curled into a little ball, with her hands on her face. He stroked her hair and back and arranged himself behind her, wrapping her in a protective crescent with his body. "I'm here, my moon," he whispered, "I've got you. And I'm not going anywhere," and held her tight.

CHAPTER 34

AUSTIN WOKE UP LATE THE NEXT MORNING, ALONE. HE RAN HIS HANDS across his face—he would've thought the entire prior night a dream, except for the fact that he still smelled like her. Once she'd stopped crying, they'd talked for a long time about silly things—the shows she watched with Andi, some Korean dramas that had stories that reminded her of home, and how nice it was to see so many pretty dresses in one show, and then they'd started kissing. He'd checked in every other kiss until she'd growled at him not to anymore, which'd made him laugh, and then he started at the soles of her feet and kissed his way up to the top of her head, just making her let him *be* there, feeling her tense and relax beneath his attention, like a skittish horse, until she told him she would be angry at him if he didn't take her, so he made love to her. Every prior night in his entire life, he would've found that phrase abominably cheesy, but as she fell asleep in his arms beside him, both of them sweaty and exhausted and locked, it was the only thing he could think of to use. He loved her, he told her so, and he fell asleep, too.

But now…. "Ryana?" he called out, because maybe she was in the next room, eating the eggs benedict that were rightfully his. He grinned at the thought of it, and pushed himself up when she didn't answer. He looked over and found her notebook on her pillow. With a sinking feeling in his stomach, he flipped to the last marked page.

My wolf,

Trust me as I now trust you,
don't look for me till sundown.
-- Your moon

And the page opposite it was the perfect picture of a full moon, with all the highlights and lowlights and shades.

Her wolf.

He folded up her notebook, held it to his chest, and closed his eyes.

Hours after that, his phone buzzed. He'd been dozing, sleeping well for the first time in what felt like weeks, even if there was a full moon approaching. Being around Ryana had calmed something deep inside him—it was like he'd been looking his whole life for her, and now that he'd found her, he could finally rest.

His phone buzzed again, and he picked it up, finding texts from Damian.

Andi says I need to tell you to come back now, read the first one, closely followed by, *And I agree,* as the dragon-shifter attempted to reclaim some part of his manhood.

Austin grinned at his phone. *Are you sure? Or should I ask Andi?*

The next three texts were in quick succession:

Fuck you, Austin.

Stop drinking all my liquor.

Come home.

Austin looked around at the spacious penthouse that'd been his home away from home for almost a week. *Will do. There's just something I need to finish, first.* And then he got out of bed, grabbed some slacks from the closet, and detoured into the office with Ryana's notebook.

THE ONLY PERSON who knew she'd left the castle via mirror to see Austin was Grim—and he was waiting outside her mirror when she returned. She stepped out of the cold nothingness inside the mirror to find his crossed blue eyes giving her a judgmental look, complete with a tail-swish.

"It's not what you think," she said, defending herself immediately.

Grim tilted his head up and scrunched his nose as he sniffed the air around her. She knew very well he could scent Austin on her—it wasn't worth trying to pretend otherwise, really.

"Okay. That part *is* what you think," she said, giving up. "Not that it's any of your business," she said primly.

Grim gave her a *meow* that rose and lowered, to let her know what he thought of that.

She stared down at her brother's guardian, as he stared back up. "Can you keep a secret from Damian?" she asked him.

Grim seemed to consider this. She didn't have a way to understand him; Damian was the only one who could—well, him, and Lyka, but she wasn't here right now.

But now that Ryana had plans, they'd be a lot easier if the cat was on her side.

Grim sat on his haunches, hissed, reared back, made some swipes at the air claws out, then jumped three feet to the left with all his hair standing on end.

"It's not about the werewolves," Ryana said, kneeling down. "I think I have a way to get her back—and I'll tell you all about it—but first, you have to absolutely promise you won't tell Damian."

Grim paced around in a figure eight, shaking his head and yowling. If Damian discovered that they'd left to handle things, they both knew he'd be pissed.

"It's the only way this can work, Grim." If she told Damian, he'd never let her go alone—and if any of the Kagaroth saw Damian, everything would be over. All of them would still know her brother on sight, and all of them still feared him, surely. They'd take Lyka away, and they'd never return.

So she was the only one who could get close enough to save Lyka. None of the Kagaroth feared her—quite the opposite, in fact: they seemed to think her a laughingstock. And she'd done nothing at the lake's edge to improve their impression of her. Any of them that had truly seen her that night would've known that she froze.

"Please, Grim. It's our only chance. And we need to do it soon—tonight." Under cover of darkness. So that they could hope to have any chance at surprise at all.

Grim grumble-purred, giving her a cross-eyed stare.

"It'll work. I'm sure of it." The cat shifted from side to side, and swiped a paw out, slapping it across an imaginary face.

"Definitely no werewolves," she promised him.

He gave her an indignant stare and then collapsed to the ground in front of her, showing her his furry belly, and she petted it. "Thank you," she said, and pulled the compass out to show him. It'd been nothing to pretend to fall asleep and then steal it away from Austin. He'd been so restful at her side, she'd almost felt bad about it—and then she'd drawn the moon for him, realizing she'd have to leave him something to keep him off her scent.

Because she'd meant it when she'd said she couldn't see a future with him—not until she was finished with her past.

She placed the compass on the ground in front of the cat. Its dial glowed light green now—it'd only taken her a few minutes of tinkering to reverse the original spell's intention, and she could now spend the rest of the night and day in her laboratory, preparing everything else.

"It points at Baran now—the man who took Lyka," she explained. And the fact that it pointed anywhere at all meant that Baran was still on earth. Grim's eyes narrowed, and he growled. "Exactly," she agreed, as the cat looked up at her. "Shortly before sundown—come meet me."

AUSTIN DROVE BACK to the castle, with Ryana's notebook in the passenger seat of the Prius, his only 'luggage' really. He'd put his own clothes from the night in the forest back on, and he needed a shower, but everything was going to be okay.

Apart from the part where Damian killed him….

But Ryana was on his side. And Andi, too. Between the two of their calming influences on the dragon, he just might survive.

And who knew, in time, when Damian saw how hard he would work to keep Ryana happy, surely eventually he'd earn the dragon-shifter's grudging respect?

Okay, that might be a step too far. Maybe…tolerance?

Benign neglect?

Sure, that worked.

Just as long as he could be with Ryana. He grinned at himself in the rearview mirror after parking the Prius and walked into the house with a spring in his step. "Honey, I'm home!" he announced, and the house echoed with no response.

Not even a snide comeback from Grim. He had a feeling the cat had probably booby-trapped his room, though; he'd have to be extra careful tonight.

Still grinning, Austin ran up the front stairs, straight for Ryana's room—and toward her still very red door. His hand hovered over it, wanting to knock—but he knew she'd left it red for a reason. He could manage to wait till sundown, like she'd very reasonably asked. What were a few hours more, now that he had the rest of his life?

More than a few hours, really, seeing as the full moon would hit him when the sun went down. But he could have his fun playing in the forest with Zach tonight and then come back to be with her in the morning.

And every day after that.

He knelt down, shoved her notebook back under her door for her, so she'd know he was home and could start drawing at will, then went downstairs to his own room—and found Zach waiting for him, sitting on his bed and frowning at a laptop.

"You're back!" his brother announced, brightening at seeing him, shutting the laptop closed.

"I am," Austin told him, smiling.

"You're, uh, also oddly happy." Zach's eyes narrowed. "Why?"

"Why do you think, brother?" There was no way he could keep a straight face; he couldn't lie now if he tried.

Zach's eyes widened. "I'm not sure I want to know."

"...that I'm mated to the most beautiful and amazing woman I've ever met? You don't want to know that?" Austin taunted.

"Oh God," Zach said, getting out of bed and walking over. He put a hand on Austin's forehead.

"What are you doing?"

"Seeing if you have a fever."

Austin laughed. "I'm a fucking werewolf, Zach."

"A magical fever that makes you insane is more believable than Ryana deciding to be with you. Absolutely no offense."

"Uh, some taken. Jesus, bro, would it cost you anything to be happy for me?" Austin ducked away from his brother's concerns, and his brother sniffed after him.

"You do smell...God. Really?" Zach's eyebrows rose high on his head.

"She came to see me last night. And it was good, Zach. So good." He sighed at the memory. "And underneath the moon, and—"

"No thank you, I do not need to hear particulars."

Austin snickered. "Then you'd better leave and let me shower."

"Done," Zach said. "Same plan as usual tonight?"

"Yeah—I'll see you in a few hours," Austin said, pulling off his shirt.

"Good," Zach said, heading for the door. "Oh, and Austin?"

"Yeah?" Austin asked, his hands on the waistband of his jeans.

"You kiss and tell on this one, and Damian'll rip your tongue out."

Austin grinned, and mimed zipping his lips and throwing away a key.

. . .

AUSTIN HEARD his phone beep on his bathroom counter halfway through his shower. On the off chance it was Ryana, he stepped outside to answer it and found a text from Dominic:

Austin—you free?

He frowned at his phone. The Kagaroth had left right after capturing Lyka, and Dominic had driven him back to his car in silence. He'd texted the rhino-shifter a few times since to try to find out more about Baran's plans on Zach's urging, while seeming casual. His share of Baran's money for capturing Lyka had landed in his bank account three days ago, according to a text from Jamison, so he had had less and less reason to be talking to Dominic, and the rhino-shifter had been ghosting him besides...until now, the afternoon before a full moon night.

He texted Dominic back: *Now's not a good time. You know why.*

I do. But it's important. Come out to play and I promise I'll have you back before curfew.

Austin started growling without realizing it. If Dominic's request was Kagaroth-related, it'd be the first lead they'd had since that evening in the forest...and maybe he could do a favor for Ryana.

He dried off quickly and texted his brother. *Dom wants to talk—I'll find out what I can about the Kagaroth's plans. Meet you at the forest.*

And to Dominic he sent back: *I'm in.*

DOMINIC SENT him an address he didn't recognize not long after—but it was on the way to the forest, which made him feel more comfortable about going there. He'd wanted to put on all of his military gear, but with the moon mere hours away there was no point—he'd just kept his favorite gun—which he was glad about when he realized Dom wanted to meet him at a meat packing factory.

He pulled through its open gates, noticed how empty the parking lot was, and drove around until he saw Dominic's Humvee in back, and a cavernous open door up where they connected the cattle trucks to channel the cows inside where the slaughtering began.

He parked the Prius beside Dom's ridiculous vehicle and got out.

"Dom?" he shouted loudly.

"Austin!" he heard the other shifter bellow from inside the building. "Get up here!"

Austin breathed the air in deep. He couldn't scent anything other than the carnage this place was used to, rendering down cows from living animals to their component bits, and the bleach they sprayed everything with to clean it down. "What the fuck, Dom," Austin shouted back. "I don't consent to being in a horror movie."

Austin heard a dull thumping against the inside of the metal lined chute—like a herd of angry ghost-cattle were coming back out—and then Dom's head peered down at him. "Wuss."

Austin shrugged. "Possibly," he said, and Dominic laughed.

"What I like about you, Austin, is you never have anything to prove. It makes you considerably more trustworthy than most."

"Thanks, I think. Why the hell are we here?" Austin held up his empty wrist and tapped it meaningfully—he was on the moon's clock, and Dom knew it.

"Baran's cooking something up, and he needed to be on guard against all comers. Asked me to grab some extra muscle, and I thought of you."

"But the moon, Dom –"

"After your performance in the forest, Baran doesn't care if you're a wolf—and neither do I." He leaned down inside the chute and offered Austin a hand.

If Baran is here.... At the least he had to let the others know. Austin reached up and took Dom's wrist, letting him help pull him into the factory.

DOMINIC'S wider bulk took up most of the tunnel as it narrowed to a point where Austin knew they slugged the cattle. No amount of bleach could drown out the scent of old panic embedded in the walls. "Here? Really?" Austin asked.

Dominic grunted. "Yeah." He ducked out of the chute at the end of it, toward the factory floor, and Austin followed. There were still carcasses hanging from the ceilings on massive hooks, in differing states of disassembly—and it was like all the humans involved had just abandoned their posts.

"But these places are twenty-four-seven operations, Dom."

"Don't worry, we've got the run of the place tonight."

Austin shook his head in disbelief. "No. This is hundreds of thousands of dollars-worth of product here—they didn't just leave."

"I don't know if you'd noticed, but those assholes from the Realms have deep pockets." Dominic took a casual punch against one of the hanging sides of beef, sending it swinging violently against its neighbors and making the chain it was hanging from squeal. "And, according to Baran, a lot of things—they're going to come through hungry."

Austin grit his teeth. *Fucking A.*

"Apparently it's going to be quite a spectacle," Dominic went on as they walked through a narrow room together, half-sliced carcasses of cows hanging from the ceiling. The bounty hunter turned toward him in front of a final set of doors. "Which is why I'm going to need your phone."

Austin frowned, taking Dominic's measure. "We both know that in about half-an-hour I'm not going to be able to use it, anyways."

"True. But—no flash photography before then, Austin. You know how it is. Just like in museums." Dominic gave him a placid smile that didn't reach his eyes, and Austin realized then the game was up. There was no point in reaching for his gun; he knew Dominic was too fast and too close, he'd break his arm before Austin could even reach his holster.

Austin stared the rhino-shifter down as his jaw clenched. "How did you know?" And more importantly—*how much did he know?*

Dominic gave him a real smile then, not taking his eyes off of him. "The little things, really. People assume bounty hunting's just a physical art, but it's not. Bodyguarding, maybe," the rhino sniffed. "I suspect Blackwood's got a cyber-security team, and to him you're just muscle. In any case," he said, twitching his head toward the doors beside them, "these fools here have no idea how vehicles on earth work, but you and I do. I know you're enough of a car person to be appropriately embarrassed by that Prius, and you gave me shit for my Humvee—and I have fond memories of your Betsy. So there's no way you didn't notice that convertible Bentley with dealer plates outside the park that night. But *you* didn't mention it. Strange, eh?"

Austin let nothing on, but he felt a settling inside his soul. His wolf knew its time was nearing, if only he could keep Dominic talking until then....

"There's only one Bentley dealer around here, and they were close-lipped about who'd purchased the vehicle, as would befit their status...but it turns out that one of their desk-girls took a picture of an absolutely luscious woman and her—at the time—red parrot, and put that shit on Instagram."

Austin fought not to narrow his eyes at hearing Dominic talk about Ryana, in any capacity.

"So I went and asked her if she'd noticed anything else strange about that day and imagine my surprise when she described someone who sounded like you. I told Baran, and all of a sudden he wanted to meet with you again." Dominic chuckled and leaned in. "So hand your phone over, or I take it from you, and we both know you wouldn't like that."

Austin made a show of lifting his hand, slowly putting it behind himself to where his phone was in his back pocket, and pulling it out. Every second longer he took was a second closer to his wolf, and he had a feeling he knew what Dom would do with his phone.

The rhino-shifter took it and crushed it in one hand, easily.

Which Austin knew would immediately alert Jamison, who would now be aware of his last known location. And if he was smart enough to talk to Zach before Zach changed—like Austin knew he would be—then everyone at Damian's would know why he'd come here and what had happened.

Nice to know his potential death at the hands of a rhino-shifter wouldn't have been entirely meaningless.

And if he played his cards right, he might still get to take out Baran.

CHAPTER 35

Once she'd taken stock of her supplies, Ryana moved into her closet. She needed to dress as ostentatiously as she could, and it was hard; her selection was very limited, seeing as usually she just had Lyka make her whatever she felt like wearing, transmuting one outfit to another, rarely keeping the individual pieces.

But it was particularly important this time to get her outfit right.

She had to play into everything Baran had ever thought about her and act like nothing had ever changed. That her time after him hadn't broken her...and that her time on Earth hadn't slowly started to rebuild her once again. She needed to remind him of the girl he remembered growing up, suited only for palace life, tragically unprepared for any other reality.

So she pulled on a very structurally sound orange silk dress with far too many ruffles, which had a train that spilled down the floor. If she wore very high heels she could get an extra six inches of space at the bottom—and cover that up with a long black tulle skirt.

It was perfect—and perfectly hideous—and she spent the next several hours sewing.

After that came hair, and make-up, and Grim's arrival. He hopped up onto her bathroom counter.

"Still with me?" she asked him, after taking stock of herself in the mirror. She looked dewy-eyed and innocent. She'd painted her lips dangerously full with the softest pink and she'd flushed herself with blush from her cheeks down to her cleavage.

Grimalkin meowed a yes, and she nodded at herself in the mirror.

This would work, or it wouldn't, but she was going to fucking try —and Baran was going to regret ever having crossed her.

She strode out to her bedroom door and saw her notebook on the ground—which meant Austin was home. Probably waiting for her. Well, he could wait a bit longer.

She smiled softly, picked her notebook up, and put it in one of the many new pockets her dress now had.

"Now the gun," Dominic told him, and Austin handed it over, making the same slow show. The bounty hunter tucked it inside his waistband, and pressed the doors beside them open with a meaty hand, letting out a burst of frigid air—they were heading into a cooler. "And for the record, Austin, as far as I know, he just wants to talk to you."

"Uh huh," Austin said, ducking himself inside—and finding twenty Kagaroth in a loose arc, waiting for him. "Oh yeah, this totally feels like a conversation waiting to happen."

None of the Kagaroth ran for him, though, so he dared to look past them—and saw Lyka, in some kind of plaited cage woven from metal, suspended from the hooks in the back. And beside her was another Kagaroth, with his helmet removed, standing beside a stack of carcasses he'd turned into a kind of a desk, with an old-looking book opened on top.

Baran.

Austin was faced with a choice. Kill him now—or kill time till Damian showed up? Because Baran was doing *something* to Lyka's cage. There were writhing tendrils of brightly colored magic snaking from its edges, and he could feel the power pouring through. As much as he knew Baran needed to die, he didn't want to accidentally trigger an apocalypse.

Lyka spotted him and gave a pitiful squawk.

"There," Baran announced, closing the book in front of him up and looking over. "Make a path," he told his men, and they did so. Austin walked down it, with black-armored warriors on either side. "So how long have you known Ryana?" he asked Austin as he neared.

"Long enough."

"Long enough to grow tired of her?" Baran snorted, and then one of his eyebrows rose as he took Austin in. "Although I heard that vehicle you purchased her was quite expensive."

Austin jerked his chin at Lyka's cage. "Well seeing as I got paid to give you her bird, it's a wash."

"Couldn't stand Lyka looking in on you, could you, eh? I know how that goes." He chuckled darkly. "You wanted her all for yourself."

"Something like that," Austin growled, trying to figure out where the other man was going.

"And did you like her?" Baran asked, watching Austin intently. "Did I train her well for you?"

Austin's wolf almost breeched and not just because the moon was almost here. What he and Ryana were to one another was none of this foul man's business, and his wolf wanted to pull Baran's throat out with its fangs. "I feel like talking about whatever the fuck you want me here for is more important than my sex life."

Baran laughed. "Well, wolf, you're here because you have a choice now. You can choose to die for the love of a woman you will most certainly grow tired of, as I did, or you can choose unimaginable power, when my spell here is through." He gestured at Lyka, lying despondently at the bottom of her cage. "I'm going to need to take my men back home when this is over, to retake the throne that is rightfully mine. But there will be plenty of opportunities left here on earth, after all the chaos."

Dominic came up to his side. "Birds come and birds go," the other shifter whispered to him.

"Do you realize he is talking about completely destroying society?" Austin quietly hissed back.

"You see, Austin, I'm hoping you're the kind of callous man I need, willing to seize an opportunity and take it, like when you gave me Lyka at the lake or when you tried to kill my men while fighting. Someone with an untapped well of cruelty I can divert for my own purposes—someone who won't be afraid of standing at the edge of a rift to keep it open, as the terrors I direct pour through."

Baran was so blinded by his own cruelty he thought Austin had given him Lyka on purpose and not on accident—and he thought Austin was his like.

Maybe someone else could've been a better actor and prolonged the moment—Zach could have, were he here—but deceit had never been in Austin's wheelhouse. He shook his head and closed his eyes. "And if I'm not the man you think I am?" he called back to Baran, knowing full well what would come next, but it didn't matter. He had had a good run. Parts of his life had been rough, yes, but he'd gotten to have the kinds of adventures most men only dreamed of. Zach had gotten out of their childhood whole, and was safe, Damian would see to that—and Austin had managed to have good friends, which was something he wouldn't have believed if you had told him as a child, that one day he'd get to work side by side with people he loved and whom he trusted in completely.

And then beyond that—how for one shining perfect night, underneath the moon, he'd known true love.

Maybe Ryana hadn't figured out how to tell him that, or even show him, really, but he'd had it in his heart, and he'd given it to her, and he knew that was enough. She'd never have to wonder how he'd felt about her. He was her mate.

She'd know.

"Austin," Dominic sighed beside him, deeply disappointed in his choices.

"Sorry," Austin said—and sprang on the nearest Kagaroth.

This close to the full moon it was easy to be savage. He twisted the man's neck sideways, twice, snapping the buckles that attached its helmet to its armor and killing him—just as he felt huge hands grab him by his back and spin him sideways, throwing him to the ground. He covered his head and ducked as the first kicks landed—grabbed a foot, twisted it, and heard a femur break—before he leapt up and grabbed another's throat. Their stupid armor—he needed a weapon—or he needed his teeth—

A Kagaroth came running into the room, shouting. *She's here!*

What? Baran asked, twisting away from his spell book again.

Austin made the mistake of pausing—and Dominic swept him up with both hands, hoisting him into the air. "Baran—what do you want done?" Dominic shouted over his shoulder, and Austin could see Baran's glittering eyes.

"Oh don't kill him now—I want a wolf-fur coat."

Dominic grunted as Austin thrashed, trying to shout Ryana away while kneeing the bounty hunter in the stomach and kicking at his sides. It was like the man was made of stone. "I just want you to know that in no way or shape is this personal, Austin. It's just sheer profit at this point." The rhino shifter lifted Austin up and then dropped him on a bifurcated meathook—he felt the metal prongs slide underneath his ribs, one puncturing each lung. He was suspended in midair, gasping helplessly, as Dominic unfastened his wide leather belt and gagged Austin's mouth open with it, almost dislocating his jaw. He couldn't have screamed even if he'd wanted too—there wasn't enough air in his lungs—he felt like he was about to drown—and moving only made the ripping of the hooks worse.

Dominic grabbed hold of his arm and dragged him, via the serpentine chain above, into the darkness at the back of the room as he heard Ryana's heels approaching on the cement floor.

Baran? I know you're in here! She forced herself to sound playful, sweeping through the hanging carcasses of cows. *I've never been this close to a kitchen before. Come out and save me from it?*

A Kagaroth appeared. She recognized the carvings on his helmet;

she'd been introduced to him before, even if she'd long since forgotten his name. *Show me where Baran is,* she demanded, just like she was back at court.

The Kagaroth made a show of leading her further into the horrible...cow factory?...and made sure that she could tell by his attitude that he was mocking her.

When he opened up a final set of doors, he practically shoved her inside, and she had to catch herself before she fell over on her heels and the gig was up.

She smoothed a hand along her skirts and regathered herself to stare coolly at the assorted helmeted men. *Warriors,* she addressed them with a pout. *Where is your leader?*

Here, my love, came a familiar voice from the back.

Hearing his voice and words felt like a punch. For so long she'd thought what Baran had offered her was love, but now she knew better. It'd been nothing but lies.

Are you a ghost? she asked, walking slowly forward, as the Kagaroth on either side pulled back, making room for her and her dress's train.

Baran turned toward her from where he'd made an altar of sorts out of animal carcasses. *Hardly. Although without you in my life, I did want to die.*

Strange, that. Seeing as I thought I'd killed you. She swallowed as she faced him. She needed to seem scared, and she actually was scared, so that worked in her favor. *How did you survive?* she asked him, because she needed to know.

He patted his shoulder, where his needle of poison was. *I took enough to seem dead to the untrained eye.*

My eyes were not untrained.

Your eyes were busy crying, he told her. His voice was not entirely cruel.

She hugged herself and looked away, as the flush she'd painted on slowly became more real.

Why are you here, Ryana? he asked her, coming around the pile of meat and bones and heading her direction.

I'm the one who should be asking you that. I'm here for my guardian.

Why ever did you take her? She could see a few of Lyka's red feathers peeking through the bars of the magically electrified cage, but nothing more. It was hard not to run past Baran to free her, but she knew she needed to follow her plan.

Because it's my turn to rule.

She snorted softly. *You say that like it's a simple thing. Like the reason my family's ruled isn't a curse that's stretched for ages.*

True. Which is why I turned to my own arcane options.

She took a reluctant step up to him and twisted her head as though she were tugging on a bridle. *What if I were to offer you a trade?* she asked, wringing her skirt with her hands like she always did when she was nervous, so he could see.

He laughed. *Princess, what could you possibly offer me that I haven't already had?*

Ryana closed her eyes. It felt like she'd been slapped. *Legitimacy,* she said and swallowed. *My life for hers. You give her back to me and we both go back with you, and I can be the cruel queen of your dreams. I will learn from the best, will I not?*

Baran made a soft sound of surprise then, and standing in front of him she could practically hear him think. *And you would sign a blood pact not to harm me, nor any of my men?*

She took an eager step forward. She was so, so close. *I would sign it right now, right here, if it meant getting her back.* Genuine tears welled in her eyes.

His gaze roved over her body, and she remembered when she'd welcomed that, but now it made her stomach turn. *Supplication in all its forms flatters you, my love.*

I am glad, my love, she answered him in a whisper. *Because this is me, begging you.*

A wicked grin lit up his face. *Do you remember that first time in the throne room?* She nodded slowly, filled with the memories as she watched him run his tongue across his teeth. He circled her like a wary predator. *I knew then that someday I would take you there again. And I will—the second we get back.*

And I would welcome your touch, Baran. Only give me back my guardian.

I don't think so, he said, lunging for her, grabbing a hand in her hair and twisting her neck so her back was at his chest. *I think I will take you, and your guardian, and no one gives a fuck if you're willing.*

Oh, Baran, she whispered, sinking back into his chest as though she were small and frightened. *That is very much what I thought you'd say.*

He tensed behind her, realizing something was wrong too late, as she ripped the front panels of her skirt open and hundreds of tiny progenitors raced out of innumerable pockets to flood the floor in a skittering wave. They rushed for the line of Kagaroth nearby as Grimalkin bounded out from underneath her train to run for Lyka.

Baran hesitated—none of his training had prepared him for this version of reality—and she elbowed him hard, sending them both stumbling backwards into a wall of cow meat. She fell with him, laughing.

This time, she began, whirling on him, freeing herself from his arms and backing up. *I will kill you for real.*

CHAPTER 36

THE WORST MOMENTS OF AUSTIN'S LIFE—EVEN WORSE THAN WHAT WAS currently happening to him, as his body did its level best to fucking keep him alive, despite all of the meathook's internal efforts to stop it —were being forced to watch Ryana beg for Lyka's life at the cost of her own pride.

He heard her call Baran, *my love,* and the things in him that were human wanted to let the meathook win and die—but the wolf that was so fucking close knew better than to doubt her. And so, as she released a wave of glossy, spidery death on the armored warriors, his wolf gave a triumphant howl—even muffled by the belt—and took him.

One of the painful perils of transformation is that not all of you transforms at once. But enough of him was mutable in that moment, between human and wolf, that as he sized up to become an animal, the meathook was ripped free.

Did it hurt even more? Fucking yes. But could he breathe now? *Finally.* He landed on all fours and applied several hundred PSI of jaw strength to snapping Dominic's belt off.

"Don't do anything you're going to regret, wolf," Dominic counseled him. The bounty hunter had a hand out in his direction, but his attention was split between Austin and Baran—and Austin realized the rhino needed Baran alive more than he needed Austin dead.

But....

Ryana and Baran were fighting. Her hair was wild, and she'd torn a high slit in her skirt to move more freely, and her hands glowed green. He knew she was conjuring all the magic that she'd written about. She flung a wave of green light at Baran, which he seemed to have difficulty shielding himself from, and Austin wanted to run to her—but then he remembered it was the kind of magic she wore a blast shield for.

And what was more—it was her fight.

He wouldn't let her die, of course—but he also wasn't going to stop her from winning.

Or let anyone else.

He leapt over Dominic to land on the rhino's far side, placing himself between Dominic and Ryana.

Dominic squinted at him. "So that's how it's going to be?" he asked. "Remember—you brought this on yourself," he warned—and shifted.

RHINOS FEEL IMPOSSIBLY FAST UP CLOSE.

They may not actually be that fast in reality, but when 800 lbs. of meat with a foot-and-a-half long horn comes racing at you with intention, it provides an impression of speed that his wolf was not immune too. Austin dodged, then raked his claws down the rhino's side as Dominic twisted violently, trying to get his horn down and up into Austin's guts.

Austin wasn't about to let that happen for a second time today, though—he raced around behind the rhino and then leapt onto its back, trying repeatedly, and failing, to get a grasp onto its neck with his teeth. His fangs were sharp, but the rhino's skin was tougher, and Dominic shook him off.

Meanwhile Kagaroth were screaming and running in assorted directions, some of them hitting themselves, others pulling off pieces of armor to get at the little spider-like creatures that had wriggled in between their armor's crevasses, which was a bad idea because it only provided more access for the things. Austin ignored their frightened howls and wove back and forth in front of the rhino, trying to keep Dominic's attention.

Dominic's bulk prevented him from helping Baran directly—Ryana and Baran were fighting too closely for him to interrupt without possibly hurting both of them. And, as if realizing this, he focused all of his attention on Austin's wolf at last.

Dominic lowered his head, pawed the ground, and stormed him.

Austin waited until the last minute to dodge as the rhino thundered by like a freight train, snapping ineffectually at the rhino's hindquarters, risking getting kicked. He could...wear the rhino out? By himself? No. That would take too long. And no matter how magical the moon was for him tonight, if he went under the rhino's hooves, he'd be through. You couldn't recover from a split skull.

He glanced sideways and saw where a tiger-sized Grim was apparently meditating in front of Lyka, and yelped.

One of Grim's blue eyes rolled over to look at him, and Austin felt a frisson of magic surround his body shortly thereafter.

What have you done, Ryana? Baran yelled, watching her small army of progenitors take out his men.

I've done nothing, she said, placing an innocent hand to her chest. *It's not my fault that they're small, there's so many of them, and that they're so, so hungry.* She concentrated all of her energies into her hands, felt the charge of power roll across her body, making her hair stand on end. She shot it out at him, and he blocked it, barely, deflecting it so that it hit a nearby piece of cow and the scent of cooking meat blossomed in the room. *You should've thought of that before you shoved their father through the rift!*

It'd taken her awhile to figure out what Baran's game had actually been, but it seemed obvious in hindsight. The correlation between a progenitor's powers and Lyka's, and the particular type of magical netting they'd taken off of the ones that they'd killed when they'd captured one—plus finally being able to believe what her captured Kagaroth had told her about creating a Conjunction—she'd realized they were trying to use Lyka's power like a battery and rip a hole between different Realms with it. The same powers Lyka and Grim used to rearrange reality, only on a larger scale, and by means of force. They'd been practicing it with the progenitor, but they'd only wound up opening one small rift and just shoving the poor thing through.

But if Grim could safely free Lyka, and she could defeat Baran—and then she saw a flash of fur out of the corner of her eye.

Austin was here somehow! And he was fighting a tank-like creature with a horn?

Oh no.

But then it was like there were three—no—five different Austins out there, running.

Had he somehow summoned a pack?

Did he even have a pack, with the exception of his brother?

Why did they all look exactly like him? she wondered.

She rose her hand to deflect one of Baran's spells on instinct and realized whatever was happening with Austin didn't matter. This was her fight now.

Baran had lifted up his spellbook during her distraction and was sidling back toward Lyka and the cat. *You don't really want to kill me, Ryana. I remember how much you cried the first time.*

I am a different woman now, she said, hitting him with a powerful bolt in his shoulder. He shouted, dropped his book, and then caught it with his other hand. *I always was stronger than you, did you know that?* she asked, advancing on him.

He stared at her and laughed. *Why do you think I wanted to control you?*

And that had been the truth of it, all along.

She'd never been loved.

Just controlled.

Until recently.

And the flood of that realization—the untapped well of anger that'd been growing inside of her for years upon years—combined with the knowledge that that was never, ever, going to happen to her again, not with Austin—she screamed with power and channeled it directly at Baran's chest—no—his heart—no—the space where his heart would've been if he'd ever had one, if he hadn't been hollow.

Her power blew past his defenses as if he had none, and he went sprawling to the room's other side, and this time he really did look dead.

She was about to go over and check when she heard the sound of an animal getting hurt. She whirled and one and only one of the wolves was limping. The other wolves were harrying the tank-like beast, but while it was winded, it was ignoring them now, focusing in on the one that was different. She raced to that one's side.

"Don't you dare hurt him!" she shouted, letting magic pour out of her hands at the massive beast. It absorbed a ridiculous amount of magic, and she gave it even more. And the wolf that she was sure was Austin slunk up beside her, growled low in warning at the tank-thing, and leaned against her thigh.

He'd been at her back and now he was at her side—just like he'd promised.

The tank-thing paused and seemed to consider what was happening, as a horrible metallic screeching began overhead. Ryana whipped out her wings to shield Austin and ducked as she looked up to find her brother's dragon literally tearing the factory's roof off to peer inside.

"Damian!" she shouted and began waving at him. The tank-creature thundered past, just as she felt the release of whatever magical netting had been holding Lyka down. A red streak flew straight to her side and nestled against her neck as Grim loped over and the rest of the wolves disappeared.

"Austin? Ryana?"

Familiar voices called their names outside, and she heard a howl—which Austin answered from beside her. She flung herself down and around his neck, enveloping him with her arms and wings. There was blood on his fur, but it didn't look like he was still bleeding. He huffed hot air against her neck, and a cold nose nudged her ear, and they had both done it. They were alive, Baran was dead, and now it finally felt like she was free.

She laughed in relief against him. It felt like he was laughing back, and now that Damian had so kindly pulled the roof off of the factory, she could see the night sky. They were together again, this time beneath the full moon, and it was perfect.

CHAPTER 37

"HEY!"

A shout made Austin tense, and Ryana looked up.

"Hey!"

There was a very, very large naked man over by one wall, pointing down at where Baran had been. The Kagaroth's head had been squished as flat as the book he'd been holding. "Hey! I just did everybody a favor! So can someone take care of these things?" the man demanded, flinching as baby progenitors started to scramble up his legs. He cupped his hands protectively over his dick and balls.

"Was he still alive?" Ryana asked, standing, one of her hands wound in Austin's fur. Austin growled at the other man, protective of her.

The unknown man shrugged. "He's definitely not now," he said as Zach-as-a-wolf, Max, Jamison, and Mills burst in.

Zach raced for Austin's side, running himself beneath his brother's furry chin.

"Ryana—are you okay?" Mills asked, picking her way through the destruction and piles of both Kagaroth and cow corpses.

"I am," she said, as Austin rubbed his muzzle against her hand. "For the first time in a long time, really."

. . .

IT TOOK LONGER than she'd thought it would to find all the progenitors again—she'd had to spend some time with Grim and Mills, coaxing them out of the little spaces they'd gotten into, inside of Kagaroth, inside of cows, inside of walls. But eventually they were all accounted for, and back into one very large box, which Jamison refused to acknowledge existed.

"Damian is flying that shit home," she heard him mutter, and she tried not to grin.

Her brother had shifted back to himself after opening up the factory like a food-can. He'd put on clothing from their vehicles before coming inside, and he had choice words for the naked stranger in their midst.

"I'm assuming someone present would like to pay me?" the man who had been the tank-like animal was insisting. "I mean, I did play a valuable role at the end."

Damian looked to Austin, and Austin growled. "Should we kill him?" her brother clearly asked the wolf. Austin growled again, and then hesitated.

"He was fighting you, Austin!" She pouted at the wolf. *Her wolf,* she thought, and it erased her pout with a soft smile. "You're too kind," she complained, but she didn't really mean it.

Then Zach raced out of nowhere, to chomp his jaw around Austin's nose and bowl him over, and they fought like puppies, in the midst of all the carnage.

"Fine," Damian said, returning his attention to the man. "Whoever you are—just know that you fucked with the wrong family. And you are helping out with clean-up. I think we can fit a good ten corpses in your Humvee."

"Will I be getting paid for cleaning expenses?" he asked Damian.

"No," her brother growled.

. . .

RYANA RODE home in the back seat of the SUV with Damian beside her. Mills was up front, Jamison was driving, and Zach and Austin were in the back of Max's truck, wedged in beside the bodies. She'd caught them all up on what'd happened before they'd gotten there, and as satisfied as she was to have won, she really couldn't wait to get out of her dress.

"So you went out all on your own," Damian said, enunciating each word so it was clear what his opinion on this was, even though he wasn't yelling. Grim was on his lap, looking asleep, but he opened one blue eye to give her a clear *I told you so,* look.

She did her best to give the cat a *Well, it worked, didn't it?* look in return.

It sounded like, after Jamison had realized Austin's phone was down, they'd come looking for him—and then when they realized she and Grim weren't in the house anymore, Damian had gotten a little wild.

She *probably* needed to apologize to Andi. Or she could just watch another three episodes of *Hwarang* with her, which would be very *like* an apology and actually fun.

"I wasn't ever really in any danger, Damian," she told him. "I mean I was transporting a hundred carnivorous spiders—"

"Don't remind me," Jamison muttered from the driver's seat.

"—and Grim!" she finished.

Damian made an unsettled sound at that. "Yes. We will be talking about that, too, later." This was directed at Grimalkin, who purred innocently.

Lyka was still wound around her neck, where she'd first landed, and Ryana raised her hand to pet the tiny feathers on her head. Ryana had meant everything she'd told Baran, she would've gone back with him if she'd had to, to save Lyka—it was just good that she'd also made alternate plans.

And now—Baran was really dead. Unceremoniously tossed in the back of Max's truck, with all the other traitors. She had his notebook with all of his thoughts on how he could abuse Lyka—and she would be burning it in her furnace the first chance she got.

"I think things turned out swimmingly, Ryana," Mills said, twisting back to look at her with a grin. "I mean, you single handedly prevented a Conjunction. I think that deserves some kudos."

Ryana grinned back at the witch. "Thank you. But I wasn't actually alone."

ANDI WAS EXCITED to see them when they returned, and Ryana got to repeat her story, only this time with ice cream, as the boys went and unloaded the bodies. And then after that the wolves went with Damian to his dragon's bathing pool, and she finally got to shower, washing a very long day off of her body and out of her hair.

She'd just finished putting the silk negligee she slept in at night on when she heard a whine outside her door—and she remembered she'd left it red.

She walked over to it barefoot, opened it up, and found Austin outside, sitting on his haunches, head slightly bowed and looking up.

"Are you clean now?" she asked him, attempting to sound stern.

He tilted his head exaggeratedly at her.

"What? You're an animal. It's worth asking," she said, biting back a smile. "And in any case, wolf, my door is red."

His eyes narrowed at her, but then they closed, and he rose up to retreat down the hall. She waited until he was five steps away before hitting her door. "Oh, Austin, look at that—it's green now."

The wolf looked over his shoulder at her, then his tongue lolled out and he wheeled to race at her. She squealed and ran inside. "You're not sleeping on the bed though!" she said as she leapt up onto it, turning back.

He huffed in affront as she fell onto her bed, laughing.

"Have you looked at yourself? You'll take up all my space!"

AUSTIN WOKE up the next morning with Ryana in his arms, and if it were possible for him to freeze a moment in time it would've been this one, with him wrapped around her, keeping her safe, and her utterly trusting him.

"Moon," he whispered, rubbing his face into her hair. "Wake up."

She stirred and smiled before her eyes opened. "When did you get here?"

"Not sure. Didn't look at a clock." It was a lot nicer waking up in bed to Ryana than it was waking up nude outdoors, or in a Jeep bed. "Just grabbed hold of you after I changed and kept on sleeping."

She turned toward him in his arms, the silk of her slip sliding delectably against him. "I want to hear everything about what happened with you yesterday."

"And I, you, but, uh...can I talk and work at the same time?" he asked, leaning against her meaningfully. He was a hundred percent hard and, honestly, talking was going to be really difficult because there might not be any blood left anywhere else in his body.

She giggled against him, which only made him harder—his brain was bloodless now, for sure—and then there was a sharp rap at her door.

"Put some clothes on Austin, because I'm not killing you while you're naked." Damian's voice came through the door loud and clear.

Ryana's eyes widened. "Brother!" she protested.

Damian hit the door again. "I mean it. Hurry up."

Austin groaned, as blood redistributed itself inside his body. "Can you have Lyka make me some?" he asked her, getting up.

She frowned and shook her head. "She's still recuperating."

"Ah." He ducked inside her bathroom—a place he'd never been before, and grinned to see all her things there. Maybe soon he'd have a toothbrush here—or she'd have some make-up in his bathroom. He grabbed a towel, wrapped it around his hips, and returned, picking her phone up off her nightstand to hand to her. "If he's still yelling in five, text Andi? And only let him hit me two times—three max." He leaned down to kiss her cheek, and went to get the door.

Damian glared at him outside from the hallway. "That isn't clothes," he complained.

"Well, this isn't fair, so here we are. Would you like to come in?" Austin said, and swung open the door.

Damian stepped into the room, eyes moving between them. "I didn't want to do this in front of you, Ryana, but maybe it's better this way."

"What is? You ruining my morning?" Ryana sounded pissed, and Austin loved her even more for it.

"Yes. This is a band-aid kind of thing. It's better to do it fast, or so I'm told."

Ryana squinted at him. "I still don't know what a band-aid is –"

"Ryana," Damian said, cutting her off, his tone implacable. "I love you, but you don't know Austin like I do. And while Austin has many charms—some might say *too* many—being loyal to one woman is not among them. I don't want you to get hurt."

"I'm actually standing here, Damian," Austin complained.

"Shut up, you know it's the truth," the dragon said, glaring at him. "If you were even remotely honest about any of this, wolf, you wouldn't be in bed with my sister right now."

"I tried, Damian—I really did," he said, and looked to Ryana for confirmation.

She blinked and nodded. "And actually, I'm the one who first asked him—"

Damian made a low growling sound and didn't stop. "I don't actually want to know the details. I'm just saying this has to stop, now, before it ends in tears. I don't want to lose either of you, and that's the only way this can go." He looked directly at Austin. "When you hurt her—not an *if*, because I know you; it's *when*—and when I take her side, because I will, because she's blood, where will you go? To live in my penthouse for all eternity? I don't think I can afford to keep you in booze, and you'll scare off all Zach's secretaries by writing weird shit on your door!"

The dragon actually looked pained, and when he put it like that, Austin could see why he felt the need to intervene.

Austin realized there was no way for him to prove how he felt to Damian—he'd told Damian about too many other women before.

Unless....

"Hang on," he said, and ducked into Ryana's laboratory. The progenitor's box on her hearth now was three times as large, and she'd lit a fire in one of her furnaces for it, but he still managed to find what he was looking for. The truth-telling potion she'd created for the Kagaroth—the bottle had fallen to the ground when he'd swept up the table leg, but hadn't broken. He went back to Ryana's bedroom with it, with a half an inch of a thick brown liquid still inside. "You know what this is?" he asked Damian.

Damian's frown only increased. "No."

"This is the truth-telling potion your amazingly intelligent and magically powerful sister created to crack the Kagaroth." He popped the cork and downed the liquid. It tasted like death and he immediately fought not to gag. But he steeled himself to face Damian, despite the thin sheen of sweat breaking out all over his body. "I am in love with your sister, Damian." He spared a glance at Ryana and saw her gawking at him. "Ryana is my mate. Now and forever—and whether you like it or not."

Ryana's hand went to her mouth and she was easing out of her bed to come to his side, a look of rising panic in her eyes. "Austin?"

"Yes?"

Maybe he'd pushed it too far, too fast. If she denied him now in front of Damian, well—he'd figure out how to deal with that later, once he stopped feeling like he was dying.

She took both his hands in hers. "Austin—please believe me when I tell you I love you, too. Which is why we need to go make you go throw-up right now, because I believe that what you just drank is *significantly* poisonous to shifters."

"You do, wings?" he heard himself ask her. It felt like a sun was exploding in his heart—but also in his stomach.

"I do, wolf," she said, pulling him frantically across the bedroom and into her bathroom. "And Damian?" she called back over his shoulder. "Mind your own business!" she shouted, and slammed the door shut behind them.

THREE HOURS LATER, Ryana was fairly sure Austin wouldn't die. They were still naked in bed together, talking, and he'd told her the full story of his day alone. After she'd told him hers, she caught him grinning at the ceiling. "Just remind me not to piss you off," he said.

"I think you'd have learned that already," she said, snuggling against him. She started tracing a finger around the tattoos on his arm, as he turned toward her.

"Did you get your notebook back?" he asked, knowing full well she had. She nodded. "And did you get caught up in it?" It was his turn to trace a finger over her, following the curvy outline of her body with a fingertip.

She rolled her eyes. "I hardly had time to save the world, Austin, much less get caught up."

"Go get it," he told her with a nudge.

She pouted, but got up to do as he asked. She picked it up from where she'd placed it in her lab, safe by the progenitor, and returned with it to lie back beside him, flipping to the last page she'd drawn on with her words and the full moon bright, and she held it over both their heads, as she leaned against his shoulder. "See? I knew you'd find me."

"Technically, you found me, since I got there first." He wrapped his arm around her more tightly. "Turn the page."

She did and...there were drawings on the next page.

Not hers.

Her heart started drumming as she sat up, taking the images in. A paw, a circle, some lines and none of it was her doing. "You wrote in my book Austin!" she said, her voice rising in horror.

He sat up beside her. "You left it alone with me."

"I—I didn't tell you that you could write in it!" she sputtered.

"You...also didn't tell me I couldn't?"

She stared at his additions, feeling physical pain. "Austin, the more personal your spell book is, the more of your own power you've put into it. This—this interrupts the book's entire flow—I—"

He groaned, at himself not at her, she knew. "I didn't know it was a spell book, Ryana."

"Why do you think I put all those spells in it then?" She set it down in her lap and ran her hands through her hair.

"I don't know. I thought it was more like a scrapbook."

"Why would I put food scraps in a book? Who would do that? And why?"

"It's okay, it's okay," he said, reaching for it. "I'll erase it, it's all right."

"No—you can't—then erasing it'll be part of the book too—it's hard to explain." She should've never left it alone with him. It wasn't his fault. He'd already told her he'd make mistakes, and she knew he didn't mean it. She practiced breathing and looked down at what he'd done. "What…is this, anyhow?" She picked the book back up and squinted at his art—then realized it was just like all of his tattoos. "It's wolf tongue!"

"It is," he said, moving the book so that they were sharing. "This is my name here—my secret name, the name only other wolves from my pack know." He pointed to where he'd drawn a disembodied paw. His drawing was much more rough, but it had a certain brutal directness —like the rest of his tattoos—and Ryana realized that that was because he'd probably done all the art for them, as well. "Black Paw— because, you'll be surprised to hear, one of my paws is black."

"Then is this the wind?" she asked, tracing the next image, the wavy lines that were so frequently repeated on his own skin.

"Yeah. For Wind Racer."

"Then what is this?" Right after the wind was a simple circle with a series of angled lines shooting diagonally out of it.

"That's you. My Light from the Moon."

"Light from the Moon and Wind Racer," she said, adding on the next piece he'd drawn.

He nodded subtly. "I just wanted you to see this and know how serious I was about you."

Ryana made a soft sound of surprise, finally understanding. "Because you want me to be in your pack."

"Yeah. Such as it is, seeing as it's just Zach and me. But still."

She closed the notebook in her lap. "So would I then be Ryana Blackwood, princess of the Realms and queen of the wind racers?" She kept her face deadly straight, even though she was teasing. "Because if today your pack has grown by one, Wind Racer, maybe someday it will grow by more. And someone will have to rule them."

Austin looked pained—but still in love. "Technically, I guess," he admitted slowly. "But packs don't really have queens, and I don't think Zach would ever call you that."

She got up on her knees to peer down at him. "But would you?" She asked him like she meant it, putting a firm hand down on his chest, pushing him back to the bed.

He stared up at her and she could feel his love for her radiating off of him. She knew he wasn't lying—she really was his moon, she could see it in everything he'd ever done for her, all along. From the way that he'd first looked at her, to how he'd always made space for her, protected her, how he'd never once been cruel, or mean, or unkind. If she was his moon, then he was her sun, and she wasn't afraid to feel his light anymore and reflect it back at him.

"How about I just treat you like a queen instead of calling you one?" he asked her.

"I think I would like that very much," she said, folding herself down to kiss him.

EPILOGUE

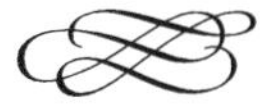

AUSTIN WAS RELIEVED WHEN RYANA OPTED NOT TO GO OUT TO CLOSE A rift with them that afternoon, deciding instead to stay home with Andi. He knew how powerful she was, and she'd saved his life on more than one occasion, so he was aware that it was a foolish fear... and yet. He'd never tell her that out loud, though—because he knew that when they went out to fight, she was just as worried, about him.

So he was pleased to come home whole and hungry: for food, and for his woman. He helped restock the SUV, then ran upstairs—he would eat out Ryana first, and an actual lunch could come far, far later.

But their shared chambers were oddly empty. Perhaps she hadn't gotten the text and was still upstairs, curled up with Andi watching their shows. "Ryana?" He called her name out just in case, and was surprised to hear her answer from her laboratory.

"One second!" she called out to him.

She'd kept up her experiments after they'd gotten together, working on whatever felt right to her or on things that Mills requested, but she'd never gotten quite as obsessed as when she'd been working with the Kagaroth, a thing that he was grateful for.

He waited patiently in their main room, all the better to be nearer their bed, and was considering how she'd react if he went in there and just *got her* to bring her back, when she emerged, holding a gossamer net between her two outstretched hands.

"What's that?" he asked.

"A gift from the progenitor. He appreciates our help."

Austin had decided to say nothing about the proliferation of boxes near her work furnace. As long as Ryana and Lyka thought it was okay, it was all right by him.

Mostly.

"Which is?" he asked, walking over to her, his curiosity getting the better of him.

She approached him, clearly trying to keep a straight face. "It's for holding children."

He made a thoughtful growl. Because either he was going to have to confess to Jamison that the number of boxes in her laboratory were getting much, much larger, or.... He pulled the netting from her hands to inspect it. It was deceptively delicate, yet impossibly strong—just like she was.

"Somehow the monster in the next room understands what my wolf doesn't," she said, finally letting the smile she'd been hiding tickle her lips.

He looked from her to her stomach and back again. "Because the monster in the next room hasn't been waiting half his life for someone to tell him that." He stared into her green eyes, barely daring to breathe. "Are you for real, Ryana?"

"Boop." She put a finger up to his nose and lightly touched it. "Seems so."

An unexpected wave of emotion rose up, rendering him speechless, as the net fell from his hand. He'd wanted this, but he hadn't dared to tell her. Their relationship was only a few months old, and just because he was eternally sure of things didn't mean that she was. But she took his hand and rested it on her belly, twining her fingers with his as she so often did.

"I thought...we would have to decide...together...." he said, mystified.

She smiled up at him and he helplessly smiled back. "Every time we were together, it was so clearly written on your face, I decided to decide for us." She shrugged, and brought her free hand up to touch his cheek. "And then I waited, because I wasn't sure that it would take. But I think that we're safe now," she said, and laughed even though she was starting to cry happy tears. "And for what it's worth, the progenitor agrees."

There were no words for the feelings that suffused him. To think he'd spent his whole life empty and searching, trying to do the right thing and getting hurt for it, only to now be made full and whole.

He swept her up against him, whispering in her ear as he pressed her as tightly to him as he could. "Ryana—my moon—my mate."

She threw her arms around his neck and let him spin her, laughing joyously. "That's Ryana Blackwood to you," she reminded him, sounding imperious even though she was beaming with delight. "Princess of the Realms—and the mother of your child."

Austin held onto her, just breathing in her scent, bonded to her body and soul, and then did what any man in his situation might—he picked her up in his arms and carried her to bed.

THANKS so much for reading Wolf's Princess! Here's an EXCLUSIVE excerpt from Wolf's Rogue, coming out late fall 2022 (or early 2023!)

"I think you should call me Giancarlo tonight."

Zach looked up from his work phone at his brother Austin, who sat beside him in the back of a limo. "Excuse me?" he asked archly.

They were both wearing tuxes and their appearances had been magically altered for the evening. His brother, instead of being an auburn haired werewolf with an easy going nature, now looked like a very serious dark haired man who might've stepped out of a perfume advertisement.

"This," Austin said, gesturing at the face he wore, before glancing at it in a tinted window. "I feel mysterious. And broody. And also like I possibly own an Italian villa."

"Oh my God," Zach muttered, rolling his eyes.

"I don't know how you manage to wear this much magic all the time though…." Austin's hand rose up to his neck and scratched at the edges of the spell.

Zach was used to the way the magic felt, having been the public face of Blackwood Industries for most of the past ten years, pretending to be CEO Damian Blackwood the Elder – aka 'the Beast'.

He'd learned to ignore the stinging sensation of the magic that rode him like he stoically ignored almost everything else – up to and occasionally including his own brother – for the good of the team. "I'm actually trying to work here, Austin."

"By staring at that phone like it owes you money?" His brother lunged for the phone but Zach was faster, bringing his hand into his chest with a growl of warning.

Blackwood Industries had been in court and splashed on the local news for months. As his Beast persona, Zach had vehemently spoken out against the unprecedented danger of workers cooperating to ensure pay was fare and breaks were adequate, because that was what his shareholders expected.

But from the inside, he'd been crippling his own case, secretly making sure the provocateurs were protected, and he'd dead dropped a USB stick with confidential conversations he'd had with his board to a reporter earlier in the day.

If he'd played his cards right, by this time tomorrow the Beast's name would be in the papers again, but now tarred with mud and—if he lost this case artfully enough—it would set a precedent into law. His company would face a fine, and he might as well personally, his shareholders would be pissed—but he'd also have plausible deniability.

The Beast would be growlingly contrite, just enough for plausible deniability, while everyone listening would know he hadn't changed.

And no one would believe that he – while pretending to be Damian Blackwood the Elder – had sold his own shareholders out.

If it happened.

When it happened.

A text flashed across his screen as his phone buzzed. He looked down and saw messages from the reporter, who had no doubt taken his time confirming the recorded conversation's authenticity.

Got it!!!!

We've got the Beast!!!!

Zach stared down at his phone with a snort, tempted to text back: *Yes. You have.*

"Is that...a smile?" Austin asked him, peering forward with keen interest. "Careful. You might break Mills's magic spell."

Zach tilted his screen so his brother could see the texts from the reporter, and watched Austin's face – looking like 'Giancarlo' – light up. "Well-fucking-done, brother!" He reached over and clapped his upper arm, hard.

"I know," Zach agreed, finally relaxing. He turned off his phone and caught a glimpse of his own reflection in its screen.

When he played the Beast, he was early fifties but still muscular, with short cropped black hair just beginning to go gray. The Beast had a lantern jaw, green-gold eyes, a nose strong enough to hold its own with his chin, and lips that curled naturally into a sneer of disdain. He looked like someone with a private chef and a personal masseuse, and as the Beast he was personally responsible for thousands of jobs and eleven-point-three billion dollars of his and his shareholder's money. When he wore this face, he was a man who casually bent other people's wills around him like a gravitational field.

Whereas the man he truly was – Zach – was always hidden underneath. He was early-thirties, had longer hair – still black though – with a more angular jaw but stronger cheek bones and ice blue eyes that'd seen too much.

Would he ever get used to spending half of his life looking in a mirror and finding another man's reflection? He assumed he would when he'd taken this role on for his best friend Damian, the dragon-shifter, years ago. It'd seemed challenging at the time, like being a Cold War spy, going so deeply undercover. And when he'd started, he'd worn the Beast like a costume, puppeting another man, like a roleplaying game that required a magical outfit change.

But over the years the stakes had become higher, and the responsibilities of running a billion dollar company began weighing on him like a mantel carved out of stone. The longer he stayed 'under', pretending, the more it wore on him. Making him wonder where the Beast ended, and where he began.

Especially because he was a werewolf to boot, and he could truly be *beastly* – when it was called for.

"You know what this means?" Austin asked him.

"I hesitate to wonder," Zach said dryly, putting away his phone.

"It means my new name tonight is Giancarlo-the-wingman," Austin told him, appearing sincere.

"Austin," Zach said, in a tone of exasperation.

"Zach," Austin said the exact same way back, and then grinned. "Come on, brother. You've got to get back out there – and tonight's the night. You need to celebrate!"

"Did you not notice that we were wearing tuxes? This is a charity ball. There's not going to be a woman there under the age of sixty, which may be age-appropriate for the Beast, but –"

"Newsflash: I don't care," Austin announced, cutting him off. "I would be happy if you got laid by the Queen of England at this point. You need to do something to break your dry spell –"

Zach began a growling sound again. "If and when I do, it will be no business of yours." Ever since his brother had gotten happily mated Zach'd had to hear about how magical it was to find a life-partner – it was verging on obnoxious. He knew his brother only wanted him to be happy, but Austin refused to accept that Zach was going to do it on his own time.

Which was, if he was honest with himself, quite possibly never. Because he already knew he and the only woman he'd ever wanted were not meant to be. He frowned and considered pulling out his phone again, as he so often had in the intervening months, to stare at the unanswered text he'd sent her.

When will I see you again, Little Star?

It was the first time he'd tried calling Stella that, instead of her real name, but something about it seemed to fit. She was smaller than him, and at the time he'd had the feeling the name might piss her off some, in a good way – that it might make her text him back just to yell.

Because the last time he'd seen her she'd been so angry at him, she'd just walked away instead of fighting back.

If he'd had even the slightest clue that that would be the last time he'd get to see her, he'd have never let her out of his sight.

The rattle of the limo pulling onto the cobblestone pavers in front of the Natural History Museum distracted him from his thoughts and refocused him on the present. He'd been to what seemed like a million of these functions as the Beast, making a brief appearance because his philanthropic secretary had begged him too, and then he would leave after giving some senator's wife a check to rescue kittens, or somesuch — these events were about the pretense of being seen to care, in public, for a group of people whose wealth usually protected them from caring about anything at all.

Which was why there would not be any short, blonde, well-armed women with multiple tattoos here tonight.

The limo came to a stop as Zach clenched his jaw.

"Just remember – *Giancarlo*," Austin said, using a hint of an accent, as a valet ran up to the limo's door to open it for them. Zach strode down a red carpet path without waiting for an obligatory photo op, and Austin closely followed him, acting like a bodyguard.

IT WAS after hours and the only other people at the museum were also attending the gala. Velvet ropes channeled women in sweeping floor length dresses and other men looking dapper in tuxedos, all of them walking through the main doors and following the red carpeting in, past an atrium full of mammoth skeletons and towards a broad hall labelled the American Midwest.

There was a pit in the center of the hall where a taxidermied bison was being beset by wolves, and other dioramas lined the walls.

"Friends, Romans, countrymen," Austin muttered, at seeing wolves on display.

"Have you never been here before?" Zach whispered back, giving his brother a slight glare.

Austin shrugged. "I chose truancy over field trips as a child." He moved away from Zach's side to actually look at the exhibits, and Zach followed him.

One diorama showed ducks in flight over a plexiglass pond with fish frozen inside, another had a colony of prairie dogs sliced in half to feature the creatures above ground and in burrows below. Zach had the idle thought that it would've been a Hunter extravaganza, if any of the animals in it had been magical like Zach and his brother innately were, as werewolves.

Layered on top of all the educational opportunities was a strange veneer of glamour. Hip height vases had extraordinary spills of flowers coming out of them and waiters circulated freely with caviar crudités and flutes of champagne. After making a slow thorough circle, Zach had the feeling whatever check he gave them here tonight would likely only cover a portion of the catering bill.

A small chamber orchestra played modern music in a classical style, and the high-ceilinged room was full of echoing conversations that nervously quieted or stopped as he strode near. As the Beast he didn't pretend to be interested in anyone else's business but his own, and did his best to maintain the illusion that talking was beneath him.

It'd been a protective measure at first, coming into this job – it was almost always safer to say nothing than to try to participate in the vagaries of conversation with men and women who he literally had nothing in common with, other than perceived wealth. By the time he'd learned which boarding schools were well thought of, and who had access to the best private islands for vacations, his reputation as someone who chose to glower rather than speak had been sealed.

Between that, the magic that protected his face, and the real Damian Blackwood's actual past – coming over from a different Realm entirely – there was no way for Zach to bridge the gap between who he pretended to be and the humans he was surrounded by on a daily basis. Nor did he truly want too – although sometimes that didn't stop them from trying to storm him.

"I would've thought this dog and pony show was beneath you, Damian!" boomed a voice from not far away. If the birds inside the diorama nearest him had been alive, they would've startled at the sound.

"Lionel," Zach said before he turned, acknowledging the other man's presence. Lionel Carter was an oil baron in a time that had no need for him anymore. Zach knew that the once wealthy man was now over-extended. Policies had shifted to favor renewables over petroleum, and he'd been too stubborn to keep up with the times. "And I would've thought it'd be too expensive for you to attend?" he said with cool disinterest, not afraid in the least of being rude.

"I've always supported the natural sciences." Lionel gave him a tight smile. "And while you and I probably belong in the fossil hall – have I introduced you to my niece?" He gestured to his right and a young girl flew to his side: early twenties, petite, brunette, with violet eyes. "This is Rosalie."

Austin returned like a boomerang to elbow him in his ribs. Zach let nothing on. He let his eyes slide over the woman without rancor, because it wasn't her fault her uncle was possibly attempting to whore her out. "How lovely to meet you," he said flatly.

"And you are?" she asked Austin next.

"Giancarlo," Austin informed her, as Zach snorted.

"How do you two know each other?" she asked, beaming with innocent sincerity.

"Rosalie, we don't speak to bodyguards," her uncle complained.

"Oh that's okay," Austin said, brushing the other man's concern aside. "While I am his bodyguard, we met in college."

College was the key phrase to unlock the protection of the magic that surrounded them – it made everyone's memories of their attendance a little more blurry than they might otherwise have been. No one noticed the change in the moment, but after they went home they'd have trouble remembering exactly what it was they'd discussed.

"Funny you should mention that then, because I was just telling Damian here how interested Rosalie was in science," Lionel said, redirecting his niece's attention toward who he wanted her actual target to be.

"I am. I'm pre-med," Rosalie announced to the two of them, before giving Austin a shy glance. Zach knew she definitely wasn't in on whatever her uncle had planned, and so she would be spared the Beast's ire.

"Pre. Med," Zach repeated slowly, giving Lionel a glare. Even as himself the age gap would've been a stretch – and that was before he factored in his lycanthropy. Zach put his hand out for hers and shook it like he might a man's. "Best of luck in your scholastic endeavors," he said and moved on, angling for the nearest waiter with booze.

"What're you doing?" Austin asked him in a quiet voice as he quickly followed, picking two of the flutes up for himself.

"Not taking advantage of a child," Zach quietly answered back.

Austin snorted. "If you keep making excuses to not get laid you never will."

"Pride's not an excuse."

Austin moved to block him from departing. "You and I both know pride has nothing to do with it." He slammed back a flute of champagne, set the glass down on the edge of a pedestal, and eyed Zach over the second one. "You're still hung up on Stella."

Zach ground his teeth together. "So what if I am?"

"She ghosted you," Austin enunciated quietly. "You're not her mate, Zach. She knows that, I know that, the whole world knows that – so why the hell don't you?"

"You're making a scene," Zach muttered with a growl.

"Oh, everyone's used to you being angry, why should tonight be any different?" Austin slammed the second glass, and a waiter came up to take it from him. "College," Austin said, waving the man away. The waiter blinked and wandered off as if he'd never been nearby. "If you weren't being angry here you'd be being angry at home besides. You've been in a foul mood for months. Which is why," Austin began, and then continued, saying more words – Zach could hear them, but they no longer held any meaning for him as a woman walked in the door. She crossed the room, heading to the far side of the bison exhibit, and Zach watched her every move.

She had overly long sandy-blonde hair that hung in loose face-framing waves, her eyes were brown – not blue – and the slit on her golden dress, which swung open every time she took a step, revealed creamy thighs which did not possess a singular tattoo.

And yet at seeing her, something shifted inside of Zach, like a compass put too near a magnet.

"Zach? Hello?" Austin said, sounding affronted, until he followed Zach's eyes. "Oh, thank God – yes – she'll do. I'll come and help."

"You'll be nothing of the sort. Stay here, or else."

One of Austin's eyebrows arched. "You do realize I'm not actually your employee, right?" he asked as Zach brusquely handed his drink over, and then stalked across the hall toward the woman's side. "I'm going to drink this!" Austin called after him.

ZACH CIRCLED WIDE. The strange curiosity he possessed about the woman now was almost overwhelming, although it wouldn't do to let anything on, no matter his level of interest. He was too important to let anyone gain power over him. Austin's estimation of events with Stella might've been blunt, but it was also accurate, and Zach knew he'd been a fool to care so much about a woman who clearly thought so little of him.

No, he wasn't allowed to hope, or dream, or relax, in either of his guises. He was too important as the Beast to the company he ran, and as himself to his crew. Him, his brother, and other assorted friends helped the real Damian fight off monsters from other Realms. He couldn't afford to be distracted in either arena.

So his feet slowed as he rounded the tableau, watching the woman relax herself against the railing, dangling her half-empty champagne glass over the edge, her slender wrists crossed. The deep-V of the back of her dress showed the curve of her spine, and she had one golden strappy heel kicked back, the only part of her that was currently moving, rocking back and forth like a slowly wagging tail.

"Mr. Blackwood," she said, as he moved to lean beside her, looking forward like she was, close, but not too close. The sensation of her presence was even more intense nearby.

"Who are you?" he asked bluntly.

She glanced over and batted her eyelashes at him. "Why do you care?"

"Because I feel like I know you," he stated, as it was the God's honest truth.

The corners of her lips curled up in clear amusement. "Is that a compliment—or a complaint?"

Zach let himself study her, rolling his gaze up and down her body. Lean, but muscled. She was dressed for the occasion, but something in her bearing said she wasn't the usual type that ran in these circles. "Too soon to tell."

She laughed quietly then, almost inaudibly, but it made the gold of her dress shimmer before she turned toward him. "I bet you sleep with a lot of women, Mr. Blackwood. So if you can't keep track of them all, I suppose I understand." She finished off her champagne and gave him a dazzling smile that made her lips look like a like brick-red bow, hiding a present that he wanted to unwrap.

"Would you like to know a secret?" he asked, pushing off the railing.

"Of course," she answered, without hesitation.

His eyes narrowed as he considered her. "I don't."

The next hall beyond them had been curtained off as some sort of staging ground for the party, and a series of waiters emerged from it carrying fresh trays of drinks and hors d'oeuvres. The motion of their arrival and subsequent departure created the smallest of breezes, which carried the faintest hint of honeysuckle from her, to him.

"Don't...keep track of them?" she guessed. "That's rather rude."

He took a step forward that ate up the space between them and breathed her in deep. There was no denying it now, he would remember that delicate floral scent, breathing it in as he curved over her, until he was in his grave.

Stella.

Wearing the guise of another person, same as he was, hidden by magic.

Surely for some good cause and not just to torture him.

Surely.

Her eyes read the new knowledge in his. "Shhh. Please. People are watching."

She was right, more guests had come in the interim, the room was filling up, and the orchestra was playing slightly louder to fight the ambient sound. Zach's mouth went dry as he suddenly felt scared not of discovering her, but of losing her again. "Why on earth are you here?"

"Because." She casually turned back toward the taxidermied beasts and he followed her example. "I need your help."

"You lost my number and forgot where I lived?" Zach murmured. "How inconvenient."

She flashed him a look. "Let me rephrase: I need your help here. Tonight. And I can't explain why, so don't ask—it's a pack thing."

Stella was a member of the Starry Sky pack—the same pack that'd killed almost all the Wind Racers in existence, leaving just himself and his brother alive. As such, he should've hated her on instinct, like his brother did…but he couldn't.

How could he hate her when he couldn't get her out of his head?

His pride was still injured though. "You think you can ignore me for months –"

She softly sighed. "I only ignored the one text."

So she had gotten it, after all.

Her words felt like a punch in the stomach – because up until now he could pretend there was a chance that it'd gone astray somehow, or that she'd lost her phone – something, anything, as a reason to ignore him, rather than it being a deliberate choice.

He knew they weren't mates, but, "I thought we were friends," he said, and dared to look at her, catching her closing her eyes, as if in pain.

"We were, for a time. In a way," she whispered, before opening her eyes to look at him again. "But I can't truly be your friend, Zach. It's not in my nature."

"I don't believe that," he said, with the Beast's gruff voice.

"It doesn't matter what you believe," she said, turning slightly toward him again. "Because it's the truth."

Zach saw Austin approaching and wasn't able to warn the other man away with his eyes. "It looked like you were blowing this, brother, so," he whispered with a warm smile as he came up, angling in to introduce himself to Stella with his hand out. "Giancarlo."

"Really?" Stella asked, knowing full well who he was. She didn't take his hand, and he squinted at her. Zach watched Austin's nostrils flare, and put out a hand to hold his brother back.

"What the fuck are you doing here, Starry Sky? And why shouldn't I fold you up like a paper airplane and toss you in there with the bison?" Austin demanded, leaning into Zach's outstretched arm.

Stella pouted up at him. "Nice to see you again too, Austin."

"I thought we were *done* with her," Austin hissed with emphasis.

"I helped save your friend –" she complained.

"Oh don't pretend it was ever altruistic. You just liked killing Hunters," Austin whispered.

"Well, who doesn't?" Stella said, laughing loud enough for it to carry, flipping her hair back and taking the final sip of her champagne.

Actions, Zach realized, that were not for him, nor his brother, but for the crowd.

She did have an agenda of her own here, after all.

He sank into himself and swallowed. "Exactly what is it that you need from me?"

Her attention focused back on him and for the briefest of moments all of the rest of his concerns disappeared. They were no longer in a crowded room full of people he mostly hated, fighting because they didn't know how else to talk. For one bright second it was just him and her, and it didn't matter that they were wearing magic, because they both knew the hearts that beat beneath it.

Her red lips twisted to the side, then frowned, breaking the bubble he wished they could stay in. "You're not going to like it."

"Try me," he suggested, encouraging her.

That's the first chapter of Wolf's Rogue! To find out when it's released, please sign up for my mailing list (and also scoop up a free book and hot bonus content!)

WARDENS OF THE OTHER WORLDS
WOLF'S ROGUE
CASSIE ALEXANDER

ALSO BY CASSIE ALEXANDER

PRINCE OF THE OTHER WORLDS (co-written with Kara Lockharte)

(Andi & Damian's story)

Dragon Called

Dragon Destined

Dragon Fated

Dragon Mated

WARDENS OF THE OTHER WORLDS (co-written with Kara Lockharte)

(each book is a standalone)

Dragon's Captive (Sammy & Rax)

Wolf's Princess (Austin & Ryana)

Wolf's Rogue (Zach & Stella)

Dragon's Flame (Tarian & Seris)

...and don't forget to join Cassie's newsletter for access to an exclusive Andi and Damian prequel story, *Dragons Don't Date,* plus *Bewitched,* a Jamison and Mills novella!

THE DARK INK TATTOO SERIES

Blood of the Pack

Blood at Dusk

Blood by Moonlight

Blood by Midnight

Blood at Dawn

Cassie's Stand Alone Books

The House: Come Find Your Fantasy -- a choose your own adventure erotica

Rough Ghost Lover

Her Future Vampire Lover

Her Ex-boyfriend's Werewolf Lover

The Edie Spence Urban Fantasy Series

Nightshifted

Moonshifted

Shapeshifted

Deadshifted

Bloodshifted

Sign up for more news from Cassie here!

ABOUT THE AUTHOR

Cassie's a nurse by day and writer by night, living in the Bay Area with her husband, two cats, inside a massive succulent garden.

Follow Cassie's newsletter for a free book and bonus content! https://www.cassiealexander.com/newsletter

Made in United States
Orlando, FL
06 July 2022